# THE EPHESIAN ARTIFACTS

By

Patrick W. Ledray

**The Ephesian Artifacts**

ISBN: 978-0-9853567-1-2
ISBN (ebook): 978-0-9853567-2-9

1. ADULT FICTION/Action and Adventure
2. ADULT FICTION/Historical
3. ADULT FICTION/Religions
4. ADULT FICTION/Mystery I. Title

Library of Congress Control Number: 2015954895

Printed in the United States of America

First Printing: 2015

Romanian Dragons, LLC
10740 Zieglers Drive
Brooklyn Park, MN 55443
**Romaniandragons@aol.com**
**Website: Patrickledray.com**

# ACKNOWLEDGMENTS

My gratitude to Kim Gordon, Minneapolis professional artist and art instructor, for her encouragement, editing, and insightful cover design. Visit Kim at: www.opencupboarddesigns.com

To Book Architects, and particularly Pat Morris and the late Dan Odegard, for their candid critique, recommendations, and encouragement.

Thank you to Bill Hammond and Gregory Ledray for their thoughtful editing and comments.

Copyediting by EbookEditingServices.com

Formatting by Amit Dey

Our publicist is Rachel M. Anderson, RMA Publicity

To Sparky the Dragon, the star in my children's book, "The Dragon in the Christmas Tree," for invisible encouragement.

Thank you to Lynda Ledray for her encouragement and website design, and for her development of our award-winning web site for Sparky at: www. Romaniandragons.com.

To Laura Ledray for her encouragement and love of history and travel.

And to my wife Susan, for her support and companionship during our travels from Minneapolis-St. Paul to Ephesus, Izmir, London, Vienna, Salzburg, Melk, and other locations in and out of "The Ephesian Artifacts."

*Bill and Esther*

# THE EPHESIAN ARTIFACTS

A novel

Patrick W. Ledray

# PROLOGUE

# AUGUST 12, 30 BC

The Supreme Living God, Pharaoh of Egypt, Ruler of the Upper and the Lower Nile, walked for the last time to her balcony and stared down upon the land she ruled. Alexandria lay at her feet, a silent city holding its breath in fear of retribution from Rome.

The high priest entered the royal bedroom, now arranged as a throne room. "Pharaoh," he said, "Your sons and daughter are in the outer chamber and await your summons." The queen of the Nile did not respond. She continued gazing out upon the city founded by Alexander III, King of Macedon, after he liberated her people from the Persians three centuries earlier.

The priest followed her gaze, allowing the silence to linger. Behind them, the queen's young female attendants waited somberly. Her fate would soon be theirs.

"Let them enter after you have prepared me for their eyes," she said, in a voice she hardly recognized.

"My queen," the priest acknowledged reverently.

Pharaoh turned and forced a smile toward her attendants. She nodded as she walked to the throne, specially constructed for her last act, on behalf of the Egyptian people. She sat and removed the coiled cobra crown she had worn throughout her rein. Placing it on the stand beside the throne, she glanced at the head of the cobra, raised at the forehead, an apparition that had so often intimidated others, as it was intended to do. For nearly forty years, she had ruled Egypt by striking down her enemies, or being prepared to strike them down. She knew the ways and secrets of the asp.

Two young women attendants set a small empty table before her. One, named Phoebe, looked into the face of Cleopatra.

"Leave us now," commanded their ruler, and they hastened away, tightly closing the richly adorned twin doors of the entryway behind them.

The priest approached with a basket, and placed it upon the table. Removing its woven lid, he quickly stepped back, watching, entranced, as the cobra lifted its head and flared its neck hood. Slowly, from the shallow depth of the basket, it rose from its coiled five-foot length into the strike position. Out darted its tongue as it cocked its head and opened its mouth, revealing sharp venomous fangs poised to pierce the flesh of its victim.

The ruler of the land of the Pyramids sat erect, staring into the dark-blue eyes of her assassin. Resigned to her fate she suddenly thrust forward her right arm in offering.

The asp hesitated.

Suddenly a vision appeared above and beyond the waving head of the serpent. Artemis, ancient goddess of the hunt, chaste protector of women and children, whose magnificent temple of sanctuary had been violated, stared with eyes more intense than the cobra's into the soul of Cleopatra. With quick and determined motions she drew an arrow from her quiver, fitted the notched end of its shaft onto the bowstring, pulled the string back with two fingers, took aim, and let the arrow fly as the cobra struck.

The arrow and asp merged into one form, piercing the forearm of Cleopatra VII, the last true pharaoh of Egypt.

* * *

Upon being dismissed from Cleopatra's presence, the attendant Phoebe had walked through the outer chamber occupied by the children of Cleopatra. They each schemed to seize control over Egypt once Pharaoh was dead. Just as their mother had done.

*Caesarion, whose father was Julius Caesar, will surely prevail,* Phoebe thought. *The brother and sister twins fathered by Mark Anthony and their younger brother are no match for his cunning and the alliances he has formed.*

At fourteen years of age Phoebe had entered the service of Cleopatra during one of the queen's stays in Ephesus. Now seventeen she was destined to be killed and entombed with her queen in order to serve Cleopatra in the afterlife, forever.

Phoebe had other plans. She was born into an ancient Order devoted to serving a true goddess, Artemis. Raised in Ephesus in the shadow of the great temple, she had been inducted into the Cult of Artemis at an early age. Phoebe had sworn to protect the sanctity of the temple, to assist in childbirth, to aid children in need, to fight for the rights of females, and to protect and continue the bloodline of her ancestors, the Amazons.

When the cobra struck Cleopatra the high priest had not seen Artemis, nor the swift arrow. He stared for some time in disbelief at the asp that now lay dead across Cleopatra's lap. He removed it and coiled it back into the basket before summoning Cleopatra's children into the bedroom. They seemed preoccupied with watching one another through their tears.

He then called for the emissary from Rome so that an eyewitness could report to Caesar that the rebellion was over.

The priest then summoned Cleopatra's court.

Phoebe reentered the bedroom and looked upon the queen until certain that death had filled the body. Then, as others pressed closer, Phoebe slipped out of the bedroom intending to escape her fate, flee to Ephesus, and spend the rest of her life serving Artemis. She would bear daughters to serve and worship her goddess.

Cleopatra's legionnaires had secured the palace and its grounds hours before. They were posted at all exits from the palace.

Once out of the bedroom and outer waiting rooms, Phoebe began running down the narrow hallway that led to the first door. She glanced over her shoulder, sped past it, then past a second exit, before stopping at the third. She was breathing deeply and her heart was pounding like a beating drum. After taking a deep breath she pulled open the door with both hands and burst out, into the armored chest of a palace guard who held aloft his drawn sword. He grabbed her arm fiercely and looked into her face. His jaw dropped.

"Yes, my love it is your Phoebe. I have come to tell you that our Cleopatra is dead. I am to die soon but desired to see you before my death. To see you tonight and," she sobbed, "I am with your child." He softened and released her slowly. Phoebe touched his left cheek, smiled through her tears, and disappeared into the night, and from his life.

# CHAPTER ONE

## APRIL 29, 1975

The UH-1H helicopter, with faint Air America markings, whop-whopped in at very low altitude, spun into the wind, and dropped onto the white fluorescent LZ marker. The waiting five-man army evacuation team and First Lieutenant Scott Frank from the 1st Special Forces (SF) Battalion, 10th SF Group (Airborne), stationed at Bad Tölz, Germany, pressed toward the opening door. They stopped. The Huey was already full. Of wide-eyed children. The person occupying the co-pilot's seat spun around. Between the flight helmet and chin, the person was wearing oversized aviator mirror sunglasses and a helmet mic for communicating with the pilot and air traffic control.

"Get the fuck in or get left!" a woman's voice shouted. "You'll fit."

They crammed in with their rucksacks and weapons but there was no room left for the lieutenant. Abruptly the slicks' turbine engine screamed louder, its blades accelerated, and the Huey rose. Lieutenant Frank jumped up onto the rising landing skid as the pilot banked hard and nosed the chopper down a road causing the young officer to fall toward the door whereupon an NCO grabbed his arms. Scott Frank looked down on what had once been the Military Assistance Command, Vietnam (MACV) headquarters, and was now the Defense Attaché Office (DAO) compound. Across the street lay Tan Son Nhut Air Base littered with the charred remains of aircraft that were bombed the day before. They flew at treetop level to the American embassy in Saigon, popped up, spun into the wind and landed on the roof of the chancery. A marine lance corporal stood on the rooftop watching with his finger resting lightly on the trigger of an M-16 assault rifle.

"Get out!" she screamed as the lieutenant backed off the skid and the five soldiers sprang out. The door slammed shut, nearly catching the last grunt's arm as the chopper lifted off. And was gone.

The team descended the stairs into the embassy's main building as Scott looked in the direction the Huey had disappeared.

"Damn that woman!" a marine major shouted.

"I'm Lieutenant Frank, sir." He didn't salute the major. Snipers liked to shoot officers being saluted. "Sir, there were a lot of kids crammed into that Huey."

"Figures. She'll have Bronco fly them out to the fleet. I told her we'd stage here and get them to the ships later! But she's not in the receive mode anymore…" His voice trailed off.

"She's American?"

"A former army nurse corps captain. Got discharged over here. She works with war orphans. Most with long-gone American fathers. Listen Lieutenant, we're light on force here and there's ten thousand mad and desperate Vietnamese ready to tear down the gate and demand a flight out before Saigon falls. As soon as I get the order we're on our way to Navy task force 76, twenty miles off the coast. You make damned sure the five grunts get out. With you. Until we're aboard a ship, stay out of my way. I've got a sick, delusional ambassador, and an embassy staff that's drinking while burning documents and millions of Yankee dollars." He paused, and studied the six-foot-tall, trim, Green Beret lieutenant. Forcing a smile, he stated with conviction, "I'll see you on the high ground."

"Yes, sir." Scott responded, as the major vanished down the stairs.

Scott Frank walked toward the edge of the roof overlooking the clamor at the gate.

"Sir," the marine on guard said. "Best stay back. They will shoot to get your attention, or worse."

Scott stopped and listened to the angry noise. "It sounds like more than ten thousand."

"They'll quiet down after being shot by the Commies. We're not being authorized the lift to get 'em all out. Just those in the compound and those with proper documents."

Scott nodded and began walking down the stairs. He soon came face-to-face with an army specialist who was running up.

"Sir, a full bull wants to see you now! We're breaking down those inside into lifts to beat feet when the choppers arrive." He turned and began a fast descent down the stairs. The lieutenant followed closely.

"How many?"

"Too many, sir. Way too many. About twenty-five hundred. Follow me, sir."

The specialist led Scott to a closed door near the center of the embassy, on the third floor of the six-story white chancery. The lieutenant knocked once on the door which was immediately jerked open by an army full colonel who brushed past him.

"Come!" he barked as Lieutenant Frank quickly followed. "Why are you here?"

"I'm the advance party for a Special Forces Mobile Training Team coming to work secretly with an ARVN brigade."

"Just you?"

"I had an NCO but he got sick and I left him in Thailand."

"That plan's out. Two marines died last night at the DAO."

"I know, sir. Rocket hit guard post one."

"Lieutenant, we expected to see Soviet-made tanks pushing through the gate by now, but they've stopped about ten clicks away. The Commies want us to get out. And, we're gettin'."

Scott did not respond. He walked close behind the colonel who moved at a brisk pace while talking over his shoulder. "The evac team knows its business. The embassy's marine detail will be beefed up by a two-rifle company task force and a marine general is expected. We're being micro-managed by Washington and the fog's thick."

"Yes, sir."

"Stay away from the front gate. Vietnamese and foreign nationals who thought they were getting out with us are locked out. They're a beehive that's been hit with a stick, but they can't sting their potential saviors. Pleading is all they have left."

"Sir, can I get a map of the area?"

"Do a foot recon in case things fall apart and we have to improvise. Maps were burned."

"Yes, sir."

The colonel raised his hand for Frank to stay out as he entered a conference room guarded by a marine private. The door closed.

Scott walked briskly through all six floors of the chancery, noting the layout before exiting the building, and scouting the buildings and grounds which were cluttered with debris. There were guards on top of the gate and posted around the inside of the perimeter fence. The noisy crowd outside the fence stretched around the entire compound. The marines were strategically posted in pairs. He turned a corner and saw the mob at the front gate. The scene was frightening and sad. Men and women with their hands thrust inside the fencing were waving papers at the guards. He heard screaming, shouting, crying, and angry, primeval noises coming from the mob. Scott was spotted by the front rank and they made eye contact as their pleading escalated. A new American. New hope.

Recognizing that he was adding to the panic Lieutenant Frank turned to retrace his steps and get out of sight. As he turned, the sun flashed off something shiny outside of the gate. For some reason he turned and peered toward the flash and saw mirror aviator sunglasses for an instant before they disappeared into the mob. No discernible face, but Scott was curious and for some reason felt a strange hopefulness. He walked briskly toward the fence and the people outside surged toward him.

"Halt!" a marine shouted at him as he pointed an M-16 in Scott's general direction.

"I saw something."

"Sir, you're not helping the situation."

Outside of the gate, the former US army nurse was being elbowed and pulled back from the iron fencing. She could no longer see inside the compound and was being crushed by the crowd. She was deafened by loud pleading voices in Vietnamese, Korean, and Thai as someone knocked her to her knees from behind. Her breathing came hard in the heat. Reaching up inside her blouse, she unclasped the smoke grenade from the front of her bra, pulled the pin with her teeth, took several deep breaths, holding the last, and let go of the grenade's handle as she rolled the canister toward the fence. With a "pop" green smoke began bellowing from the grenade. Coughing and screams began around her. The crowd in front pushed backward as she crawled forward, still holding her breath, her eyes closed. Someone cursed her as they fell over her. Waiving a hand in front of her, she finally felt an iron fence bar, grasped it, and pulled herself up as a slight wind eased the smoke behind her and away from the gate.

"American!" Scott said firmly, pointing toward the smoke as he ran toward the woman. Shouts behind him. He and a marine went up the fence and reached over as the glasses turned skyward. The marine grabbed an arm as Scott grabbed the head, then her hair. They pulled as she struggled, hand over hand, gasping, sweating, eyes inflamed. She flipped over the fence, held by the two men. Something hit Scott's stomach as he hit the ground with his back. He was gasping. He blinked up into his elongated reflection in her sunglasses.

She staggered onto her feet.

"Where's Major Kean?" she demanded of the nearest leatherneck.

"Parking lot," came the response whereupon she stepped over Scott and disappeared around the building. Lieutenant Frank was pulled onto his feet by the marine who had helped pull her over.

"Thanks."

"Semper fi," came the response as the marine turned toward the chancery and looked up.

"Sir, it's raining money!"

Scott Frank looked up and saw smoke billowing from the rooftop incinerator. Black ash, some document size, swirled down and mixed with charred Yankee currency. As the blackened paper and ash descended, loudspeakers in the compound began broadcasting an Armed Forces Radio program. The program was interrupted by a short announcement. "The temperature in Saigon is 112 degrees Fahrenheit and rising." After a short pause, Irving Berlin's *White Christmas* began. It was the signal to all Americans, and others with priority, that Operation Frequent Wind, the helicopter evacuation of American civilians, embassy staff, and "at risk" Vietnamese had begun. The lieutenant and marine stood side-by-side, faces skyward, watching the black flakes descend as Bing Crosby crooned, "I'm dreaming of a white Christmas, just like the ones I used to know…"

The sounds of an incoming chopper broke their thoughts and Scott began walking, following in the path the woman had taken toward the parking lot. There, trees were being cut down and a landing zone was being marked with luminous paint in anticipation of the heavy CH-53s that could not land safely on the rooftop. Vehicles were being driven to spots around the LZ so that their headlights could illuminate it for night operations.

Vietnamese firefighters were preparing to hose down the area with water in order to keep dirt and trash from flying up into helicopter blades. Lieutenant Frank approached a fireman having trouble coupling hoses and they worked together until the LZ was well watered. The firemen had, to a man, volunteered to be among the last evacuated in case a chopper caught fire and they were needed.

The operation began and after nightfall choppers landed every ten minutes, were loaded with people, and flown to the fleet. Time sped by and three platoons totaling one hundred thirty marines arrived from the DAO compound to beef up embassy security. The remaining marines back at the compound were evacuated to the fleet at midnight, after they used thermite grenades to ignite the buildings and destroy telecommunications equipment.

Scott Frank guessed that fewer than fifty marines had been guarding the American Embassy and compound when he arrived. *The few and the brave,* he thought, while standing in the darkened entrance to the chancery.

"Where's your green weenie?" a female voice questioned from behind him, referring to his Green Beret, that was not on his head.

"Got it here," he responded while slapping his right leg just above the cargo pocket. He looked at her face. She was still wearing the mirrored glasses.

"Bit hard to see, isn't it?" he asked.

"I found the marine from the fence and now I've found you. Come on. A drink's in order."

Scott noted that the nurse carried a glass jar with some sticks and leaves in it. He was led inside the chancery, up a few floors in an elevator, and to a door. Locked. She took a step back and kicked it in.

"Bar's open," she stated matter-of-factly. The bar had apparently been wide open recently and almost all of the liquor bottles were open and on the bar or on tables, and a few were on the floor. Many glasses were scattered around the room.

"The embassy staff helped themselves I see," she muttered while placing the glass jar on the bar. She grabbed two glasses and a bottle of Old Crow bourbon.

"General Grant's favorite, you know," she said, holding up the bottle before pouring the glasses full. She handed him a glass, and as he grasped it, her left hand slid over his. Scott looked at her hand and saw a silver ring with a crescent moon and arrow. He looked up and their eyes locked.

"Thank you," she whispered. Before he could respond she released his hand, picked up her glass, and toasted, "Here's liberty, loyalty, and family." She tapped his glass with hers and took a gulp. He followed suit.

"This is for you," she proclaimed while handing Scott the glass jar. "Her name is Rose. She prefers to eat ivy or rose leaves."

Scott peered into the jar and only focused upon the eight-inch-long brown insect after it had moved very slightly.

"She's a Ramulus artemis. Commonly known as a Vietnamese stick insect. She blends in. Also, she's a parthenogenetic. And, be careful, she wears a dagger at her belly." Scott sipped whiskey as he stared at the small barb on the end of the bug's stomach.

There was a loud shout outside, and Scott went to a window and looked around the blind. A marine NCO was below, pumping his right fist up and down over his shoulder. Double-time signal.

Scott turned around to speak and caught his breath. She was gone. He eyed her empty glass. His was still half-full. He left it next to hers and moved quickly, grabbed an abandoned book bag from a chair, slid the jar inside, and departed the bar leaving its door wide open.

The marines, army evac team, and civilians were directed to the parking lot LZ where the marines formed a final perimeter. The flights out continued from the rooftop, as well as the parking lot, all night long. In the early morning hours Major Kean appeared and ordered everyone into the chancery. Scott scanned the crowd for the woman. She was not present.

A crash thundered as the scared and desperate crowd, now realizing that they were being deserted, broke down the gates and flooded into the compound. The chancery door was slammed shut and bolted seconds after the last marine jumped inside. Outside, an abandoned Vietnamese interpreter, who had worked for the embassy staff for eight years, crashed a water tanker through the door and the crowd surged up through the building toward the rooftop LZ.

The elevators were locked and, as the marines withdrew up the stairs, they locked the gates behind them. The top doors were sealed and mace was sprayed in the stairwell to discourage the mob.

Scott heard gunfire and then someone shouted, "Tiger is out," meaning that the ambassador had been flown to the fleet. A CH-46 landed. Most of the remaining personnel were ordered to board including Lieutenant Scott Frank, who sprang into the helicopter carrying the book bag like a fullback protecting a football as he crossed the goal line. He went to the front of the helicopter and looked out over the pilot's shoulder as they lifted off. Looking down, Scott saw someone going through the wall that separated the American compound from the French embassy.

The nurse looked up and light from the helicopter's landing light flashed from her sunglasses. Scott felt numb. He was attracted to her from the time she had sworn in the chopper. He admired her fierce independence and she was pretty. Such a sudden attraction for Scott was very rare and he questioned how he could experience such feelings in these circumstances.

The fleet was soon visible. Ships, Vietnamese junks, boats, and a mixed array of watercraft were scattered among the naval task force, gaining refuge.

Someone tugged at Lieutenant Frank's right sleeve from behind. It was the young marine from the fence. Smiling broadly.

"Look at this," he said, holding up a bottle of Old Crow. "She gave it to me!"

"I got a bug," the lieutenant laughed back.

"Sir, where are you ordered to?"

"Don't know, Corporal, but I *very* recently decided on law school."

"You kidding me? What's the excitement in that?"

Scott smiled back, cradling the jar.

Major Kean and the last ten marine security guards departed an hour later, at approximately 0753 hours, and landed on the USS Okinawa. Operation Frequent Wind, the helicopter evacuation of Saigon, had saved seven thousand. Additionally, 2678 Vietnamese orphans had been evacuated earlier by fixed-wing aircraft.

The Vietnamese firefighters, many orphans, and thousands of others were left behind.

# CHAPTER TWO

## JULY 23, 1980

Scott Frank took his last look through the sixteenth floor window of the law offices of Kohn, Lager and Erickson in downtown Minneapolis. These fine views, he mused, would soon be replaced with eye crossing bar examination review materials he would be studying in his drab apartment. He studied his own reflection in the window. *A lean six-footer with a moustache*, he mused. After being honorably discharged from the army, he'd completed law school and was about to sail a solo path as an attorney. Now his brief job as a law clerk was over. The only task he had left before departing for his farewell party at the Haberdashery restaurant was to pack up his few personal items.

Returning to the glass-covered desk, he scooped up his eight-inch-diameter world globe. The countries he had visited were outlined in black. It was a favorite possession of his, replete with vivid memories, and he placed it carefully inside a cardboard box alongside a framed Army Commendation Medal.

For several months Scott had searched advertisements in *Bench & Bar* magazine for used law books for the office he planned to open in Excelsior, a nearby community on Lake Minnetonka, once he passed the bar examination. The latest magazine was open on his desk. Scott saw that someone had left a telephone message slip for him. The typed message read simply, "Law Books for Sale" with a telephone number.

Intrigued, Scott grabbed the telephone and rapidly pressed the numbers into the keypad. He heard the ring of a telephone on the other end, not the dull rolling clicks of a modern phone, but actual ringing, reminiscent of a small bell being shaken by a child. It rang three times before a woman's voice warily said, "Hello?"

Scott chose his words carefully, suspecting he was speaking to the widow of an old barrister whose possessions she was in the process of disposing.

"Good afternoon, ma'am," he said, trying to sound professional and not overly eager. "My name is Scott Frank and I am looking to buy law books for my first law office. May I ask, have the books you advertised been sold?"

"Oh, no," the voice responded. Then, after a pause and with a note of encouragement in her voice, she added, "They're still here."

"What kind of law books are they?" Scott asked pointedly. Above all he wanted to avoid driving a long distance in the summer heat if the books were of no use to him.

"Used books," the woman replied.

"Yes, of course," Scott replied politely. "But what type of books?"

"They're in very good shape," she said.

Scott could not suppress a smile. "Are you familiar with the books?" he asked, and when he received no reply, he rattled off some possibilities "Are they encyclopedias, Minnesota Reporters, textbooks, horn books, or Minnesota Statutes?"

"Different types, at a good price," she responded.

"Yes, but what about titles? Are they titled or numbered volumes? For instance, do they have an "NW" and a number on them or do they have names?"

"All types, different types, some with numbers, some with names; but all types, all sizes," she countered.

Scott Frank paused to formulate a different approach.

"What type of law did the lawyer practice?"

"He was a general practitioner."

Scott Frank was getting nowhere but he didn't want to give up just yet. "Are you selling anything else," he ventured, "such as office furniture or any office equipment?"

"Perhaps."

"What would be those types of things?"

"All types."

Scott thought to say good-bye to this woman and hang up. But there was *something* in the woman's tone of voice that drew his interest. He asked her where the items were located.

"Where are you coming from?" she responded.

"Downtown Minneapolis," Scott said. Silence ensued. "Where could I see the books and other items?" he added tentatively.

"We have rural route numbers out here, and you'll need directions," came the reply. "Do you know where the historic town hall in Chanhassen is located?"

"Do you mean the white building that looks like a prairie schoolhouse, the one near the Chanhassen Dinner Theater?" It was the only structure that sprang to mind. He rarely ventured to Chanhassen, and even more rarely attended plays or other stage events.

"Yes," she replied. "That's the one."

After Scott received directions from the old town hall to what the woman described as a farmhouse, he asked if he could come out the following morning at eleven o'clock. That would give him ample time to sleep in after what was likely to be a loud and long farewell party.

"Yes," came her reply. "You may come tomorrow at that time."

An hour later, Scott arrived at a popular downtown bar featuring the usual accessories, plus a carpet of peanut shells casually tossed on the floor by a variety of what looked to be lawyers, bankers, and other white-collar professionals. Even on this Wednesday evening the establishment was crowded. After fourteen or fifteen employees of his law firm had each consumed a minimum of two drinks, glasses were tapped with spoons, knives, and forks to create slightly less noise for the farewell toasts.

"Johnny, we hardly knew thee!" a not so sober Brad, the most junior lawyer in the firm, shouted out.

"I think his name is Scott!" a secretary corrected.

"Whatever," Brad crowed. "He won't amount to much if he sails past the bar, though. He could have dragged out the assignment given to him over the entire summer and milked it for all it was worth until fall. But no, not our Johnny! He actually worked, even on weekends, and so he has worked himself out of a job. Far worse, it will be hard for us to over-bill that client again. Must be that army mind drumming on duty and honor and all. So raise your glass and toast Scott Frank, the sorriest excuse for a lawyer ever!"

"To the sorriest lawyer ever!" his cohorts chimed in.

"Good luck, Scott," a colleague named Susan said when the cheers had faded. "We have a card signed by everyone in the firm, and I signed it twice, wishing you the best now that you have eased my workload. And as a parting gift we present you with this beautiful silver-plated letter opener purchased with firm funds. It's engraved with your very own initials, *S F*."

To another round of cheers Scott Frank rose, took the card, read it, and opened the box containing the letter opener which he then held aloft for all to see.

"Thank you for this and thank you for coming out this evening to wish me well," he said in a steady voice. "I know your being here has nothing to do with the firm paying for dinner and the bar tab."

"I hope that you all invite me back here some evening after I pass the bar exam. Be sure to bring the firm's checkbook again, Meg!" That comment summoned yet another round of applause and cheers. Scott raised his glass, and offered a toast, "Here's liberty, loyalty, and family," he said with feeling.

"Hear, hear!" came the enthusiastic response.

*  *  *

At ten-forty the next morning, Scott arrived at the old wooden town hall in Chanhassen. From there he followed the woman's detailed directions into the countryside, to where a split-rail fence was interrupted by a long driveway leading from the main road through a thick growth of tall pine trees planted so close together that many would have to be cut down before any could fall flat. Nestled behind this protective green barrier stood the farmhouse.

Scott's first impression was that the house had been built in the early 1900s and that a coat of white paint had been applied the previous summer. He stopped the car, turned off the ignition, and searched about for dogs. Farm dogs, he knew well, did not take kindly to strangers arriving on their home turf in unfamiliar vehicles. He recalled his uncle Ernie's enormous wolf-like German shepherds keeping terrified children at bay inside the car, until Aunt Alvina called them off and shooed them into the barn. After a minute or two had elapsed with no dogs on the prowl, Scott stepped out of his car, removed his baseball cap, and threw it onto the passenger's seat. Glancing around he noted that the farm was orderly and unusually quiet. He saw no signs of farm animals or farm equipment, just a few birds fluttering about a feeder.

With a shrug Scott walked up the steps of an open porch and tapped on the wood edge of a screen door. Several moments later, the door opened to frame a blue-eyed sophisticated-looking woman smiling at him. Her appearance was far different from the mental vision he had of her during their telephone conversation. She was trim and dressed in a short-sleeved safari jacket and matching long pants.

"Please, do come in," she said pleasantly, holding open the door.

"Thank you," Scott replied, making a point of carefully wiping his feet before crossing the threshold into her residence. The woman smiled as if in understanding, and then led him down a wide hall toward what Scott took to be a spacious living room or parlor. As he followed behind her Scott marveled at the photographs, paintings, and furnishings he passed along the way. But what he found upon entering the large room utterly astounded him. The room was similar in design and contents to a small-town museum to which every family in the town had donated its oldest and most precious heirlooms.

Scott glanced up and around. He gauged the ceiling to be at least twelve feet high, and he noted with appreciation the correspondingly high windows, each with a curved top crowned with stained glass. Light radiating through rich colors cast intricate patterns on the decorative wallpaper and illuminated an enormous Waterford crystal bowl set in the center of a circular oak library table. Just beyond the table, Scott noticed an old polished brass telescope perched on its tripod, pointing skyward through an opening in the trees. A European-style matchlock gun hung above a fireplace so immense that a five-foot-tall person could walk into it, turn around, and walk out without touching the sooty walls. Inside the fireplace was a side stone bench for warming oneself on cold Minnesota nights, and the iron pot hangers, once used for cooking, were still in place. Further enhancing the hearth area was a harpsichord and three Victorian loveseats that faced the fireplace. They were sitting on an elaborate Oriental rug.

Scott stared at one object and then at another as the woman waited patiently.

"This is fantastic," he muttered to himself, his gaze captivated seemingly at once by what appeared to be a seventeenth century landscape oil painting, a brightly colored Tiffany lamp, and a nine-foot-high brass birdcage. "I've never seen anything quite like this."

"Oh, thank you," she replied. "I'm so very pleased that you have such an appreciation for antiques. Incidentally, the office is in the next room." She pointed at a pair of French doors, which opened out.

*An office?* Scott thought. *Out here?*

The office, too, was neat and orderly. A large black stove dominated one corner and he noted a substantial red brick fireplace with two comfortable-looking straight-backed chairs placed strategically close by it. At first glance

Scott was disappointed not to see an antique desk. But on second glance he noticed a stand up desk with a tall stool located near the chairs. The desk was small, about the size of a podium. It featured a leather-inlaid top and drawers on one side. The bottom was open with long legs supporting the structure in such a way that it appeared both artistic and strong to the eye. What came quickly to Scott's mind as he studied the desk was the image of old, crotchety Ebenezer Scrooge in his counting house in London, leaning over its top edge and giving poor Bob Cratchit another earful.

And then there were books: classics, poetry, books whose titles Scott recognized, and books whose titles and authors were unfamiliar to him. Shelf upon shelf, they rose to the ceiling high above, occupying an enormous bookcase covering a wall, filling a corner, and half of the adjoining wall. A long ladder on wheels, affixed to a ceiling track, made every book accessible. Even in its own time the office would have been remarkable, whatever "time" that might have been. More than anything Scott wanted to be alone in this room. As an admirer of antiques and antiquities—and as a future lawyer who yearned to dive into what must be fascinating information in the client files—this room held a cornucopia of treasures.

"Is everything in this office for sale?" Scott asked, unable to keep his enthusiasm in check.

"Oh, no; no, no," she stammered. "In fact nothing's really for sale. Not now, anyway. You should have given me your telephone number. I realize I never asked. I'm sorry, but nothing's for sale. Certainly not the books," she added with a smile, pleading for forgiveness.

"It's my fault," Scott replied, noting her relief that he didn't seem upset with her. "We didn't confirm anything on the phone and besides, I should have given you my number in case you couldn't be home for some reason. But I am glad for the opportunity to see your beautiful house." He gave her a questioning look. "Why, may I ask, have you decided not to sell the books?"

"Oh, he called last night and told me not to sell the books" she replied. "He also told me to rent the office if I could."

"Who is *he*?" Scott asked curiously. "Whose office is this?"

"Why, it belongs to none other than Mr. Rutheford Ruffescott," she told him.

"Mr. Rutheford Ruffescott," Scott repeated the name softly, thinking it was one of the strangest names he had ever heard.

"Yes," she answered warily, "the same."

Scott stared at the woman who stared back at him questioningly. After several awkward moments had elapsed he said, "How much is the monthly rent for this office?"

"One hundred dollars is all," she sighed. "It's a bit out of the way."

"I'll take it," Scott stated without pause, as if it were a reflex. An unthinking, unguided, irrational reflex to a hesitant, undirected offer.

She stared at Scott, or rather through him, before letting out a breath. Her facial expression conveyed a curious blend of relief and circumspection.

"Can I offer you a spot of tea?" she inquired with a tentative smile, as Scott again glanced around the room. She must have sensed his urge to explore the room for she added, "Mr. Ruffescott stressed that the lessee was to have use of everything, and to work around his things."

"How long can I lease the office?" Scott asked.

"Until he returns," she responded.

Despite himself, Scott smiled at her. There was something about the graciousness and forthrightness of this woman that appealed to him. "I'd love that cup of tea," he said.

She returned his smile and motioned for him to follow her.

Scott was pleased with himself. For one hundred dollars a month he had secured a retreat from the twentieth century. An antique study, a private library, and apparently someone to tidy up, were now his for the taking. His decision may have been a bit abrupt, perhaps even foolish, but it was a compulsive response to a unique opportunity, and he had no regrets.

The woman escorted Scott into a cozy, well-appointed dining room that featured a long, formal table with ten chairs. "We can have tea in here if you like, or in the living room at the small table if you prefer."

What Scott preferred was not drinking tea surrounded by empty chairs and formal portraits of austere men and women staring down at him from their fixed positions on the walls. At the far end of the room was a suit of armor, holding aloft a sword by its blade. The helmet was bowed down, beneath a cross formed by the blade, hilt, and handle. *The cross of redemption*, he thought to himself, before saying out loud, "The small table will do just fine."

"Very well. By the way, the downstairs water closet is just off the hallway if you'd like to freshen up."

"Thank you, I would."

When Scott returned to the living room he noticed that the small library table had been covered with two linen cloths, a white one on top offsetting the indigo blue beneath, the combination creating a decorous look to the area. Teacups and saucers were set out on the table accompanied by several silver spoons, four wedges of lemon, and a small silver tealeaf strainer.

Scott sat down in the chair facing the rear of the house and waited until she glided in, smiling. She carried a teapot in its cozy and a small pewter bowl with a pestle in it, surrounded by tealeaves and cuttings that emitted a pleasant, fresh fragrance.

"How do you prefer your tea?" she asked, as she unscrewed the tea leaf strainer and laid it aside. "Weak or strong?"

"Strong," Scott replied, watching her perform her tea ceremony with obvious delight.

"Good. As do I." She winked, and Scott noted her high cheekbones and smooth complexion. She was very attractive and her age was a puzzle.

With the pestle, she carefully broke up the tea leaves before tapping them into the strainer and refastening its top. Scott expected her to place the strainer into the pot but instead she placed the strainer in the cup directly in front of her, and poured the hot water from the teapot into the cup beside it. She then transferred the strainer into the cup with water, lifted it up and down a few times, and added more water. After waiting a while to allow the teas to brew, she placed the cup before her.

"I'll keep the floating bits of tea for myself," she said matter-of-factly, before repeating the process in the second cup, which she placed before Scott.

Scott took a wedge of lemon, squeezed the juice into his spoon, and deposited it into his cup.

"My, my, who taught you to enjoy tea?" she asked delightedly.

"My grandmother, rest her soul," Scott told her. "She and I once had tea in Langley, Washington. Langley is a small town about a mile or so from where my parents have a summer place on Whidbey Island. When we walked into town one morning she explained to me how to take tea properly, as the British do, and I have never forgotten her words. It's the one incident in our relationship that has survived most vividly in my mind."

"You know," his hostess said, "in England high tea is traditionally served in the late afternoon, and can actually be a substitute for supper. Many people prefer not to eat a large meal in the evening, and the tea can be taken with almost any food of substance. Was your grandmother English by chance?"

"Yes, she was," Scott replied, "and proud of it. She was particularly proud of the fact that she returned to London during the Blitz and survived that ordeal."

"Much like King George and the Queen Mother," the woman said, smiling. They talked and drank tea, and after what seemed to Scott too brief a period, the grandfather clock in the corner struck four. He glanced in its direction.

"I have to get going," Scott said, wondering how so much time had vanished. "I'll be back on Saturday morning if it's all right."

"It's your office. Here are the keys. They also open the front and back doors." She handed him a number of large brass keys attached to what appeared to be a watch fob, but on closer inspection it turned out to be some sort of military medal.

"Thank you," Scott said. He took the keys from her and headed for the front door. "And thank you for the tea and the conversation. I look forward to more of them."

"You are most welcome," she called after him warmly.

*This is odd*, Scott thought to himself, as he slipped onto the front seat of his car and started the engine. Although he had enjoyed himself and felt good about the day, he could not deny that indeed there was something almost surreal about how easy it had been to rent this wondrous office in the middle of nowhere and have access, if not ownership, to all those books and pieces of furniture. And then he wondered how in the excitement of it all he had failed to even once ask the woman her name?

"This is very odd," he said out loud as his car headed out the driveway toward the main road.

# CHAPTER THREE

## JULY 26, 1980

On Saturday Scott Frank returned to his new retreat. The drive seemed shorter than he remembered but today he had a lot on his mind. After being discharged from the active army he had joined a local reserve unit. For three years he had been assigned to a civil affairs company at Fort Snelling, near the Minneapolis/St. Paul airport. Now, however, he needed to pass the officer's advanced course if he wanted to remain in the reserves. It was a good part-time job with the opportunity for paid active duty training throughout the year. He planned to take the bar exam, attend the army's Civil Affairs Advanced Course at Fort Bragg, North Carolina, and then open his own law office in Excelsior. By then, he thought, Mr. Ruffescott might want to sell his office furnishings and law books. Unfortunately, the office at the farmhouse was just too far removed from the real world to efficiently serve a green lawyer.

Scott knocked on the front door of the farmhouse without hesitation, waited a moment, and knocked much harder. When he heard no activity from inside, he withdrew the keys from the front pocket of his pants. The doorknob turned easily but the thrown bolt held the door firmly against its jamb. When he inserted the largest key and turned it he heard the bolt slide smoothly aside, unlatching the door. Scott swung the door in. It seemed to gently pull his arm as he followed. The house was still.

"Hello?" he shouted, as he pushed the door open. "Is anyone here?"

Hearing only the rhythmic ticking of the grandfather clock in the front hallway, he tentatively walked inside. Immediately he sensed the presence of all the magnificent possessions and the aura of all those who had once stood in this room admiring them.

Scott walked to the French doors of the office and gently pushed down on the door's handle. It was locked. After using a small brass key to unlock one of the twin doors he entered a world that was at once both majestic and strange.

Since the office's large window curtains had been tightly drawn, the only light came from beams of sunshine playing through the half-round stained glass windows located above them, casting shafts of soft, deep colors that imbued the room with an ethereal quality.

Near the center of the room was a large, square, maple card catalog box which rested on a round oak library table. The table had its legs bolted to the floor. Perched upon the top of the box was a small brass telescope-like instrument. The box featured card catalog drawers with twenty-five drawers per side. One hundred small drawers. As Scott walked around the box, he noticed that the small telescope sat off-center so that it could easily be peered through.

The scope was supported by a brass column attached to a circular base of dark-green marble. A brass arm affixed to the back of the telescope descended into a point. Scott took a second turn around the box wondering why the scope pointed away from the windows and toward the bookcase. He bent over it carefully and peered into the scope. It contained crosshairs like a hunting scope and they crossed over the title of a book. The room was too dark to read the letters so Scott turned on the light and again looked through the scope. What he read was "Turkey."

Puzzled by what this signified, Scott stood up and opened the nearest drawer. What he found were index cards. Each card contained the title or subject of a book, the author's name, and notes. He studied the first card and then the second. They were in alphabetical order. Each card also had a small hole and a number with a dot next to it.

Acting on a hunch Scott placed the card titled "Jerusalem" onto the recessed brass plate under the scope and rotated the scope until the dot next to the number 37 was aligned with the same number on the marble base. He then placed the elevation pin projecting from the barrel into the hole and peered through the scope. Sure enough, a book with the title "Jerusalem" appeared near the center of the crosshairs. With such a system, he now understood, books could be added at the end of the collection and the scope's crosshairs would target them. A card for each book could be made out and punched and the cards placed in alphabetical order within the drawers. The books could then be located easily, without the necessity of their being arranged in alphabetical order. This could also aid in locating books purchased together.

"Pretty damn clever," Scott muttered to himself.

He opened the curtains and surveyed the room. The standup desk was just as he recalled, and after he walked over to it, he attempted to open its top. Finding it locked, he opened the file drawers which contained client files, alphabetically arranged. He leafed through the files, not wanting to remove any. He then sat in the client's chair, and after that he tried out the stool, thinking to himself that this was one of the finest offices he had ever seen. Every piece of furniture had been placed where it could best be used without interfering with any other furnishing. And the bulk of these furnishings were truly an antique dealer's dream.

Scott opened his briefcase, withdrew study materials for the bar exam, and walked to the stool to begin studying. Sometime later he glanced up and noticed to his surprise that it was evening. Shards of red-colored sunlight flooded the room, again seeming to highlight the small scope perched on top of the large box. Feeling suddenly weary and sore from sitting, Scott decided to take a walk through the house. After he slid off the stool and turned around, he noted that both of the twin French doors were wide open. He remembered leaving one of the doors closed and suspected that unbeknownst to him, the proprietress had returned home and opened up the room. As he walked over to the doorway he felt a cool breeze on his skin and caught the aroma of brewing tea. She rose from a chair near the fireplace and Scott noted that the woman seemed even taller and more self-assured than he'd remembered.

"Good evening!" Scott greeted the woman as he entered the living room. "It's nice to see you again."

"The pleasure is mine, also, my dear sir," she responded in a strong, self-assured tone of voice. They exchanged smiles.

"You know," Scott said, somewhat shyly, "I really must apologize for not asking your name the other day. I'm not usually that rude. I must have been in a daze or something. Can we start fresh?" He held out his hand. "My name is Scott Frank."

She took his hand and Scott felt her firm grip. "Not to worry," she said. "I knew we'd be getting to know each other as time progressed. My name is Rebecca Jean Solmquest."

"Are you related to Mr. Ruffescott?" Scott asked.

"Only by virtue of association," she replied.

"Are you his secretary?"

"Not officially. Although I do help out from time to time. You see, I am the fiancé of his associate, Jacob Arthur Youngquest. He's better known as Jay, from his initials."

Scott said no more although he yearned to find out more about Jay, the associate. *The office contained only one desk, and if Rebecca is Mr. Youngquest's fiancée, why is she living in Mr. Ruffescott's house?*

He sat down at the library table which again had been transformed into an altar for the consumption of tea. Today's menu included, in addition to tea, a selection of scones with raspberry jam and slices of orange.

Rebecca poured the tea and settled back in her chair.

"How are your studies for the bar exam coming along?" she asked pleasantly. Her eyes held his, and it seemed to Scott as though she was searching within him for answers to unasked questions.

Scott did not recall mentioning anything to her about the bar exam.

"Not as well as I had hoped," he said. "However, I did manage to get through quite a bit of material today. The office here is quite conducive to concentration and getting things done. But of course, you already know that."

"It's your office now and I am so glad it's working out. I must say, you seemed very intent on your studies when I checked in on you this afternoon."

"You're right. I didn't hear you return. You were as quiet as a mouse."

She smiled at that. "Well, I was glad to find you here. I miss having Ruff and Jay around to talk to, and you seem very interested in antiques and history, which as you can deduce, are two very important subjects to us. In many ways those subjects define who we are and what we do."

Scott paused and replied, "And I would be very interested to learn what it is that you and your colleagues actually do. I believe I can assume at this point that it is not restricted to the pursuit of law."

Rebecca nodded. "No," she said vaguely. After placing her cup back on its matching saucer, her soft blue eyes bore into him again. "I can tell you a story, if you'd like to hear it."

"I would indeed."

"And you have the time for it?"

"I'll make time."

"Very well," she said with a smile. "You have been warned." She paused a moment to collect her thoughts.

"This story may take some time; for I have a gift, or perhaps it's a curse, for details. You may have guessed from my accent that I am British. And darling Jay was a soldier in the British army. He was a lieutenant, as dashing then as he is now. We met in the lobby of the Shepheard's Hotel in Cairo when I was on holiday there in '37. Although he was kind and romantic, and oh so very attractive, I offered him no encouragement at first. He told me he had been schooled in England, and at a university in Austria. He received his commission in the same regiment in which his father, grandfather, and great-grandfather had served. Quite a good, solid English family, with generations of service to king and country."

"Eventually we became engaged. But shortly after we did, in '38, the war started. I was with the Royal Air Force, and Jay was with his infantry regiment on the Continent. The Germans attacked and his company was cut off from Dunkirk and the boats. His unit was stranded in France and ordered to exfiltrate as individuals and small groups. That's when he decided to flee to Austria. He remained behind Jerry lines for most of the war, serving the Allied cause as a spy."

Rebecca paused to take a sip of tea. "Are you with me so far?" she asked. "Please feel free to help yourself to more tea and another scone."

"I will, and I'm with you, Rebecca. Tell me, what happened to Jay when the war was over?"

"Well, that's the sad part," she said softly. "Jay's family in England all but shunned him. They really didn't want him to come home."

"Why, for heaven's sake?"

"It was rumored that he'd collaborated with the Germans in order to gain information."

"Did he?"

"No. He did not. And the information he gathered proved to be quite valuable to British Field Marshall Montgomery."

"Well, then. Couldn't the truth be told in order to exonerate him?"

"There were strict laws about discussing such matters. He could not make the revelations he wanted to divulge. Not to anyone, including his own family. They forever remained suspicious. Mind you, Jay was never called a traitor by anyone who mattered. But he was never called a hero either. So, Jay and I decided to leave dear old England in our wake and move to Australia, where he had more accepting relatives. But not before a trip to Paris, a city we both loved and where we could renew our love. We were on quite a tight budget, but at ten o'clock one Saturday night, we decided to splurge and go to Café Le Procope, the café that claims to be the oldest operating cafe in the world. And who do you suppose we found there?"

Scott shrugged. "I don't know. Who?"

"None other than Mr. Rutheford Ruffescott. Or Ruff, as he preferred to be called even then. I must say, I was quite taken by his manners and jolly disposition. The café was crowded that night, and there was no place for Jay and me to sit. When Ruff saw us standing there, waiting for a table, he waved us over to his table for four in the corner."

She paused to sip some more tea. Scott took advantage of the break to pick out a scone, cut it in half with a butter knife, and spread a dab of jam on each side.

"Keep going," he urged. "I'm all ears."

"I recall every detail about that night," she reminisced. "The table glowed in the candlelight. The candle dripped wax down the sides of the wine bottle holding it. It was a red candle. The tablecloth had a small tear on my side. There were four chairs around our table. One chair was piled high with books, and maps, and a coat. Some of the books were open and stacked one on top of the other. I sat across from that chair, between these two young men. We were an instant smash with one another. We each took turns talking and listening, no one interrupting the other. It was all so wonderfully pleasant."

"Ruff had been an officer in the American forces during the war. And when we three met, he was in Paris searching for rare books and manuscripts. He had purchased quite a number of books in French and German, and those he was planning to ship home to America. He was also searching for paintings and antiques that the Germans had hidden before abandoning Paris. His story was quite compelling. When we told him we were soon to move to Australia, he sat back in his chair and gave us a rather curious look."

"What sort of look was it?"

"It was the sort of look that said, 'Oh no you're not. You're coming back to the States with me!'"

"His look conveyed that?"

"That and more. And then he asked us flat out to come with him to the States. Actually, Jay and I had discussed going to America but we didn't know anyone here. When we told Ruff that he invited us to stay with him until we found our own place."

"A rather generous fellow."

"That and more," Rebecca confirmed. "We talked all night, tipping to stay well past closing. We drank wine, ate a wonderful meal, and talked about ourselves, about Paris, about life, and how much needed to be done to restore normalcy after the war. It seemed there was never a silent moment at that table. Once, when Jay couldn't remember the name of a small town where our train had stopped to make some repair, Ruff searched through his stack of books and produced an atlas with foldout maps, complete with notes on the names of the best restaurants, and names, addresses, and the telephone numbers of people he had met. It was an enchanted evening. Magical. We were captivated by the excitement of each other's lives, and by the opportunities awaiting us. And there I was with my beloved Jay, a man I would follow anywhere, a man I..."

She smiled at Scott. "I'm rambling on like a silly goose, aren't I?"

"Not at all," Scott assured her. He was sure there was a poignant point to this story, and he was determined to find out what it was. Plus, he was enjoying this woman's company, and the crisp patrician lilt to her voice. "Please, continue."

"Well, Jay and I obviously came to America with Ruff, and through the years we have had many adventures here, in Britain, and elsewhere. At Ruff's insistence we each kept a journal, starting from when we all first met. It got so I couldn't get to sleep if I hadn't recorded at least one sentence of what had occurred that day. We journaled volume after volume about everything: from how to grow tomatoes, to the names of the best restaurants in Berlin. And age didn't slow us down. Each year brought greater challenges and opportunities, and more volumes to add to our library of journals."

"Question," Scott interjected. "Does Mr. Ruffescott practice law?"

"He does. Or, at least, he did at one time, in the office you have rented. But it was a sporadic practice with few long-term clients. Whenever he seemed to settle in to a comfortable routine, he'd sit down to tea one day and say, 'Something extraordinary has come to my attention and it presents an interesting opportunity.' Then we'd be off. Doing research, then planning, directing, organizing, coordinating, and controlling some sort of expedition. It could be obtaining a rare book or painting, or recovering some lost or stolen treasure for a museum, an insurance company, or a family. We developed many contacts. And then, after a brief respite, just when we thought we could settle back into the real world, there he'd go again with, 'Something extraordinary has come to my attention and it presents an interesting opportunity.'"

"I must say, I would love to read your journals," Scott said, intrigued. "Dare I ask where Mr. Ruffescott is now?"

"He is in Ephesus," she responded. "I need to explain to you why he's there before I leave."

"Where are you going?" he asked, leaning toward her.

"I will answer your question in a moment, Scott. Before I do, let me give you some background. Have you ever heard of the ancient city of Ephesus, in Turkey?"

Scott shook his head. "No," he replied, "I haven't."

She paused and looked pensively at the young man sitting across the table from her, as if weighing the pros and cons of revealing a great secret to him. Ultimately she nodded to herself, her mind made up.

She began slowly, deliberately.

"When Jesus of Nazareth was alive," she launched in, choosing her words carefully, "Ephesus was one of the wonders of the world. A marble city. A jewel in the Roman Empire."

"The lands surrounding the coastal city of Ephesus were among the most cultivated on the north Mediterranean coast. Each year the abundance of produce resulted in a surplus of food, which in turn made traders wealthy, and the city a hub of activity. But this basis of the city's economy became her demise. After hundreds of years of cultivation and cutting of forests, the soil eroded and spilled into the River Kaystros and from there into the harbor, filling it with silt and dirt to form a delta. That delta grew like a cancer. Years later, the fields turned to sand and desert. Today, Ephesus lies six miles from the sea, behind a barrier of land formed by the soil from the fields."

"Ephesus had been the government center for the Roman province of Asia during the first century AD, and was a great political, administrative, commercial, and religious center as well. It was, in essence, a crossroads. The main east-west road into the interior of Asia Minor passed through it, as did the north-south road through Turkey."

"Because of the disaster which befell it, Ephesus was abandoned around the year 1350, and was lost to desert sands until it was excavated by Austrian archaeologists toward the end of the nineteenth century. Ever since then, the Austrian Archaeological Institute has continued its work at Ephesus. After six years of incredibly laborious work, J.T. Wood, one of the original archaeologists, located the Temple of Artemis, what is now referred to as the seventh wonder of the ancient world. Five more years of work elapsed before the temple ruins were reclaimed from the desert."

"What a magnificent piece of architecture the Temple of Artemis was! Sixty feet high, 180 feet wide, and 377 feet long. The roof was supported by 127 columns, each of which was six feet in diameter. In 1904, another archaeologist, D.G. Hogarth, found the great altar, which contained a treasure trove of jewelry, coins, and art. Those objects were probably imbedded in the altar in the fourth century BC during the construction."

Rebecca paused briefly to sip what was by now tepid tea.

"Are you a college professor or history teacher?" Scott asked, enthralled. "How have you come to know so much about this site?"

"At one time Jay studied archaeology in Vienna, and he got to know several of the archaeologists quite well. He visited the site in Turkey on several occasions. He loves talking to me about it, even today."

"Apparently so. This is all quite fascinating, Rebecca."

"It is. And it gets better."

"Carry on, please."

Rebecca nodded.

"The Austrians are doing a marvelous job excavating Ephesus. They have unearthed a great theater which, can hold twenty-four thousand spectators. A marble arcade, thirty-six-feet wide, once led down to the harbor a half-mile away. That street, lined with shops, must have been a wonder."

"While the Apostle Paul was in Ephesus, a silversmith named Demetrius was openly hostile toward Paul's new Christian ministry. Demetrius made silver miniatures of the Temple of Artemis, and probably the goddess Artemis herself, although none have been found. Demetrius held a public condemnation of Paul in the great theater which resulted in a near riot, prompting Paul to flee the city. Paul's faith eventually led him to martyrdom. After he was beheaded during the destruction of Jerusalem, the Apostle John headed the church at Ephesus. The sixth century Basilica of St. John was located north of the temple of Artemis. It was here that John wrote the fourth book of the New Testament."

"Did he die there?"

"Yes," Rebecca replied. "They found his tomb there, untouched. The temple of Artemis has been plundered many times, but never the Basilica of St. John. John was, after all, a disciple of Christ."

"Go on," Scott urged when there came a pause.

"At that time, the population of Ephesus was perhaps a half million. The city became the focal point of the Catholic Church's power and influence. The famous Council of Ephesus met in 431 AD to deal with theological controversies surrounding the nature of the historical figure we know as Jesus Christ. The Council was held in the great Church of Mary, which has been partially reconstructed just northeast of the theater near the original harbor at Ephesus."

"Ephesus was thus a very important religious center. Ancient paganism flourished before Christianity. Members of the cult of Artemis merged with the cult of the Virgin Mary after St. Paul and St. John began preaching there. The Artemis cult was probably founded in pre-Ionian times, during the thirteenth century BC by the Carians and Lelegians. They settled around the temple of the godmother, Cybele, as Artemis was then known. That early reliance on the power of first a god-mother, and then the Virgin Mary, resulted in closely-guarded secrets concerning the Virgin."

"What secrets?"

"I'm coming to that. Constantinople, now called Istanbul, was a forceful competitor of Ephesus in claiming a special relationship to the Virgin Mary. Of great importance to Constantinople, and particularly to the Byzantines, was a core belief concerning the importance of religious relics. Any objects associated with a saint, and particularly the remains of a saint's body, were solemnly revered. Relics were brought to Constantinople from its inception, and churches were literally built to house, guard, and honor those relics. Were a person to see, or in a rare case, touch one of these relics, power and virtue were conveyed to that person. For this reason, both civic and religious leaders sent out emissaries to purchase, and if necessary steal, these relics. Thousands were taken."

"The Emperor Constantine founded Constantinople on the site of ancient Byzantium after he had assumed power in 306. Constantine saw himself as the thirteenth apostle, Christ's earthly representative. He dedicated Constantinople to the Virgin Mary and people from far and wide sought her divine protection from capture and plunder at the hands of their enemies. The city held the robe worn by the Virgin Mary, which the Byzantines regarded as their ultimate safeguard, and they displayed it on the city walls whenever they were under siege. They also claimed, at various times, to possess other religious artifacts. These included the axe which Noah used to build his ark, the stone from which Moses had drawn water in the wilderness, some of the Virgin's milk, the crown of thorns Christ wore on the cross, nails from the cross, some of Christ's blood, the sponge and reed used at the crucifixion, and even the stone slab on which Christ was laid in his tomb. All were claimed to be in the possession of the Byzantines."

"Incredible," Scott breathed. "I never knew any of this."

"Byzantines scoured the Holy Land for more relics," Rebecca continued, her voice never wavering, "but the cult worshipers, and Christians in Ephesus, had secretly hidden their own treasures that had protected them through the centuries. If their most precious relics were taken from them, what would become of the inhabitants of Ephesus? Why, they most certainly must have asked, should Constantinople possess all of God's most powerful objects?"

"Although Jesus was a prolific orator, he apparently left no writings. Others recorded his miracles and sermons many years after his crucifixion. The accurate recording of His life was clouded by folklore and human frailties, and dimmed by aging memories. His teachings were surely repeated time and again, but generally only one version of each of His sermons ever found their way into the Bible. True, His disciples were often with Him. But often they were not, and Jesus had to constantly remind Himself of the lessons He was conveying to His flock. The stories recorded in the Bible may well have been repeated many times by Christ in order to make a point, or emphasize proper behavior. In other words, to make the story as meaningful as possible."

"Now then, Scott, I am telling you all this in order for you to understand our logic in believing that even Jesus needed a method to ensure that His teachings would be passed on accurately. Paul wrote, as did other disciples, that when they came together Jesus would speak His sermons. The disciples would repeat them back to Him, or record them for His inspection, so that the word of God could eventually be spread to every corner of the earth."

"Understood," Scott acknowledged, as he glanced at his wristwatch, "But where is all this leading?"

"Sorry. I realize this is a lot of information to present to you. But please, bear with me. Here's where it gets interesting," Rebecca assured him. "Not long ago, Ruff expressed one of his awe-inspiring theories. He had a photograph of one of the copper scrolls found in a Dead Sea cave. It was a map that had never led to any real findings of significance. On the bottom of the scroll was an inscription in Aramaic. It read: 'With Mary, Signs of God' and it was followed by a series of Egyptian hieroglyphs. A few of the thousands of fragments discovered in cave four also contained portions of hieroglyphs, all scattered around a single broken jar."

Scott raised a hand, "What caves?" he interjected. "And where and what is cave four?"

"In ancient times, in the village of Qumran, there was a collection of biblical manuscripts maintained by the ascetic people who lived there. Qumran was located a mile from the Dead Sea's western shore, and about seven and a half miles south of the city known as Jericho."

"The manuscripts were in scroll form, written on animal skins, and hidden in clay jars in caves in a cliff. These, of course, are the Dead Sea Scrolls that were discovered in 1947. Because of the war going on then between the Israelis and Arabs, the area was not thoroughly searched until the years between 1949 and 1956. During that period, hundreds of caves were scoured by archaeologists, and also by local Bedouins seeking treasure. Only eleven of the caves were found to have hidden manuscripts, and those were dated from the third century BC and the second century AD."

"Cave one contained a copy of Isaiah, a Habakkuk commentary, and other important writings. In cave two, they found more than a hundred fragments of biblical books. Cave four had thousands upon thousands of fragments of manuscripts, only about four-hundred of which have been identified to date. Nearly all of the Old Testament was represented in fragments, except for the Book of Esther. A small fragment of the First Book of Samuel, from 300 BC, is believed to be the oldest known piece of biblical Hebrew. Caves five through ten were also found to possess many scroll fragments. Cave eleven held a psalm scroll containing forty-one biblical psalms, and I believe a portion of Leviticus. But in cave three, the excavators found something truly extraordinary."

She paused for emphasis and refilled her teacup, warming her hands around it. Scott leaned forward, expectantly.

"Cave three contained a copper scroll approximately twelve inches high. It held directions to more than sixty caves where hidden treasure were rumored to be buried. Twelve copies of the scroll were made, and a thorough search of the caves was conducted. Afterward, when nothing was found, the paper copies of the scroll were burned and the scroll declared a hoax."

"Was it, do you think?"

Rebecca shrugged. "Maybe. Or maybe the Bedouins had already used it to locate the treasure. In any event, Ruff believed that Jesus might have written signs to himself, small notes in the form of personal hieroglyphs that he used to instruct his disciples. Jesus had lived in Egypt as a child, which was where his father Joseph was living when the Holy Spirit first visited Mary. When Jesus was dying on the cross, he entrusted Mary to the care of his disciple John, and together Mary and John traveled to Ephesus. Or so claims the historical record. In the mid-eighteenth century, Pope Benedict XIV decreed that Mary had died in Ephesus."

Rebecca returned her teacup to its saucer. She then gave Scott a meaningful look which almost begged the question that Scott now asked. "What is Ruff's theory?"

"That perhaps Jesus had given his writings to his mother, and those writings are buried with her, in Ephesus."

"Imagine," Scott replied, "the original words of God as communicated through his son, Jesus Christ, and left with his mother – the only direct communication between God the Father and the Virgin Mother. She would have been entitled to them. It makes sense."

"There is a logic to it, and some time ago Jay set about to either prove or disprove Ruff's theory. He read everything he could about Ephesus and Mary's whereabouts after her son's death. After considerable research he came to the conclusion that she had indeed been living in Ephesus at the time of her death, or assumption into heaven. The Basilica of Ephesus had been dedicated to Mary, and in the days of its dedication, canon law required that a church could only be dedicated to saints who had lived or died in the place of the church's creation."

"Just recently, Jay announced that he had received a letter and a journal from a professor emeritus at the University of Vienna, who was also a leading archaeologist of the Austrian Archaeological Institute. Jay went into his office and returned with an odd octagon-shaped diary. It was badly damaged. Professor David Meister had sent it to Jay, after Jay had written him inquiring as to where Mary may have been buried. The diary was in German and had been written by an assistant to archaeologist Otto Bennedorf beginning in 1897."

"You have my attention," Scott said. "Please continue."

"The young man, Herbert Weber, was a proficient writer. He told of the petty jealousies that had arisen between the archaeologists excavating Ephesus and the trouble they were having securing additional funding for the project. However, the last two pages proved to be very mysterious. Here, let me read them to you."

Rebecca rose and started walking toward the office. Scott stared after her. *She has just rattled off the history of an ancient city, a comprehensive review of the Dead Sea scrolls, and a college-level lecture on Jesus Christ. This is no ordinary country lady shacked up with two men in a farmhouse filled with antiques.*

She returned with a roughed-up eight-sided leather book.

"Here it is," she announced, sitting back down in her chair and opening the book. "I'll translate. 'September 4, 1898,' " she glanced up at Scott, and began reading.

'I cannot sleep, not because the night is hot, but because I know what secret Johan and Derek share. I followed them up the hill and listened to their conversation. They have been working on their own, apart from our site. They had hired local men to help them dig near the home of the Virgin Mary. Then they suddenly dismissed them, paying them to leave Ephesus.'

'At first I thought that the jar they have uncovered contained the ashes of Mary. But no, as they studied the jar and spoke of it, I realized the jar was empty, save for some cloth without markings. But the jar had a message written on its side and also inside its lid. From what I could hear from my hiding place, the inscription declares that the remains of Mary and the signs had to be hidden, apparently because Constantinople was sending priests and legionaries to claim the Blessed Virgin's bones. Ephesus had lost all other relics of the Virgin and Christ, and with Mary's bones removed, what protection would Ephesus have? The answer is none. So the body had been exhumed, and found to be wrapped and well preserved. And the Cult of the Virgin Mary placed within an ossuary the Virgin's remains, and a parchment with the symbols of the pharaohs. The jar also said that the star of Artemis is also therein. The jar is kept in a steamer trunk in their tent,'

Rebecca stopped, drank tea, and then continued.

'Tonight, when Johan and Derek are away at the port seeing off our sponsors, I will sneak inside their tent and study the jar. God forgive me if I am disturbing something sacred. I only want to understand and share my knowledge with the world, without profit, only for the glory of Lord Jesus and his Virgin Mother.'

"That was the last thing Mr. Weber wrote," Rebecca said, closing the book.

"According to the expedition records, the next day his body was found where he had apparently fallen through the roof of an ancient bath, and died on the marble floor below. His neck was broken. The jar was apparently never reported by anyone else in the expedition. No trace of it seems to exist, save for these references in the unfortunate man's diary. The diary was returned to the university with his few belongings, and was then given to his mother who bequeathed it to the university upon her death. It took its place along with many others in the university archives. Apparently no one bothered to read it very carefully until Professor Meister came across it when scanning the journals for Jay."

Scott considered that, and then nodded at Rebecca, signaling her to continue.

"Ruff urged Jay to take advantage of this remarkable opportunity and to go to Vienna to study everything relevant that Professor Meister has access to. He thinks they should do everything in their power to trace the whereabouts of that jar. He thinks if they can find it, then perhaps they can determine where the body of the Virgin Mary is buried, along with the hieroglyphs, and star. Ruff believes that Professor Meister in Vienna is on a similar quest, and so he and Jay could be of service to each other."

"So Jay left for Vienna. He's called twice. I remember the second call well because he was so angry. He'd found that there were pages missing from the old journals. Apparently, someone has been tearing pages out from key works written by archaeologists. He also reported that his research into the circumstances of Mary's death has aroused the curiosity of a Jesuit priest who Jay believes is watching him closely."

"As for Professor Meister, Jay found him in poor health and without much energy. He had been working long hours writing a book about the second century library of Celsus, which is now the finest reconstruction at Ephesus. The professor wanted to return to the excavation but doctors talked him out of the trip. Meanwhile, Ruff and I were here. Ruff was working a little on his law practice, but mostly reading everything he could about Ephesus and its connection to Jesus, Mary, and the Roman Empire. We found nothing about any personal notes Jesus may have made in the form of symbols or hieroglyphs. He was presumed to be illiterate."

"Then one morning, I came down to the sound of a music box playing the *The Blue Danube* waltz. Ruff was wearing his gray tweed traveling jacket and he had his packed bags by the door."

"He told me he was leaving for Turkey. Ruff had tried to call Jay regarding some questions on the excavation and was informed by Professor Meister that Jay had left unexpectedly, without saying good-bye. When he asked the professor if Jay had left a letter with him to mail to us, he said no. The only departing communication from Jay was a telephone message left with Dr. Meister's former secretary, Frau Weber, saying that he had to leave unexpectedly, and that he would contact Professor Meister after returning to the United States. "

Rebecca paused and studied Scott's face for a brief period before continuing.

"That was both odd and unsettling, you see, because we have a very strict rule to always leave a letter with a colleague to be mailed to whomever isn't traveling with us when we switch locations. These letters also contain messages in code to ensure that if a letter were to be intercepted, nobody would be able to determine our intentions."

"Codes?" Scott asked, perplexed. "What kind of codes?"

"We use the Paris edition of the *International Herald Tribune* newspaper. We date each letter, and use the paper from two days before that date, to encode our brief messages. The day of the month denotes the page from which the encoding and decoding are to be done. In the small area where the stamp will be placed we write a series of numbers with dashes between them. 1-1 indicates the first line, first word from the page identified by the letter's date. 15-6 indicates line fifteen, word six, and so on. The space to write numbers is small, so the penciled messages are brief. It's a handy system though. We steam off the stamps over the teakettle."

"Is such a system really necessary?" Scott ventured. "I mean, is your work really that secretive?"

"Yes," Rebecca replied simply.

Scott Frank sat back in his chair, feeling an adrenaline rush. His mind spun around the dissertation, and his surroundings.

"In the office there is a huge painting of women at a lake. Some are armed, and some appear to be nymphs bathing. The description beside it says: Artemis at Lake Nemi."

"Very observant. Yes, it is titled, Nemorensis and Egeria, by the artist L. Stuytz of Germany. Painted in the first years of the 1800s and depicts Artemis being worshiped in a grove on the shore of Lake Nemi. Worshiping nearby is Egeria, a nymph of a nearby stream. It shows a celebration... the Festival of Nemorensis on the Ides of August. We are safeguarding it until its return to the bar in the St. Paul Hotel, after renovations there are completed. We've enjoyed wonderful times beneath that painting."

He stared after the woman who got up and disappeared, apparently to refresh herself. When she returned, she smiled at him, apparently sensing his many questions.

"I wonder if you'd mind taking me to the airport in the morning?" she asked.

"Where are you going?"

"Why, to Vienna, of course. To gather what clues I can find there. Then I am off to Ephesus. I fear that Jay has been taken."

"Taken? By whom?"

"That is the question that I seek the answer to," Rebecca Solmquest responded.

"Why take him to Ephesus?"

"I don't know, but I suspect to help find either the jar, or Mary's gravesite, or both. He won't cooperate, of course. But he'd lead them on a pretty convincing wild goose chase."

"It's been a while since Jay left," Scott pointed out.

"I am painfully aware of that," Rebecca said quietly. She stared down at her hands folded on her lap. "I have heard from Ruff. He called me from Ephesus last night. He has not found Jay, but he is on to something. I have decided to do some investigating on my own, starting in Vienna. Ruff did mention to me that he is looking forward to making your acquaintance."

"I wish I could help you," Scott heard himself say.

"You can," Rebecca stated. "Would you mind staying here and checking the mail and answering the phone in case Jay calls? We will compensate you, of course, and this is a good place to study for the bar exam."

Scott nodded before he could stop himself.

"Thank you. You are very kind. And please, eat whatever you want, and the guest room is comfortable. Oh, and be a bit careful, as we have been trespassed. Throw the bolts at night. Do you have any questions for now?"

"Just one," Scott said, as he struggled to make sense of this evolving mystery and of his role in it. "What time does your flight leave tomorrow?"

# CHAPTER FOUR

## JULY 27, 1980

The next morning, after Scott drove Rebecca to the airport, he returned to his apartment in Minneapolis and packed for his house-sitting assignment. He had not asked about how much he would be paid to stay at the house, and he really didn't care. It would be a quiet place to study, well removed from any distractions.

The guest room was large and comfortable, and there was plenty to eat in the refrigerator and freezer. Scott settled in and studied.

The two-day bar examination began on the last Tuesday of the month, and that day found Scott surprisingly relaxed. He answered the questions, turned in his answers, and upon arrival back at the farmhouse, found a letter postmarked from Turkey. He glanced at the address and to his great surprise, realized that it was addressed to him! There was no return address on the envelope, just his name and the address of the farmhouse. Scott took the letter inside, sat down on the loveseat in front of the fireplace, and opened the letter with an old brass opener from Thailand. He unfolded the paper and read:

19 July

Dear Mr. Frank,

Rebecca has by now left to pursue Jay. I know she was going to invite you to enjoy our home, and to move in if possible.

It would be a comfort to me knowing that someone trustworthy was watching the old fort.

Appreciatively, Rutheford Ruffescott P.S. Please steam off some tea for yourself and wish us success!

Short and to the point, Scott thought to himself as he slid the letter back inside the envelope and laid it face down on the table before him. Suddenly a shadow passed over his face, one of apprehension mixed with excitement. He sprang up from his chair and strode purposefully into the kitchen where he turned on the front burner and placed the teakettle upon it. As the water heated, he walked into the office and began pacing back and forth across the room, his eyes darting about and his mind spinning. When he heard the piercing shriek of the kettle, he returned to the front room, picked up the envelope and spread it open.

"Could it be?" he mumbled to himself, as he walked quickly back to the stove.

After holding the stamp over the kettle for a few seconds he tried pulling on one corner. It remained affixed so he tried again, and then again. On the fourth try, he managed to peel off the stamp. With growing excitement, he squinted down at the small square area in the upper right-hand corner where the stamp had been placed. A long series of tiny numbers greeted his gaze. Scott took the envelope and letter into the study and placed them on the desk. He again unfolded the letter and looked at its date: 19 July. Scott went to the sitting room where the *International Herald Tribune* papers were stacked and found the issue dated July 17. He computed eleven sets of numbers, and using the formula Rebecca had explained to him, he soon had the code deciphered;

"Cabinet as return bishop on new date coming cloth and wait."

*Jesus*, Scott thought to himself. *That makes no sense whatsoever.* Carefully, he reselected each word based on the numbers. The end result was the same message. He listed every possible meaning from the dictionary for each word and still nothing made sense. Worse than that, it was utter nonsense. Scott rubbed his eyes and then the temples on the side of his head. A glance at the grandfather clock revealed why he felt so tired and why his head ached. It was three in the morning and dark outside. With a heavy sigh he heaved himself to his feet and shuffled upstairs to bed.

The next morning Scott was tired as he began the second day of the examination. He found it hard to concentrate and kept thinking about the coded message. He finished just as "time" was called and drove back to the home with some apprehension. Sure enough, there was another letter for him, this one addressed from Selçuk, Turkey. It was dated 20 July and it too, was short:

"Am looking forward to meeting you soon! Best, R. R."

Folded into the letter was a small square piece of cloth that was at once both delicate and brittle. Scott held it up to the light. Nothing appeared woven into its fabric. After steaming the stamp from the envelope, he recorded eleven sets of numbers. Following the same procedure as he had on the previous day, but more quickly this time, he decoded the message: "Chosen at relocated bank or now date this cloth and wait."

Scott battled away another wave of frustration and studied the two messages. Five of the last six words matched. He wrote the six words from the first envelope across a page and the second set of six words underneath them. The first letters matched. C-A-R-B-O-N. Carbon. Carbon date coming cloth and wait. Carbon date this cloth and wait.

"Carbon date the cloth?" he said out loud. "Great. Just how am I expected to do that?"

He held the small piece of cloth up to the light and stared at it. Again, he noticed nothing that offered a clue. With a shrug, Scott sat down with the telephone book, flipped through the pages, and within a few minutes was calling the University of Minnesota. After four transfers, a disconnect, and several minutes of waiting, he was connected to Professor Raymond Kimes.

"What is it you want analyzed?" the professor asked, after Scott had explained his need for carbon dating.

"A piece of cloth."

"How old a piece of cloth?"

"I don't know," Scott responded. "That's why I want it analyzed. But I have reason to believe it's very old."

"How big is it?"

"About one inch square."

"Oh, I'm sure they can't analyze a piece that small," the professor responded.

"Could you, if it were a larger piece?"

"I don't have a spectrometer here, if that's what you're getting at. But I know that Dr. Edmund Halverson at Arizona State University works with one, and they also have one at Oxford."

Scott waited while Professor Kimes hunted down Dr. Halverson's telephone number. As soon as he had it, Scott called the number in Tempe.

"Dr. Halverson's office," a receptionist answered.

"Is Dr. Halverson in?" Scott asked.

"No, he's in class at the moment. May I ask the purpose of your call?"

"I have what I believe is a rare piece of antiquity that I need to have carbon dated. I was referred to Dr. Halverson by Dr. Kimes at the University of Minnesota."

"I see. May I have Dr. Halverson call you?"

"Yes, thank you. It's long distance, I'm afraid. The area code is 612." He then gave the receptionist his name and number.

"Very well, Mr. Frank. I will give him the message."

Thirty minutes later the telephone rang.

"This is Ed Halverson," the voice said matter-of-factly. "I am returning the call of a Mr. Scott Frank."

"I am Scott Frank," Scott responded. "Thank you for returning my call. Dr. Kimes from the University of Minnesota referred me to you. I have a very old piece of cloth that I need to have carbon dated. But I'm afraid that it's quite small."

"How small is it?" the professor asked.

"About one inch square," Scott replied.

"Well, we can radiocarbon-date that size of remnant. How old do you believe it is?"

Scott paused, thinking. "Three thousand years old," he answered.

"Really? And from where did it originate?"

"Jerusalem," Scott lied.

"Well, if it's not a University project, we may have to charge a fee for the service," the professor said. "You're coming from Minneapolis?"

"From Minneapolis."

"To whom does the piece belong?"

"Ruthef…" Scott started, and then caught himself. He was receiving secret messages, working without pay, for some very eccentric people. Maybe they wouldn't want their names revealed.

"That's fine," Scott replied, side-stepping the question. "I will bring a check to pay for the service."

A period of silence ensued, and Scott feared that this Dr. Halverson might have hung up. "Hello?" he said tentatively.

"I can analyze it on Friday," Halverson said abruptly. "Are you bringing it here or mailing it to me?"

"I'll bring it," Scott said, all too quickly. "I'd like to see how it's done."

"Very well. Please be here at nine o'clock on Friday morning," the professor said in a personable tone of voice. "I look forward to meeting you."

"And I, you, Professor. Thank you."

Scott arrived at the Phoenix airport on Thursday evening and took a cab to his hotel. The next morning he was at Arizona State University just after eight. He admired the campus as he walked to the building and office specified by Dr. Halverson. There he found a short, slim man of about forty years of age, wearing wire rim glasses and sporting a medium beard, which was graying on the sides.

"Dr. Halverson?" he asked, when invited inside the office.

"Yes."

"I'm Scott Frank. I called you on Tuesday about carbon-dating a piece of cloth."

The professor stood up and seemed to study Scott for a moment before extending his hand in welcome. He smiled at Scott in a way that suggested they had met before.

After they shook hands, Halverson patted Scott on the shoulder before leading him down the hall to a locked room. Once inside, Scott was faced with an array of devices that reminded him of a cross between a physics lab and a high school chemistry classroom.

"How does carbon dating work?" Scott asked.

"Well," Halverson explained, "because cloth is made of plant fiber, we can radiocarbon-date it. The flax plant absorbs carbon-14, a radioactive isotope of the element carbon, which comes from cosmic rays. When the plant dies, it stops taking in carbon-14. The carbon-14 it has absorbed begins to disintegrate at a predictable rate. Since it has a half-life of 5,730 years, a piece of cloth that old would contain half the radiocarbon content of a new piece of cloth." He paused and was pleased to note that Scott appeared anxious to hear more.

"This tandem mass accelerator spectrometer dates material through a complicated process. First, the sample is burned to produce a gas, that in turn is converted into bits of graphite carbon. When we direct radioactive cesium to the carbon pieces, a beam of charged carbon atoms is expelled. This beam passes through an accelerator, then into a cloud of hot argon gas that changes the charge and accelerates the atoms. A magnetic field separates the carbon-14 atoms, and this computer calculates the relative amounts. The sample's age is thus determined." He stood smiling, his hand on top of a machine with an atomic symbol and a DANGER sign affixed to it.

"How long does the process take?" Scott asked.

"Well, a teaching assistant and I will begin as soon as she arrives. We should have the results for you this afternoon around three. I'm afraid we aren't allowed to have anyone not employed here with us when we do the actual testing."

Scott handed him the envelope containing the cloth. "Thank you very much. I really appreciate your assistance."

Dr. Halverson nodded. "It's my pleasure," he said pleasantly. "I'm anxious to see the age of the treasure you have brought us."

After a self-guided tour around campus, and a leisurely lunch followed by another walk, Scott returned to Dr. Halverson's office at the appointed hour. He knocked on the door and Halverson greeted Scott with a frown.

"I'm afraid we have some disappointing news," he began. "Your specimen is indeed very old, from about the first century AD. So it's approximately two thousand years old. But there's something odd here. You said it was from Jerusalem?"

"I did," replied Scott, trying to look disappointed. Instinct told him to divulge nothing about this cloth, even though he knew precious little.

"What was the piece a part of?" Dr. Halverson inquired.

"I don't know exactly, but I think it may have been from a piece of clothing. How much do I owe you for the test?"

"The university can pick up the tab on this one if you would fill out this form," he said, handing a sheet of paper to Scott. "Please describe the whole piece as best you can, including where it was found, and answer the questions on the back."

"I'm sorry, I don't know that information," Scott replied. "I wish I did. I want to help you, but my employer only told me it was three thousand years old, from Jerusalem. He's there now and when he returns I will know more."

Dr. Halverson stared at Scott for several moments as if weighing something in his mind. He then retrieved an envelope from his desk with a return address written on it. He affixed a stamp to it, then handed the envelope to Scott.

"I ask you to please mail me the information as soon possible," he said.

"Will do," Scott promised, and he departed the office quickly, wishing to avoid further questioning.

Professor Edmund Halverson stared after him, a smile spreading across his face. "Rutheford Ruffescott," he sighed.

\* \* \*

Scott felt fatigue pressing on him as his plane landed at the Minneapolis-Saint Paul International Airport and he drove west toward the old farmhouse. When he got there he went straight to bed.

Four days later, Scott discovered another letter addressed to him from Mr. Ruffescott. He was excited to see it but hesitated before opening it. He heated the teakettle, as he was sure the stamp was obscuring yet another mysterious message. It was. It decoded simply: "Come here." In the envelope was the message:

> "If you should ever come to Ephesus, I recommend flying to Izmir. From there it's a reasonable car ride to the ruins and to the Tusan Efes motel, where I have enjoyed many restful nights."

There was also a postscript which referred to two books. Apparently, he was to review them before leaving on his trip. Scott placed the letter and envelope on the fireplace mantel, and then slumped into a loveseat. He could not afford to drive to Northern Minnesota for a weekend, let alone fly to Turkey and become involved in some wild-eyed escapade about which he knew precious little. Not only that, he had received orders to report to Fort Bragg in North Carolina in less than a week. Additionally, he had charged the flight to Phoenix on his credit card, and was nearly broke. How would he ever recover financially once he returned? How could he explain things to the army brass if he sought to cancel his active duty? Why was he being summoned in the first place, and why, oh why, was he being so damned compliant?

*Sweet Jesus, what have I gotten myself into?* Scott wondered.

When sleep finally came to him that night, he dreamed about being alone in a rowboat, straining against the oars. It was a small red pram, with a hard, wood thwart for a seat. He wore no life preserver, and his back ached from the strain of the oars as he stretched his arms forward, dipped the oars into the calm blue water, and then pulled the little boat forward in rhythmic bursts of speed. Suddenly, the bow lifted into the air and he turned to look forward in horror at a large green wall of water capped with wind-whipped white spume. He crouched low as the wave crashed upon him, flooding the boat and throwing him into the fierce hurricane-force winds, his cries of terror drowned out by the shriek of wind as he tumbled down to his doom.

Scott woke with a start. He had been lying on his left side with his right arm dangling over the bed's side. A wind-blown tree branch was snapping against the bedroom windowpane, and he could hear the telephone ringing downstairs. Sleepily he checked his wristwatch: four o'clock. "Damn," he muttered to himself as he dragged himself out of bed, switched on a light, and gingerly made his way down the stairs.

What brought him fully awake, was the unexpected sound of a car engine starting up outside. He peered out the staircase window and saw the headlights of a car come on just before the car started down the driveway and out toward the main road. Scott picked up his pace; at the bottom of the staircase, he felt a chill breeze wafting in through the wide-open back door. Scott stood stock still, listening for a telltale creek or groan from someone walking on the wood floors. Hearing nothing beyond the pleasant tick-tock of clocks, he walked guardedly into the dining room, retrieved the sword from the suit of armor, and ran his finger lightly along its edge. Satisfied it remained a lethal weapon despite its age, he began turning on every light in the house as he went from room to room, sword in hand, looking in closets, behind drapes, and in any other possible hiding place. Finding nothing out of the ordinary, he put down the sword and walked into the parlor toward the fireplace.

Suddenly he felt a chill run up his spine. He remembered the letter and envelope that he had left on the mantel. To his relief, they were still there, undisturbed. He picked them up and held them securely in his right hand, as he searched through the desk drawer where he kept his notes and the other letters he had received. No doubt about it, someone had rifled through them, and it appeared that one envelope was missing.

# CHAPTER FIVE

## JULY 15, 1980

Jacob Arthur Youngquest arrived in Vienna, fourteen hours after departing Minneapolis-St. Paul, a tired man. From Wolfsthal airport he took the *Schnellbahn* to Center Station, then the subway to the Ober St. Veit station before walking up the hill to the Gössl Hotel, a favorite haunt of his. It was located on a quiet street and offered good food and a hospitable staff. Few Americans, or Brits, stayed there and that was part of its allure. Perhaps it was too far off the beaten path to appeal to most tourists. But the train ride into the heart of Vienna presented an ideal opportunity to relax while observing the city's magnificent Baroque-era construction. Many of the more imposing buildings had been erected during the eighteenth century reign of Empress Maria Theresa, the last sovereign of the Habsburg Dynasty.

Jay had not contacted Dr. David Meister about his visit. He would be forever grateful to the archaeologist for concealing him during the war and employing him as his research assistant. University records had been falsified to reflect Jay's having worked there between 1937 and 1939. His collaboration with Dr. Meister from 1939 until the summer of 1945 had been of enormous value to them both. Jay had burned his uniform and all other traces of his being an officer in the British army. If caught by the Nazis he would not have been afforded any protection under the Geneva Convention. He would have been interrogated and then shot as a spy. Therefore, he had kept to himself as much as possible while gathering information about German war movements and passing that information on to an underground contact he never met face-to-face. His primary task, as prescribed in one of only three messages he received during the entire war, was to obtain as complete a list as possible of all German Nazi officials in the city, together with a description of their duties, and with whom they associated. It was a task that required little effort on Jay's part, since the *rathaus* was within easy walking distance of the university, and parading around to every social hot spot in Vienna seemed to be the favorite occupation of Nazi officials.

After an early breakfast the next morning at the hotel, Jay walked down the hill to the train station and soon was on his way into Vienna. Upon arrival, he went directly to the university and was told by a receptionist that Dr. Meister was expected to return later that afternoon. Jay left his business card with the secretary and departed but not before having a quick look around the office that had been his haven those many years ago.

Jay took the walk down the *Ringstrasse* to the Ephesus Museum where, on its balcony in 1938, Adolph Hitler had stood and declared the *Anschluss* that annexed Austria to Nazi Germany.

Jay entered the museum feeling the love of history upon him.

In 1977 the Turkish government, in a show of appreciation for the Austrian archaeologists' efforts at Ephesus, donated many fine pieces from the excavation to Austria. The collection was housed in the magnificent New Berg Museum, whose elegance and beauty heightened the appearance of the well-displayed artifacts. Jay walked around the exhibition all day, reading in German from the guidebook . He strolled to the large model of Ephesus and climbed up the steps to the observation porch, where he gazed down upon the finely-detailed model. He was studying it when interrupted by a sharp voice from below.

"You up there, Englishman! Be careful or you'll fall into antiquity!"

Jay looked across the model to where Dr. Meister was standing, smiling. As soon as he was down the stairs, they embraced.

"I suspected you'd be coming here soon," the professor said, clasping Jay's right hand in both of his. "You'd have to start here just to make sure my old eyes hadn't missed something in the archives, right?"

Jay smiled. "And to see you again," he said. "And to make sure you are taking care of yourself."

Dr. Meister returned the smile. "Don't bother. Of course I'm not. There's nothing in this tired old body worth taking care of. I can hardly concentrate, my eyes are bad, my legs are weak, and I can't travel. What's the point of living life as a fossil?"

*He doesn't look bad,* Jay thought. *He doesn't look bad at all.*

"I was at the library next door and just came in here on a whim – and there you stood, older and certainly wiser, staring down at our model of the excavations. Quite a display, isn't it?"

"Yes, it's well done," Jay responded.

"Well done?" the professor asked, arching his eyebrows. "Is that all you can say? My dear sir, it's splendid! This building, the layout, the descriptions– it's one of the finest displays anywhere in this world. Well done indeed!"

Jay laughed. "It's nice to be corrected by you again, Professor."

"Where are you staying in Vienna?"

"At the Gössl."

"Oh, yes. You've stayed there before, haven't you? I wish I could offer you a decent place to stay, but alas, I am unable to do so. I live in a small room on the first floor of a house owned by my former secretary, Frau Weber. I'm sure you remember her. She's retired now. And she has me to order around. I can't believe how a woman who served me for over twenty years as a faithful, dutiful, dedicated secretary could have developed such a tyrannical and judgmental disposition during her time away from the university. She delights in making me feel like an invalid. She nearly smothers me."

"I remember her well," Jay responded. "Can we have a cup of tea or coffee together?"

"Indeed we can. I know a good café nearby. And I have a few revelations to share with you."

The professor studied Jay carefully. His former student appeared to be in excellent health. Although his hair and moustache were now gray, he could pass for a much younger man. He glanced at his watch and then noticed that his primary research assistant, who was also a doctoral candidate, was approaching them.

"Jay Youngquest, I am pleased to introduce you to Bassam Safar, my fine assistant."

The two shook hands and soon Jay and the professor were on their way to the café.

# CHAPTER SIX

## JULY 16, 1980

Bassam Safar watched quietly as his mentor, Professor David Meister, peered through the large magnifying glass at the Latin text before him. The text was on parchment, sandwiched between two sheets of glass to prevent it from crumbling when touched. The old professor was breathing heavily; tiny beads of perspiration had gathered on his brow. After a good number of suspenseful minutes had elapsed, he placed the glass carefully on the table.

"Nothing here, either," Dr. Meister said with a sigh. "No mention, no clue, nothing."

"Well, Professor," Bassam sympathized, "it is indeed unfortunate that thousands of documents from the Library of Celsus were systematically destroyed by the Christians. Surely at one time there were references..." His voice trailed off, leaving in its wake a question more than a statement.

"Yes, I know. But Jay will be disappointed. Is he still searching through the journals from the Ephesus expeditions?"

"He is," Bassam acknowledged. "He told me that he has found a number of journals with pages torn out of them."

"I heard. I'm amazed we still have the journals. They've been studied by the English, scrutinized by the Nazis, and translated by the Jesuits who have been coming here for years to copy them and ask questions of our staff. The Jesuits are very thorough."

"Yes, they are," Bassam conceded, before taking his leave and returning to his office. That evening he worked later than usual on the translations of an Aramaic text recently supplied to him from a museum in Athens. He heard a noise and looked up from his work. Standing before him was Dianna, the department's tall, svelte, and very attractive secretary. He had asked her out twice, and she had politely rebuffed him on both occasions. He understood. He was a Muslim, born in Iran. It was unusual for her to be in the office so late. The wall clock registered six-twenty. She was normally on her way out shortly after five.

"Working late?" he asked.

"Yes," she said. "I have some things to get out before I leave town Friday morning." She smiled at him and his heart leapt. *Damn*, he thought. *She radiates sexuality and she knows it.*

He returned her smile. "How late will you be working tonight?"

"Well, I'm about finished. I thought I'd come over and remind you of your meeting tomorrow with Professor Meister."

"I'll be there. Where are you going on Friday? On a holiday?"

"No, that's for later. I'm just going to the country. I want to get away for a long weekend and relax a little. I took my last examination this morning and I must say I'm a bit tired from all the studying. A few days away from the rat race here in Vienna and I'll be fine."

Her eyes locked on his and he felt himself go weak. Despite being fully prepared to be rejected a third time, Bassam could not help himself. He had to ask.

"Will you have supper with me tonight?" he inquired tentatively, as if he already knew the answer.

"That sounds very nice," she said without pause. "When will you be ready to leave?"

Bassam sat speechless for a moment, his jaw agape. Then: "As soon as you'd like."

"Good." She glanced at her wristwatch. "I'll finish a last letter and meet you out front at, shall we say, seven o'clock?"

"Seven o'clock it is," he replied, forcing himself to sound as if what had just transpired was nothing out of the ordinary.

He finished for the night at quarter to seven and waited by the front door until she arrived, five minutes late.

"Where are we going?" she asked as a cab pulled up.

"To Café Landtmann. I called a cab and here it is. Perfect timing."

"Perfect timing is my specialty," she said to him coyly, as he opened the door to the vehicle. He followed her in and to his surprise she did not slide over to the other side of the seat. Instead, she sat in the middle where his body touched her left side. He was delighted, nervous, and excited as he launched into idle but earnest conversation until they arrived at the restaurant. It was an expensive meal even by Viennese standards, but he paid without regret and they departed for her apartment after a short wait for a taxi. He wanted her, very much; the wine they had consumed made her even more radiant and desirable. Her long, beautiful legs showed below a tight skirt, which had crept midway up her thighs, and there was an air of sensuality about her that no man of normal persuasion could deny. He waited for a pause in their conversation, then leaned over and kissed her. She responded by turning toward him and pressing her hand on his upper thigh. They kissed deeply, passionately, their tongues touching until the taxi driver called out the address of her apartment.

"Can I come in for a few minutes?" he asked, almost as a plea.

"No," she replied. "But I wouldn't mind your company this weekend if you can get away."

He swallowed hard, unable to fully accept what she had just said.

"That sounds wonderful," he managed to say. "I have a car and we can drive wherever you'd like."

"Good. See you here at nine on Friday morning?" she asked, her hazel eyes wide with anticipation and seduction. Or so it seemed to him.

"Nine o'clock? On Friday? Yes, that will do nicely. Nine o'clock. I shan't forget." Silently he cursed his fumbling. Never had he felt so inept in the company of a woman.

"I should hope not," she said teasingly, and kissed him softly on the lips, her hand drawing slowly down his face in a final caress. She then opened the door, got out, and closed the door behind her, before hurrying into her apartment building. He watched her go, inhaled a deep breath, and gave the driver his home address. *Good Lord, is it only Wednesday? Can I make it to Friday?*

The next morning he arrived early at his office. He looked for Dianna several times at her desk but apparently she hadn't come in. *Odd*, Bassam thought. When he heard the professor arrive, he strode to his mentor's office.

"Good morning, Dr. Meister," he greeted. "Are we still planning to meet with your American friend this morning?"

"Yes, Bassam," the professor acknowledged. "He'll be here at noon. He called earlier from the museum and told me that he also wants your insight into his theory. You are both rather alike in your approaches to archeology. I believe you can be of some assistance to him."

"I'd be happy to assist him in any way I can," Bassam asserted, adding, in as casual a tone as he could muster, "By the way, do you know if Dianna is coming in today? I want to ask her for some typing assistance."

"Dianna? No. I'm afraid she won't be back until next week. She was planning to come in today but called this morning and said she needed to take today off."

"Oh," Bassam responded, again trying to stifle his true emotions. "I hadn't realized."

"After that," the professor continued, "she is leaving for a month-long vacation. It's well deserved. She is quite bright, and now that she has finished her studies, I will recommend her for a position at the museum, as an assistant to the curator."

"She would be excellent in that position, Dr. Meister."

"I quite agree. Her final paper was brilliant."

Jacob Arthur Youngquest appeared at Professor Meister's office doorway. He had arrived ten minutes late and apologized to both Dr. Meister and Bassam Safar for his tardiness. He laid his briefcase on a chair and rubbed his red-streaked eyes.

"Hard times?" Professor Meister asked. He gazed affectionately at the handsome, well-dressed man whose life he had once saved.

"I'm stumped," Jay said in a defeatist tone of voice. "Utterly stumped. I've gone through every journal, every article, and every scrap of paper in the archives about the 1898 expedition, and I haven't been able to find any reference to a jar and lid with inscriptions. I found no relevant references to hieroglyphs. I don't understand. Such a discovery would have surely surfaced sooner or later. Nor could I find any references to findings near the house of Mother Mary. I did note, however," he concluded, "that pages have been carefully torn out of a number of archaeological journals."

"So we have heard," Bassam commiserated. "But of course writers often throw away pages from their journals. They make mistakes, think better of their former conclusions, and decide not to leave anything for future research that might not be viewed as rational or scholarly."

"I realize that, Bassam," Jay said, "but these pages were torn out recently. Very recently, according to the torn paper. I have studied the edges of the paper meticulously with a magnifying glass, and there can be no refuting the conclusion that someone has been stealing from the archives."

"Damned fools!" the professor muttered contemptuously. "I'd like to find out who has done this. It's criminal! I will make them lock up the archives and restrict access to supervised readers. Everyone, including me, will be scrutinized. We have guards in the museum watching and listening for those who would so much as touch the artifacts while we let unknown idiots loose in the writings to desecrate the originals and copies of archaeological logs and journals. It's criminal, I say!"

"Copies?" Jay asked, a ray of hope expressed in his eyes. "Did you mention something about copies?"

The professor frowned before staring intently at both men. "Yes, I did," he confessed. "In 1936 I saw what was happening in Germany. Books were being rounded up and taken to Berlin. Books were being banned. Books were being burned. I began removing certain scholarly works to a secret place. Some of these were well-known journals that could lead archeologists of the future to new discoveries. These I systematically checked out and asked my students to copy the better known ones that might be missed. We kept the original works and placed the copies back as originals. Whole collections were thus saved, sealed up in a secret place that only a priest, and Joseph Katz, and I knew about. But, as it turned out, the Nazi invaders removed nothing! At least nothing related to the ruins at Ephesus."

"Where are these journals?" Jay asked.

"In a cemetery at an old church in Salzburg. Packed into a wall crypt."

"Salzburg is hours from here!" Jay exclaimed.

"Yes, yes, I know. But I wanted them away from Vienna and I had a trusted friend who was a priest at a Salzburg church. Joseph Katz and I took them there by train, in trunks and suitcases. The priest then put them in the crypt."

"How many works are there?" Bassam asked.

"Oh, quite a few."

"My God, what an undertaking," Jay said. "Have you ever gone back there to look at them?"

"Never."

"I don't remember you talking about any Joseph Katz when I was here during the war," Jay ventured. "Who is he? What happened to him?"

"He was a friend who assisted me before the war. He disappeared in 1938. Disappeared from Vienna. Then one night his wife disappeared too.

They were Jewish by ancestry. We never heard anything more from them or about what happened to them."

The old professor's shoulders drooped and his eyes misted.

"I did nothing to try to save her," he said in tones of self-deprecation.

Jay felt a tingling sensation in his spine. The thought raced through him that perhaps the professor had hidden Jay himself from the Nazis as repentance for this earlier failure to act. His eyes welled with tears and pity for the man as he placed a hand on the professor's back.

"I need to go to Salzburg," Jay said quietly. "I'll leave tomorrow."

"I'm going with you," the professor stated as a fact. "You'll never find them without me. But please, let us wait until Saturday morning."

Jay did not respond. He needed the professor's help but feared that the trip would be hard on him physically.

"Don't worry about me!" the professor responded, as if reading Jay's mind. "I can survive such a short trip. And it will do me good to get out of Vienna."

Bassam Safar swallowed. He wanted to go also, but his plans for the weekend had a strong grip on his tongue.

"Should I go with you?" he finally asked.

"No. I don't think that'll be necessary," Jay responded. "Besides, we may have to arrange for the return of the books to Vienna."

The professor nodded. "That is true. Now that I know that they are more complete than our works here, they must be safeguarded so that they arrive back safely."

"Doctor, I would like to help you, and Mr. Youngquest, but I have made plans for the weekend," Bassam admitted. "In fact, Professor, I want to ask you for the day off tomorrow."

"Permission granted, Bassam. You deserve more time off than you've given yourself. Is there a girl involved, perhaps?" His lighthearted tone suggested that this would not be the first time Bassam had asked for time off because of a woman.

"No such luck, Professor," Bassam lied. "A cousin is coming to visit me."

"Another royal cousin, I suppose. Well, you two enjoy yourselves."

"Thank you, Professor. I'll spend the balance of today making sure that space is made available in the archives. I'll draft a letter for your signature, Professor, concerning the stolen pages and your insistence that the archives be made secure. We can have the locks changed. I believe we should also inform the police. The thieves need to be caught, or at least made aware that their criminal behavior is being closely monitored. We can't have more journal pages disappear."

"Good man," the professor said. "Be on your way now."

Bassam departed on his self-assigned mission, happy to contribute to the cause without sacrificing the upcoming weekend with the woman who by now completely dominated his thoughts and fantasies.

At eight-thirty Friday morning, Bassam got into his Jaguar sedan and drove to Dianna's apartment building. Traffic was light and the day sunny with a light breeze. As the silver Jaguar rolled to a stop, she opened the front door of her building and came toward him with a lilt in her step. She had a small suitcase in one hand and her purse in the other. She wore a cherry-colored pantsuit and her dark hair bounced playfully as she walked to the open trunk, where Bassam stood admiring her.

"Good morning," she greeted him happily.

"Good morning, Dianna." He took the suitcase from her and secured it inside the trunk before closing it. "How are you today?"

"How do I look?"

"You look fantastic."

"Well, I feel fantastic," she replied, and kissed him lightly on the cheek. Her bright eyes danced. "What do you say we go to Melk? I've always wanted to see the monastery there."

"So have I," he said, adding, "the way you look right now Dianna, I'd drive you to Siberia if that's where you wanted to go. Consider me your humble servant."

"Flattery is one of your best traits," she said, laughing. "Especially when it is directed at me. Besides, my dear Bassam, when it comes to good looks you are hardly a slouch."

They got into the car and were soon on the autobahn heading west. He drove, while she withdrew a small map from the glove compartment and calculated the approximate distance.

"We should be there by noon," she announced, "if you keep your foot to the floor. We can eat lunch once we arrive, and then find a cozy hotel for the night. We can decide where to stay tomorrow night later."

Bassam was becoming increasingly relaxed as the reality of his good fortune took hold. Dianna obviously felt very much at ease with him as they discussed her examinations, living in Vienna, and especially Dr. Meister, while cruising along the autobahn at 130 kilometers per hour. She seemed to admire the professor and his work as much as Bassam did.

"Professor Meister told me that your paper was excellent," he said at one point. "In fact, 'brilliant' was the word he used."

"Thank you for telling me that. Yes, he gave me an excellent grade, but he never says anything to me, either about my studies or about my work for him."

The sun warmed the car's interior and they continued their drive to Melk without incident. They ate lunch at a restaurant in the heart of the town and then found a hotel. He hadn't touched her yet, but dearly wanted to. He was anxious and excited as a woman from the front desk led them up to the second floor where she showed them two rooms. Both were spacious, comfortable and well appointed, with excellent views of the Danube.

"I prefer the first one," Dianna said to the woman, who nodded her understanding. Bassam went downstairs to register, and then moved the car into the small lot behind the hotel. When he returned to the room with her suitcase and his leather overnight bag in hand, she closed the door behind him. She had drawn the shades closed, he noted, as he set the bags down. He turned toward her and immediately she was in his arms, kissing him tenderly. Desire exploded through him. As her mouth opened and her tongue found his, she began unbuttoning his shirt and unzipping his pants. He responded by kissing her neck and fumbling with the buttons of her blouse.

"Get undressed while I change," she whispered. He undressed quickly and stretched out on the bed. A moment later she emerged from the bathroom wearing an ivory-colored camisole and went to him. An hour later they both lay exhausted.

"That was wonderful," he sighed, not entirely truthfully. Despite his appetite for sex, he had rarely enjoyed it with a woman the first time they were together. He couldn't seem to relax, and more often than not, had ended up leaving the woman less than satisfied.

"It'll get much better," she said smiling, as her hand skimmed up his inner thigh and gently gathered him in.

"I must have been blessed from above," he muttered, and he utterly abandoned himself to her warm, sensuous ministrations. "I'm in heaven," he whispered in her ear sometime later as she lay moist and spent on top of him.

"Heaven is a good place to be," she whispered back. "Let's stay here together all weekend."

"I can be talked into that," he murmured.

They stayed. For Bassam, it was like a dream. She was so aggressive, and yet so very sensual. She slept wearing the camisole, and a bra she would not let him remove, except for the time she pulled down the left shoulder strap to expose a full breast, a sight that caused his loins to stir. They left the bed only for a long evening meal during which she drank no wine or beer, and he talked incessantly to her about how incredibly beautiful she was. They returned to bed at the hour of midnight and fell asleep an hour later after another round of heated passion. He woke in the morning with a heartfelt groan of encouragement as she aroused him with her lips.

"Today let's explore the abbey," she said later at breakfast, as she poured him a cup of thick black coffee.

"Agreed," he said. "We can walk there from here. Shall we get going?"

"In a minute. First I have to get my purse from the room. Will you come with me?"

"Of course."

No sooner had they returned to the room then she put a "Do Not Disturb" sign on the doorknob, closed and locked the door, and pulled him into bed.

It was afternoon before they walked across the bridge spanning the channel, and then through the woods to where the Danube flowed. They talked of nothing important. She seemed so happy to be with him on one level, and yet on another, so reluctant to talk about anything that might come across as personal.

*What are you complaining about?* he reprimanded himself. *This is a man's fantasy. She wants your body. She desires you. She is satisfying in bed, and yet no feelings seem to be developing between us. I am a Muslim who may well return home next year to meet and marry a Muslim woman. I want no love to be between us. This arrangement is ideal, and I should be ecstatic.*

Unfortunately, he wasn't ecstatic. He was troubled. They were simply using each other, without sentiment. It was simply not his way. Bassam sighed and shook his head. *I'm troubling myself about nothing. Enjoy her this weekend. See what happens.*

Sunday morning he woke to the sound of the shower running. Bassam went into the bathroom to relieve himself, and glanced around at the items on the shelf above the sink. After he had closed the door behind him, he walked back to the bed and lay there supine with hands clasped behind his head. When Dianna emerged from the bathroom they made love more passionately, it seemed, than ever before. When she catnapped, he got up and went into the bathroom to shave.

"Are you feeling all right?" he asked, when she came in to watch him.

"Yes. Why, Bassam?"

"I saw the thermometer in here while you were showering," he said. He glanced at her and noticed her cheeks flush pink.

"I was feeling a little warm during the night and wanted to see if I was getting a fever. I'm not. My temperature is normal. I feel fine today."

He finished shaving and then showered before they went down to breakfast. Most of that morning they spent in their room. At two o'clock they checked out and drove back to Vienna. Bassam was quiet during much of the trip. Dianna seemed to have little to discuss with him. He assumed she was absorbed in thoughts of her studies ending and where she should apply for a position. And about her coming holiday.

"What's the American like?" she asked suddenly, as they reached the outskirts of Vienna.

"Jay? He was Professor Meister's research assistant during the war. Very interesting man. He's in search of the burial place of Mary, the Mother of Jesus. His hypothesis, based upon nothing other than a journal entry from an 1898 expedition, is that the prophet Jesus also wrote sermons that might be located with the body of Mary, along with a statue."

Dianna appeared nonplussed by that piece of information.

"Is he making any progress in his research?" she inquired.

"No. He contends that certain books in the archives have had pages torn out of them. That, in turn, has made him more suspicious than I believe is warranted. Pages often fall out of crumbling old books. The paper they used back then was of poor quality."

"That's too bad. Is he going to be in Vienna long?"

"I'm not sure. I expect that he'll be busy for some time, examining journals that the professor had hidden away in the thirties before the Nazis could get at them."

She arched her eyebrows.

"He hid books from the archives?"

"Yes. In Salzburg. Jay and the professor are arranging for their return this weekend, in fact."

"He shouldn't travel," she stated with conviction, as the Jaguar pulled up to her apartment. Bassam popped the trunk open and Dianna immediately got out of the car to retrieve her suitcase.

"Can I walk you to the door?" Bassam asked her.

"I can manage, thank you." She gave him a forlorn look. "Thank you for this weekend, Bassam," she said softly. "I really enjoyed it."

Then, without another word, she turned around and disappeared inside her apartment building.

# CHAPTER SEVEN

## JULY 17, 1980

The Jesuit superior general, who was personally addressed as *Father General*, worldwide head of the Catholic Jesuits, picked up the telephone and listened carefully to Father Martelli's solemn recital. One of Father Martelli's assistants had learned while in Vienna, that an American possessed information which supported the existence of the Blessed Virgin Mary's grave in Ephesus and that the grave might contain writings by Jesus. When Father Martelli paused, the superior general said nothing right away. Neither man wished to intrude upon the other's thoughts. They knew each other that well. But while they respected each other's abilities, that respect had never blossomed into a friendship between them.

"Tell me, Father Martelli," the head of the Order asked. "How many times have we chased such stories around this world?"

"That is irrelevant," came the reply after a sigh. "We have no choice but to investigate the matter."

"You're probably right. We should never jump to conclusions. So I suggest we each appoint an advocate. Yours the proponent supporting the theory, and mine the devil's advocate against the theory. We will see where their investigation takes us."

"Yes, that sounds appropriate," Father Martelli replied.

"They can meet at your convenience, Father. I want this matter to remain strictly confidential. You and I can discuss it again after we receive additional information. I don't need another confrontation with the Polish this month," he added, referring to Pope John Paul II, who was born in Poland. "Do you understand?"

"I understand."

"Father, on a related matter, I have recently acquired a copy of a most aggravating memorandum about our Order prepared for Cardinal

Lombranski. It is not flattering. In fact, it contains many accusations and insults directed against Jesuits. So you see how sensitive this investigation can become. We must handle it quietly and discreetly, as a team. Agreed?"

"Agreed. A Jesuit has never become pope, Father General. Perhaps we have encouraged too much introspection?"

There was silence for nearly ten seconds.

"Perhaps, one day. So, Father, who will you designate as your proponent?"

"Father Antonio Gianti. A bright young priest of unquestionable faith."

"Well, I have a young priest here who prays many times each day for the opportunity to slip out from under my thumb. Father Joseph Baronio. He is from Milan, serves as the assistant to my priest secretary, is thirty years old, enjoys exercise, and is quite competent. He silently questions just about everything I do. I've relied upon him a great deal during the past year since my priest secretary, Father Lucerso, became ill. He will welcome the challenge and will welcome his freedom even more."

"He is the long-distance runner I have heard so much about?"

"The same."

"How did he do in the New York Marathon?"

"Three hours, twenty-six minutes, sixteen seconds," the Jesuit superior general responded, chuckling.

"That is most impressive. Thank you, Father General."

"No. Thank you for bringing this matter to my attention at the onset of your investigation. I'll have Father Baronio report to you tomorrow afternoon, at fourteen hundred. Good-bye. Be well."

"Good-bye."

Father Jerino Martelli, Director of Jesuit Missions and Marian Authority, gently placed the telephone receiver back on its cradle, his outstretched palm lingering above it momentarily.

*Well, well,* he thought. *Report to me. Here! The father general apparently doesn't want to be seen as the originator himself, and no one in his office would apparently be designated to monitor this matter. He's left it entirely in my hands. He even thanked me for bringing this to him. Well, that can only mean one thing. He is marshalling his forces against those who would desecrate our Order and attack us. We must stand united behind Father General. He is a brilliant man.*

He picked up the phone and told his receptionist to send in Father Gianti, who had informed him about the American's theory and research in Vienna.

Antonio Gianti was a vibrant member of the Society of Jesus who had been blessed at birth with a most important Catholic credential. He was Italian. What's more, he was born into wealth and privilege, was well educated, articulate, and boyishly handsome. After graduating from the seminary in Rome, he was assigned to serve as assistant to Father Jerino Martelli, the director of the Jesuit Missions and Marian Authority. His intelligence was reflected in the breadth and depth of his studies, particularly in the field of languages. Fluent in Italian, German, Latin, and English, he could also read ancient Aramaic. A strong interest in archaeology led to his study of Mediterranean civilizations of the first and second centuries.

Father Gianti entered his superior's office quietly, taking his usual long strides across the carpeted room to stand before the large mahogany desk.

"Sit down, please, Father," Martelli said, beckoning toward one of two chairs placed before the desk. Sunlight streamed through a series of windows, casting a soft light upon a space that closely resembled a college dean's office. After Antonio, or Tony as he preferred to be called, took a seat, Father Martelli began.

"You and an advocate from the father general's office will meet here tomorrow, with me, at 1430 hours. You will be the advocate for the proposition that there exists a grave containing the remains of our Holy Mother, as well as writings from the hand of Jesus. You will both report only to me. You will speak to no one else about this. And I mean *no one.* Is that clear?"

"Absolutely."

"Good. I expect you to have an outline on my desk tomorrow morning at 0900 detailing how you plan to proceed with this investigation."

"I will have it to you," Father Gianti promised.

At nine o'clock the next morning, Father Martelli carefully read through the plan that had his young associate and his opponent flying to Vienna. There, they would begin researching the Austrian Archaeological Institute's archives for any mention of a holy gravesite. They would discreetly talk to Dr. Meister, and shadow the American whose origins were English and whose name was Jay Youngquest. The plan went on at length about the probability of flying to Izmir, renting a car, and driving to Ephesus. There was a cost estimate, assuming they would have to travel to Turkey.

"Very well," Martelli said, after reading the plan and laying it on his desk. "This is a good beginning. But I must again stress our need to be careful. We must be very, very careful. Nobody from the outside must know about your investigation. You surely recognize the serious implications all of this poses for our faith?"

"I do, Father,"

The Director of Marian Authority thought, *Do you indeed?* But as he rose to his feet, he simply said, "Leave this report with me. Return here this afternoon at 1430 hours."

Father Gianti stood. "Thank you for giving me this assignment." His superior nodded solemnly, and Father Gianti turned and departed. Despite himself, a giddy feeling bubbled up inside of him as he clicked the door shut.

Not far away, the Jesuit superior general sat pondering before he summoned in his acting priest secretary.

"Father Baronio, bring in your notepad. I have something to send out immediately."

In the outer office, the wiry looking Father Baronio stood slowly and pulled at his collar. It sometimes seemed to choke him. The supervisor of two clerics, he was also a nursemaid to the ailing secretary of the Jesuit superior general, and an observer of people coming and going. Although he rarely knew what was happening behind the scenes, his fellow priests believed him to be a close confidant of their superior general. That thought always made him smile. The superior general confided in no one, not even the pope. He picked up his gray pad and pen, and after knocking once, entered the Jesuit superior general's office.

"I am writing a report on you for your file, Father," the superior general began. "I will have it completed later today. Is there anything about your service since your last evaluation which you believe deserves special recognition?"

The young priest gave him a quizzical look.

"No, Father General," he said. "As you know, I just had a review of my performance in February."

"I do know, but this is an assignment termination report."

Father Baronio felt the blood drain from his face. A chill ran up his spine. "Have I done something wrong?"

"No. I have decided to hire a new assistant as my secretary. One who is more clerically inclined."

He only enjoyed this creation of agony because of the joy he would soon bestow.

"You will report today at 1400 hours to Father Jerino Martelli. Do you know him?"

"I know his position," Father Baronio responded.

"Good. I am offering you the opportunity to be a devil's advocate." He then described to Father Baronio the information that Father Martelli had relayed to him.

Father Baronio listened with teeth clenched to hide his smile. But inside he was beaming. An advocate! He'd travel without need of his clerical robes. He'd be with crowds of real people. He'd be independent.

"Now, this I must warn you, young priest of Jesus. You are an advocate on an assignment that may challenge the very basis of our faith. You will be seeking evidence that the body of Mary, Mother of Jesus, was not assumed into heaven upon her death, as our Catholic doctrine teaches. You will be searching for her grave, and you will be searching for possible writings of Jesus. Hieroglyphs. And whatever you find is to be kept as secret as though it were encased in a tomb. Avoid notes. Safeguard what you find. The case for the death and burial of Mary is to be made logically, and as completely as possible. It must be fully researched. I doubt that any hieroglyphs from Jesus ever existed. Your proposed findings must be based upon *facts*, not hearsay or intuition. Understand: you are not the final judge of what did or did not occur. Your investigation will be presented to Father Martelli. He will decide the implication of your discoveries, balance the arguments, and decide how the final report will be written. Not you. Do you understand me?"

"Yes."

"Do you have any questions so far?"

"Yes. Who will I be working with?"

"Your old roommate from the seminary, Father Gianti."

Despite the solemnity of the moment, Father Joseph Baronio could not resist a smile. The superior general frowned at him, then looked down.

"Now, the next thing you must understand, is that although I am making this assignment, you are working directly for Father Martelli. I want no information coming to me."

"I understand," he replied, thinking, *Very sly. This man would not be even the indirect source of any heresy.*

The superior general continued, "Now, Father, you are an intelligent priest. You must also understand that this assignment could be very detrimental for you politically. It could ruin your career. So I want you to think about this. Pray about this. Think and pray. Tomorrow morning after breakfast I want your confidential decision. Then, if you decide to go forward with it, delegate your responsibilities until your successor is appointed. As a reminder, you are to be at Father Martelli's office at 1400 hours. Questions?"

"None, Father General. Just a thank you for selecting me for this assignment."

Both men stood together and looked directly into each other's eyes. The superior general felt that his priest understood his mission. The superior general offered his hand and Father Baronio shook it firmly before departing the office.

"God be with you." As the door closed behind the young priest, the Jesuit superior general said to the now empty room, "You are my best and that is why I am sending you to demolish this theory that Mary's remains are on Earth. You must succeed whatever the cost. The defense of our teachings must prevail over all else."

At precisely two o'clock that afternoon, Father Jerino Martelli had the superior general's advocate admitted into his office. He briefed the plan, as outlined to him that morning by Father Gianti, as if it were his own. He wanted both priests to understand who was in command, and to whom they were to report. As a result, Father Gianti would not be joining them until later.

"Father Baronio, do you have any questions about your assignment?"

"No, Father."

"Do you have any doubts about it?"

"No, Father."

"Do you fully understand what I mean when I ask that?"

"Yes, Father. I have been well trained."

Martelli nodded. "Did Father General have any additional instructions for you?" he asked, his nonchalant tone suggesting he either already knew the answer, or didn't care about it.

"Only that I was in your service and no longer in his. He told me that you have supreme authority in this investigation and that I am to report directly to you."

Father Martelli was certain the priest spoke true. Father General was already distancing himself from the investigation.

"I hope you find your assignment to this directorate meaningful. I will now ask Father Gianti to join us and we can conclude."

Father Gianti entered the room and stood rigidly before his supervisor, as would a soldier before his commanding officer. When invited to sit, he sat, after glancing askance at the devil's advocate. Joseph Baronio sat motionless, offering no recognition of his old friend.

"I understand you know one another?" Martelli asked.

Both men nodded.

"I will pray for each of you. I will pray that the truth be revealed through each of you. But I must stress once again that whatever facts you uncover be reported only to me. Each of you understands the serious nature of your assignment. I need to be kept current concerning your activities, but only when you are absolutely certain your calls are not being overheard or monitored. Put nothing in writing. I have made ample funds available to you, so if you are in need of detailed guidance, return to Rome and report to me. May God be with you."

He leaned forward and stared deep into each of them, his hands clasped before him on his desk. When he had their full attention, he continued.

"Remember – we are Jesuits. The Society of Jesus. The pope's servants. Our contributions to science, the arts, writings, teaching, and exploration are unequaled by any other society or organization on this planet. For centuries, we have been the defenders and promulgators of papal authority and teachings. I need not remind you, however, that during the past century we have been accused of channeling our skills, passion, and zeal into attacks against the papacy and its teachings. I fear knowledge of your assignment by some would be viewed as an attack against not only the papacy, but against all of Christendom."

He stood, and as if on cue, they followed suit. "I ask that we go now to pray together, as equal servants before God, to seek physical strength, clarity of mind, and understanding in all that we do."

Father Jerino Martelli led the way to a small, private chapel. The elderly Father Majesky had hobbled in to say mass and was surprised and seemingly unnerved to see Father Martelli there with the two younger priests. Father Majesky said the mass as the three men of God prayed devoutly. *Something*, he thought, *is up*.

After the service Father Martelli returned to his office, and the two advocates strode purposefully to Father Gianti's room where they spoke softly of their mission, inquired about the other's family, and rekindled their friendship. They had rarely seen each other during the past year. Both were grateful to have this strange sequence of events reunite them in such a critical mission.

"So my friend," Father Baronio said, "you are the priest who was doing research in Vienna. You found out about this theory concerning the Blessed Virgin!"

"Yes, Joseph. I was researching a paper on Timothy's life after John left him in Ephesus. In the course of my research, I was informed of an American named Jay Youngquest who had been a professor's assistant during the war. My confidante told me that this man was searching for records that might indicate where the Blessed Virgin is buried, and where sacred scrolls may be hidden. I had to return to Rome the next day, so I don't know much more. Except that I am amazed that we two lowly servants in the Roman Curia have been blessed with this responsibility."

"Blessed." Father Baronio chuckled, "Are you so naïve, Tony? Surely you are so blinded by excitement that you forget that as priests, we have no business going on such a mission unless so ordered by the Congregation for the Doctrine of Faith who carry the official concern for orthodoxy and soundness. As Jesuit priests, we are being sent off to possible future glory or damnation, either of which would certainly cause resentment at the Sacred Congregation of the Universal Inquisition."

"Well, they let Galileo off lightly," Father Gianti chuckled.

"Yes, and they burned Giordano Bruno at the stake in 1600!"

"I'll bet that the Cardinal Prefect knows about all this at the C.D.F. and where we're off to," Father Gianti said slowly. The way he said it made it sound more like a hope than an affirmation.

"Don't count on it, my friend. Don't count on anything. This investigation concerns some of the most basic doctrinal truths of our religion. If he knew what we know, the Cardinal Prefect would have sent us off himself, or dispatched a team of his own investigators."

"I knew this flight from bureaucracy would not be any sort of vacation," Father Gianti sighed. "But I had hoped it would be rejuvenating. But don't worry. I do understand how sacred our mission is. And how politically dangerous it might turn out to be."

Moments of heavy silence ensued before Father Baronio said with forced gaiety, "Of course it will be rejuvenating. These sorts of inquiries always are. Yes, we have serious work ahead, but tonight is for celebrating our assignment. Dinner is on me. Do you still fancy French cuisine?"

"Do you really need to ask?" Father Gianti said with a smile.

At eighty-thirty that evening they met at L'Eau-Vive, a popular French restaurant not far from the Vatican. The meal was superb and as usual, at ten-thirty, everyone in the establishment set aside their dessert and wine glasses, put down their cigarettes, and joined with the Catholic sister waitresses, who were dressed in their elegant national costumes, in an evening prayer and the singing of the Lourdes hymn, *Ave Maria*.

After the hymn, the restaurant patrons resumed their joyous ways with no sense of incongruity save for two priests who, moved by the song's sacred lyrics, left their unfinished desserts and departed the establishment in silence.

# CHAPTER EIGHT

## JULY 19, 1980

On Saturday morning, the day after Bassam and Dianna drove to Melk, Jay Youngquest traveled by train and then bus to the residence of Frau Weber in Vienna, where he was to meet Dr. Meister at eight-thirty. As Jay walked up a cobblestone walkway toward the front door, the door opened and a beaming Frau Vesta Weber greeted him.

"Jay Youngquest!" she exclaimed joyously. "We are so happy to see you again! Come in, come in."

"And I, you," Jay replied with feeling. He noted that Frau Weber appeared to be in good health. She wore wire-rimmed glasses with round oversized lenses, and although she was only about five-foot-five, she was trim.

He entered the hallway and followed her into a small dining room where three place settings had been laid on a cloth-covered table. Jay hadn't eaten breakfast – he had overslept and had to hoof it to arrive by the agreed upon hour of eight-thirty - and his stomach growled at the anticipation of food.

"How are you, Frau Weber?" he inquired, smiling at the woman who, as Dr. Meister's secretary, had both tormented and consoled him during the war. Her sovereignty in the office was never questioned, even by Dr. Meister, who ignored her often cutting remarks directed at students who showed up late for appointments. And her cutting remarks directed at research assistants who handed her sloppy handwritten reports for typing. Jay's clear and flowing penmanship could be traced to having spent many hours practicing calligraphy, in part to quell Frau Weber's criticism.

"*Ich bin so, danke,*" she replied in her native tongue.

"I like your home, Frau," Jay commented. "Are you enjoying your retirement?"

"Thank you, and yes!" she said, reverting to English. "I must confess, at first I was angry at being sentenced to a life of boredom. But I quickly learned that for years I had no time for myself and had forgotten many things I had once loved, such as writing poetry, taking long walks, and reading. I have also resurrected my garden, and I travel whenever I can."

"It's hard to imagine you being retired. You worked so hard and seemed to enjoy all the activity at the university."

"Ach, that is true. I did love our work. But I wouldn't go back to that rat race, as you Americans say, for anything. No, I am most happy here in my quiet Viennese home."

"Does Dr. Meister know I'm here?"

"I knocked on his door when I saw you coming. He should be out shortly." She took a step toward him and lowered her voice. "You watch him. You watch him closely. He won't slow down. I told him not to go to Salzburg, believing you would be traveling by train. But if you drive his car, it's all right, yes? Even so, make sure he stops for rests. He tires for some reason, even in a car, and he needs frequent stops. Don't let him walk too fast either." She was about to add something further when Dr. Meister entered the room.

"Leave the poor boy alone," the professor said. "Jay, don't listen to this woman who believes we still work for her." He gave Jay a wink.

"You both be careful or you will get no fresh bread and tea from my kitchen," Frau Weber harrumphed before disappearing into the kitchen. She reappeared moments later with a silver tray laden with hot tea, rolls, bread, marmalade, and raspberry jam.

"I am joining you for breakfast and I promise not to say another word about your trip except that it always rains in Salzburg so you must take an umbrella and wear your rubber boots and don't get wet. Otherwise you'll catch your death of cold."

"Imagine," Dr. Meister chuckled under his breath. "She said all that without taking a breath."

"I heard that," she said, as she sat down at the table.

After breakfast, Jay and Dr. Meister drove off in the professor's Volkswagen Beetle, with Jay behind the wheel. They stopped once for a rest, and as they approached Salzburg, the skies became overcast. To the south they saw ominous, dark clouds approaching with muddled, slanted lines falling down from their bottoms.

*It would seem Frau Weber's forecast was correct,* Jay mused to himself just before the professor interrupted his thoughts.

"I called various officials here yesterday," he announced, "to get the word out that the books and journals need to be returned. Apparently our inquiries have created quite a stir."

"How so?" Jay asked.

"Local church and civil authorities have to obtain an order from the coroner to open a burial vault. And it's no easy matter to obtain one. I've brought along a written explanation from Father Speier, the priest who helped me hide the books in Salzburg. I'm glad we documented everything in his hand. He is still highly regarded in these parts."

"But he died, you said."

"Yes, in an automobile accident in 1964." The professor sighed. "I hope we won't have too much trouble with this."

"Me too," Jay agreed.

They drove directly to the old church where the journals were hopefully still secreted away. After parking the car, Dr. Meister led them toward the grounds below the cliff. He soon located the fenced-in crypt he was looking for. Fresh flowers adorned many of the monuments, but not this crypt. A smile creased Professor Meister's lips as he stared at it.

"Are you sure that this is the right place?" Jay asked.

The professor glanced askance at Jay.

"Let's hope so."

They heard a murmur of voices behind them and turned to find, striding toward them, two robed priests and another man wearing both a frown on his face and a drab, ill-pressed suit on his body.

"Let the games begin," the professor whispered.

"Dr. David Meister and Mr. Youngquest, I presume?" the taller of the two priests said with a smile. He offered his right hand in greeting.

"You presume correctly," answered Dr. Meister. When he shook hands, he felt the priest's soft grip.

"Well, it's good to meet you. Your fame precedes you. I'm Father Reike and this is Father Piene. And this gentleman," referring to the non-cleric, "is Mr. Niklas Frick. I'm sorry we didn't have more notice of your coming as your request is really quite unusual. Mr. Frick is from the city coroner's office and has graciously agreed to visit with us on his day off about the procedure which must-"

"Can we go inside and sit down?" Dr. Meister interrupted. "I'm not as strong as when we hid the journals and books." Father Reike managed a smile. "Of course. Please come with me."

*Good,* thought Jay. *We all need to be calm and reasonable about this.* They walked into the old church and sat down around a table in a small meeting room with nothing on its white walls but a small wooden carving of Jesus on the cross.

"May I have some water?" asked the professor. Father Piene left the room to fetch some glasses and a pitcher of water. Dr. Meister wasn't thirsty; he simply wanted to take control of the meeting, a skill he had mastered after years of practice on students, faculty, and officials of all stripes.

When Father Piene returned, he poured a glass full and placed it before the professor.

Dr. Meister took a sip. "Thank you, Father," he said. "Now to business. I believe that the church, and local authorities, need assurance that there are no bodies entombed in the crypt in question? What's secreted away in it are books and journals belonging to the university and the institute that I hid from the Nazis in the late thirties. Mr. Youngquest and I will do whatever is necessary to obtain proper clearance to take them back to Vienna, where they rightfully belong."

"That is most reassuring, Professor," Father Reike replied. "Thank you for recognizing the sensitive nature of your request."

Dr. Meister took another sip of water. "Jay," he said calmly, "be so kind as to give Father Reike the letter from Father Speier."

Jay produced the document and handed it to Father Reike, who studied the two-page document before passing it on to Mr. Frick.

"I recognize the handwriting," Father Reike commented. "After you called us yesterday to alert us of your intentions, I obtained samples of Father Speier's writing. I then reviewed church records and found that the bodies in that crypt were exhumed from a cemetery in Stockerau and brought here. Thus, it appears that there was an opportunity for you to use the crypt for the purpose you claim. However, as you must appreciate, to open a tomb requires authority, and not only from the church and the government, but also from any descendants of whomever is suspected of being buried in the crypt. In addition to all of that, we must avoid stirring up *any* publicity about this. The next thing we know, anyone who is the least bit curious will want all the old crypts opened. The desecration of a final resting place is a matter for grave concern," he said, smiling as he added, "so to speak." They all chuckled. "I believe that this matter can be expedited, and that the crypt may be opened yet this year," he concluded.

The muscles in Jay's jaw tightened.

"Well, I would like to be alive when that happens," the professor countered, "and 'within the year' sounds far too long. Bureaucracies take the maximum time possible to get anything done. It's the nature of the beast. We need these documents. Let's do this quietly and quickly. The longer it takes to move those books to Vienna, the greater the chance that there *will* be publicity. Everyone with approval authority should meet here Monday at the latest, issue the necessary orders, and we should get on with retrieving the books. We have no time to delay." He sat back and sipped more water.

The two priests glanced at one another, and then at Frick who sat rigidly in his chair.

"We will move as quickly as possible," Frick said matter-of-factly. "Be assured that I have been thinking about this matter since I received the call from Father Reike. Your presence, Dr. Meister, will not be necessary at our meeting on Monday, and we will do whatever we can to expedite your request."

Jay and Dr. Meister looked askance at one another. Their facial expressions revealed the simple truth that they had no choice but to comply with the proposed timeline. They'd be delayed in their quest, but at least the wheels were turning.

"Thank you," Dr. Meister said. He scraped back his chair and rose to his feet. "Jay and I appreciate your consideration in this matter. My secretary will call you on Monday, Father Reike."

The professor turned toward the city official. "If we could please have your address and telephone number, Mr. Frick? I will stay in contact with you until the crypt is opened. We understand your concerns. I would like you to keep us informed. Please expedite this matter, as you have just promised to do. Jay is an American and he is here to do research using the materials you are holding. Let's please assist him."

"Dr. Meister," Father Piene asked. "I am curious. Why have you waited so long to claim these books?"

"I was under the impression that our library had duplicates of the most important of these books. But it has recently come to my attention that this is no longer the case. Plus, new revelations have come to light about the Virgin Mary and--" Professor Meister cut himself off in mid-sentence and silently cursed himself. He had said too much.

The men shook hands all around and Jay and the professor departed the room and the church.

"Let's have another look at the crypt site," Jay suggested, once they were outside. The professor nodded in agreement.

"Very interesting," Mr. Frick stated, after the professor and the American were out of earshot. "I'd like to be present when the crypt is unsealed. The documents clearly are of great value to the professor. What did he mean about revelations concerning the Virgin Mary?"

"Yes. Of great interest," Father Reike replied, ignoring the question as the two priests and Frick walked out into the churchyard. Frick turned toward Father Reike.

"I'll call you on Monday morning, Father. Nice to meet you, Father Piene. *Aufwiedersehen.*"

As the two priests watched Frick depart, Father Reike gave Father Piene a solemn look and said, "After forty-four years my question is – assuming that the crypt contains books and not bones – does the Church have a legal right to them, or at least to studying them before turning them over to this professor from Vienna? I think we had best consult the bishop. Or better yet, we must seek guidance from Rome. I have a friend in the Vatican who has extensive knowledge of the Blessed Virgin. I will call him this afternoon."

Jay strode silently alongside the professor as they approached the gate to the crypt.

"They're being careful about this," the professor said in a lowered voice, even though they could see no one nearby. "They have a right to be concerned, of course, but I fear bureaucratic trouble. Frau Weber was correct when she predicted yesterday that they would delay turning the books over to us. As a follow-up to my call, she spoke to Father Reike to make arrangements for the meeting this afternoon. He said it was important that we all meet this weekend, to give the impression that he'd expedite the matter. But she told me that the way he said it indicated otherwise. Wise woman."

"You've still got her working for you!" Jay chuckled.

"Damn right. She's not one to gossip, and she knows how to get a foot in the door. Besides, my current secretary is out of town, and I had trouble breathing yesterday. I didn't feel my best."

"You should see a doctor!"

"I've seen too many doctors. Rest more, they say. So I rested most of yesterday in bed. I do feel much better now, though." At the small fenced-in area in front of the crypt he gripped Jay's elbow.

"This is exciting, isn't it? Yes, I'm feeling much better. We'll spend the night here and drive back tomorrow afternoon, after church." He squeezed Jay's elbow. "Let's sit in the front row during mass, as a reminder to them."

Jay nodded. "First, let's eat lunch. I'm famished."

"Fine. Lunch, then accommodations."

\* \* \*

That same Saturday afternoon, Father Martelli, Director of Jesuit Missions and Marian Authority, was summoned to the telephone for a long-distance call. He exchanged pleasantries with Father Reike, whom he had not seen in two years, and remembered only vaguely as one of many students whom he had taught while serving as a visiting lecturer in Austria. His mind came to full alert when the priest mentioned Professor Meister's name. After taking a moment to consider the priest's request for guidance, Father Martelli spoke slowly and carefully into the telephone.

"I am already aware of Dr. Meister's activities," he informed Father Reike. "I have sent two of my most trusted assistants to Vienna. Fathers Gianti and Baronio will be contacting you. Please give them your full cooperation. Do not, I repeat, *do not* divulge that they are there to assist you in this matter. Professor Meister and this Jay Youngquest should be put off firmly until the three of you are in complete agreement on how to proceed. However, Father, as the head priest, you have final authority. My assistants can help you on matters of procedure and protocol, and they need to know everything that transpires. They may need assistance from you also, to obtain information concerning the contents of the crypt. Again, assist them as you would me."

"Understood," Father Reike said. He hung up and walked into Father Piene's office where he sat down, shaking his head.

"I just talked with Father Jerino Martelli in Rome," he told his colleague. "He is the Vatican official in charge of all matters involving Mother Mary.

He already knew about the professor's visit, and in fact, has two assistants on their way to advise us. Mark my words: there is more to this affair than some old books hidden from the Germans during the war."

Father Reike returned to his own office to finish correspondence to the bishop. He decided not to mention the two priests or his conversation with Father Martelli. At the very least the bishop would feel circumvented.

Back at the Vatican Father Martelli wasted no time following his conversation with Father Reike. He contacted Father Gianti and then recorded the substance of his calls on a message log form which he tore from its tablet before placing it in a file. The file was a necessary evil. Disbursements of money required proper documentation with references to working files, concerning each investigation. He would keep this file locked in his own desk. He had opened the file himself, and had obtained the file number from Poly, the file clerk. She had brought the typed reference card and folder to Father Martelli and asked for the usual information: priests assigned, description of investigation, and location of research; but she was told only to leave the file folder, reference card, and label, and that he would fill in the information later.

"As you wish, Father," she had said respectfully, before departing his office.

It was Poly's turn to work all day on Saturday, and to be available for typing services. At four-thirty in the afternoon, she knocked on Father Martelli's door. Hearing no response, she entered, glanced around the empty office, and walked to the desk, upon which she placed the day's typed correspondence. She chanced a glance toward the open door. Nobody was coming. She could hear no footsteps or voices. All was quiet. With cat-like precision, she removed the top blank page from Father Martelli's message log pad, rolled it up carefully, and placed it up her sleeve before leaving the office and closing the door behind her.

Within the hour she was home, brushing the paper's top surface lightly with a soft leaded pencil, and reading the memorandum that Father Martelli had locked in his desk. She smiled. *Good, the pencil trick worked.* Within minutes, she had typed out a copy of that message.

Within the hour, she was relaying the message from a public telephone to an associate in Izmir, Turkey.

# CHAPTER NINE

## JULY 20, 1980

The clock radio clicked on and Jay Youngquest reached over to shut off the Sunday morning music. He looked across at the aged professor sleeping peacefully in the other twin bed, and once again considered his own mortality. He'd been thinking more and more about that lately. He did not fear death; he simply wondered about it. He also reflected upon his own life. There was so much about it that he loved, especially Rebecca. He was a lucky man.

"Professor Meister?" he intoned. "Professor, it's nine-thirty. Time to rise and shine."

"Then that is what we will do," the professor said with surprising vigor, as he threw off a blanket. "First we'll have breakfast and then we shall attend mass." He sat on the edge of the bed and stretched his arms. "It's a good morning, Jay," he said with a smile.

"Yes, a good morning, Professor," Jay said in affectionate reply.

Jay showered while David Meister dressed. After breakfast, they walked for half an hour before heading toward the church. They sat in the front pew, in full view of Father Piene and Father Reike, who performed the timeless rituals. After the service they checked out of their Salzburg hotel and then drove back to Vienna, where they scoured through indexes at the university, searching in vain for any information or legal precedents that might help them in their quest in Salzburg. At seven o'clock Dr. Meister called it a day and asked to be driven home.

After parking the Volkswagen, and seeing the professor to his door, Jay took a train to the stop for his hotel. Although mentally and physically exhausted, he felt the need to relax and unwind before going to bed. He deposited his overnight bag in the room and then went downstairs to the hotel restaurant to enjoy a beer and perhaps a light meal.

As he entered the Schneider-Gössl, the merry sounds of accordion music and rounds of laughter and applause greeted him. The restaurant was warm and comfortable; lightly-stained knotty pine tables matched the paneled walls. Most of the tables were filled with two or four people.

A large group celebrating a birthday near the stove in the back room was being entertained by the restaurant's accordionist, who sat at the head of the table playing songs that poked fun at the middle-aged man whose birthday it evidently was. Jay sat at a table near the party, enjoying the music and the good cheer. The waiter greeted him politely and Jay ordered a Stiegl beer. He sat back and studied the people in the party. As were most of the Austrians in the room, these folks were well dressed in either traditional lederhosen or more modern cuts of cloth. As he studied them, Jay felt a pang of loneliness as his mind, drifting back to similar kinds of events he had once enjoyed with close friends.

The waiter placed his stein of beer before him and as Jay took a deep draught, he was caught off guard by a not unattractive woman in a simple yellow chemise dress sliding into his booth across from him.

"Herr Youngquest?" she inquired.

"Yes. And you are…?"

"Alex Harmon. I have been waiting for you."

"How so? Have we met? I'm sorry, I don't remember you."

Her hazel eyes bore into his. "We have never met, Herr Youngquest, but I know about your mission here. I, too, have an interest in finding that gravesite in Ephesus and I believe I can help you. Perhaps we can help each other."

Jay studied the woman. He estimated she was in her late forties, although her svelte body reinforced by a gentle disposition could peg her as someone considerably younger. She appeared as a person he could intuitively trust, which by itself was enough to put him on his guard. But he could not deny his keen interest in what she had to say.

"Before you tell me how you can assist me," he stated, holding her gaze, "I would like you to tell me just how much you know about my mission."

"Well," she replied after a quick glance this way and that to assure their confidentiality, "I know you are looking for missing pages from journals written by archaeologists who excavated a site in Turkey during the late 1800s and early 1900s. I know that you have apparently been given the journal of Herbert Weber to study and that Professor Meister is arranging to recover books and journals he hid in a crypt in Salzburg before the outbreak of war. I also know that you will not find what you are looking for in that crypt." She paused to let that last sentence sink in.

Jay took a sip of beer, his eyes never leaving hers.

"Okay," he said, placing the stein back on the table. "Let's say for the sake of argument that I agree with everything you just said. So how can you help me?"

"I have access to the missing pages," she said without pause.

"Do say? Then show them to me," he countered.

She smiled. "They aren't here. In fact, they aren't in Vienna. But I want to take you to them and to assist you in finding the grave site you seek."

Jay took a long pull from his stein, draining it empty. "Forgive me if I seem a bit put off by your suggestion," he said in a voice edged in sarcasm.

Her smile remained. "And why is that, Herr Youngquest?"

"Because," he said forthrightly, "I am more than a little concerned when approached by a lovely lady I have never met, who knows so much about my business, and who proposes to accompany me to God only knows where, to help me in a quest I may need no assistance in completing. Is that a fair start? I could go on. In fact, I'm just getting warmed up."

Alex leaned forward and her smile disappeared.

"Herr Youngquest, let me be blunt: we are not alone in this search. Other parties are, at this very moment, racing to find the burial site of the Virgin Mary. They are not interested in the truth of what this site may hold. They are only interested in protecting their religious beliefs."

Jay did not flinch. "You, on the other hand, are only interested in the truth, yes? For starters, how did you know where I was staying?"

"I have been following you."

"How convenient. Perhaps tomorrow we can meet at the university to discuss this." It was his turn to glance around the room at the other patrons. She might not be acting alone.

The woman shook her head emphatically. "Herr Youngquest, we must leave tomorrow morning for Turkey. The missing pages are there. However, no one must know about our collaboration. I repeat: *no one*. First thing tomorrow morning, I want you to call Dr. Meister and tell him that you are running out of time and that you fear further delays in obtaining the books. You *must* believe me: the Catholic Church has already decided that you will not obtain access to the books until after Church officials have had ample opportunity to study them. That will take valuable time, time we do not have. Tell the professor that you are going to Turkey, to Ephesus, before you return to America. That is the truth. However, he cannot help you obtain the missing pages."

"Why all the mystery?" Jay asked, clutching at straws to make sense of what was, by any standard, a baffling turn of events.

"You just have to trust me. There is far more at stake here than you realize. Your enemies will stop at nothing to prevent you from finding what you seek."

"Even if I do trust you, you have to admit, this is all rather sudden?"

"Is it really?" the woman asked, frustration entering her voice. "Herr Youngquest, you are hardly a neophyte in such matters. I have heard of similar kinds of exploits in the company of Rebecca Solmquest and Rutheford Ruffescott."

"All right. I am only in Vienna to conduct research. I admit, I don't have a reason to mistrust you, but can you give me a reason *to* trust you?"

"I can give you this," she said, handing him a single page of photocopy. He didn't recognize the handwriting, and as he began silently translating the quarter page of German text, he noticed that the left edge of the copied page had a slightly jagged appearance. The original had apparently been torn from a journal. The cursive writing read, "The body of my friend Johan was found today, three days after he disappeared. He must have been in a knife fight, as he had many cuts on his left hand and arm, and his own knife, which he held in his hand, was covered with dried blood. Our jar has been stolen. I fear that others now know about our discovery. Perhaps one of those bastard diggers. We should never have tried to keep the secret to ourselves. I am afraid that they might also know about H.W. and why Herr Dell was not in his tent this evening. I will tell him tomorrow morning."

Jay paused before asking, "Whose journal was this?"

"It belonged to a man named Derek Liebert."

"Very well, I believe you. Did you tear out the pages?"

She shook her head no. "I am staying in the room next to yours," she said in a business-like tone. "We should get some sleep. Tomorrow will be a tiring day. Your airline reservation has been made, and the flight departs tomorrow at twelve noon for Istanbul. I will be accompanying you, but I don't want anyone to know we're traveling together. In the morning, please call Professor Meister at home and tell him about your change of plans but do not mention me. Understood?"

"Understood."

"Very well. Good night."

The woman named Alex departed the restaurant before him, and he paid the waiter before walking up the stairway to his room on the second floor. She hadn't told him which room she had checked in to. He paused in the hallway hoping to hear sounds indicating which room was hers, but he heard no sounds of any kind.

Jay entered his room and searched it thoroughly. Nothing appeared disturbed. Nevertheless, he braced a chair under the door handle, pulled the window drapes together, and removed a copy of the *International Herald Tribune* from his briefcase. Within ten minutes he had written his message in code. Jay placed the stamps over the small numbers he had written on the top right corner of the envelope, wrote a short note to Rebecca, addressed and sealed the envelope, and turned out the lights. He sat in a chair for an hour listening intently for any telltale noise. Confident at last that no one was astir on his floor, he removed the chair barring the door and crept downstairs to leave the letter among the outgoing mail on the counter. He then went back upstairs to his room, locked the door, and fell into a deep sleep.

Jay dreamed of driving in a fierce snowstorm. As his car rounded a corner, it skidded on black ice and crashed into a ditch. His head slammed against the steering wheel, and the car stopped, although the engine kept running. Semi-conscious, he smelled the car's fumes but was unable to raise his head off the steering wheel. Gasping for breath, he fought in a panic to force away the hand that held the handkerchief against his nose and mouth. It smelled strongly of ether.

"Relax or I'll kill you," a man's gruff voice said in German, and Jay realized with sudden horror that he was no longer dreaming. Mustering what strength he could, he bit down hard on the man's hand.

"You bastard!" the man growled. Instinctively he reached for a black jack attached to his belt. As he raised it to deliver the knockout blow, a wide shaft of light emanated from the doorway, illuminating the room and the knit ski mask covering the assailant's face. Startled, the attacker turned toward the light's source just as an arrow struck him on the side of the neck, its steel tip piercing flesh, shattering vertebra, and releasing a gush of blood. The assailant, his eyes bulging and his mouth agape, gurgled something incomprehensible and then collapsed in a heap upon Jay.

Jay, stunned to his core, heard someone in his room first closing the door, and then the window, before pulling the man off him. A small but powerful flashlight blinded Jay in one eye and then the other.

"Relax, Herr Youngquest," a gentle feminine voice urged him. "You have been drugged and it will take time for the ether to dissipate. In the meantime I'll get rid of this intruder."

Jay closed his eyes and woke in what he thought was only a few minutes. Alex sat in a chair drawn up to the bed, watching him intently. It was light outside. He wiggled his toes, then moved his arms and legs. In a few minutes he was sitting up, his head throbbing as never before.

"Damn, that hurts," he muttered, rubbing his temple.

"You'll feel better shortly. The ether is wearing off. Which is good since we have to leave as soon as possible. Here, take these." She gave him a glass of water and two white pills, which he assumed were aspirins.

"Who was that man?" Jay asked, after he had swallowed the tablets and gathered his wits about him.

"I don't know," Alex said. "There was another man, a fat man, waiting in a small Mercedes. He was watching your room very carefully. I used the rope your assailant had to lower the body down to him, after I wrapped it into a bedsheet. He no doubt thought I was the assailant and you were the body in the blanket. The fat man tossed the body into the trunk of his car and sped away. He'll have quite the surprise when he discovers that the body in the sheet is not yours!"

"Yes, and in the meantime my head hurts like my worst hangover," Jay lamented.

"I'm sorry. The pain should ease shortly. Those pills I gave you are powerful ones." She glanced around the room. "Now then, we must check out right away. I've packed for you. We must check out separately. I'll take some of your things to the car. It's a small gray Opel parked one block up the hill. Meet me there in fifteen minutes."

"Yes, ma'am," Jay said, feigning a half-salute.

He dressed as quickly as he could manage and took the one remaining small bag down to the checkout desk where he produced his credit card.

While the woman behind the desk prepared his bill, Jay studied the stack of letters on the counter. He did not see his.

"Has the postman come yet today?" he asked.

"No, sir. Not until this afternoon. Do you have something to go out?"

"I guess not," Jay responded.

He exited the small hotel and glanced about for anyone observing him. He noted only a few people, nothing out of the ordinary. He turned to his right and walked up the street to the gray Opel. He opened the rear door, and after placing his bag next to the others on the seat, he slid into the front passenger seat.

"Did you call Dr. Meister at home?" Alex asked him.

"No. In all the excitement I forgot to."

"I know someone who can contact him for you," she assured him. She turned a key in the ignition and edged the Opel out into the street.

From a side street, not far away, the fat man watched through his rear-view mirror as the gray Opel approached. As it sped past, he turned his blue Fiat around and followed it from a distance.

"There was blood on your pillowcase and fitted sheet, so I have taken them with us," Alex said, guiding the car in and around traffic.

Jay was lost in thought as his gaze took in the narrow streets and clusters of homes speeding past him. Her words brought him back.

"Why was that man trying to kill me?" he asked.

"I don't think he was trying to kill you. I think he was trying to kidnap you."

"But *why*?"

"He must have known that you possess valuable information about the gravesite, which, under the right set of circumstances, you would be willing to share with him."

"Not on my life."

"That's exactly my point. As I said, under the right set of circumstances."

Jay Youngquest sighed. "Well, he would have been disappointed. I don't have much information to share."

At the airport, Alex made several telephone calls. Jay checked in and boarded the flight to Munich. Alex followed suit a few minutes later and took a seat far removed from where Jay was sitting. On the flight from Munich to Istanbul, and then the evening flight from Istanbul to Izmir, she sat directly behind his aisle seat. They didn't speak to each other and after a time Jay was able to relax and consider what had happened in his room at the Gössl Hotel in Vienna. Without a doubt, Alex had saved him from being kidnapped, or something worse. Based upon the rope that the intruder had brought with him and the car parked below the window, sedation and kidnapping were the most likely objectives, as Alex had surmised. But why? He had no meaningful information yet about the writings of Jesus or the tomb of the Blessed Virgin, nor had he observed anyone who appeared hostile or overly curious. Furthermore, what a remarkable coincidence it was—if one believed in coincidences, which he did not—that this woman should contact him at his hotel, just happen to appear in his hour of peril, and kill his assailant with an arrow. A woman named Alex, brandishing a bow and arrow, and an excellent shot to boot. What was she, a member of the Artemis Cult? He could think of no other explanation.

Admittedly, he knew little about this cult, but decided to ask her about it when they talked next in private. She kept a sharp eye on him to be sure but he could have fled from her on any number of occasions, assuming of course, that she was indeed acting alone. Or he could simply have refused to go with her. It was then that Jay realized that his sudden departure from Vienna would have to be explained. Also, failure to report a death was surely a criminal offense in Austria.

It was dark when the jet landed in Izmir and after claiming their baggage, Alex led Jay outside to a waiting car. The driver remained stoic and behind the wheel as they placed their bags in the car's trunk. Alex motioned for Jay to sit in the backseat, diagonally across from the driver. As he opened the rear door another woman walked up to the car and took a seat next to the driver. After Alex had settled into the backseat next to Jay, the car was driven away from the airport.

After what seemed like a half-hour to Jay, the car was driven through an iron gate and into a parking lot behind a warehouse that was adjacent to a pier. Jay was asked to get out of the car and into a van parked nearby. He did so, first making sure that the driver transferred his suitcase and travel bag. A fourth woman, who had been in the driver's seat of the van, got into the car and drove it slowly away. Jay noted that the van had no side windows behind the front seat. Again, he was asked by Alex to sit behind the front passenger. After he complied, the van started up and followed the car they were just in.

*What the hell?* Jay thought to himself. *Why all this maneuvering around?* It seemed like something out of a spy novel.

The car, with the van following behind, proceeded back through the darkened warehouse area with its headlights off until it approached the open gate. Then, the headlights flashed on and it accelerated through the gate on toward the center of the city. The van's driver held back for a moment, as if to make sure that nothing unusual was afoot, and then accelerated toward the gate with the headlights switched on. Suddenly the gate began to close, and as it did, the van's driver put the pedal to the floor. No one in the van spoke as it surged forward and the gate continued to close. Just then, a flatbed truck shot forward from out of nowhere and stopped abruptly at the gate, blocking what little chance the van had to escape through it.

The van's driver spun the steering wheel in a 180 turn, causing the wheels to screech and the van to shake violently, nearly rolling over. She lost control, regained it, and bolted away from the entrance. Ahead, two sets of headlights, side-by-side, were coming at her.

"We're trapped!" Alex shouted.

"Not yet we're not," the driver yelled defiantly. Again, she spun the van around in a 180 and sped back at full speed toward the closed gate.

"Hang on!" she cried out.

The driver forced a sharp left as she braked the van, slamming it straight into a closed warehouse door, bursting it open. The van's windshield shattered, the side mirrors flew off, and the van veered sideways as it skidded across the interior of the warehouse before crashing into the opposite wall. With steam seeping up from beneath the van's hood, the three women struggled free through the open doors.

Alex pulled Jay out, who was dazed by the van's savage impact. "Run!" she yelled, and the four of them took off toward the back of the warehouse, Jay hobbling along as best he could.

"Keep going!" the driver yelled as she smashed a glass box with a broken shard of wood and pulled down on a fire alarm switch. Bells began ringing and battery-operated floodlights were activated as the group ran forward, their route still illuminated from behind by the van's one operable headlight. Jay glanced back over his shoulder, and to his alarm, saw armed men pursuing them with pistols. He strained to run faster.

"Hell," he muttered to himself.

The driver suddenly turned right and pushed open a door.

"Go!" she commanded, and the three others were quick to comply.

Outside the warehouse, Jay saw a railing twenty feet away and water directly below. Cars and trucks were coming at them from both ends of the warehouse.

"Who are they?" Jay heard himself shouting, as they ran toward the railing.

"Black Pope!" Alex shouted back.

"Into the water!" a woman commanded. Jay saw Alex spin toward a man who was ahead of the others. He was waving a pistol.

Alex reached behind the waistband at her stomach and pulled a dagger from its sheath. Turning, she lunged at the closest pursuer. "No! Get out of here!" she shouted at Jay, who had turned back to help her.

The man with the pistol fired just as Alex threw the dagger at him. The bullet nicked her in the arm as the blade stuck into the man's protective vest. He lost his footing, stumbled, and fell forward. Alex ran up to him and kicked him in the groin as Jay gave him a hard rabbit punch to the back of the head. The pistol discharged again and Jay heard it strike a wood light post on the pier behind him. They sound of other men running toward them grew close.

"Into the water!" Alex shouted again. Jay felt two women grabbing him from behind and they pulled him to the railing. They pushed him through between the deck and lower rung, and he fell as another shot rang out. Then, one by one, the others plunged after him into the cold water of the bay.

The left side of Jay's face hit the water first. Saltwater filled his nose and his entire left side throbbed with a violent pain. He felt light-headed as if he were dreaming, as he weakly treaded water before sinking again into what seemed more like bliss than misery.

Underwater, sinking ever deeper, he mouthed the word, "Rebecca," and the final words he heard from inside his head before succumbing to the inevitable were, *Oh no. Jay. Please, Jay. No. Don't leave me.*

# CHAPTER TEN

## JULY 21, 1980

The old clock clanged out its alarm, awakening Professor Meister instantly. He shut off the jarring sound and sighed. He hated Mondays. Instead of staying awake he drifted back off to sleep, only to be reawakened, this time by the telephone ringing in Frau Weber's room. Reluctantly he rose, showered, and got dressed. He went into the dining room and saw, to his dismay, that his tea had already been poured.

"This tea is cold," he called out to the kitchen.

"No it's not," came the miffed reply. "I just poured it."

He sat down, eyeing the tea with suspicion. He picked up the cup and took a sip, burning the roof of his mouth in the process. "Damn," he whispered irritably to himself, "the dame was right."

"I received a message from Jay," Frau Weber announced, entering the dining area from the kitchen.

"He decided to go to Ephesus and will try to reach you this morning at the university. He said he has a theory to check out before returning to America. Apparently he thinks that it will take a long time for the documents to be released from Salzburg and he's running out of time."

She took a seat across from the professor.

"Are you exhausted from your trip?" she asked him, with more than a note of concern.

"Of course not. It did me good to get out of Vienna."

"You didn't get up with your alarm," she observed.

"I have nothing to rush off to today."

He was lying and she knew it. But she said nothing further about it.

"I can't understand why Jay would dash off so suddenly," the professor commented. "It's so unlike him."

Frau Weber shrugged, "Perhaps he has exhausted his research here and is going to the Ephesus Museum to continue it. He certainly sounded well and he apologized for not speaking to you directly."

"You should have awakened me," he scolded. "I would have wanted to speak to him."

"I looked in on you but you were sleeping so soundly I didn't want to disturb you."

"Ach! Women!" was all the professor could say to that.

By noon, he was dressed and at his office. He arrived just as Dianna returned to her desk.

"Good morning, Dr. Meister," she greeted.

"Good morning. Did you have a nice weekend?"

"I did. Very refreshing. A Father Reike called from Salzburg. Wants to talk to you as soon as possible. Said it's urgent." She handed the message slip to Meister.

"Good news, I hope," the professor mumbled. He picked up the telephone and placed the call. He was quickly put through to Father Reike.

"Dr. Meister, I have very good news," the priest enthused. "The crypt will be opened tomorrow morning at eleven o'clock. Can you be here by then?"

The professor felt his heart pounding. "Tomorrow? That soon?"

"Yes, Professor. Both civil and church authorities were quick to approve it, in deference to you." As he said that Father Reike smiled across the table at Fathers Gianti and Baronio.

"Please pass along my heartfelt gratitude. I will be there tomorrow morning."

"Excellent. The court order will have been signed by then. It turns out that the Kollers, whose name is on the crypt, had no surviving relatives and thus no one to object to the crypt being opened. Mr. Frick was therefore able to obtain a judge's preliminary approval and has arranged for police security. I hope you appreciate our responsiveness."

"I most certainly do, as I just stated. I will see you in the morning."

"Until then, Dr. Meister."

The professor hung up the telephone and called in Bassam, his assistant. They made plans to leave early the next morning for Salzburg.

At that moment, in Salzburg, Father Reike smiled again at the two young Jesuits seated across the table from him. He was delighted that they had arrived so swiftly from Vienna—delighted as well that they had each signed documents that he had prepared which absolved him from any consequences that might arise as a result of the crypt being opened.

The next morning Bassam Safar, with Professor David Meister seated beside him, drove his Jaguar to a parking spot near the Salzburg church. As they strode toward the vault, Professor Meister noted that considerable preparations had been made since he was there last. The church grounds near the crypt were closed off by ropes, and posted signs warned that this section of the grounds was "off limits" until further notice. The crypts were cave-like chambers carved into the hillside, one of which had a large gray canopy set up against it. A police officer in full uniform sat on a chair near the entrance to the crypt, apparently to discourage curiosity seekers and to ensure privacy.

Dr. Meister led Bassam into the church where Father Reike and a priest who the professor did not immediately recognize, greeted them.

"Professor Meister, this is Father Gianti," Father Reike said.

"Oh yes, I believe we have met," the professor said, his memory jogged. "You are a Jesuit doing research at the university and museum are you not? Why, we spoke together not too long ago, as I recall."

Father Gianti smiled. "Thank you for remembering me, Professor."

"May I introduce you to my graduate assistant, Bassam Safar," the professor said. They shook hands all around and Father Reike led them to his office.

"Mr. Frick has called," he announced, when they were all assembled. "The order is signed and documented. He will present a copy to us soon. As I informed you yesterday, Doctor, the Church has consented to the unsealing. However, we just learned that we will be required to hold onto the books here, until their release to the university has been formally approved by both Rome and the Austrian Archaeological Society. And the university, of course. I'm sure you understand."

The professor's heart sank. "But it's clear from Father Speier's letter that the books and documents belong to the university," he protested.

"No doubt. We do not contest that. However, we must avoid any possible liability to both us and the university. You must also accept responsibility for any damage to them and also attest to the fact that they are all here."

"I have brought a list with me, if that's what you mean," the professor scoffed. There was rancor in his voice and a scowl on his face.

"Father Gianti here expedited the approval we felt was required under these unusual circumstances," Father Reike said, apparently nonplussed by the professor's sour reaction. "He is prepared to assist you in making a complete inventory of the books as they are removed from the crypt to a room in the church which is being prepared with temporary shelving. Does that meet with your approval, Doctor?"

Professor Meister thought not. He didn't want anyone else meddling with the journals. Besides, this whole mess was the result of his trying to assist Jay in finding lost pages from books and journals. He didn't even know which books and journals those were! But what choice did he have? Suddenly he felt like a pawn in an unwelcome game of chess.

"It does," he said with resignation.

"Excellent!" Father Reike exclaimed. "Now all we need to do is wait for Mr. Frick." He made a show of glancing at his watch. "He should be here at any minute."

As if on cue, Frick appeared at the office at eleven sharp. He was wearing the same suit of clothes he had worn three days earlier, and the same scuffed brown shoes. Without further ado he produced the order which was passed from hand to hand. No one took issue with the wording of the document or the signatures at the bottom.

"Everything seems to be in order," Father Reike finally pronounced. "Shall we proceed to the crypt, gentlemen?"

Fifteen minutes later, they were watching intently as two workmen removed large slabs of the marble wall from the front of the crypt. The marble had enclosed the crypt, concealing its interior. Each worker then picked up a lantern. A third lantern was hanging from the canopy's center pole. Everyone drew a breath as the light from the lanterns flooded into the crypt's cavern, exposing two large marble sarcophagi set behind a formidable locked iron gate.

"I don't see any books in there," Frick said. All eyes fell on Professor Meister who was staring intently at the nearest sarcophagus.

"I was not here when Father Speier sealed the crypt," he reasoned out loud. "But I am as certain as I can be that all of the books are there." He pointed at the sarcophagus set behind the iron gate. "Let's have a look inside."

One worker handed his lantern to his companion and took an ancient skeleton key from Father Reike who wiped his hand against his robe after handing it over. The worker fumbled getting the key into the keyhole. When he finally did, he carefully turned it while gently moving the gate's door back and forth in case the mechanism had bound up. A loud click greeted his efforts and he nodded. He turned the key around again, causing a second, lighter click as the double action easily pulled the bolt from its position in the gate's post. He pulled at the gate and it slowly gave way, its hinges creaking and screeching in protest.

Professor Meister walked quickly into the crypt. "Pull off this top stone," he said to the workmen, indicating the marble slab on top of the first sarcophagus.

Father Reike walked up and blocked their path. "Not so fast," he declared stiffly. "We have no permission to open a sarcophagus. Only the crypt! The books were assumed to be in here, not in a sarcophagus. If you open the sarcophagus, and see the coffin, what would you then have us do? Expose a body laid in sanctity? No! There is no civil or church authorization for such a desecration."

He turned to Father Gianti, who offered no hint of his own sentiments on the matter. Instead, he walked around the crypt and studied the floor and walls.

"I believe we can justify opening the top of the sarcophagus," Father Reike finally said softly. "If there is a coffin inside, we shall reseal the crypt. Perhaps, fearing discovery, Father Speier was very clever."

"He was indeed a clever man," the professor remarked.

Father Reike nodded toward the two workers who attempted to lift each end of the sarcophagus's top. The lid would not budge. Even when they both got on one side and strained with all their might, the seal would not break. Then Bassam and Father Gianti both stepped forward and added their strength to lifting the lid.

With a sudden crack the lid separated and the men pivoted the lid and left it on the sarcophagus at an angle. Father Reike stepped forward with a lantern he had taken from one of the workers and they all stared down into the twin voids of a human skull.

"Lord forgive us," Father Reike whispered, crossing himself three times.

They all stepped back except for Professor Meister who had long since become accustomed to the hollow stare of the dead. He reached into the cold box and then held up a small brass clip. Father Reike was about to say something, but was cut short by the professor who held up his hand demanding silence.

"Something's not right here," he declared. "First of all, where is the coffin? Did you see one in there? No, you did not," the professor answered for them. "And second, why does the skull lie so far up in the sarcophagus? Now, if one of you would be so kind as to bring me a light, I believe I can reveal to you the secret of this crypt."

Father Gianti took the lantern from Father Reike, stepped up to the sarcophagus, and held the light over the opening. Peering below, he saw what the professor had seen, a second skull placed just below the first one. There were two skeletons inside.

"The bodies were entombed without coffins so that they could share the limited space in this sarcophagus," the professor exclaimed. "The crypt is marked with only two names: Joseph Koller and Hilda Koller. If my theory is correct, and I am certain it is, the books will be found in this second sarcophagus."

Father Reike glanced over at Mr. Frick, who was staring aghast down at the two skeletons. For whatever reason, emotion had him by the throat. He looked up and shook his head disgustedly.

"We have no proof of this most recent theory of yours. Let's get out of here."

He moved toward the gate.

"Do you see this?" the professor asked, holding up the clip from the sarcophagus. Frick stopped short.

"Yes," he replied bitterly. "You took it from the dead."

"Yes, I did. But it did not belong to them. It is a brass page marker that was widely used at the university in the early part of this century. Look, you can see the university's crest."

He handed the clip to Frick.

"Because our books could not be removed from the library, they had to be re-shelved every night. We all used these page markers, which you will notice has an arrow on one side, to mark the page to be studied next. The clip was lying between the skeleton's fingers and the arrow was pointing toward the second sarcophagus."

Father Gianti and Bassam Safar walked to the second sarcophagus. The two workmen followed in their footsteps after receiving a quick nod from Father Reike.

Surprisingly, the lid lifted up without much effort. After sliding the stone slab to an angle, Father Gianti lifted his lantern and they all peered down.

What they saw made Professor Meister smile, but when he reached beneath an overhanging layer of canvas and began groping around, his smile rapidly disappeared. He pulled out his hand, which held a journal that bore smears of blood.

# CHAPTER ELEVEN

## JULY 22, 1980

The sergeants commander was admitted into the private office of the superior general of the Jesuit Order of the Roman Catholic Church. He wore no readable expression on his face as he strode purposefully to the front of the desk of the superior general. He bowed his head, and cast back the black hood on his head, waiting for permission to speak.

"Please, be seated," he was told, "and tell me why you are here."

"Father General, I must remain standing before you as I am a man in disgrace. I failed in our mission in Izmir. I did not capture the American, Joseph Youngquest. He escaped our trap."

The superior general eyed him closely.

"Your plan was well conceived and you have never failed our Order. What is your explanation and where is the American now?"

The sergeants commander raised his head. He bore the hardened look of a criminal, which is what he had been prior to his admission into the Jesuit Order. Precluded from the priesthood due to his criminal record, he had become a sergeant brother in the service of Christ through the auspices of the Black Pope. The moniker "Black Pope" had been attached to earlier superior generals for a number of reasons. They preferred to wear the black priestly vestments of their Order, and as the head of the "papal cavalry," their mission was to serve the papacy.

The White Pope—so named because of the more ornate white robes of that office—relied on that support despite a key difference in ideology. Whereas the pontiff was historically a conservative cardinal, who defended and extolled the beliefs of the Catholic Church, the superior general was the head of Jesuits, whose ranks were filled with those who questioned certain beliefs. They had established many of the schools and universities that educated Catholics and non-Catholics alike. Young minds were taught to question, and Jesuits were known to continue questioning well after taking their priestly vows. The white-robed Holy See's revelations and exhortations were often questioned by those in the Jesuit Order whose symbol was IHS.

The sergeants commander spoke matter-of-factly.

"He eluded us by dropping from a pier into the water soon after he changed vehicles. Those who worship the pagan goddess Artemis rescued him from the water in an instant. They were under the pier in two speed boats. I saw him escape."

He paused and studied the superior general who had entrusted him with the planning and execution of this sensitive mission. For five years he had served faithfully as the sergeants commander, and they had been the most fulfilling years of his life. He fully expected to lose his command as a result of his failure. As a man disgraced, he could do nothing but look down dejectedly at the red cross embroidered on his black mantle.

"Father General," he added quietly, "one of my men heard one of the pagan women shout out the term Black Pope during our intervention."

The head of the worldwide Jesuits stood up from behind his desk and walked to the window, where he stared out at the Jesuit's marble-lined headquarters on Borgo Santo Spirito. From there, his gaze went to St. Peter's Square, just a short walk away from where the White Pope reigned supreme.

"Black Pope," the superior general said flatly.

"Yes, Father General."

"Our operational security has been compromised. Did you follow all protocols?"

"I did, Father Superior. The sergeants were cloistered even before I reported here for the mission order."

The superior general turned slowly toward his sergeants commander. *Here is a fine leader of men,* he thought to himself. *He must be given support and reassurance. My continued faith in him will strengthen the bond of personal gratitude and service to the Jesuit authority.*

"I must ask that you perform a personal favor for me, Sergeants Commander," he said. "You must tell your men that we were betrayed. The mission that we sought to execute in secret was most surely compromised. Without that breach in security, I believe that Mr. Youngquest would now be in our care, and rescued from that pagan sect so opposed to us. We shall have another opportunity to succeed, and I have no doubt that we *will* succeed.

Give your sergeant brothers my assurances. They have not lost my confidence, and you continue to have my full support."

The sergeants commander swallowed hard.

"Your confidence in us will be earned back, Father General."

"It was never lost. Now please return tomorrow, Commander, at 1600 hours."

The sergeants commander came to ramrod attention, and for a second his eyes locked with the superior general's. He did an about face, brought up his hood, and exited the inner office.

There had been no handshake signifying that the mission had been accomplished. *That,* the sergeants commander promised to himself as he closed the door behind him, *is the last time I depart Father General's office without his shaking my hand!*

The superior general sat down at his desk, folded his hands, and prayed. He reminded himself that he had not sought this office. He had been elected for life following four days of intense discussions among delegates representing the Order's worldwide geographical provinces. Had he shown any ambition for the high office, he would have been disqualified. His piety and organizational abilities had resulted in his election. He had found strength in prayer from the first time he had been taught to pray by his mother, and he prayed now for the ability to defeat the pagans who sought to undermine the teachings of the earliest followers of Christ. This mission had always belonged to the superior general of Jesuits.

The assignment that he had entrusted to Father Martelli was a diversion. Those two schoolboy priests would never have any chance of even coming close to the artifacts. That he knew.

On a lower floor of the Jesuit building, the sergeants commander entered the special quarters of his command. The Jesuit Order had been founded by Saint Ignatius in the sixteenth century. Sergeants historically were warrior monks, foot soldiers, and light cavalry, who had served the crusading Knights Templar, an order founded in 1118, hundreds of years before the "pope's cavalry" or the Order of Jesuits, was established. Although few in number, they were fit, well trained, and lived a life of celibate service. In part, because of the avowed secrecy of their activities, they had long been at odds with the Swiss Guards, the highly visible guardians of the Vatican and Holy See, which is why the superior general forbade any contact between the two groups.

The Jesuits' focus was on frontline missionary work worldwide. At times Jesuits became involved in the politics of nations. As a result, the lives of Jesuit priests, nuns, and staff workers were sometimes placed in jeopardy. Having a quasi-military force at the Black Pope's disposal had proven valuable time and again.

The need for secrecy was acknowledged and appreciated by the sergeant brothers, whose past records blocked their entry into the priesthood. They were suited for their role, and each had come to embrace his secret status with pride. Some had served in regular military units and had assisted with weapons training and small unit tactics.

Kidnapping a person being held by an adversary, without being able to kill that adversary, had been the subject of only one POI, or Program of Instruction. The sergeants commander had not trained his men to standard and he knew it.

Underlying their commitment to serve the poor and oppressed, the Jesuit spirit was founded upon an understanding of poverty and oppression. As ex-cons, the sergeants were in effect, social lepers. Most were unable to find decent employment due to their criminal records. They had felt the scorn of an unforgiving public and knew poverty and oppression.

When the sergeants commander entered his orderly room, a clerk jumped to his feet, bowed his head, and placed his right hand over the red cross on his black tunic.

"Is everyone here?" the sergeants commander asked.

"Yes, sir."

"Then let us get on with it."

The clerk entered the drill hall and announced the sergeants commander. Immediately, everyone in the hall snapped to attention, keeping their heads bowed. On a small table in front of the formation was each man's lapel pin, placed there by each sergeant as they entered the hall. Each pin was a miniature shield with the top half colored in black and the bottom half in white– a tiny replica of the shields carried by their brethren from the time of the Crusades. Their presence on the table signified that each sergeant was prepared to offer his immediate resignation from the Order. The pins were arranged in the same order as the sergeants standing at attention before their commander. Should he choose to do so, the sergeants commander could simply sweep the pins up and depart the room. In that event, within the hour, every man in his command would be gone from the building. He could sense the anxiety in the silent hall, but not a man looked up at him in either hope or resignation.

"Be at ease, my brothers," he said with authority.

As one, they raised their heads and stared stalwartly at their commander. He was not looking at the pins.

"The father general has reaffirmed his faith in us," the commander announced.

"Operational security was breached, and he is personally investigating how that happened. Somehow our enemies knew we were there. Their escape was made to look like a spontaneous reaction, but it wasn't. They had boats under that pier. Within minutes they were gone."

He paused to let that sink in.

"I am to return to the father general's office tomorrow at 1600 hours. You are confined to your quarters until I return from that meeting."

The commander gazed into the eyes of one soldier in Christ who stood before him, as though frozen in time. The commander then reached down and picked up one pin before departing. The men noticed his hand trembling as it held the small shield.

Rabbino was the last to leave the assembly hall. His comrades had departed quickly, a few expressing sorrow at his abrupt dismissal from the sergeants. He thanked them without showing any outward sign of emotion. Inside however, he felt shock which manifested itself in a numbing, semi-conscious awareness of what was happening. He had sealed his fate when the third bullet he fired, during the fight on the pier, had struck the Amazon. He was to only fire warning shots. To force surrender. Unfortunately, after being kicked hard in the groin and struck on the back of his neck, he lost his composure and shot the woman.

Soon, he was alone in the hall. Rabbino stared despondently at the table's polished top as if half-expecting his small crest to magically reappear. He heard someone moving outside of the closed door, and his heart leapt as he imagined the sergeants commander re-entering the hall and declaring that it had all been a horrible mistake. But no, he surmised, it was an escort come to take him to his room and supervise him packing up his possessions. He would, of course, be required to hand over his Vatican identification card, keys, uniforms, and mantle.

Rabbino walked around the hall for the last time. He studied the pictures on the wall: photographs of his cohorts engaged in training exercises or engaged in operations. In his room, he had only one picture of himself, and that was the one of him sandwiched between his two closest friends, both sergeants, taken in a café in Venice.

He had no family, no girlfriend, and no friends at all outside the Jesuit secret service. He was alone, as he had been for most of his life since growing up in a Naples orphanage. Sadness had been his lot in life but it had always been tethered to hope.

Rabbino walked out of the drill hall and paused briefly as the door closed behind him. He walked to his room without acknowledging the escort. He changed into civilian garb, packed, and placed his keys and identification card on the desk. He departed the building carrying a suitcase, an overnight bag, and a knapsack on his back. In it he had placed the rope sash that the sergeants used to fasten their mantels about their waists. He had coiled it and placed it in the knapsack without any objection from his escort, although it was a uniform accessory owned by the Jesuit Order.

The rain had stopped and there was a fresh, clean scent to the night air. He walked slowly away from Vatican City toward a hotel where he had once spent the night with a woman he had met in St. Peter's Square. Even the memory of that rapturous night could not coax a smile from him.

Rhea, office assistant to the superior general, watched the sergeant's progress as he strolled down the street, with eyes that thirsted for revenge. She followed him for several blocks until, to her surprise, he entered an expensive hotel. Even by Rome's standards. She watched as he registered and then shadowed him until he entered his room on the fifth floor. Rhea then returned to the lobby and passed the time reading a book before checking into a seventh floor room under an assumed name.

At two in the morning, Rhea left the hotel and walked across the street. She stared up at the fifth floor window to the room occupied by the assassin. It was still ablaze with light. Rhea fingered the passkey in her jacket pocket as her eyes remained riveted on the window. *No wonder he can't sleep*, she mused. *A man discharged under such circumstances, who had killed another, would have many sleepless nights.*

"Soon, you bastard, you will be sleeping for eternity," she muttered.

The young woman scanned the deserted street for a minute before re-crossing it and entering the hotel lobby. No one was at the front desk, and Rhea went directly to the fifth floor. At the door to Rabbino's room she stopped, looked up and down the hallway for observers, and then quietly unlocked the door with the passkey. Rhea pulled the dagger from the front of her waistband. She silently pushed the door open and was met by the sight of the sergeant's body, hanging listlessly from his mantle's rope. A noose was around his neck and the other end he had tied to a ceiling beam. An over-turned chair lay beneath him.

"Mother, you are avenged," she whispered savagely as she tucked the blade away and stole out of the room.

The sergeants commander woke at 0500 hours, as was his custom. After dressing, he proceeded to the workout room and exercised for an hour before going to the mess for breakfast. He picked up a newspaper before heading to a table; the morning news radio broadcast, as usual, was piped into the room. The broadcaster spoke of a suicide in a prominent hotel in Rome, near the Vatican. The man's name was not immediately available for release, but his description riveted the commander's attention to the announcer's voice.

There was little doubt in his mind as to whom the decedent was. He walked briskly out of the mess and to his office. Within a few minutes, he had dialed the superior general's quarters and relayed to the him his belief of what had happened as a result of his actions toward the sergeant. There was no response from the head of his Order. The line simply went dead.

The head of the worldwide Jesuits stared at the top of his bedroom desk. He had withheld information of importance concerning the Virgin Mary from a pope whose coat of arms contained the Marian Cross and an M in personal reverence to Mary, the Mother of Jesus.

The Jesuit father general dressed and then called the pope's personal secretary.

# CHAPTER TWELVE

## JULY 22, 1980

Mr. Frick took out his handkerchief and mopped his brow. "We need the head coroner here," he said shakily.

"I thought you were the head coroner," Professor Meister said dryly.

"I'm the senior clerk. I don't deal with dead bodies. I deal with proper documentation."

Father Reike looked down at his feet and spoke softly.

"We have desecrated these graves, and I believe that we have been misdirected. There are bodies here."

"And my books!" Professor Meister interrupted. "This blood surely comes from a recent burial. We need to take this stone off and see who's in there and get the books out."

They all stood transfixed, staring at the darkness within the coffin.

"Father Reike," the professor began firmly, "there appear to be three bodily remains in this crypt. Your records indicate only two. My books are here. Let's at least take off the stone slab and see what, or who, is inside!"

Father Reike motioned the workers forward, and he and Father Gianti followed behind. They lifted off the stone cover and leaned it against the side of the sarcophagus. Lamps were brought close and they gazed down into a dead man's open eyes and mouth.

The corpse lay on a bed of books, a look of fright and pain frozen on him. There was a gasp, and one of the workers grasped the sarcophagus to steady himself.

The dead man appeared to be about forty years old and quite muscular. A small hole in his neck had dried blood caked around it, and they could see blood on the front of his shirt. He was lying in a hollowed-out space within the bed of books so that the front of his body was flush with the top of the stack. Professor Meister staggered back a few steps and fought to regain his composure.

"He is recently deceased," Father Reike whispered.

The professor shook his head and stared at the body with a face aghast. "What has happened here? We need to call the police," he exclaimed. His eyes searched the crypt as Frick hurried away to summon the authorities.

"You know," the professor said in a faraway tone of voice, "there were many more books than could fit in this one sarcophagus. Now what do you suppose Father Speier did with the rest? Or have certain books been removed?"

What crossed the professor's mind at that moment was the image of Jay Youngquest suddenly leaving Vienna for Turkey just as this body appeared in a crypt full of books that Jay apparently no longer had an interest in studying. *Is there a connection? If so, what is it?* he silently questioned.

The professor glanced at Reike.

"Father, would it be alright if Bassam and I get a bite to eat? I am hungry and tired. We can come back later to give our statements."

Father Reike offered a brief nod. "See that you return as soon as you have eaten," he replied firmly.

"Of course. Come, Bassam, let's find us a nice restaurant where we can relax for a while."

A light rain had begun to fall.

"Damn Salzburg, always gloomy and rainy," the professor grumbled, as they walked to a nearby restaurant. Soon they had coffee warming their hands and lunch ordered.

"You've been very quiet, Bassam," the professor said, after the waiter departed. "What's on your mind?"

Bassam was stirring his coffee, deep in thought.

"Dr. Meister, I have had a lot to think about! I have never been involved in a modern day mystery before. It's like a dream—or in this case, a nightmare." He paused as the waiter returned with silverware and napkins. Bassam then went on.

"I am wondering about your friend, Mr. Youngquest? He leaves just when we are about to be presented with the journals he apparently needed to complete his research. I am more than a little suspicious. Should we inform the police about his sudden departure from Austria?"

The professor gave him a knowing look.

"I too have been thinking about Jay's possible involvement in this. Let's discuss our official story. You can bet we will be asked those questions."

They talked through breakfast, keeping their voices low. They would let on about Jay's interest in the journals and how that interest led to their recovery. These facts were known. However, they would say nothing about his leaving, unless and until, they were asked about it.

They paid the tab and walked back to the church, where a circus-like atmosphere awaited them: several policemen, a coroner, Mr. Frick, priests, vehicles with blue flashing lights, a television news team, and many onlookers, all scampered around the street and the graveyard.

As they approached the crypt, a police officer stopped them.

"We are witnesses and are here to see Father Reike," Bassam told him. "Inside there," the officer responded, pointing toward the church.

Once inside, they were ushered into a room that had been hastily converted into a waiting room. Due to the number of workers, priests, and others who the police needed to question, they had decided to interrogate people in Father Reike's office. Unfortunately, the police had neglected to inform the priest of their plans, and Dr. Meister walked into the office to the sound of Father Reike angrily berating someone.

"Officer, you may certainly ask your questions of me and Father Piene in my office. The others, however, can be questioned at police headquarters. Not here. This is a sacred place. You may gather your evidence, make your lists, but then you must respect the sanctity of this cathedral!"

"I understand, Father," the officer replied dryly. "I assure you we will be brief. It will be so much more convenient for us to ask each witness a few questions here. I'm afraid I must insist."

"Officer," Professor Meister interrupted, "I am Professor Meister from the Austrian Archaeological Institute and University of Vienna. I am largely responsible for creating the disruption within this holy place. I am anxious, as are you, to have this investigation completed so that I can procure my books and return to Vienna. However, we must respect this house of God. I know that your good chief—my former student, Chief Honaker—is demanding a thorough investigation. I will be the first to leave you my name, and I will depart immediately for your headquarters where I can renew my friendship with my old student and await your questioning."

The police officer, caught off guard by this smooth-talking academician, backed off. *Perhaps,* he thought to himself, *discretion is the better part of valor, as the Shakespearean hero Falstaff once said.* He didn't need a conflict with the Catholic Church *and* a friend of the police chief.

"You are right, Father Reike," the officer apologized. "We can obtain our witness list and then have everyone questioned at headquarters. Please meet me there in one hour. I will speak with you first Father Reike, there."

The priest recognized the twisted compromise and accepted it graciously.

"I will be there Officer, as you request," he replied.

The officer smiled at Professor Meister and then turned his attention to Bassam.

From the officer's hard expression, Dr. Meister concluded that he was none too pleased to be in the presence of a Persian. The professor acted quickly to cut through the silence.

"This is Mr. Safar," the professor introduced his assistant, "He is completing his doctorate degree under my supervision. He is also my senior research assistant. He kindly drove me here from Vienna and will also come with me to your office. He was with me when I discovered the body."

The officer drew a notepad from his raincoat pocket and wrote on it.

"Very well," he said in conclusion. I will see you all in one hour at my office."

After the officer departed the room, Father Reike walked over and closed the door behind him. He gave Dr. Meister a warm smile.

"Thank you, Professor, you were most influential."

"Do they know who the dead man is?" the professor asked.

The priest shook his head. "Not yet but they are taking pictures, measurements, fingerprints, everything you would expect. Quite thorough."

They walked out together into the courtyard where the crowd was watching the sheet-covered stretcher being loaded into an ambulance. The crowd was much larger than when Dr. Meister had arrived.

"I'd like to send a truck here tomorrow to pick up my books, Father," the professor said to Father Reike. "You might need time to approve my request. However, I am old and would like to begin my inventory of the works in Vienna this week. Will you help me?"

Father Reike was taken aback. He had promised Father Gianti from Rome that they would hold the books in Salzburg until the Church had studied their contents.

"I promise to try," the priest said without much conviction.

"Thank you, Father Reike. Well Bassam, let's drive to the police station right after we see how many books are in the sarcophagus."

The professor walked quickly toward the canopy with the priest following behind Bassam, both of them surprised at the professor's sudden quick pace. He walked resolutely past a guard and approached the open crypt where Father Gianti and Father Piene were removing the books and journals from the sarcophagus and placing them in boxes. Professor Meister's sudden entrance startled them.

"Good!" Meister said. "Packing up my works for shipment to Vienna, I see. Excellent. Quite efficient! I see you are making a list, too."

He looked at Father Reike.

"Can I have a copy of that list before I return to Vienna? Please be extra careful with my books there. Bassam and I will gladly assist you in cataloging them."

The priest shrugged.

"Why not?"

With Father Gianti recording, and the four of them calling out titles and authors before arranging each work in the boxes, it took nearly an hour to empty the sarcophagus. Dr. Meister inspected the inventory and compared it to the partial list he carried with him.

"We are late for our appointment with the detective," he commented, when the brief inspection was completed. "Bassam and I will go on ahead. Please copy the list and bring it with you to police headquarters, Father. It's important evidence."

He moved to exit the tent and then turned back.

"I believe you should know that some of the journals and books are missing. I don't know how many at this point. They may be hidden in the walls, or under the flooring in the crypt, or maybe Father Speier placed them elsewhere in or around the church. But it would seem that most of the older journals are not in these boxes."

With that he again motioned Bassam to follow him and they walked out through the tent and into the cool drizzle of the rainy day.

"Now, to the inquisition." He chuckled as he opened his umbrella.

They arrived at the police station a half-hour late and were told that they would have to wait to give their statements due to the large number of people involved. They sat down on a bench and waited.

In short order, an impeccably uniformed and tall man with an engaging smile approached them.

"Dr. Meister!" he intoned in a booming voice. "What a great pleasure to see you again! Come with me to my office, please. Let us visit for a few minutes."

"I would like that, Herr Honaker," the professor enthused. "But first, may I introduce you to my associate, Bassam Safar, who brought me to your fine city amongst the clouds."

Honaker gave Bassam a broad smile. "It's my pleasure to meet someone who surely admires this archaeologist par excellence as much as his former students, especially myself."

The two men shook hands warmly.

"Mr. Safar, I will see that you are interviewed next while I chat awhile with my old mentor."

"That would be fine, Chief Honaker," Bassam said. "Thank you."

The first thing Honaker said, when the professor was settled in a comfortable leather chair in his office was, "I can't believe you're here. One of my investigators mentioned your name and assured me that yes, you were here, and that you said you know me. He is a good man. A true professional, although he can have a short manner in dealing with people."

"He was doing his job," Dr. Meister responded.

Honaker nodded. Then, changing the subject: "I hear that you are still very active: teaching, writing, and even traveling."

"Not so much anymore, but I try to be useful. The institute, the museum, and the university have been my whole life, and I am thankful to be employed at my age!"

"I was pleasantly surprised to hear that you remembered me, as it has been over twenty years! I was only in a few of your classes, and was taking courses primarily to further a career in law enforcement."

"Well, I do remember my students, and I did hear from Professor Wantar that you had become the head of the police department here a number of years ago."

"I have largely you to thank for that. I found the archaeologists' methodology to be very instructive when applied to police work, as did my superiors." He grinned. "Fortunately, we investigate incidents when they are fresh, whereas you often investigate matters that occurred thousands of years ago. I'll never forget your classes. You made the past come alive for me."

"Thank you. I live for such compliments."

"Then you have a lot to live for. I hear that you hid books in a crypt before the war and then returned to claim them only last week." He paused, waiting for a response. When none was forthcoming, he continued.

"As I understand it, you and an American acquaintance of yours came here from Vienna to see the crypt opened, but had to delay matters due to church and governmental regulations. Is that correct?"

The professor nodded.

"And then you found a dead man in the coffin containing your books."

"It was a sarcophagus," the professor clarified.

"Yes, sorry, a sarcophagus, Doctor. And I understand that the American"—he consulted his notes—"this Jay Youngquest, has left the country?"

"He has," the professor admitted, wondering who had passed that information to the chief. "He continues his research at Ephesus."

"Do say? Is he also a fellow professor?"

"No. He was my assistant during the war, but he didn't know about the books until he found pages missing from journals in our library. I had no need of the hidden journals before because the Nazis never took the other copies we had, and many of the hidden journals were never missed or requested. Also, I seem to have put them out of my mind after all these years."

"Did you ever see the dead man before, Doctor?"

"Not to my knowledge. Who is he?"

"Well, confidentially, he has an extensive criminal history. Interpol made an identification within the hour based upon the man's fingerprints and the police photographs. He was a thief and a reputed murderer with ties to the underworld. He was German by birth, but resided in many European cities."

"Was he stabbed?"

"Yes, but whether or not that killed him we will only know after an autopsy. He had been dead for about thirty-six hours. I would like to show you a picture of him now, and others taken a few years ago. I would like to see if perhaps you might recognize him."

He handed the professor four eight-by-ten photographs. The top three photographs were in black and white. They depicted a progressively older man. The fourth one, in color, was of the corpse.

The professor studied the photographs before handing them back.

"Sorry. I don't know him."

"Professor, do you know of any reason why anyone would kill for these books?"

"Not a single reason."

"Then can you tell me what your acquaintance, Jay Youngquest, was searching for?"

The professor did not blink. "Pages from old journals which might lead him to the final resting place of the Virgin Mary."

"In Jerusalem?"

"No, in Ephesus. He believes that Mary died in Ephesus and was buried there." Honaker sat back in his chair, which creaked under the burden of his weight.

"Fascinating," he said, shaking his head. "This man is searching for a grave that is nearly two thousand years old, and I am looking for reasons why a man was slain two days ago. Fascinating. We will need Mr. Youngquest's American address, where he stayed in Vienna, and where he would stay in Ephesus."

"Yes, I have that information in my office, except I don't know where he'd stay near Ephesus. In Selçuk, probably, but I don't know where."

"I would like what information you have as soon as possible. Can you telephone your office?"

"From here? Now?"

"Please, it will save you the long distance charges."

Honaker reached for the telephone on his desk and placed it in front of the professor. The professor placed the call. A few minutes later, he handed the chief a slip of paper upon which he had written the requested information.

"I understand that some of the books are missing," the chief said, as he examined what was written on the paper.

"You sure work fast!"

"Yes, we do. Can you provide me with an exact list of those titles?"

"Yes, surely, but I'll have to compare the current inventory with a comprehensive list I have in Vienna."

"Very well, then. I will personally call on you tomorrow or the next day."

"Personally?"

"Yes, Professor. This is a perfect excuse for me to go to Vienna! I wouldn't want a subordinate to have to drive so far for work!" He laughed a delighted laugh. "Perhaps we can even have dinner together and catch up a little. You name the restaurant, I pay the tab. A deal?"

"Only if you agree to leave this wretched weather in Salzburg."

They shared a laugh and then the professor said, in a more serious tone, "I will tell Professor Wantar that you're coming. He will look forward to seeing you as well."

They stood together.

"Bring the rest of your questions with you, Chief of Police Honaker, I am prepared to assist you in any way that I can."

# CHAPTER THIRTEEN

## JULY 22, 1980

Father Anthony Gianti sat on the straight-backed chair that he had placed in the corner of the room that was farthest from the door. He was slumped forward, his hands clasped as if in prayer, and his bloodshot eyes stared down at them. He disdained death. Its sight made him feel cold and clammy. A man was dead, and here in this room were all but three of the books he'd lain upon in death. Those three books had blood on them and currently they were being analyzed in a police laboratory to determine blood type. Surely, Anthony mused, the blood on the books was that of the deceased. The dead man was a known thug. Then there were the other books and journals from the last century and the early twentieth century. He and Father Piene had been scouring the journals until the professor and his assistant had walked into the crypt, startling them.

The door to the room opened and Father Joseph Baronio, the former assistant to the priest secretary of the Jesuit superior general, dressed in street clothes, entered.

"Hello, my dear friend," he said cheerfully. "You will be pleased to know that the good professor and his Arab assistant have now departed for Vienna with their inventory list. They never saw me so I can nose around the university without arousing suspicion! If you care to join me we can leave once we've gone through these books. Late tonight or tomorrow morning, I hope."

"Joseph," Anthony began deliberately, "don't you think that we should inform Father Martelli that a man has been killed here, and that the police will soon be made aware of our investigation? Someone, maybe the American, has given us a stern warning not to meddle in this quest for the Virgin's burial site. Do you have any idea what we've been caught up in? I doubt you do, and this death is really affecting me. I don't care if the man was a criminal, he was clearly murdered. Also, Bassam is Iranian. A Persian and not an Arab."

Joseph gave his friend a long look.

"I understand, Tony," he said. "I haven't had a lot of time to think about what's happened since we left the Vatican. It doesn't make any sense to me that someone was murdered because of some old books and journals. Father Reike told me that Professor Meister is convinced that some of them are missing. Father Reike is having the workmen search the walls and flooring of the crypt for possible hiding places. The prime suspect is the American, Mr. Youngquest, and that's what troubles me. It makes no sense. He wouldn't leave Austria unless he'd found what he'd been searching for. Apparently he is now in Turkey. But why would he throw the body of an underworld figure on top of the books? What does he gain by doing that? It makes him a suspect in a murder case and that's the last thing he'd want?"

"I agree it doesn't make sense," Tony replied.

"To answer your other question, no. I don't think we should call Father Martelli until we have something more definitive to report. Our first task is to skim the books and journals for clues concerning the theory of Mary's death and the possible existence of Christ's writings. Then we should go to Vienna *after* we learn more about the journals with the missing pages."

Joseph walked over to a box of books, lifted it from the floor, and then placed it upon a large rectangular table. He removed a book, and after noting its title, scanned through its pages. Finding nothing of note he placed it aside and took up a second book, repeating the process.

"Want to help, Tony?"

"Yes, of course."

Anthony joined in the process. He tried to concentrate on each book but found it difficult to do so. The dead man's face kept staring up at him from the pages. Finding nothing insightful from their cursory inspection of the books in the first box, they were about to go through the books in a second box when the door opened and Father Reike entered wearing an expression fraught with concern.

"My friends, the police are on their way. They want all of the books and have dispatched two officers to fetch them. Chief Honaker just telephoned me. He will not accept my attempts to put him off. He has obtained the necessary paperwork. There is nothing more I can do. You have only a few more minutes with them."

"Why are these books being taken from us?" Anthony demanded to know.

"For the investigation, I presume. I know only that they'll soon be gone."

"Then we have a problem," Joseph Gianti stated emphatically. "Our own investigation requires that we review them before we surrender them."

"What investigation?" Father Reike asked.

"The investigation into the contents of the books and journals, and whether you should continue to hold them or deliver them to the professor," Anthony explained.

Father Reike raised his arms in a *What am I supposed to do?* expression. "I need this like a hole in the head. I've just had my church turned upside down by the police," he complained bitterly.

Anthony approached the priest and placed a sympathetic hand on his shoulder.

"Very well, Father Reike," he said. "Thank you for your hospitality. I am impressed by how you handled this delicate and unusual situation. You can contact us later after the books have been returned. It is reasonable for the police to want to examine every piece of this mystery. I wish that we could have examined them first, but we will report to our superiors on the careful and wise way you handled everything." The two priests shook hands.

"Thank you, Father Gianti. Are you both leaving Salzburg then?"

"I suppose so," Anthony replied. "Under the circumstances there's not much point in remaining here and we have other matters to attend to in Austria before returning to Rome. Incidentally, Father Reike, have the workers found other books hidden in the crypt?"

"Not yet. We have ripped up some of the floor, and we are planning to drill inspection holes in the walls."

Father Reike walked over to the closest box of books and bent down to pick up a journal when the door opened. Father Piene led in a uniformed officer and two plainclothes policemen. Within twenty minutes the books were gone.

The two priests investigating the matter returned to their hotel to prepare to depart from Salzburg.

After Joseph finished packing, he went into the next room where his friend was changing out of his clerical robes. "You know, Tony," he said. "We probably should stay together in order to review the same documents and jointly gather evidence. As advocates serving on opposite sides of this investigation, we should be exposed to the same facts and information, from the same source. But in the situation we find ourselves, things are happening very fast. Professor Meister has returned to Vienna, the police have the books and journals here in Salzburg, and Jay Youngquest has gone to Ephesus. Here we sit in Salzburg. So do we go to the police and ask to review the books under their supervision to learn what we can? Or do we go to Vienna to review the materials in the university library and at the archaelogical institute? Or do we go to Turkey and pursue this Mr. Youngquest?" He paused momentarily. "Or do we split up and stay in contact by telephone?"

"You obviously have an opinion, Joseph hedged. "What is it?"

Anthony looked at his friend and responded slowly. "I believe that Mr. Youngquest has taken the important journals. I don't know what to think about the dead body. But we know that Mr. Youngquest has gone to Ephesus in Turkey, which is where this quest will inevitably lead us as well."

"Then why don't we both make immediate arrangements to go there?" Joseph Baronio asked.

Anthony responded, "My instincts tell me that we may learn valuable information by going to Vienna. Professor Meister has duplicates of the books and journals that are missing from here. His copies have missing pages. Nevertheless, what they reveal may help. I believe that since Professor Meister and his associate do not know who you are, you are the one who should work undercover there. I, meanwhile, should go to Ephesus. I could look for Mr. Youngquest and see about doing some research there at the museum. I know what Jay Youngquest looks like. In any event, we could speak together by telephone or relay messages through Father Martelli. If either my investigation or yours bears fruit, one of us could be in a position to follow up on leads. The key seems to be what Youngquest is up to. What do you think?"

Joseph paused briefly before replying. "You raise good points. So why don't we drive over to police headquarters? You go in and find out if, and when, you might be permitted access to the books. Tell them the Church's inventory was not completed. Let's try to find out more about the dead man, then we can decide on our next moves."

"Good idea," Tony agreed.

They drove to the heavy stone building that housed police headquarters. After an hour inside, Tony came out and walked purposely to where Joseph was waiting for him down the street in the car.

"The dead man is Adolf Asher," Tony said excitedly, once he was inside the car and had closed the door. "He's a criminal with an extensive record in Germany, France, and the Netherlands, for openers. He stole art and antiquities from galleries, museums, and private collections. Art! I just learned that five thousand pieces of art are stolen every year! He stole art not for himself or for ransom, but for private, wealthy collectors! Unbelievable! His last known whereabouts were in Amsterdam about eighteen months ago. His death was caused by a stiletto knife--or an arrow if you can believe it--that went through his neck. The police can offer no motive for the murder, although Mr. Youngquest remains the prime suspect in the investigation. Probably because at this point, there is no other suspect."

"When will you have access to the books?"

Tony frowned. "They won't let anyone touch them until they've been properly inventoried and reviewed. They claim that they are important evidence and will only be released at the conclusion of the investigation."

"Who made that claim?"

"Chief Honaker himself. He met with me and was sympathetic to my position, but was unyielding nonetheless. He wants to unravel this mystery step-by-step and has taken over the case himself. He is going to Vienna soon to speak with Professor Meister and to investigate what Mr. Youngquest was doing there. But as I said, he was adamant that the books would only be given back to Father Reike, and then only after the police investigation has been concluded."

"I expected as much," Joseph grumbled. "Well, now what's our plan?"

" I will go to Selçuk. Joe, you should proceed to Vienna. I was going to use an assumed name, perhaps even wear a disguise, but we only have our official passports. Let's plan to communicate through Father Martelli every day. Once you are done in Vienna, plan on joining me in Selçuk. By then I should have learned something of value."

"Your spirits have soared since this early afternoon," Joseph laughed.

"Yes, because I am beginning to see things more clearly. We should part here. I can take a bus or train to Munich and fly to Izmir from there. You can return the rental car to Vienna. In two days, we begin our daily calls to Father

Martelli. It will be very exciting for us both, but it could also be dangerous. For our careers as priests, and for our very lives, if the events of today offer any indication."

Two hours later, Joseph Baronio waved good-bye to Tony as the train for Munich departed the Salzburg station. Five hours after that, Joseph was lying on a bed in his hotel room in the western section of Vienna. Closing his eyes, he imagined Tony on a flight to Izmir and from there in a rental car to Ephesus, hard on the trail of the mysterious American, Jay Youngquest. In the meantime he, Joseph, would enjoy being in Vienna while searching through journals and museum archives for clues referencing the alleged death of Mary more than nineteen hundred years ago!

He fell asleep and dreamed about a girl with whom he had been a friend many years before. His cousin appeared in a blue dress that was embroidered with small white flowers. She had been so beautiful, so loving, so close to him during their last two summers together before he made the fateful decision to become a priest. He envisioned her lying naked on the bed in his father's home, and as she opened her eyes, he saw tears welling and overflowing down her cheeks and onto the pillowcase. When he reached down to touch her lips, his hand suddenly made a fist and it struck her, causing her lower lip to split open. Blood dripped down her chin, mingling with her tears, as she gazed up at him in disbelief. He cried out in anguish, and when he tried to embrace her, she disappeared. Hearing a noise behind him, he whirled around to see his father standing at the door, his arms wrapped protectively around his cousin. She was sobbing and he was consoling her. Joseph collapsed to his knees, crossing himself repeatedly, and then fell forward onto the floor in utter despair. His father came to him and started shaking him angrily.

A news reporter's voice blared from the clock radio and Joseph jerked awake. Switching off the alarm, he lie back on the bed, rubbing his eyes, trying to dispel the horror of the lingering dream and get his bearings. He got up, dressed, and went down to the hotel restaurant for breakfast.

By mid-morning, Father Baronio had exited the train that had sped him into central Vienna and was at the university library inquiring about books and journals related to the subject of Ephesus. Directed to the card catalog, he skimmed the works listed and then returned to the reference desk.

"Good morning again," he said to the efficient-looking librarian stationed there, "I am doing research on Ephesus and was told that the archaeologists' journals were here. I could not find them listed in the card catalog. Might they be kept somewhere else?"

"They are, sir," the librarian informed him. "They are downstairs in the archives. However, you will need permission to access them. Would you like to fill out a request form?"

"Please."

She removed a form from a file drawer and handed it to Joseph. It was written in German and English. Its introduction explained that the form was for those seeking permission to examine archives otherwise closed to the public. He filled out the form using the name Joe Baronio and his parent's address. After completing it, he handed it to the clerk who read it and asked, "You aren't associated with any school or organization?"

"No, ma'am, I'm not."

"Well, the collection is locked up now because of vandalism. If you are an individual without credentials, it might not be possible to see those texts. Have you ever done research here or checked out anything from this library?"

"Alas, no. I am on holiday here from my home in Italy, and I drove all this way to do my research. I am a sort of amateur archaeologist, and I am fascinated by the excavations in Turkey done by the Austrian Institute. I became interested in reading more about these excavations after I saw the exhibit at the museum." Joseph paused, then added, "They kindly recommended to me that I come here to read the journals."

"I see. Well, I will ask someone who has authority over the archives to review your request, but I can't promise that you'll be able to see the journals." As she picked up a telephone and dialed, Joseph wondered what he would do if he were denied access.

"Someone will be here in a few minutes," the librarian told him.

"Thank you for helping me," he responded sincerely.

Shortly, an attractive woman walked up and spoke to the reference librarian. As she approached Joseph, she carried the form he had filled out.

"*Buon giorno*," she greeted him. Then, in English: "Can I be of assistance?"

"Buon giorno. Yes, I came to read the journals about Ephesus left by the archaeologists and their assistants from the expeditions."

"Which journals are of interest?"

"Well, I don't know how many there are. I was hoping to learn about each archeologist's methodology, and how each came up with his theory about how Ephesus might have looked thousands of years ago."

"I'm very sorry to disappoint you, Mr. Baronio, but we've had some vandalism here recently and as a result the archives are locked. Only authorized researchers are allowed to enter."

Joseph gave her a forlorn look and then asked hopefully, "Can the journals be photocopied, at my expense? I would hate to have come all this way for nothing."

"I'm sorry," she said again. "There are many books and journals, and we just don't have staff available to copy them."

"I see. What is your name, if I might ask?"

"Lydia."

"Well, Lydia, thank you for your time," Joseph said, not trying to hide his disappointment. Lydia gave him a perfunctory smile and returned to the reference desk.

Joseph returned to the card catalog, having decided to at least read a general work on the excavations. He found two books of interest and sat down at a table to read them. Two hours later, he replaced the books and left the building. He had to think but because he didn't want to be alone, he decided to have a cup of espresso at the Café Landtmann as recommended by a reference clerk.

It was busy, but lunch hour was over and he found a table in a corner. A tuxedoed waiter appeared and Joseph, changing his mind, ordered a stein of Heineken beer. After casually surveying an afternoon crowd of tourists and business patrons, he engrossed himself in one of the many newspapers provided for customers. After a bit, Joseph stretched and glanced around the room. He was drawn to the profile of a woman sitting alone reading a book with a bright red cover. He thought for a moment and then recognized where he had seen her before. She was the woman from the library.

"Excuse me," he said, leaning over his table toward her.

She apparently didn't hear him and Joseph repeated himself, louder than he had intended, "Excuse me, Lydia." She looked up, and gave him a puzzled look. "I want to thank you for explaining things to me at the library."

She raised her eyebrows and then a hint of recognition crossed her face.

"Oh yes, I remember you," she said. "I'm afraid I wasn't much assistance."

He waved that away. "Perfectly understandable. If vandals have been at work, everyone should be concerned about protecting the journals, especially you. I was just hoping to do some real research from source materials for a change."

"Will you be in Vienna long?"

"I was planning to be here a number of days. Say, would you mind if I joined you? Then I wouldn't have to shout."

"Of course, please do. Your name is Joseph, isn't it?"

"Yes, but please call me Joe," he replied as he sat down at the table across from her. "All my friends do. By the way, where did you learn Italian?"

"In Rome. I studied there."

"But you're not Italian, are you?"

"No, I'm Greek, born and raised in a suburb of Athens," she responded.

He felt a strong attraction for this woman which he tried to force from his mind. They talked for a few minutes about Rome. Joseph told her that he had worked there for a number of years before returning to Milan, where his family lived. She nodded knowingly and then glanced at her watch.

"Please excuse me," she said, standing up. "I must return to the university. Have a nice holiday."

"Thank you," he said, standing politely. Lydia took a few steps and then turned around.

"If you return to the reference desk tomorrow morning at nine, Joe," she said, "I will help you access those journals you have come so far to see."

"I'll be there!" Joseph enthused. "Thank you very much. *Grazie tante.*"

He watched her depart and looked appreciatively at her shapely legs and derriere. Yes, there was no denying it. He felt a definite attraction for her. Joseph sat down and ordered another Heineken.

The next morning, Joseph was at the library fifteen minutes early. The same young efficient-looking woman who had helped him with the form the day before was again on duty, and she was joined at nine by Lydia, who was wearing a bright yellow dress that attractively set off her shoulder-length ebony hair.

"Good morning, Joe," she greeted him. "Please, come this way." She led him toward the back of the library, then down two flights of stairs. In what was essentially a well-lit and impeccably clean basement, she withdrew a key from her purse and opened a door into a large rectangular-shaped room filled with thousands of books and journals. She then directed him to an enclosed study room and asked him to wait. In no time she reappeared with a card catalog.

"The journals you are probably interested in are listed here on the cards," she said, placing them on the table. "Most are written in German. Write down what books you require and I will get them for you. And, I will need to keep your passport or other photo identification. Questions?"

Joseph shook his head no and she handed him a copy of the paper he had filled out the day before. He produced his driver's license from the bag he carried and she studied it before departing.

For the next hour, he examined descriptions of books and journals typed on the reference cards in the catalog. They all sounded fascinating. Every one of them seemingly held potential answers to so many questions. He made a lengthy list, which represented a cross section of those who had participated in the excavations in the late 1800s and early 1900s. From time-to-time he was distracted by others who also had access to the materials. Some looked like they might be instructors. One uniformed man was involved in security, judging by the way he kept looking in on him.

After completing the list, Joseph decided to see if Lydia was in the stacks. He found her in the area where the card catalogs were located. She looked up and smiled at him; the dark green of her eyes sparkled and Joseph felt his heart skip.

She took the card drawer he was holding.

"Have you finished your list?"

"Yes. Do you think I can find them?"

"No, I'll get them," she insisted. "Some may be in another room where students are working on a special project. I'll bring a couple of them to you right away to get you started. You've made quite a list. How long were you planning on staying here?"

"A few days. I don't really have a schedule. When I'm done here, I'll tour the city before going home."

"Are you vacationing alone?" she asked.

"Yes. I'm just following an interest in archaeology, and in the process, have become fascinated with Turkey."

"It's a fascinating country. I'll bring the books to the study room, Joe."

"Thanks."

Joseph returned to his room and sighed. She was so attractive. So warm. He pushed those thoughts aside and forced himself to think about Tony, wondering if his friend had made contact with Jay Youngquest, either in Selçuk or at the ruins in Ephesus.

Lydia appeared at his side and plunked six journals down on the table.

"I'll re-shelve these when you're done and get you six more. You can find me by the card files where I was before."

"Thank you, Lydia." She turned and walked away, his eyes following her every movement. Joseph shook his head and opened the first journal, written by an Austrian aristocrat who had helped finance an expedition in 1903. Unfortunately, it dwelt upon the man's inflated ego and his monetary contributions to "researching the gods" who had once ruled Ephesus and Asia. Joseph's grasp of German was good but by the time he got to the fourth journal he had developed a headache. He glanced at his watch– almost twelve-thirty. He was skimming the fifth work when he noticed that a page appeared to be missing. He read the pages just before and just after the tear, but they held scant interest, describing as they did the marking of column pieces from the fallen "oktogon" structure which had been removed to Vienna and then reassembled in the museum.

The last book dealt entirely with mapping the locations of the harbor during the various periods of Ephesus' history. He finished with his notes, picked up the books and walked to where she was standing, speaking with two girls who were dressed in student's uniforms.

Lydia took the books from him and smiled.

"Were these of any interest to you?"

"Yes. I only wish that I had more time to read them carefully. Because of my limited time, I've had to skim them."

"Well, I'll get you six more."

"Are you having lunch with anyone today, Lydia?" he heard himself ask. "I'd like to treat you to lunch for turning a potentially futile trip into a most pleasant experience."

She appeared slightly taken back by his offer, but then smiled.

"I'm sorry, but I have plans to meet a friend this afternoon and am quite busy."

"Maybe some other time," he responded, blushing. He hadn't blushed for years. He hadn't come on to a woman for years either, and he felt foolish.

"I'll get you those journals," she said.

Joseph walked back to the study room, his mind unable to focus on much of anything. *Remember, you are a priest,* he reprimanded himself as he sat down in the chair. He sat staring at the tabletop when she returned.

"If I'm not here when you are finished with these, just leave them in this room. Please lock the door on your way out."

"Thank you," he said, smiling into her eyes. She gave him a quick smile in reply and then departed.

Joseph forced himself to concentrate on the journals, seeking anything even remotely related to his search for information about Mary or writings by Christ. After another couple hours of fruitless study, he carried the six books to the card catalogs where he found Lydia seated at a desk.

"Excuse me," he said.

She looked up. "All finished?"

"Yes, with these. I'm getting pretty tired and I've only searched through fourteen journals. How many more are there?"

"Many, many more," she laughed.

"Well, I think maybe I've read enough of them, so I may not return tomorrow. I'm not sure my aching posterior can take much more of this." He noted her slight grin and added, "You have been most kind. I had forgotten how tiring studies can be."

"I suppose then that you won't be repeating your offer of lunch?"

Joseph arched his eyebrows.

"What about supper after work this evening?" he blurted out.

"At the Landtmann?"

"Wherever you like," he said, trying to appear unruffled.

"I can meet you there in four hours, at nine o'clock, if that's not too late for you."

"To the contrary, it's perfect. I'll see you then."

Joseph rushed back to his hotel room feeling every bit the schoolboy about to go out on his first date. As he was selecting a clean set of clothes from the armoire, he saw his clerical collar and robes. Without a second thought, he removed them from their hanger and placed them on the bed. If he was to travel incognito he had to dispose of these, he rationalized, as he walked to the front desk to inquire about obtaining a small cardboard box. The clerk produced one quickly and Joseph took it up to his room, and packed his robes, collars, and black shoes in it. Removing the crucifix from around his neck, he placed it in the box, sealed it, and addressed it to himself at the Vatican.

Just before nine, Father Joseph Baronio arrived at the Landtmann and was seated at a table for two in a side room. He ordered a glass of Bordeaux and waited expectantly for Lydia to arrive. When he spotted her coming in, he stood up and waved.

"Good evening," she said.

"Good evening, Lydia," He pulled out her chair for her. "You look lovely. The very image of Aphrodite."

"What a flatterer," she chided. "But I want you to know that I approve of flattery when it's directed at me." A waiter appeared to take her drink order. "I'll have whatever he's having," she said.

"Very good, madame."

After the waiter walked off Joseph asked, "Have you worked at the university long?"

"Yes. I was a student there for three years, and I have worked there for two years since my graduation. I studied archeology and cultural anthropology, and I have even taught these subjects from time to time."

"That sounds interesting. I, too, am a teacher, in Milan."

"Oh? What do you teach?"

"Religious studies at a private school."

"How very interesting."

For the next hour they exchanged stories about Rome and the marvels of Vienna. They ate their meals slowly and finished with coffee and a liqueur.

"Well, Joe," she said, near the conclusion of dinner, "I'm sorry to see you leave so soon. I have enjoyed your company and hope you have good weather for the remainder of your vacation."

"Thank you, Lydia. The feeling is mutual."

Joe sipped his liqueur. His head was spinning slightly and he couldn't remember how many glasses of wine he had consumed. The waiter walked by, and Lydia summoned him. She paid the bill and Joe sat there trying to remember what day it was.

They left the restaurant and took a cab to his hotel. In his room, they drank more wine as Joseph struggled to make coherent conversation. A voice in his head kept repeating, *You're a priest, you idiot. You're a priest!* until he pulled her shoulder toward him and they embraced. How he got her into bed, or wherever they went to make love, he could not later recall, but he did remember the brief thrill of her naked flesh and the hot flow of passion before he blanked out and felt nothing.

The sound of someone knocking on the door startled him awake. Through a fog he saw a maid sticking her head into his room. Seeing him there, she quickly withdrew and closed the door. He fell back to sleep and awakened sometime later feeling hot and achy. He stumbled into the bathroom where he downed three aspirins and stared at himself in the mirror. To his shock he was still dressed. He still had his shoes on. His pants were held up by the button over an open zipper, and his belt hung loose.

"Dear God, what have I done?" he moaned.

He showered and then inspected the bed and the room. He found no trace of her. Not even her scent. He looked at his wristwatch. Two o'clock in the afternoon. Heaving a heavy sigh he packed his belongings, placing the box with his name and address next to his suitcase. Surely she hadn't seen it in the corner of the room.

Father Joseph Baronio was confused and ashamed. He decided to flee Vienna, rationalizing that nothing of value would be found there. Then he called Father Martelli in Rome. He was out, and to the receptionist's knowledge, Father Gianti had not called from Turkey. Joseph decided against leaving a message, planning instead to call from the airport and talk directly to his superior. His head pounded as he checked out of the hotel, loaded the car, and drove to the airport, where he mailed the box. His flight to Munich was uneventful, and the one to Izmir equally so.

Father Martelli was not available when Joseph called him from Munich, so the priest decided that he'd call again from Izmir. It had only been three days since he and Tony had parted company. Even so, he needed to see his friend. Joseph felt guilt when calling the Vatican, after his one-night stand that abrogated his priestly vows, and he also felt guilty about not calling Lydia before leaving Vienna. What would he say, anyway? He knew what had happened between them physically, but his mind could not bring the details into clear focus however much he wanted to remember.

In Izmir, Joseph obtained bus and train schedules for transport to Kuşadasi, a coastal town near Ephesus. Tony was to have rented a car, and after comparing travel times and expenses, Joseph decided to travel by train.

# CHAPTER FOURTEEN

## JULY 25, 1980

Father Joseph Baronio, Jesuit priest assigned to the personal service of Father Jerino Martelli, Director of Jesuit Missions and Marian Authority, arrived in Selçuk, tired from the long trip from Vienna. Father Baronio hoped that his close friend, Father Antonio Gianti, would be at the hotel indicated by Martelli's secretary. He had found nothing of importance during his cursory efforts in Vienna. Worse, he had wasted time. And worse than that, he had sinned.

Being preoccupied with what had happened between him and Lydia left him exhausted, and almost incapable of focusing on the sacred mission he had been sent on. Every lead that he and Tony had followed seemed to go nowhere. They had received little guidance, and the plan that Father Gianti had presented to Father Martelli had soon proven pale in comparison to the task at hand. Their position was tenuous at best if they wished to satisfy the Vatican. Even his previous posting, under the thumb of the Jesuit father general, now seemed like a wonderful job.

Father Baronio entered the hotel's lobby and approached the registration counter. A young man appeared from a side room.

"May I be of service?" the desk clerk asked cordially.

"Yes, thank you," the young priest replied. "Is a Mr. Gianti registered here?"

"Sir, he is. You may use the telephone there on that desk if you would like to call him."

"Can I just go to his room?"

"Of course, sir. Room number 102, just down that hall." He pointed to Joseph's left.

Joe knocked on the door, and in short order, it was flung open. Father Antonio Gianti beamed at Joseph from the room.

"Hello, my friend," Tony gushed. "Come in, come in. You must be tired. Have you checked in? I have a room reserved for you right next door, and the food here is wonderful! By the way, the ruins at Ephesus are unbelievable! I had no idea they were this spectacular. Much different than the sites in and around Italy. Less developed perhaps, but very impressive!"

Joseph slumped into a chair. Tony noted that his friend looked glum.

"You do not look well," Tony stated. "Can I get you a drink of water? Something stronger? Name your pleasure."

"No. I am fine," Joseph assured him. "And I am pleased to find you in such good spirits. I'm afraid I wasted time in Vienna," he commented, as an image of Lydia drifted across his mind's eye. "I take it from your tone of voice that you have made some progress here, though?"

The expression on Tony's face shifted to one more somber.

"Well, I too must admit that I have nothing of great value to report. I have become acquainted with the area, of course. And I have checked hotels to see if I could find where Jay Youngquest is staying. Alas, no success. Going to see where Mary had lived before her death was an experience that renewed my faith, and perhaps I did a little too much sightseeing. However, I was informed that you were on the way, and I had contact with a woman who appears to be a key player in all this."

"Someone found you here?"

"Yes," Tony confirmed. "I don't know what to make of it, and was going to report it to Father Martelli, but I decided to await your arrival."

"Who contacted you?"

"Well, she wouldn't identify herself other than to say that she knew I was here to do research on some hieroglyphs, and that she had been assigned to help me. She even mentioned your name."

"*She* contacted *you*?"

"Yes, Joe. You find that surprising?"

"Just a little! Apparently our plan to sneak into town has not worked out quite as well as we had hoped. When do we meet her?"

"Well," Anthony said, thinking, "I believe she will call here again as soon as she has more information. From what I could gather, she is not the one making decisions. Since she knows of our mission, and said she was a designated contact person, I assumed that she works for the Vatican."

Father Baronio whistled softly and sank further into his chair.

"Have you been to Mass here?" he asked.

"No. Why?"

"I have something to confess. I want you to hear my confession, and I want my confession heard in the sanctity of a church."

Tony raised an eyebrow. "We can go to the church near the temple ruins at Ephesus."

"That will do. I'm not thinking clearly and should take a nap. I haven't slept well in a number of days. Let me check into my room, get some sleep, and then maybe you can show me the ruins, and take me to the church. I need to do this as soon as possible."

"I'll go with you to the registration desk. Is the suitcase and bag all you have?"

"Yes. And thank you. I hope you understand that I'll be in a better mood to talk once I get some rest."

"Of course, my friend, of course," Tony said. "Let's get you checked in."

After Joseph was checked in and asleep, Tony took a stroll around the town. He watched as shopkeepers hocked their wares to the many tourists who had arrived by bus and cruise ship. It was high sales season, and sales of souvenirs, leather goods, pottery, and a host of items were in full swing amid a sea of shouting, haggling, pleading, and other elements of local salesmanship. Anthony sat down in a sidewalk café, and after ordering an espresso, he unfolded an Italian newspaper he had brought with him from the hotel. He was engrossed in the sports pages when the table shook slightly as someone sat down across from him. He looked up into the eyes of an attractive young woman who had a pleasant smile. She looked at him as if they knew each other.

"Hello, Father Gianti," she greeted him. "I am Cy and we spoke on the telephone. Has your friend arrived from Vienna?"

The way she asked her question suggested she already knew the answer.

"Yes," he replied. "He is resting in his hotel room, and I have told him about your call."

"Thank you. I am waiting for some information about how to assist you, and expect to have that information soon. Then I would like to meet with you and Father Baronio, either at your hotel or mine."

Anthony nodded. "Where are you staying?"

"In a small hotel about a kilometer from here."

"Since you know your way around, perhaps my room at the Kalehan Hotel would be best?" he suggested.

"Fine. I am sorry but I must go now as I have another appointment. I look forward to our next meeting. Say hello to Father Baronio for me."

He stood up and watched her walk a short distance before looking into her purse. She then walked into a small shop. Anthony weighed the value of following her as he watched the shop's entryway. After half an hour, he concluded that she had exited the shop by another doorway. Without further ado, he paid the tab and started back to the hotel after first verifying that the woman was indeed no longer in the shop.

The next morning, the two priests entered an old church overlooking the foundations and lone pillar at the site of the Temple of Artemis. Without seeking permission from the parish priest, they proceeded to a confessional booth in which Joseph devoutly beseeched God's forgiveness for his intercourse with the young woman in Vienna.

Anthony listened intently. After the confession he gave the necessary advice, assigned a penance, and asked his friend to say an Act of Contrition. He gave the absolution. The two Jesuits exited the church, chastened by the frowning look of the church's priest.

From the church they walked the archaeological site, often sitting or standing in the shade periodically, to read a description of what they were viewing from a guidebook. In spite of Tony's support, and his confession, Joseph still felt terrible. The knot in his stomach remained, and it was taking its toll on him. He feared that his glum disposition was beginning to rub off on his friend, for which he apologized. Anthony brushed that away, assuring him that a few days were all that was required to put this unsettling experience behind him. Joseph prayed that his friend was right.

The two Jesuits had set out on their mission with such glee and enthusiasm that it was hard to believe that they had fallen to such depths. Both of them wished for an end to this assignment and a return to the Vatican, regardless of what that might mean to their careers in the Society of Jesus of the Roman Catholic Church. They returned to the hotel and Anthony called the Director of Jesuit Missions and Marian Authority. He was immediately put through to Father Martelli.

"Father Gianti. Is Joseph with you?" the director asked in a hopeful tone.

"Yes," Anthony replied. The sense of relief on the other end of the line was apparent.

"I have some important guidance for you both," the director announced.

"We are anxious for any guidance from you," Anthony replied. Except for the contact with the woman, Cy, they were floundering, with nothing of any value to report.

"Listen carefully to what I'm about to tell you," Martelli said quietly. "The Austrians are about to begin excavating near the house of the Virgin Mary, which as you may know is located a few kilometers from Ephesus. They have received information that leads them to believe that important artifacts relating to Mary may be uncovered through a new excavation. I know this because the Director of Excavations from the Austrian Archaeological Institute contacted me personally."

"I see."

"Yes. He does not want to excavate near the house without our cooperation, and even requested that we send a team to assist him. I told him that I had two Jesuit priests on station there who could join in the effort immediately. He seemed happy that they could begin soon, and asked me to have you contact him as soon as is convenient." The director paused, to allow that information to sink in.

"I can contact him right after this call," Anthony assured him.

"Excellent. Excellent. His name is Dr. David Freiberg and his telephone number is... wait just a moment, I have it here..."

Father Martelli gave them the number in Selçuk, carefully repeated it, and then had Father Gianti repeat it back to him.

"Now. Do not reveal the nature of your work there. Dr. Freiberg was told that you both are on a pilgrimage, and on a well-deserved holiday that will be extended as long as you are of value to his efforts. This is, perhaps, directly relevant to your mission. Something, or someone, has prompted this new excavation."

"I am very optimistic," Father Gianti replied.

"As am I. Now if I may, I would like to speak with Joseph."

"Yes, but first let me tell you about a woman who has contacted us." He then explained the telephone call and the brief discussion at the café. The only response was an even "thank you."

"Joseph," Tony said, turning to his friend, "Father Martelli wants to speak with you."

An apprehensive Jesuit Father Joseph Baronio took the telephone.

"Yes, Father," he said, trying to sound firmly in control of emotions frayed by feelings of guilt.

Martelli repeated the same information he had just told Anthony. He was both demonstrating direct authority, and re-emphasizing the fact that they were advocates on opposite sides of a critical/doctrinal presumption. Joseph assured his superior that he understood what was at stake and hung up, his gaze lingering on the telephone a moment or two.

"He is excited about this new excavation. Who should telephone the Austrian?"

"You call," Tony said.

"This is David," the phone was answered after the fourth ring.

"Dr. Freiberg, I am Father Joseph Baronio, and I am with Father Anthony Gianti, here in Selçuk. Father Martelli has just spoken to us about the excavation and we can report to you at your earliest convenience."

"I am so happy to hear from you, and so soon!" Freiberg replied. "We would like to fill you in on our excavation plans here at my residence, tonight if possible. We will follow a strict protocol that as perhaps you know, begins with photographing the area to include the site, as well as the surroundings. We do this so we can eventually restore the site to its present condition. We will dig very carefully once the site is marked, and we will review our progress daily. Have either of you participated in an excavation before?"

"No, sir. I'm afraid we have not."

"That's fine. The methodology is logical, and it will be exciting, particularly if we find anything of real interest."

"What exactly are we looking for?" Joseph asked.

"Let's discuss that face-to-face," Freiberg said quietly. "We don't want to have the site compromised. Can you be here by nine tonight?"

"Yes, of course. But we'll need directions."

After Freiberg gave him directions to his residence, and the two had hung up, Joseph sat down and smiled at his friend.

"Tony, we are blessed. I have a strong sense that this excavation is linked to our mission! If so, we are two very lucky Jesuits. I will be happy to focus on some hands-on work. Besides, I have always wanted to look for ancient artifacts. Yes, truly we have been blessed. I suddenly find myself excited by this assignment again."

Father Gianti returned the smile. *The affair is becoming dimmer. This is good. There is nothing worse than working with someone who is depressed, someone you must guard against upsetting.*

They arrived at the Austrian's residence just before nine, and within a few minutes the area was a beehive of activity as many participants pulled up in vehicles at precisely nine. Austrians, known to be punctual, were not about to sully their reputation, nor to keep the "head archaeologist on site" waiting. He stood, greeting them each on the porch, a one-man receiving line.

The two Jesuits ascended the four steps to the home's porch and were greeted warmly.

"You must be Father Gianti and Father Baronio," Freiberg greeted them, as he stepped forward and shook their hands.

"I am Tony Gianti," Anthony said, finding the professor's handshake to be firm.

"And I am Joe Baronio," his companion added, in turn.

"I am sorry to have interrupted your holiday," he apologized. "I am grateful, however, for your participation in this endeavor. Without the Church's blessing we would not have been able to start our search, and we need your participation in this excavation in the event we unearth religious artifacts."

"What do you hope to find?" Tony asked. He was surveying a group of people who seemed quite comfortable with their surroundings, as well as with each other, as they helped themselves to the pleasantries of a full bar. A Turkish man wearing a white jacket approached them with a tray bearing glasses of white and red wines. The two priests relaxed. They each selected a glass of Merlot that met with their instant approval. The head archaeologist had ignored Tony's question.

"Come, let me introduce you," Freiberg said, and he took them around to meet everyone present, including his Turkish butler, now functioning as a bartender.

After a half hour of social chit-chat a small bell rang, summoning the sixteen men and women present to gather around the dining room table, where a model of the House of Mary lay upon a large sheet of engineering paper containing drawn squares, numbers, notes, and a few photographs of the area.

"We will begin Monday at seven o'clock sharp," Freiberg announced. "The site is secure and the photographs were taken today, right Harry?"

"Yes, sir," came the response from a young Englishman with a Nikon 35mm single lens reflex camera hanging from his neck. "We await your hand-picks, and shovels, and paintbrushes, string, dustpans, and buckets, Doctor!"

Everyone chuckled at that statement. It was clear to the two priests that the photographer was popular.

"Did any pictures turn out?" a woman quipped, peering over her glasses.

"None as fine as you, Florence, my dear," came the retort, which was met with more laughter.

"All right now. Just some business of a minor nature to temporarily extend the bar," an elderly man stated. The room grew silent as the man extended a collapsible pointer and tapped a spot next to the miniature house.

"We will be right up against the foundations on this side. Go gentle. We are searching for some ancient bones, most likely buried in a rather small chest. I expect that the body was shortened up and originally wrapped in cloth, and then buried for a time, as was the custom. In any event, this initial probe should take a month or so. Questions? Okay then, good luck!"

"Who is he?" Joseph asked a geologist who had mentioned he was taking a summer archaeology course.

"That is Dr. Sodbury, from Oxford. A very bright archaeologist who believes that the Virgin Mary did in fact die at this site, and was likely buried within one hundred meters of the house."

"Then why dig at the foundation?" the priest asked.

"The house serves as clock center, and each season, the digging will be directed to a new sector. Some believe that we will unearth many artifacts: pottery, bits and pieces, utensils. Perhaps even a skeleton. However, I personally doubt that we will find anything of major significance. Pilgrims have been coming here for centuries seeking sacred artifacts. I can't imagine that there is much left to discover, even one or two meters down." He turned away to speak to a contemporary.

Anthony turned to Joseph and chuckled, "You know, this is even more exciting than when I stayed up all night re-writing the director's speech to the cardinals concerning Jesuit missions to West Africa in the 1700s!"

On Monday, the priests dressed in their work clothes and drove to the House of Mary at seven to find that they were the last to arrive. Large squares, designated by thin cords, divided the area to be excavated. Those gathered there had already begun digging with handpicks, small hand spades, and trowels. The procedure was explained to them by a young male undergraduate student from Vienna. They were given tools, directed to a section, and began getting dirty. Joseph appeared to be especially happy as he carefully loosened soil in his designated area. He deposited the soil into his dustpan and sifted through it.

Their first day as archaeologists passed quickly for the priests, and by late afternoon, they felt the work in their tired muscles. They ate their evening meal at the hotel, mostly in silence, and retired early.

At the end of the second day, Anthony called the Vatican and left a message for their director. He reported that the excavation was progressing, but nothing had been found yet.

Four days later, at a depth of two meters, some pieces of pottery with a geometric pattern were found, a discovery that infused the excavators with a renewed sense of optimism.

The following days passed swiftly. On his seventeenth day of service as an amateur archaeologist, Joseph woke with the sun. Despite the promise of confessional forgiveness and the excitement of the dig, Joseph's feelings of guilt had not totally dissipated. He hid this fact from Anthony because he did not want to further involve his friend in his personal gloom. Even more troubling was the fact that his team at the excavation site included a blond coed from the University of Vienna whom he could not avoid staring at. A harsh reality was becoming clear: while the priesthood may be his life, it was no longer his passion. He had an enduring feeling of emptiness and one of being trapped. He couldn't blame the drug for his indiscretion, and questioned his own steadfastness to the Roman Church's principles. Perhaps a return to Vatican City would renew his faith, although Joseph was beginning to doubt that its walls could block out his human feelings.

Joseph's Jesuit mentors had said that such feelings and conflict were natural, and could either be tuned out or turned around with faith and steadfast purpose. This morning in particular, he questioned his resolve. Joseph went down to breakfast and sat down at the table where Anthony had finished eating, and was reading the morning paper.

"Good morning," Joseph said, forcing himself to sound chipper.

Tony peered over the top of the paper. "Good morning."

"What did you have to eat?"

"Fruit, bread, and cereal," Tony said, folding the paper and placing it on the table.

"Audrey has noticed you staring at her," Tony added, referring to the blond coed.

Joseph shook his head, either in disbelief or remorse, Tony couldn't tell.

"She said something to you?"

"No. I overheard her telling someone that you must have a sister who looks like her."

Joseph did not respond and Anthony Gianti, confessional priest to his friend, did not offer a lecture. He decided to save it for later.

They arrived at the excavation site at seven o'clock as usual, and found that the area sectioned off had been expanded, and that new sectors were being laid out.

The site coordinator approached them as the priests gathered their tools. "Joe, Tony, I would like the two of you to work this section," he said, while walking over and pointing down at a large square, sectioned off by string. "We have already taken photographs of the area, so you can begin once you have made your log entries."

Within a few minutes, they were digging into soil that was particularly easy to remove. They had gone down three feet by late afternoon when suddenly Tony struck something hard. Tossing aside his trowel, he used his hands to carefully clear away dirt and pebbles from the top of what soon was revealed as a marble slab of some kind.

"Joseph, over here!" he said excitedly, an outburst that drew others to the site. Tony, with the help of Joseph and two others, slowly carved out a two-foot trench around the container made of marble. The excavation's coordinator had long since arrived at the spot, and began directing the gentle lifting of the chest-like structure out of the ground, and onto a thick piece of canvas.

Father Baronio looked expectedly at the site coordinator who gave him a slight nod. The two Jesuit priests swept off the top of the slab with their hands, waited until the object had been photographed, and then set about, with help, to remove the cover. It finally gave way, and the priests managed to rotate it ninety degrees and slide it to the side. Tony peered inside. An old soiled cloth covered whatever was buried beneath it. Again, Tony looked to the site coordinator and again he was given the go ahead.

By now everyone at the site was gathered around. The Viennese coed gave Joseph a quizzical look that hardly registered with the priest. His full attention was on the marble chest.

With trembling fingers, he leaned down and slowly drew back the frayed cloth. A flash of a camera momentarily revealed in better detail what lay inside.

"What?" he exclaimed. For under the cloth he found three bottles of champagne, surrounded by ice and glasses.

"Congratulations!" the entire crew, save the priests, shouted in unison.

"You are now members of the secret society of old and odd things unearthed!" the site coordinator exclaimed. "By virtue of your working for over fourteen days, we salute you, and ask that you join us in celebration!"

Both priests shook their heads and laughed.

"The digging seemed a bit too easy today!" Joseph exclaimed, as the bottles were opened. The crew soon consumed the three bottles, and several more that had been stowed nearby for the celebration. After champagne, it was time to stow the tools and quit for the day.

"You have now experienced the thrill of a salted site," the blonde said, smilingly at Joseph, who smiled while avoiding any eye contact.

The telephone in Anthony's room rang almost as soon as he arrived back at the hotel, and the woman known to Father Gianti as Cy, asked if they would be available to meet the next day. He agreed, and went next door where Father Baronio was reading a novel.

"Good," Joseph responded. "Should we call Father Martelli in Rome and inform him about this meeting?"

"Yes. Let's call in the morning. We haven't learned anything of value at the site, and I couldn't support either position if my life depended upon it, but at least we have *something, something* to report. He may offer us some guidance, or maybe he has information to share with us. He must be relying on someone or something other than us?"

"Yes, I now hope so. Let's inform the site director and say we have other business to conduct tomorrow. He has more than enough workers with the volunteers who arrived yesterday."

Following an early breakfast the next morning, Father Anthony Gianti returned to his room, sighed, took a deep breath and dialed the Vatican's country code, and then the director's number.

"Father Martelli," came the firm response after only one ring.

Father Gianti explained that both he and Father Baronio were together, and told of the meeting scheduled for that afternoon.

"Wonderful job. Wonderful," came the reply. "Obviously you are working well together, and are on the verge of learning some important information. I must go now, but contact me following your meeting. Ciao."

He then hung up suddenly as Tony uttered a surprised, "Thank you."

"That was all?" Joseph asked with disbelief.

"He said he is pleased, but seems to have put us out of his mind. It was as though we have been sent to fetch a bag of bagels from the corner bakery."

At 3:04 p.m. there was a knock on Father Gianti's door, and he opened it to find a bellman who smiled and handed Tony an envelope. He nodded, and when he saw that neither gentleman was reaching for his tip, nodded a second time, spun around, and departed back down the hall.

The note was typed, and stated simply, "Please meet me inside the café across from the hotel. I have had nothing to eat today, and it will be more comfortable for us."

"It's not even signed, nor is her name even typed at the bottom," Joseph remarked, after being handed the note.

"Well," replied Anthony, "let's go and meet her."

They entered the café and a server, obviously expecting them, met the priests at the door with a big smile, and said, "Please, follow."

He led them to a large private room with several round tables, one of which was occupied by the woman Anthony recognized from the café. She stood, introduced herself, and noted, "Father Baronio, I assume," as she offered her hand. "I am Cy." They shook hands, and then she shook Father Gianti's hand firmly.

"I am so hungry. I have ordered some soup and a salad. Please, join me if you are hungry," she beckoned.

"Maybe I'll have an espresso," Tony replied. "Me, also," Joseph added toward the waiter who departed, closing the door behind him.

"This room was available, and they understand that our business is confidential," she offered. "Have you seen the ruins?" she asked expectantly. Both priests were taken aback by her casualness, given the circumstances that brought them together. They were expecting to call Father Martelli back later that day, before he left his office, with exciting news.

Tony began telling her what they had seen, and his enthusiasm for Ephesus quickly surfaced. To Joseph's surprise, his good friend carried on a monologue for some time. He was interrupted by a few knocks on the door and the entry of two waiters, one carrying the food ordered by Cy, and the second with the two espressos, which were placed before the priests.

The waiters departed, closing the door.

"Please, will you allow me to dine before we begin?" she asked pleasantly, as the two priests picked up their espressos, and began sipping the hot contents from the small cups.

Cy placed the cloth napkin on her lap, and picked up a spoon as she studied the two priests. They appeared relatively relaxed and offered no conversation as she began eating. By the time that she had finished her soup, the two men had finished their drinks. She moved the soup bowl aside, and placed the salad in front of her, while noting that the two Jesuit Priests were now looking at each another with some apprehension. Together their looks turned to concern as they stared into their empty cups and silently mouthed a few words. Joseph Baronio attempted to slide his chair back and away from the table, but was unable to do so. He looked toward Tony, who was sitting up, but apparently asleep! Within the minute, he too was unconscious, slumped back into his chair.

A side door opened and members of the Cult of Artemis placed them on stretchers before carrying them to the small ambulance which was backed up to the restaurant's rear doorway.

# CHAPTER FIFTEEN

## JULY 28, 1980

Soon after Rebecca Jean Solmquest checked into the same room at the Gössl Hotel in Vienna that had been previously occupied by Jay Youngquest, she placed a call to Professor Meister at the university. She was informed that he was out, and quickly decided against leaving a message.

Rebecca inspected the room carefully, searching in vain for any sign of Jay. Lying supine on the bed, she used a small pair of opera glasses to inspect the ceiling. *Nothing unusual there*, she thought, although she noted that the windowsill had abrasion marks on it, apparently made by a rope. The abrasions were recent and quite apparent. She also noticed a slight discoloration on the wall opposite the bed, eight feet or so up from the floor. Placing a chair under the spot, Rebecca climbed up to have a look. A hole, about the diameter of a piece of chalk, had been caulked in, and not repainted. Rebecca went down to the front desk.

"Might I look at the room next to mine?" she inquired. "I believe that was the room I stayed in last time, and I might want to move into it tomorrow."

The attendant raised her eyebrows slightly.

"Of course," she said. "That room is currently available, and we want you to be comfortable. I'll go up with you."

She took the key from its place behind the desk, and led Rebecca back upstairs. The door was unlocked and they walked in.

"Yes," Rebecca said, looking around, "This is where I stayed before, but since it's quite similar to my present room, I'll just stay there. I'm sorry to have bothered you."

"As you prefer," the attendant said. She locked the room and returned downstairs, as Rebecca returned to her room.

She had seen what she had expected to see: the same sort of covered hole in the adjoining room, in the same spot. *Maybe it was nothing*, she mused, but she had a hunch that it was important. Standing on the chair again, she scraped at the covered hole with her fingernail. It was a synthetic caulk of some type, and not plaster. She didn't know what to make of it.

The next morning, Rebecca waited in her room until there was a knock on the door. She went to open it.

"Please come in," she said to the maid. "I was just leaving."

The maid nodded and went into the bathroom to begin cleaning.

"Say, do you clean this room every day?" Rebecca asked.

"Yes, ma'am, every day except Tuesday."

"Well, about nine days ago a friend of mine, a Mr. Jacob Youngquest, was staying here and may have left a book on the bedside table. Did you happen to see it?"

The maid frowned. "I don't remember anything being left in here during the past month. If I had seen it, I'd have turned it in to the desk."

"I forgot to ask down there. Was there anything unusual about the room when Mr. Youngquest checked out?"

"I can't remember clearly that far back, ma'am," the maid said.

"Thank you anyway," Rebecca said, adding as if in explanation. "He has been so forgetful lately. It's his age, I'm afraid."

"He might have accidentally packed something from the room," the maid offered, her voice careful, almost shy.

Rebecca looked up. "Was there something that Mr. Youngquest accidentally took when he checked out?"

"Well, yes. I reported to the housekeeper that a pillowcase was missing... and a fitted sheet."

"A pillowcase?"

"And a sheet," the maid responded.

"Well, I will certainly pay for those items," Rebecca responded, her eyes asking for forgiveness.

"Housekeeping may have billed him, ma'am. I don't know. I'm sorry to have troubled you."

"No trouble at all. I'm the one who's sorry. I appreciate your frankness, and know what an inconvenience such things can be."

Rebecca returned to the front desk.

"Can you tell me who was in room number six when Mr. Youngquest checked out?" Rebecca asked the desk clerk.

The desk clerk gave her a hard look. "I am not allowed to divulge that sort of information, madam. I'm sure you can understand why."

Rebecca ignored that.

"When Mr. Youngquest checked out, he may have been having a seizure and did not know what he was doing. He's on a strict medication. I was told he took some bedding by mistake, and I will pay for those items myself. His brother, Marshal Youngquest, was staying next door in room six, I believe. They did not meet me at the university yesterday, and I'm sure they left me a message here when they checked out."

The clerk nodded understandingly. She brought out a registration book and scanned through it.

"No. There are no messages. And a second Mr. Youngquest was not staying with us when Mr. Jay Youngquest checked out. Sorry."

"They may have stayed together, I suppose. Thank you so much."

Rebecca returned to her room and again inspected the wall with the hole in it.

*There's plaster dust here. This hole's been drilled and filled recently,* she concluded. *The bedding was taken to hide something; or to use for some purpose. Perhaps something was lowered out the window with a rope made from the sheet. Something unexpected happened in here that involved Jay. Of that, I'm certain.*

Three hours later, Rebecca was at the university waiting for Professor Meister. She was surprised that he recognized her. They had met only once, ten years earlier.

"Rebecca, how surprised I am to see you!" he said with a smile, as he opened the door to his office and ushered her inside. "This is one of the most exciting weeks I've had since the end of the war! First, Jay comes to visit me, and now you."

"Is he here now?" she asked expectantly.

"Sorry. No. Jay contacted my former secretary at home and told her he was going to Ephesus. He left unexpectedly, and I'm afraid under circumstances that may make him somewhat of a suspect."

"A suspect? In what?"

"A murder in Salzburg."

"A murder in Salzburg?" she repeated incredulously.

"Yes."

Professor Meister gave her a detailed account of their journey to Salzburg and his subsequent trip. He covered it all: finding the body, the journals, and the criminal investigation being conducted by Chief Honaker.

"And you think Jay is now in Ephesus?" Rebecca asked when he was finished.

"All indications point to that."

"Was he with anyone?"

"No. I don't believe so. He was never accompanied by anyone, and he never mentioned having an associate with him. Why?"

Rebecca shook her head. "There must have been someone or something that called him to Ephesus. I don't know who or what, and I am concerned because it is so unlike Jay to leave suddenly without coming here to say good-bye to you." She paused. "Why do you think he would call your former secretary?"

"I live in her home. She didn't want to wake me the morning Jay called. He knew her quite well.

"You are sure that he didn't mention anyone he had met who was assisting him?" Rebecca inquired again.

"I don't believe that there was anyone," the professor repeated.

"And you know of no link between Jay and the dead man, other than perhaps the journals?"

"No."

Rebecca gave him a look fraught with concern.

"I'm terribly worried about Jay, Professor," she confessed. "That's why I've come to Vienna. Mr. Ruffescott, whom you've met, has gone to Selçuk to look for Jay. He hasn't found him there." She paused and noted the look of concern she was receiving in return.

"If Jay left here unexpectedly," Rebecca reasoned, "it wasn't because of anything happening in America. He either found something here in Vienna, or was contacted by someone here. In either event, this is where I intend to start my search for him."

"I understand. In the meantime, I will ask Chief Honaker about his investigation. It might shed some light on Jay's whereabouts. By now he must have contacted the police in Selçuk-- and in Kuşadasi, a larger coastal town."

Rebecca smiled.

"You know, Professor Meister, Jay owes you his life. I am so grateful for what you did for him. I can't tell you how many times he has told me how you hid him from the Nazis, and risked your own life for him. We both know that Jay could not kill anyone unless his own life was threatened. Why would he kill someone and then tell you where he was going? No. I don't believe he did that. It's improbable."

"I agree one hundred percent," the professor responded. "And please be careful. Something is unfolding here that concerns and connects us all. I just wish I knew what it was."

After she left the professor with an agreement to meet the next morning at ten, Rebecca took a subway back to her hotel. At the door to her room she inserted the key—but the door came ajar on its own.

She pushed the door open and saw a man sitting in the semidarkness. Her heart skipped a beat and the name "Jay" escaped her lips, a split second before she realized that the man sitting there was much larger than Jay.

"Please come in," the man said. "I've been waiting for you."

Rebecca took a step backward into the hallway, and glanced toward the stairway. "Who are you?" she demanded.

The man stood and flashed an official looking identification card at her.

"I'm Chief of Police Honaker, from Salzburg."

Rebecca stepped forward, flicked on a light, and studied the man standing before her.

"Do you make it a habit to intrude upon a hotel guest's privacy and sit in a dark room?" she asked him.

"I'm on official business," he replied. "I have permission from the front desk. I turned out the lights to observe the room when it's dark. Sorry if I frightened you."

"Have you found Jay?" she asked forthrightly. She noted that her suitcase had been moved from the twin bed, and that the door to the armoire was open.

"We know that he left Vienna by plane for Istanbul, and from there to Izmir. I believe he is still in Turkey."

"What specifically are you doing in my room?" she demanded to know.

"Mr. Youngquest also rented this room when he was in Vienna. I am investigating his possible implication in a murder."

"A murder?"

"Yes. I have reason to believe that Mr. Youngquest may have killed a man in this room."

"You have a vivid imagination!"

"Perhaps. But, as you know from the desk clerk and maid, Mr. Youngquest checked out unexpectedly, taking a pillowcase and a sheet with him. Let's suppose that an intruder confronted him in this room and attempted to extort him, perhaps over the old manuscripts. They fought and somehow the intruder was stabbed and died upon this bed," he said, pointing toward it. "Your friend then took the sheet and fashioned a rope to lower the body to the ground before putting it in the trunk of his car. Let's further suppose that the next morning he checks out, and drives to Salzburg, where the books and journals he covets are hidden in a sarcophagus. He waits until night, enters the crypt, removes the journals he wants, drops in the body, and then flees to Turkey."

"I believe I read about that plot once in a fairytale," Rebecca said with open disdain.

"But a fairytale you have considered yourself," Honaker rebuffed. "I'd bet a pretty coin that the woman's fingerprints in the burn marks on that windowsill are yours." He indicated the window overlooking the street. "You've inspected this room thoroughly, haven't you? As well as the one next door? Yes, I have only a theory. However, since I have no other theory at the moment, it's the one I'm going with."

Rebecca smiled at the chief, an expression which, judging by his frown, caught him off guard. He had apparently been expecting anger, not cooperation.

"How can I be of assistance to you?" she asked.

Honaker quickly composed himself. "You can begin by telling me what Mr. Youngquest was searching for. Then you can tell me what contact you have had with him since he left America."

Rebecca closed the door behind her and sat down on the chair next to the bed. "As I indicated, I will do everything I can to assist you in your investigation, Chief Honaker," she said, a statement that she doubted the police chief fully accepted. His smile in return seemed forced.

"Very well, then. I must ask a few questions, and some of them may seem personal. I'm not trying to pry into your private life. I just need to do my job."

"I understand," Rebecca said, but offered nothing else. She continued to stare at him until he blinked.

"What is your relationship to Mr. Youngquest?" Honaker asked.

"We are unmarried partners. I suppose that since I accepted his proposal, we are still engaged."

"How long have you been engaged?"

"Since forty-five."

"How old are you now?"

"No. Chief. I meant nineteen forty-five."

Chief Honaker glanced up from the notes he was taking. If she was mocking him, he saw no trace of it.

"Where do you live?"

"Near Chanhassen, Minnesota, in the United States of America."

"Why did Jay Youngquest come to Austria?"

"To do research."

"Concerning the gravesite of Mary, the Mother of Jesus?" he asked.

"Yes, and some ancient writings, and perhaps other artifacts."

"Has he ever been convicted of a crime?"

"No."

"Why have you come to Vienna, Miss Solmquest?"

"To find Jay," she replied.

"What have you learned?" the chief asked.

"Why, nothing. Nothing at all," she answered matter-of-factly.

"Isn't it true that Mr. Youngquest is not forgetful, and is not subject to seizures?" he inquired.

"Yes, that is true."

"Then aren't you trying to impede our investigation by making such claims to potential witnesses in a criminal investigation?"

"No. What I'm trying to do is learn all I can. I love Jay very much and need to find him."

Honaker gave her an arch look.

"This is a police matter. A murder investigation. And in my professional opinion, you will do whatever you can to impede it. I must therefore ask you to cease whatever it is you are doing in Austria and return home."

"I have no intention of doing that."

"This not a polite request. This is an order. You are jeopardizing my investigation by meddling in it. That will cease as of this moment."

"You are overstepping your bounds, Chief," Rebecca said calmly. "The American Embassy will support my request to remain in Austria. And contrary to what you just said, I can be of some service to you if you permit me to stay."

Honaker shook his head. "Your embassy has been contacted, and the authorities there understand my request and agree with it. Therefore, I have taken the liberty to confiscate your passport from the hotel, and have assigned an officer to take you to the airport in the morning."

"I want to contact the embassy before our discussion continues," she said without any hint of anger.

"As you wish. However, please do not leave the hotel. If you do, you will be arrested."

Rebecca decided to say nothing further to him. She went to the telephone book and looked up the number of the American embassy. As she was dialing it, Chief Honaker departed the room, closing the door behind him.

Chief Honaker left the hotel after ensuring that the young officer assigned to watch Ms. Solmquest understood that he had been entrusted with an assignment more important than it appeared.

"Under no circumstances must Rebecca Solmquest be in Austria after tomorrow," he stated firmly.

"Yes, sir," the officer replied. "I will see her onto the plane and watch it take off."

"Good. Leave a message with my secretary when the airplane is in the air."

"Understood, sir," the officer said.

Chief Honaker then entrusted the officer with the airline ticket, and Rebecca Solmquest's passport. On the way back to his office, Honaker stopped at a pay telephone to call for two men to fly to Turkey, instructing them to bring along special weapons that he specified.

# CHAPTER SIXTEEN

## JULY 29, 1980

Professor Meister sat in his office staring down at the mass of paperwork covering his desk, but looking at nothing in particular. As one of the oldest and most respected faculty members at the University of Vienna, he was given a wide latitude concerning deadlines, attendance at faculty meetings, and the submission of reports to the administration. When a serious crisis arose, one of his graduate students or his secretary stepped in to do what was necessary.

The telephone on his desk rang. He considered ignoring it, but decided to pick up the receiver. It could be a call from Jay Youngquest.

"Hello, Meister here," he answered.

"Hello, Professor. This is Chief Honaker calling to speak with you about an important request."

"I am always willing to respond to your every request," was the jovial reply. But the police chief's tone sobered him.

"Professor, I need to ask that you keep what I am about to tell you in strict confidence. Don't tell anyone. Do you understand?"

"I do," the professor replied.

"Very well, then. I have reason to suspect that your friend Mr. Youngquest found what he was looking for in your journals, and may be using that information to uncover priceless artifacts in Turkey."

"What makes you believe that?"

"We have our sources of information. What's more, it is clear that there is a direct link between the murder of the man in the crypt and Mr. Youngquest's sudden departure. If he should call you, please inform me immediately. I am personally overseeing this investigation. Can I count on your full cooperation?"

"Of course," Dr. Meister responded. "However, I still believe that when all is said and done, and the evidence accounted for, you will find that Jay Youngquest is innocent of any wrongdoing."

"Professor, I admire your sense of loyalty. But do not fail to call me if Mr. Youngquest contacts you. Don't tell him about my enlisting your cooperation, and encourage him to explain what happened and why he left. I also will need to know where he is staying. Find out all you can. All right, Professor?"

"I'll do what I can," Dr. Meister responded without enthusiasm. "I'll do what I can."

"Thank you. Also, Ms. Solmquest has been interfering with my investigation, and I have had to send her back to America."

Professor Meister did not respond. Both men hung up and Dr. Meister noted that the light on his telephone stayed on for a split second after he placed the receiver back on its cradle. Someone had been listening in.

The next morning after breakfast, the plainclothes officer who had been watching Rebecca Solmquest approached her, introduced himself, and invited her to be ready to depart the hotel at ten-thirty. An hour later he escorted her through customs, walked her to her gate, and after returning her passport, observed her board the Lufthansa jet bound for Kennedy Airport in New York. The flight was delayed for nearly an hour due to a problem with the cargo door warning light. But it was repaired and the young police officer dutifully observed the airplane as it taxied around a building, and a short while later, took off. The officer then called Chief Honaker's direct number, and as instructed, left a message with his secretary. He then went home to catch some much needed sleep.

When the jet landed in New York, Rebecca discovered, to her dismay, that her suitcase had been checked through to Minneapolis. There was nothing she could do about that, so she took her carry-on bag to a Pan American ticket counter where she booked passage on the next flight to London.

The ability—or good fortune—to turn setbacks into opportunities, had always been one of Rebecca's strengths, and her call from Kennedy Airport to Ruff at his hotel in Selçuk, had been answered by him. He had not found Jay, but he had a plan to find out where he was. It was quite possible, Ruff surmised, that the British Museum in London held a clue, or an artifact, of importance to them. He went on to explain that in the 1890s and early 1900s

Turkish antiquities were still being shipped to the British Museum. Even some antiquities recovered by the Austrians ended up in London, rather than Vienna or Izmir. At that time there had been no museum located near the ruins. Thus, the fact that no jar or lid or references to writings by Jesus had been found in Vienna or Ephesus opened the possibility that something of direct interest may have found its way to the British depository of almost two million artifacts. At the very least, the extensive collections in the museum's library warranted further study.

From Heathrow Airport, Rebecca traveled into London by train, then took the tube to Paddington Station, where she found reasonable accommodations a short distance away. Her third floor room, without bath, was most acceptable. In stark contrast was the complimentary English breakfast, which was toast unsuitably dry, in a toast rack. Also included were undercooked eggs that stared up, seemingly gasping from the experience of being drowned in oil, right next to the petrified fruit wedges. Nearby Chinese and Indian restaurants proved suitable fare, however.

Gaining access to journals at the library and artifacts at the museum, proved difficult, even with the forged letter of authorization from an official of the British Museum. She had once nodded to him over a glass of champagne during a fundraiser, after she had rendered a sizable contribution. His letter to her, thanking her for her donation, had provided the correct spelling of his name, and an example of the letterhead.

Rebecca found nothing of relevance in the journals she studied at the British Museum. She felt lonely, and it was frustrating that Ruff had not reported any progress in his efforts to find Jay. She was now convinced that she had made a mistake by listening to Ruff. She should have gone to Turkey, not England.

Rebecca wandered around the impressive museum, taking special note of the Rosetta Stone. Jay's work with Professor Meister during the war involved the many artifacts from Ephesus that had an Egyptian provenance, and he had studied hundreds of hieroglyphs and their various translations. She knew that there were hundreds of Egyptian symbols, and this was the stone that had inspired a new look into the meaning of Egypt's ancient language of the gods and pharaohs. Hieroglyphs were the writings found in the ancient tombs of Egypt. As she gazed upon the large, black granite stone, with its polished face and gray writing in ancient Greek, Demotic script and hieroglyphs, she was reminded that Professor Meister had given Jay a copy of the stone's writings. Seeing the original made her ever more fearful of losing Jay. Her eyes began to well up, and she shook her head, casting out the demons of fear and possible loss.

*I need a break. I'm in London, it's Saturday, so why not see a play?*

Years before she had seen Agatha Christy's *The Mousetrap*, although she could not remember the details of the longest running play in London. At her hotel she freshened up, changed, and made a reservation for dinner at the Ivy, an upscale and well-known eatery that had been a favorite of Winston Churchill's during the war. She would go out, relax, and enjoy herself. Tomorrow she would redouble her efforts. And contact Ruff.

The dinner was up to expectations, and in fact so pleasurable, that Rebecca soon put aside her concerns. An American couple had arrived at the Ivy shortly before Rebecca. While the man was nicely dressed, he was not wearing the obligatory coat and tie, and so had to be "fitted" in the restaurant's cloakroom from a supply kept on hand for such contingencies. During that interval, his wife introduced herself to Rebecca as Cheryl Rice from Wisconsin. She and her husband Jim were on vacation, and she was most interested to learn that Rebecca was English and living in Minnesota. When her husband returned, decked out in sports coat and matching tie, Cheryl suggested they have dinner and watch *The Mousetrap* together.

After the performance, they decided to share a taxi. During the ride they exchanged addresses and telephone numbers, both in London and at home, and made promises to keep in contact with one another. On an impulse, Rebecca mentioned that she was doing research at the British Museum, and asked if they would like to meet there the next day for lunch. It was an invitation readily accepted.

Rebecca was smiling to herself as she paid her fare and slid out of the taxi. It was approaching midnight and the street was deserted as she walked to her hotel. As she opened her purse to get a mint, her arm was suddenly seized, and she was pulled into the shadow of a stairway.

"Please don't be afraid," a husky voice said, "I am here because of Jay Youngquest."

In the feeble light of a street lamp, Rebecca recognized the man as a tour guide at the British Museum who had appeared to take an interest in her, and had seemingly followed her from time to time. She had passed off his interest as a passing fantasy.

"You're hurting me," she spat out.

"I'm sorry," the man apologized. He eased his grip on her.

"Where is Jay?" Rebecca asked defiantly, looking about for a possible escape route.

"He is in a medical facility in Izmir, Turkey," the man said forthrightly.

Shocked to her core, Rebecca let her guard down. "Is he hurt?" she heard herself ask.

"He was injured in an altercation with another man," the guide said. He released his grip entirely. "However, he is stable and should recover fully. But he will recover more quickly if you are with him. I can take you to him."

"How do you know all this?"

"I have my sources."

"Why should I trust you?"

"Because I have this."

He handed Rebecca Jay's passport and key chain. "Can you leave tomorrow morning?" he asked her.

"Yes, of course. I can leave immediately."

"I'll make reservations tonight. We should be able to leave Heathrow no later than noon tomorrow."

"Which hospital is he at?" she asked.

"It's a private clinic, but it's well staffed. I'll give you more details tomorrow. Be ready to leave your hotel by eight."

He gave her a hard stare.

"I know you recognize me from the museum, and yes, I have been watching you. My associates were working with Mr. Youngquest when he was injured. If you contact anyone-- the police, Mr. Ruffescott, or anyone else-- I will not be here in the morning and you will not be taken to him. I am doing this to help you both. Please believe me. And trust me."

"I do," she said without much conviction. "Although I don't have much choice in the matter, do I?"

"Not if you want to see Jay..." The man walked quickly away and disappeared around the first corner.

Rebecca went up to her room, partially packed, and laid down to sleep. She got little rest, ate little at breakfast, and opened the door to her room at the first tap upon it at 7:55 a.m. It was a taxi driver who handed her a business card from the British Museum.

"I have been paid to take you to Heathrow, mum," he said.

She nodded. "Thank you, I'm ready."

When she was settled into the backseat of the black taxi, the driver handed a large envelope to her. Inside, she found an airline ticket to Izmir, through Istanbul, and an open-ended ticket for her return trip to London. A typed note stated that she would be met in Izmir by "a friend." That, she doubted.

At Heathrow she called the hotel where Jim and Cheryl Rice were staying and left a message that she was unable to make lunch.

The flight from London seemed long, tiring, and was nerve-racking. She slept fitfully, in part because her mind kept racing, and in part because the air-conditioning was malfunctioning, causing her skin to feel warm and clammy. She had finally given up trying to sleep and just stared out the window until the jetliner finally landed in Istanbul. She then flew to Ismir.

Once through security and inside the main concourse, the museum man approached her.

"Please follow me, Rebecca," he said softly to her, as he passed by her side and walked outside to a waiting car. He put his bag in the trunk and got in the backseat. Rebecca did likewise and soon the car sped off.

Thirty minutes later, they pulled into a well-maintained parking lot that served what appeared to be a medical clinic. Rebecca's arrival at the back of the clinic was expected. A young woman opened the door for her.

"Good day, madam," she said politely. "Please come with me."

Rebecca followed the young woman to a small office near the nurse's station. Five recovery rooms spread out in a circle around the station, where another young woman, a nurse, sat in a chair outside a room that did not have a patient's name on the signboard next to the door. Rebecca was joined by two other women, both clad in medical uniforms. The taller of the two ushered Rebecca into an office and closed the door.

"I am a doctor," she said, "and this is my nurse. We have been attending to Mr. Youngquest. He was injured in a fall off of a pier and nearly drowned."

The doctor paused to let Rebecca compose herself. When she had, the doctor continued.

"We have been carefully monitoring his vital signs, which are stable. To avoid possible infection, we have given him some drugs. He is still under sedation but should be awakening soon. We are pleased that you will be present when he awakens."

Rebecca had many questions but chose to remain silent. She was numbed by a confusing mixture of shock, anger, and unabashed relief.

"If you don't have any questions," the doctor said, not unkindly, "please put this gown on over your clothing." She handed over a gown, along with a pair of slippers. Rebecca quickly complied. The doctor then led her to the room located directly behind the nurse seated in the chair. The other rooms appeared to be deserted. The doctor opened the door to allow Rebecca entry, and she and the nurse followed her in.

By all appearances, Jay looked dead. He was pale and unconscious. Two IV's were tapped into his arm, and a heart monitor pulsated quietly. The room smelled faintly of some sort of medicine.

Rebecca, tears welling in her eyes, walked over to the bed. She picked up Jay's hand gently, raised it to her lips, and kissed it.

"Oh dear God, my beloved Jay," she managed to say, as she gazed down upon him.

She put down his hand and walked over to where the plastic IV bottles were hung. She studied the labels and then wheeled around in a rage. "What the hell are you doing?" she shouted at the doctor.

Rebecca reached over and unplugged an IV.

"Your stupidity could have killed him," she cried out. "A truth serum is only to be administered to a healthy person!"

The doctor mumbled something incoherent and nodded at the nurse, who quickly removed a needle from Jay's arm. She then removed the drug bottle and tube from the stand, and packed them away into a brown case.

"Get out, both of you."

"As you wish," the doctor said. "I will check back later."

When they were gone, Rebecca picked up Jay's hand again and stroked it gently.

His eyelids flickered open and then closed. Rebecca leaned over him.

"Voice of an angry angel," he said softly.

"Oh, Jacob, don't leave me, don't die on me," she pleaded, choking on her words. As he lapsed back into sleep, she sat beside him, smoothing back his hair and talking incessantly to him until the doctor returned.

"He spoke a few words and I think he knew I was here," Rebecca said matter-of-factually. "What is his prognosis?"

"He should recover fully," the doctor replied in a professional tone. "He should be up and about within a day or so. He should remain here, however, so we can see to his recovery and protect him."

"Who is responsible for his injuries?"

"Jesuits working directly for their superiors in Rome," the doctor bluntly replied. "He may not have been injured intentionally. They wanted him alive to provide information about the location of their Virgin. There was a fight on a pier, which he escaped by jumping into the water. He nearly drowned. But he was rescued from the water, and brought here. One of our associates died in the ambulance on the way. She was shot while saving him from capture."

"Did that woman bring Jay here from Vienna?"

"She did. He came with her freely, in his quest for pages torn from old archaeological journals once kept at the University of Vienna."

"I see," Rebecca said, her wrath toward the doctor having now cooled. "Has he been shown those pages?"

"I'm not sure. I am a doctor and know very little about that sort of thing. However, tomorrow someone will be here to speak to you about that. Until then, the room next to this one is empty and at your disposal. We ask that you remain here until he can travel, which may be much sooner than I had originally thought. He is in good physical condition, and he is also strong willed."

Rebecca nodded her gratitude, but doubted that the doctor's knowledge about the situation was limited.

"I need to speak to someone—a mutual friend of ours in Ephesus—to tell him about Jay."

The doctor smiled but did not respond. Just then a nurse came into the room with a tray of food.

"For me?" Rebecca asked.

"Yes. Have something to eat, and then I suggest taking a nap in the next room. If his condition changes, I will wake you. I am also staying here until he is discharged, along with others. We have a guard posted outside of the door to these suites. She will not permit you to leave, nor anyone unknown to enter. In the meantime, you are free to come and go from this room as you wish. If Mr. Youngquest should use the call button, the alarm will sound in your room as well as in the nurses' station. Do you have any questions for me?"

"No. And thank you," Rebecca Solmquest added with sincerity. " But please, no more drugs not prescribed for his injuries."

"I have seen to that. It was a poor decision and I apologize for being a part of it. It won't happen again, I assure you."

Rebecca walked with her tray to the room that had been prepared for her. A table and two chairs had been set up alongside the hospital bed. And, most surprisingly, the food tasted excellent.

The buzzer in her room sounded at two-fifteen in the morning. Rebecca was sleeping soundly, and it took a few seconds for her to remember where she was and what the buzzer going off signified. Then, remembering, she donned the gown and slippers and hurried to Jay's room. To her untold delight, he was awake.

"Good morning, my darling," she said, trying to sound casual. " How do you feel?"

"Handsome," he responded.

"Oh, good. You're feeling well enough to joke around."

"You don't remember my last one about the angry angel?" he quipped.

Rebecca bent down and kissed him, lightly on the lips.

"Seriously, Jay, how do you really feel?"

The doctor entered the room and studied the monitor. She then checked Jay's pulse and blood pressure. Jay closed his eyes and slowly shook his head.

"When will I be able to get out of here?"

"In a few days, based upon your recovery to date."

"Good. I think that I can sit up and maybe get out of bed. Is it really just past two?"

"That's two o'clock in the morning," Rebecca said.

"In the morning? I'm keeping you all up, aren't I?" Jay said, gazing up fondly at Rebecca. "Hell of a gentleman I am. But I do have a question," he said to her. "How did you get here so fast?"

"I was in London at the British Museum, after the police evicted me from Austria. The chief of police of Salzburg and I don't seem to get along. He thinks that you murdered some thug whose body they found with Meister's books in the crypt in Salzburg."

"You don't say?" he responded. "Well, it wasn't me. Alex shot the man with an arrow, in my room. He was attempting to either kidnap or kill me. Since then, I've been running into a string of bad luck. That is, until I opened my eyes and saw you here."

He squeezed her hand and she squeezed back. They smiled into each other's eyes while pressing the Morse code letters that formed words into each other's hands.

"How is Alex?" he asked. "I heard a gun fire, and then a moan as she rolled me off of the pier."

"She died several days ago," the doctor replied.

Jay Youngquest stared at the doctor's face for several deep breaths.

"I am sorry to learn that. She was very personable and may have saved my life in Vienna." Jay closed his eyes and slowly shook his head.

"She died," Jay whispered to himself.

"Yes," came the response. "She was shot at fairly close range and lost too much blood. They weren't expected to fire their guns..." The voice trailed off bitterly.

"What do you mean, they weren't expected to fire their guns?"

"Just that. With that understanding, we did not use deadly force upon their approach."

Jay Youngquest leaned back and sighed noticeably.

"I don't understand why you placed us in danger if you knew what was going to take place - that there would be an attack to capture me."

"We needed to protect a source inside of the Vatican. However, that person has been apprehended and we seek her release."

"Why am I such a valued commodity? I have no information as to the whereabouts of the statue, or the other relics!"

"You understand hundreds of hieroglyphs, and have exchange value should either Rutheford Ruffescott or Professor Meister find what belongs to us, or clues to where our treasures are resting."

"Apparently, I am also wanted for murder."

"Yes."

"So, the Vatican holds one of your sect, you hold me, and everyone believes that Ruff may soon possess the relics?"

"Yes. Well summarized."

"Negotiations leading to mutual compromise results when all parties desire an accommodation; something attainable only through others," Jay pondered out loud, while staring into the woman's eyes.

"We need to get to Ruff."

"You cannot travel."

Youngquest stared through the doctor.

Rebecca Solmquest forced herself to relax and let her mind search for a plan. She recalled that upon her arrival, she had passed a closed door. She'd glanced through its small rectangular window into a room with a whirlpool bath. She had also noted the smell of chlorine.

Rebecca Solmquest suddenly appeared very tired. She clenched her right elbow with her left hand, massaging it as she looked at Jay.

"I am quite sore today," she half whispered. The doctor and nurse departed the room, leaving a guard.

Their sentinel moved closer and pulled a chair up next to the bed, obviously intent on monitoring their conversation. Rebecca took Jay's left hand into hers and squeezed it gently. She blinked her eyes deliberately. Then paused. Jay allowed his eyelids to droop until he could barely see Rebecca's eyes. She pressed "CQ CQ" in Morse code with her fingers into his palm. The attention signal. Dash dot dash dot dash dash dot dash. He twitched his left cheek, and she began her secret message as the sentry assumed he was sleeping.

After a few minutes, Rebecca gently placed Jay's hand onto the bed.

"Can I take a whirlpool bath?" she asked softly.

The woman guard frowned, and then replied, "Yes."

Rebecca went into her room. She then wrapped herself into a bathrobe that had been folded neatly on a chair near the bed. She picked up a bar of soap, her shoes, and her tube of Prell concentrate shampoo and walked into the whirlpool room, which also had a large white cabinet and enclosed shower. She opened the cabinet as the woman guard closed the door. Rebecca spotted the bottle of granular chlorine and dropped her towel over it. She removed her clothing and slipped into the whirlpool as the sentry pressed a button on the wall, starting the water jets. After twenty minutes, Rebecca lifted herself from the water and reached over and grabbed the towel, with the concealed chlorine. She entered the shower and closed the door. After showering, she dried herself, brushed her hair, and left the shower, leaving the shower door open behind her, but not before pouring the chlorine granules onto a dry portion of the floor. She dressed and then returned to the shower, and as the guard read a magazine, squirted all of the remaining Prell concentrate shampoo in her bottle upon the white grains containing THC.

Rebecca walked briskly to her room, followed closely by her escort. She closed her door.

The chlorine granules soon began smoldering and then burst into intense flames. The cloud of chlorine smoke spread quickly and the smoke detector in the whirlpool room began its shrill warning. Rebecca's guard sprang up from her chair in the hallway and ran down the hallway as shouting filled the clinic. Two women ran into the whirlpool room and saw the fire before retreating with burning eyes from the chlorine-saturated smoke. One grabbed a fire extinguisher from its wall hanger in the hallway, took a deep breath, and reentered the room, while her companion held the door open. The cloud of gas entered the hallway while the fire was sprayed with foam from the extinguisher. The fumes caused their eyes and noses to burn and water.

Eight women were in the hallway.

"What happened?" the doctor shouted.

"I don't know. Rebecca just took a bath a few minutes ago," came the response from Rebecca's escort.

They looked into each other's eyes, turned, and ran to Rebecca's room. It was empty. She had escaped in the screen of smoke and confusion.

Jay lay upon the bed, eyes closed, feigning sleep.

"Find her," the doctor commanded.

Rebecca Solmquest knew that she was somewhere in Izmir. She ran at her top pace, breathing in first every four paces, and then exhaling for four paces. After ten minutes, she had to breathe in, and then exhale, every two paces. She then slowed to a purposeful walk and proceeded down a side street toward the glow of city lights in the distance. Her bra's lining held a British passport, American currency, and a small Swiss army knife, containing a tiny compass in its handle. Ephesus was not far away, and Rebecca had communicated to Jay that she would go there, expecting that his captors would also recognize that the ancient city was the location of what they all sought. She would hire a cab.

The clinic was thoroughly searched, while three car teams fanned out and searched in an expanding rectangle.

"She can't get far without her American passport and money," the doctor had announced confidently.

The nurse entered Jay's room quietly. The smell of chlorine still lingered. She studied him carefully. He was surely asleep. He was even drooling slightly from the right corner of his mouth.

"Mr. Youngquest?" she said in a half-questioning tone. "Mr. Youngquest, please wake up so that I can check your vital signs." He blinked cross-eyed. Yawned.

"Okay," he responded, then sat up as she placed a thermometer under his tongue. She noted that he glanced around the room, apparently for Rebecca. He did not know what had happened – about her escape.

"Soon you will be recovered. We will take you to a new location," she said. "Rebecca has departed with an escort already."

Jay frowned.

"All right," he responded wearily, as he yawned and stretched his arms above his head. "What is that terrible smell?"

The nurse ignored the question and the doctor entered the room and did not smile as she examined his wound. She glanced at his chart, which the nurse handed to her. "*He doesn't know she's gone*" was written in the comment section of the nurse's notes. The doctor and nurse locked eyes briefly.

A week later, the car carrying Jay, wearing a black hood over his head, entered the ruins at Ephesus in darkness and proceeded into the archaeological site. It stopped beneath the long-abandoned hillside homes of the ancient city's once wealthy class.

"I'm going to give you an antibiotic," the nurse said, as she injected him with a tranquilizer. Jay flinched slightly and was fast asleep within minutes.

# CHAPTER SEVENTEEN

## AUGUST 6, 1980

Scott Frank was tired. He had been unable to sleep or even relax the entire night. Earlier he had turned on every light in the house to discourage the return of whoever had invaded his space. He now walked cautiously into every room and turned off the lights, until he reached the office. There, he remembered the postscript in Ruffescott's letter. He was to bring the book *Funde Aus Ephesos Und Samothrake* with him to Ephesus and read *Area Handbook* for *the Republic of Turkey*.

Scott went to the "F" drawer in the catalog system and found the German title. He placed the card in the holder beneath the small telescope, aligned the mark alongside the number 46, and placed the pointer into the card's hole. Peering through the instrument, he instantly spotted the book on a lower shelf, within easy reach. He removed the book and leafed through pages which were written entirely in German. The words apparently described the Ephesus excavations in great detail.

Putting the book aside, Scott went to the A section and found the card for the second book. Placing the card in the holder, and repeating the process, he spotted his prey on the top shelf. Scott rolled the ladder beneath the spot and climbed up. The green book was large and heavy. He had to tug at it, and wiggle it back and forth to free it from the grip of the books squeezed tightly together on each side of it. Suddenly it broke free, causing Scott to shift his weight and the ladder to roll to its right. Struggling to regain his balance, Scott thrust his left hand behind the ladder. As he did so, the book struck a shelf, dropped out of Scot's hand, and ricocheted off a lower rung on the ladder as it fell to the floor with a resounding thud.

"Damn it!" he cursed out loud. He glanced down and saw that the book had sprung open, and that the floor below him was now strewn with American paper currency. He climbed down, picked up the book, and found that its interior had been hollowed out and crammed full of hundred dollar bills.

*The money I need to get to Ephesus,* he thought with a sigh. *What have I gotten myself into?*

He gathered up the money and after totaling it, let out a low whistle. "Twelve thousand dollars," he muttered. "Jesus! That should sure as hell get me to where I'm being asked to go. I hope there's nothing illegal in this little 'antiquities and rare things' escapade."

Scott tested the back door and noted that it was still unlocked. He hadn't locked it after the intruder had fled! After inspecting the floor, he walked outside and down the steps to where the car's lights had come on, searching for a clear tire track or anything else that might help identify the intruder. He found nothing. No clue whatsoever.

"Let's see here," Scott said out loud, while standing in the driveway and staring up at the stars. "Whoever it was parked away from the house, walked up the back steps, somehow jimmied open the door, walked through the house, found the letters and envelopes, and escaped as I came downstairs to answer the telephone. One: They obviously realize that the letters and envelopes are important. Two: They may know about the codes. Three: They may know something about Jay's disappearance. Four: Someone called in the middle of the night, scaring the intruder away." He shrugged again. What items he had just ticked off were not facts. They were mere suppositions.

Scott walked back into the house and then to the living room, where he examined the fireplace mantel, and then the table on which he had left the letters. *Maybe,* he thought to himself, *I should search for fingerprints?* Maybe he should call the police. He was a victim of a burglary, trespass, and, possibly, theft. He sat down in a chair and shook his head. *I can't do that. If I do, I'll have to explain why I'm here in this house that's not mine. I'll also have to explain about the codes under the stamps, and about so many things I simply don't understand.*

Starting to feel tension building up in his shoulders, Scott locked the back door and went upstairs to take a nap.

The next day, he drove to his bank and deposited one thousand dollars into a savings account. Five thousand dollars went to traveler's checks, and another five into his checking account. He kept one thousand in cash. From the bank, he drove to the post office to put a hold on the mail. He continued on to his apartment.

Once there, Scott called a travel agent and made the necessary travel arrangements. He took his time packing and then tried to get some sleep, but without much success. He was about to take a shower when the telephone rang. He shuffled over and picked up the receiver.

"Hello," he said groggily, as the line went dead. He stared at the receiver for several moments before placing it back on its cradle. *A wrong number, or someone keeping tabs on me?* he wondered. Mentally he reviewed what he'd packed into the large suitcase and a small carry on.

The next afternoon, as the airport taxi drove away from his apartment complex, Scott glanced back and noticed a silver Buick pulling away from the curb from across the street and down a block from his apartment. The Buick seemed to be following them from a distance, even as the taxi veered onto Interstate Highway 494 east and picked up speed. Every few minutes Scott glanced back, and each time he did, he saw the Buick following from the same distance. To his relief, when the cab veered off the highway at the air-port exit, the Buick passed by the exit and kept heading east. At the Northwest Airlines counter, he paid the fare and then walked through the terminal to his gate. Two hours early, Scott sat down and busied himself looking around the nearly empty departure area. Quickly becoming bored, he decided to buy a paperback book for the flight, and get a beer.

Then an idea struck him and he started walking briskly through the ter-minal toward the upper level ramp where cars, vans, and buses drove up to let departing passengers out. Spotting a Budget Rent-A-Car shuttle parked near the doorway, he walked up to it.

"Do you rent silver Buicks?" he asked the driver.

"No sir," the driver politely responded as he slid the door closed. "Stan-dard's the only one that rents that make of car."

Scott stood waiting where he was until a Standard minivan drove up and stopped. As several passengers got out, he asked the driver the same question.

"Why yes, we do," he was told.

"Good. I'm quite partial to those. Used to own one. Mind if I tag along?"

"You're the customer, right? Hop in."

Scott got into the van and as the driver headed to the Standard office and parking lot, he weighed the pros and cons of his hypothesis. Someone, he was certain, had come to Minneapolis specifically to find those letters, or something in the farmhouse. But where had that person, or people, come from? Vienna? Ephesus? And then he had been followed. He was sure of that too, and his identity was no secret. His name was on a missing envelope, and his address was in the telephone book. Anyone coming there from out of town would most likely rent a car at the airport.

As they pulled into the Standard lot, he noted several silver Buicks parked there. Scott exited the van and went to a Buick parked next to the office. As he peered inside, a voice called to him from the office.

"Sir, that car's just been turned in. But we have others just like it ready to go!"

Scott checked out the car's exterior before turning toward the uniformed employee.

"I saw the car pull into the lot," he said, with concern written on his face, "and I was certain that someone I need to see had rented it. That's why I hurried over. But I guess I missed out. Of all the lousy luck."

"Well, that's the only car like that that's been turned in recently. The driver was a woman. Do you know her?"

"Only a little," Scott lied, shaking his head in feigned frustration. "Of all the lousy luck," he repeated.

"Well," the employee said, "if it's any help, her name is Helen. But she had an unusual last name, something foreign, maybe Middle Eastern. I rented that car to her three days ago."

"Can you possibly tell me what her last name is? And her address?"

"Not unless you're a cop."

"I'm not a cop," Scott said, in his most austere professional tone. "I'm a divorce lawyer representing a woman whose husband is having an affair with her." He took out his wallet and produced a business card of a partner at Kohn, Lager and Erickson. The attendant gave it a cursory glance.

"I just want to know who that woman is."

The employee scratched the nape of his neck, "I dunno," he said. "It's highly irregular. Can you wait for my boss? He'll be back in a half hour."

"I can't. My plane leaves in an hour. Please, it's really important. I wouldn't be bothering you otherwise."

The employee sighed. "I won't have to testify, will I?"

"No, you won't. That I can guarantee. You will hear nothing further about this."

"Well okay then, I'll let you see the rental agreement. Her name and address will be on it." They went inside and the attendant handed Scott a rental form that the woman named Helen had apparently filled out. He wrote down her name. The address listed was in a town he'd never heard of. In Turkey.

"I appreciate this," Scott said to the attendant, who was looking around warily, worried he would be caught violating office procedures. "One more question and then I'm out of here. What did this Helen look like?"

"Good looking; classy. Blond hair, medium length, wearing a blue skirt, white blouse, and sandals. That's all I can remember. Sorry."

"Nothing to be sorry about. You've been a big help. Thank you."

"The shuttle is leaving soon, sir," the attendant announced eagerly. "Will you be needing a ride back to the terminal?"

"I will. And thanks again." They shook hands.

Scott, his mind calm but working in overdrive, got in the van and took a seat. He got out at the Northwest entrance and returned to the departure gate just as his flight began to board. He scanned the passengers still waiting in line, but none fit Helen's description. *Maybe she's already on the DC-10*, he thought, *or maybe she's taking another flight so I won't suspect she's following me.* He considered asking at the boarding desk if she were on the flight, but decided against it. The flight was a long one and there would be plenty of time to scrutinize the passengers.

Scott boarded the jetliner and found his window seat without appearing to look for anyone. He settled down for takeoff, and after the "fasten seat belt" sign went off he got up and slowly walked aft toward the restroom, his gaze quickly sweeping over the passengers facing him. He noted only blond women who appeared to be traveling alone. One was obese and the other was quite elderly.

*Maybe she lost track of me at the airport. Or maybe she isn't following me at all. Well, even if she is following me, she won't be hard to spot in Turkey. Not with her blond hair.*

Just then another notion struck him. A wig. Maybe she was wearing a wig! A Turkish woman would most likely be a brunette or dark-haired, not blond. She probably changed her clothes and removed her blond wig while waiting to board the flight.

Scott was strangely confident his theory was correct, and debated what to do next. One thing was certain: nothing was going to happen soon, and there was not much he could do about it anyway. Forcing himself to relax, he closed his eyes, stretched out, and allowed himself to drift off to sleep. He woke refreshed, to the voice of the flight attendant asking the passenger in the seat in front of him whether he wanted breakfast. When she inquired the same of Scott, he gave her a nod, and as the stewardess reached across with the tray, he glanced up and into the eyes of a thirtyish brunette waiting behind the flight attendant's cart, which was blocking the isle. She looked away quickly when Scott glanced at her, and then she walked toward the front of the air-craft. A short time later, he observed her walking down the other aisle toward the aircraft's tail section. *Maybe that's her?* he thought, as he watched her disappear into a restroom. She also seemed somehow familiar.

Scott's plane landed at Frankfurt International Airport twenty min-utes early and he checked in at the Lufthansa counter for his flight to Izmir. Assured it was on time, he headed straight toward the departure concourse where he waited, one gate over from his own. The woman he had spotted on the plane appeared shortly before boarding, wearing a nondescript outfit with dark glasses and carrying a single bag. For a moment he considered having the check-in attendant announce her name and then watch her reac-tion. But he decided that any sort of confrontation at this point would be ill-advised and gain him nothing. Surely this woman was not working alone. Scott waited until all sections of the flight to Izmir had been called, and the final boarding announced, before getting onto the jet.

Helen boarded behind him. *Gotcha*, he thought to himself, avoiding the urge to look back at her. She clearly wasn't going to board the aircraft until she knew he was on it.

Scott sat down in his seat and pulled the duty-free catalog from the seat pocket in front of him. He scanned through the magazine, selected what he wanted, and then pressed the attendant call button. Shortly after the flight leveled off at cruising altitude, Scott received the items he had ordered. Min-utes later, he walked to the nearest lavatory carrying his small bag, and pass-ing by the woman sitting ten rows behind his assigned seat in the center of the aircraft. Once inside the lavatory, Scott opened his bag and took out what he needed to change his outward appearance. After purposely waiting fifteen minutes, he emerged from the restroom. Scott was clean-shaven, and no longer sported a mustache. He wore sunglasses that adjusted to the light, and a different shirt, pants, and now a tie. He also wore a hat and his face appeared tanner than it had before.

Scott slid into an empty aisle seat three rows behind Helen, took out an in-flight magazine, and sat there appearing to be reading. When the pilot announced the beginning of their descent, she stood and placed a pillow in the overhead bin above her seat. Scott watched as she peered forward toward his assigned seat, and then back toward the restrooms. Seemingly confused, she went to the back of the plane and entered the restroom next to the one he had used. In a few minutes, she returned to her seat and again looked ahead to where he had been sitting.

*The form becomes the shadow*, Scott thought smugly.

Fifteen minutes later they were taxiing toward their gate at the terminal. He remained seated until the other passengers had cleared the aisle in front of him. He then got up and walked quickly out of the aircraft, noting that Helen remained seated. Across from the baggage claim area, he watched her slowly make her way toward him, glancing this way and that from behind her sunglasses. So far he had fooled her. Now all he had to do was pick up his bags and then proceed through customs. Customs! "Shit," he whispered with a sigh. "I don't match my passport picture!" He felt his face flush. *You're no spy, Scott Frank*, he bitterly reprimanded himself. *Now what?*

Scott waited until Helen had claimed her luggage and had proceeded to the customs area. After she cleared customs, he returned to claim his suitcase that he'd rechecked in Frankfurt. He removed the glasses and went to stand in a customs line.

The customs official took his passport, stamped it, and returned it to him without so much as a glance in his direction. To his even greater relief, he was waived through without having to open his baggage for inspection. Struggling to appear nonchalant, he carried his baggage out of the customs area and into the main terminal.

Suddenly he saw her. She was talking to another woman who had her back turned toward the passengers emerging from customs. He then realized he wasn't wearing his sunglasses. He quickly removed them from his pants pocket, but before he could put them on, she set her gaze hard upon him.

Although she offered no hint of recognition, Scott had the distinct feeling that she had spotted him. *Damn*, he cursed under his breath. He prayed that he was wrong.

Scott pushed his cart to a lounge area where a small group was talking and sat down among them. He watched Helen walk to a better vantage point to survey the crowd. Not finding what she was looking for, she walked back to the customs officials and spoke to each one in turn until one of them nodded and held up an embarkation card. She then turned purposely around and signaled her companion to follow her toward the main exit doors. He smiled as he watched them scurry outside where they split up: Helen remaining by the main exit to observe passengers leaving the airport.

Scott pushed the cart to another set of exit doors at the far end of the building and stepped outside to hail a cab. He signaled the cab at the front of the line. It sped forward and the driver jumped out.

"I speak English!" the cabbie said with a smile, apparently recognizing Scott as an American, as he grabbed Scott's bags and settled them into the trunk. He opened the back door and Scott got in just as he noticed Helen in the distance, getting into a waiting car and driving off.

"Follow that white car, please," Scott said, pointing to his left. "A woman I met on the plane is in it and I'd like to see where she's staying," he lied.

"1968 Chevrolet Impala. Good car! Of course I'll follow her for you, sir. You're American. She'll like you!"

"Perhaps, but her sister sure doesn't like me. Her sister lives here, so please stay well behind their car."

"Will do, James Bond!" the driver laughed.

Despite Scott's instruction, the cabby nudged up close behind the Chevrolet as they wended their way along the main thoroughfare leading into the heart of Izmir, the third most populous city in Turkey. Scott remembered that it boasted of thirty-five hundred years of recorded urban history. Finally, the Chevy pulled off the highway and headed up a hill, then into a parking lot next to a marble building.

"Keep going to the next corner and stop there," Scott said.

"No problem for me, I am at your disposal."

As the cab pulled to a stop, Scott glanced back but could not see the two women.

"What's that building? A hotel?"

"That? Oh no. National treasures. Antiquities."

"A museum?"

"Yes, a museum of antiquities from all around my country."

"I see. Is there a tourist information center nearby?"

"There is. Near Konak Square. Would you like me to take you there?"

"Please."

"Roger that, James Bond!" the driver chortled, and put the car in gear. At the information center Scott picked up two maps in English, a guide to the city, and a small paperback book profiling the essential facts about Turkey.

"I am your guide, James Bond," the driver said, as Scott got back into the car. "I will take you wherever you wish and serve as your guide. What is your pleasure?"

"That you stop calling me James Bond."

"Ha ha. Very good. What next?"

"What's next is that you show me where that museum is on this city map."

The driver studied the map and pointed out the location. Scott circled it with his pen.

"Thank you. Now, I'd like to find a good place to stay for the night."

"Of course! My cousin works at a good hotel. Very nice. Not too expensive. Don't worry, I will be your guide!"

They sped off and they soon arrived at a hotel. Scott didn't like the looks of it from its exterior.

"Don't worry," the driver said, as if sensing his passenger's doubts. "Clean rooms. Good prices!"

As if on cue, a bellman appeared, opening the door for Scott and seeing to his luggage.

"How much do I owe you?" Scott inquired. "Sorry, I forgot to exchange American dollars for Turkish lira. Do you take American? Or can you take me to a bank?"

"Of course, James Bond!"

"As I told you, my name is not James Bond," Scott said irritably. "The name's Frank...Scott Frank. James Bond is a British agent."

"Yes, of course, Mr. Frank," the driver said, his tone turning more sober. "I understand. My name is Ahmet. First, we go into the hotel and get your room. Then I will guide you to the bank."

"Very well, Ahmet. Thank you."

At the bank Scott exchanged five hundred dollars in Travelers checks for Turkish currency, and after paying Ahmet, adding in a generous tip, arranged to have Ahmet pick him up at the hotel the next morning at nine. As Scott went to his room to wash up and change clothes, he checked his watch. Three o'clock. Overcome by jet lag and the suspense of the two flights, he considered succumbing to the inevitable and lying down to rest. But he fought off the urge. He had something to do, and an inner voice was telling him he needed to do it now.

# CHAPTER EIGHTEEN

## AUGUST 10, 1980

Scott went downstairs to the front desk in the hotel's small lobby. Thankfully the clerk spoke some English. Scott produced a map of Izmir and after asking him to locate the hotel on the map, circled the spot with his ballpoint pen. He then asked the clerk to call him a cab.

Despite the late afternoon hour, the temperature hovered close to 100 degrees Fahrenheit. It was a heat that reminded Frank of the summer he had spent in Athens. When the cab pulled up, Scott jumped inside to blissful air-conditioning, happy that the cab was not driven by Ahmet. He gave the driver the address of the museum, and in no time it seemed they were there. Ahmet, Scott reasoned, must have done some extra driving to boost up the fare.

Scott paid the driver and got out of the cab. He noticed a number of people, most likely tourists, coming and going through the front entrance, as he walked briskly around the building to the parking lot. Seeing no white 1968 Chevrolet Impala parked there, he returned to the entrance and walked inside along with what appeared to be a small group of tourists. He purchased a ticket and entered the exhibition area, looking cautiously for the woman named Helen. An English-speaking tour was about to begin and Scott joined the group. He paid scant attention to the guide, and lingered about among the antiquities until the group leader called out to him to please keep up with everyone. Startled by the request, Scott looked at her for the first time—and his face flushed. She was the woman who had met Helen at the airport.

Thirty minutes later the tour ended and Cy, according to her nametag, thanked the group and walked back through the museum toward a door marked "Staff Only." Scott watched her go, secreted behind a set of small statues encased in a tall glass cabinet. His was apparently the last tour of the day– as a woman announced in multiple languages that the museum would be closing in ten minutes. Scott's gaze took in his surroundings as he weighed his options.

Deciding that he needed to look behind the closed door, he walked to the small bookstore and picked up the first book he saw. He removed the price sticker from its flap and strode to the "Staff Only" door. Turning the knob, he pushed against the door. It swung in, revealing a narrow hallway that he proceeded to walk down, his senses alert, trying to look like someone who needed assistance to determine the price of the book he carried. No one appeared, and the small offices on each side of the hallway were empty.

At the end of the hallway, Scott found a narrow flight of stairs descending down a dimly-lit stairway. He heard a number of muffled voices from below, and was about to descend when he heard the door behind him open. Turning around, he saw that someone had opened the door about a foot, and he heard that person's voice speaking in a conversational tone. He abandoned his plan for explaining his presence in the staff area, glanced down the stairs, and quickly took refuge in an empty office. He swung the door almost shut, leaving enough space to spy on whomever was out there. He heard what sounded like a key being inserted into and turning a lock, and then he heard two sets of footsteps approaching him.

Scott held his breath as two women passed by the door, heading for the stairway leading down—to what? Just as they were about to walk down the stairs, one woman glanced back toward him. He felt certain he had been spotted, but if so, she gave no sign that she had seen him. She simply turned off the lights in the hallway and stepped into the stairwell. Scott felt his heart beat faster. The woman was Helen.

Scott listened to the voices. They were conversing in Turkish, or so he thought. Scott realized that he could not stay where he was for much longer. When the women came back upstairs, it seemed likely that one of them might enter this office. Scott waited for what his watch indicated was a half hour. Suddenly the voices ceased, and after a few minutes of silence, he crept back to the staff door. It was locked. He tried it again, to no avail. It was locked solid. Having no other option, he returned to the office and sat in stone silence, trying to figure out what to do next.

*Jesus,* he thought to himself. *The army and legal training offered little guidance for this situation.*

Curiosity soon got the better of him, and he walked slowly to the stairway, listening intently for any clues about what was below. Hearing nothing, he began to creep down the stairs. At the bottom, he found a hallway leading into what appeared to be a large meeting room. He paused, listening. No voices. No sound of any kind. He crept to the entrance, peeked inside, and noted two restrooms and several small housekeeping rooms adjacent to the main room. Satisfied they were empty, he went into the meeting room and searched for any indication of human activity. There was none. Where the women had gone, he had no clue.

Scott sat down in a corner next to a large floor-length curtain fastened close to a wall, giving the impression that the underground room contained a window. It was evidently a presentation room, since a good number of chairs were set around a small podium on a single riser, and a pull-down projection screen was curled up on the ceiling above center stage. He had no idea what this all meant, or what demonic curiosity had led him here.

Suddenly, Scott heard footsteps on the stairs. In a flash he was up and hiding behind the curtain. Someone entered the room and closed the door to the hallway. He heard a rustling sound and inched his head to the right. It was a woman, perhaps seventy years of age, who began taking off her black full-length dress. Then she removed the black scarf that covered her head. As Scott ducked his head back behind the curtain, he heard her walk across the room and open a door, perhaps to a bathroom or one of the housekeeping rooms.

Scott took the ballpoint pen from his shirt pocket, and holding the curtain tightly with one hand, poked a hole through it at eye level with the pen. He peered through the hole as the woman returned to the main room, wearing a long white priestly-looking garment. She appeared to be an elegant woman with white flowing hair, and large bright eyes. Just then, she reached above her head to a wall light, which she turned a quarter revolution to the right. When she pushed against the wall to the left of the light, it moved in several feet. As soon as she stepped through the opening, the wall closed and the light returned to its original position.

*What the hell is that?* Scott asked himself, as he inhaled a sweet flowery aroma. *Who are these people? And what in God's holy name am I going to do now?*

Feeling an overpowering need to sit down and rest, Scott decided to hide in the men's restroom until morning, at which time the upstairs hallway door would likely be unlocked. No one would know he had been here. Should he be discovered before then, he could claim he was an epileptic and must have had a seizure. He'd somehow convince them he'd blacked out. It would not be far from the truth. Scott did feel light-headed and exhausted to the bone.

And yet he was profoundly curious about the hidden door and the light fixture, and could not pass up an opportunity to examine the wall. It was paneled in teak, with sections that fit together tightly without noticeable seams. He studied the fixture and touched it, not daring to turn it even the slightest bit.

Then suddenly, he again heard footsteps in the stairwell, this time many of them. Scott glanced toward his curtain on the other side of the room. Too far away. He turned the light fixture and pushed on the wall. It gave way and he slid inside the narrow opening. There he was met with an eerie greenish glow. He pushed against the wall panel, but it didn't budge. With his left hand he searched for anything to grip on this side of the wall. He felt a short iron bar, bent down. He pulled down on it, but nothing happened. He twisted on it and the door slid shut. Panic surged within him as his vision slowly adjusted to the green dimness inside.

Scott found himself perched at the top of a steep staircase that led even farther down and to the right. To the sides of the doorway were recesses that could serve as hiding places. He stretched out his left hand as a buffer and sidestepped along the wall of the recess. It went further back, but contracted after about ten feet, preventing him from going deeper into hiding. He sensed a movement to his right, and a light was shining from within the room he had just left. He heard the door swing back. Scott held his breath as a woman, dressed in white robes, stepped inside the stairwell and began walking down the stairs. Six people followed her, similarly dressed in white. The door closed behind them and he could hear the echo of their footsteps beneath him. He exhaled slowly and waited until he could wait no longer.

Scott emerged from his hiding place and stood at the top of the stairway studying the green chemical lights that had been placed on the stairs. What compelled him, he could not say, but he soon found himself slowly walking down the steps, pausing periodically to listen intently. He heard nothing, so he kept on going, counting the number of steps in what seemed like a descent into the nether world. Finally, it got lighter, enabling him to discern an arched entryway ahead leading to a marble vestibule. Passageways of marble ran out in several directions. Chemical lights had been placed along the center pathway, and Scott continued in that direction.

Soon he came upon soft voices singing some sort of chant. Where Scott was now, small passageways shot off to the right and left. He took the second one to the right that led him around a corner and up a slight slope, before turning into a narrow, stepped passageway going almost straight up.

Scott climbed the steps, the light now almost gone. He stopped when the light faded entirely, and was about to retrace his steps when he glanced up to see a gray area of light ahead.

As he climbed carefully toward the light, the chanting ceased, to be replaced by the melodious voice of a woman. Her words became clearer to Scott as he neared the light emanating from between the columns which ran in a semicircle around the dome of what looked to be a church.

Scott reached the top and peered over the ledge. He was two or three stories above a room filled with perhaps two hundred women, each of them wearing a pearl white peplum, and all of them, except one, sitting on rows of polished marble benches arranged in a semi-circle before an altar. Along the side walls of the room were statues of a huntress, armed with a bow and arrows. Up front, behind the altar, he noted three larger, more ornate statues, each one clearly depicting both the beauty and the strength of the female body, and one adorned with an elaborate costume and headdress.

The elegant-looking older woman he had seen from behind the curtain stood facing the congregation. Before her was a low altar on which an assortment of gold and silver vessels had been placed.

She was speaking quietly, calmly, yet with a joyful quality that somehow seemed out of place. Mesmerized by what he was looking at, and unable to tear his eyes away, he watched as five young women stood up in the front row and solemnly walked over to join the elder woman at the altar. They bowed as they faced the center statue, then stood quietly, their backs to the congregation.

The elder woman, whom Scott assumed was some sort of high priestess, spoke to the assembly, her voice increasing in tone and caliber, and imbued with emotion. Then she paused, raised her arms and gazed up as if to the heavens, and called out a name. One of the five young women walked to the priestess and bowed her head before her. She stood proud, erect, and from what Scott could see, appeared almost defiant. Without being commanded to do so, the young woman then stepped up to the altar, unfastened her peplum, and pulled it down to her waist, exposing her breasts. She then lay supine upon the marble altar, smiling, staring up at the ceiling.

Scott froze. Any movement of his head might be detected by the young woman. She closed her eyes.

*Christ Almighty, they're going to kill her. A heathen sacrifice of some kind.*

He wanted to close his eyes, to pull his head back, but he could not. His eyes remained transfixed on the girl as the priestess chanted something incomprehensible, which was, in turn, answered by the congregation. The four other girls at the altar stood motionless at the feet of the statues of their goddess. Suddenly the priestess reached down and picked up a curved silver object, about a foot in length. Sliding a knife out from it, she raised the glistening blade high in the air, for all to witness, and then, after seizing the young woman's right breast in her hand, plunged the weapon down and across the young woman's chest, severing the breast. The priestess covered the wound with a large cloth, and after commanding the young woman to hold it firmly in place, she collected the severed breast and placed it in a gold container.

The priestess pulled up the young woman's peplum and fastened it so that only the right half of her chest was covered. The young woman rose from the altar, bowed first at the priestess and then at the goddess statues, before walking up the center aisle to an empty seat at the front of the congregation. From the beginning of this ceremony to its ghastly end, Scott saw no blood, and heard no cries.

The priestess called out the second young woman's name, and performed the same ritual. Then the third, fourth, and finally the fifth young woman came forward. Not one of them appeared afraid or hesitant. It was as though they felt privileged to be called upon to have their right breast taken from them. After they were all seated in the front row, they began another chant that transformed itself into a song. They stood, then silently knelt, facing the statues with heads bowed. After what appeared to be a period of silent prayer, they rose and sang out as the priestess, followed by those standing closest to the altar, filed out the doorway opposite the altar, at the far end of the underground hall.

*Good God Almighty. Now they're going to have a reception for the new initiates!*

Afraid to go down, Scott noted the walkway that led across the front of the temple to a second stairway that led down. Not caring to take his chances down there, he found a spot to hide between the double rows of columns at the top of the staircase. Overcome by the events of the day, he closed his eyes and was quickly swept away in a deep sleep.

Scott Frank woke from the sounds of his own snoring. It was pitch black. He couldn't see his hands in front of his face. *Terrific*, he thought. Scott groped with his hand until he felt the fluted surface of a column. He stood up, clinging to it. He took a tentative step, then a second step toward what he believed to be the back wall. On the third step, his right foot plunged down and he had to throw himself backward to keep from plummeting onto the altar. He lay quietly on the floor for a moment, then rolled over and crawled to the wall, feeling his way along it until he reached the steps. There he turned around, sat up, and descended the stairs on his rump in the darkness.

When finally he reached the lower hallway, he stood up and slid against the wall to where he hoped the arch was located. He tripped over something he couldn't see and fell forward, breaking the fall with both hands. A stab of pain shot up his left wrist.

"Damn!" he cursed, his anger swelling as he realized that all of the chemical lights had been removed. That meant he'd have to walk up the next flight of steps in the dark. On the way down, he had counted one hundred twenty steps, so on the way back up, when he had counted to one hundred twenty, he paused to rest and listen. Hearing nothing, he felt ahead for the handle of the door, found it, and turned it. To his relief, the door opened. He held his breath, his senses ever alert. Still he heard nothing, so he opened the door all the way.

It was dark inside the room, although at the far end he noticed a sliver of light from under a door. Scott flicked on a light switch and walked across the room and out into the hallway toward the last flight of stairs. At the top of the stairs, he glanced at his wristwatch: 5:20. If his luck held, he thought he might find the staff door unlocked, open that door from the inside, walk out the main entrance, and be on his merry way back to the hotel. Scott walked briskly to the door and pressed down on the door's handle. He smiled. It was unlocked. He pulled the door open and his smile vanished as the museum's alarm went off.

Bells began ringing and a siren screeched out in warning, sounding as if a squad of police cars were rampaging through the museum. There was nothing for him to do now but to bolt for the front entrance and escape the museum before security arrived. But when he reached the entrance doors he found them to be double-bolted. A quick search of the windows revealed that each one was protected by tightly-spaced steel bars.

"Now I'm screwed!" he muttered in despair.

Scott paced back and forth like a lion in its cage, unable to think, unable to act, calling upon his strict army training to no avail. The alarms were deafening. What to do, what to do. Instinctively, because he had nothing else to go on, he raced back into the heart of the museum, past the door to the offices to the rear of the exhibit area. There he found another staff door and went through it into a corridor containing additional offices. At the end of the corridor, the hallway made a sharp right turn into a small loading dock secured by a drop-down metal door. He saw three red buttons and pushed the top one. The door began to rise. When its base had risen two feet off the floor, Scott rolled through and fell four feet to the pavement. He struck his head on the cement and cried out in pain.

He found himself in a small rectangular courtyard filled with ancient-looking columns, pieces of sculpture, and a long wall with a multitude of faces carved into it. Above him, the alarm blared. Fighting off an urge to run, he forced himself to walk calmly out of the courtyard, away from the museum, and onto the street running past it. Cars passed him, including a police car apparently responding to the alarms, but no one paid any more attention to him than he did to them. Another police car passed by at a good clip, but the three officers inside also paid him no mind. *Why should they? Why would I be suspected of anything, walking along the road minding my own business? Who would ever believe that I just spent the night in a temple, hidden in the bowels of the earth, watching five young women having their right breasts cut off? No one, that's for damn sure!* Hell, even *he* couldn't believe it.

It was nearly six o'clock in the morning when he entered the hotel and went to his room. He sat on the edge of the bed for a while, feeling the adrenaline gradually dissipate and the pain kick in. When he finally lay down, he was dead asleep in only a few seconds, and it seemed like only seconds more, before he heard someone knocking loudly on his door.

"It is me, Ahmet, here to drive you! It is nine and I am here for you!"

"Please come back in one hour," Scott snapped at the door.

"Yes, James Bond, at ten o'clock! I will wait for you downstairs!"

"James Bond," Scott groused as he swung his legs over the side of the bed. He opened his suitcase and got out his toilet bag, a pair of trousers, a short-sleeved shirt, socks, underwear, and a pair of sandals. For fifteen minutes he stood under the shower, allowing the hot stream to massage his tired and aching muscles. When the hot water felt tepid, he stepped out of the shower, dried himself off and dressed slowly.

As he was carrying the luggage down to the front desk, he noticed Ahmet talking to the desk clerk. Ahmet smiled at him and came running toward him, taking the bags from his hands.

"I'm checking out," Scott said to the clerk.

"Certainly, sir. I will prepare your bill."

Scott paid in Turkish lira, took his receipt, and walked outside to the waiting cab.

"Ride in front with me. You see better!"

"Fine." Scott got in and closed the door, feeling rejuvenated by the hot shower and the soft breezes of the morning.

When Ahmet climbed in behind the steering wheel and gave Scott a questioning look, Scott said, "I would like you to drive me first to the archaeological museum. Then I would appreciate a tour of Izmir. After lunch, I'll need to rent a car."

"Yes, of course. Whatever you say!"

"And this time, please drive directly to the museum. I went there last night and found it to be within easy walking distance from here." Scott smiled inwardly when Ahmet offered no response to that statement.

"Pull into that parking lot," Scott said, when they were approaching the museum. A quick look around confirmed that the old Chevy was not there.

"Let's drive around the city and you can tell me about it."

Ahmet drove past many of the main points of interest in the city of two million souls. As they drove around, Ahmet informed Scott that he had once served as a tour bus guide, and had given tours in English. During the tourist season, he led tour groups by bus to Ephesus. He was now working only part time driving a cab owned by him and an older brother. He'd learned English in school, and because he had learned it well, he had recently secured a job as a waiter in the Officer's Club at the American Air Station near Izmir.

After lunch, they drove around for another half hour before Scott asked to be taken to a car rental office.

"But why don't you like me?" Ahmet asked in a whining tone. "Is it my driving?"

"It has nothing to do with liking you, Ahmet. I need to go to Selçuk. I plan to be there a week and to visit Ephesus often. It will be easier for me to get around if I have my own car."

"But I will gladly take you to Selçuk," Ahmet protested. "I will charge you the same as a rental car. If you tour the ancient ruins it will be easier for you to go by my car. I will guide you also, for only tips. I know the ruins and the museum there, also. I know all the sights – where the Virgin Mary lived, the Seven Sleepers, the baths, the stadiums, everything! Don't you like my driving? I am a good guide."

"I am meeting someone there, and don't believe that I'll need a guide."

"Okay, I'll just transport you there! Then, if you need a car, I will find one for you, cheap. If you need a guide, I will be available. What do you say, James... aaah Mr. Scott?"

"When could you be ready to leave here for Selçuk?" Scott asked.

"I can go right now if you'd like. I have all I need in the trunk. My wife packs for me, for such excursions. She is a good woman. A fine mother. Prays five times a day! If I'm home tomorrow, it's okay. If not, that too is okay. I'll get petrol and then we will go. You won't be sorry because I know the road, and can be a guide for you from Izmir to Selçuk, and then to Ephesus!"

"And the price will be the same as a rental car?" Scott responded.

"Plus tips."

"Okay, it's a deal. Let's go."

"Good, James Bond, good!"

"But on the condition that you call me Scott. No more of this James Bond."

"You are too modest, Scott James Bond! This is a good idea to hire me. Do you want to drive by the important ruins? No problem, we can do it."

As they drove off toward highway E24, Scott stared silently out the window. He had left home in such haste. He'd brought his passport and the Turkish government didn't require a visa, but he had neglected to secure a new international driver's license. The one he had was expired. If one were required to rent a car, he'd have to take the train, a bus, or a car for hire. He didn't tell Ahmet any of this. He was getting a fair price. Again, fatigue overtook him, and he dozed off until he felt the taxi's engine being turned off.

"Here we are Mr. Scott," Ahmet announced happily. "Selçuk."

Scott gazed out on a small town, dominated by a mosque and an ancient fortress, perched high on a ridge that the guidebook identified as Avasoluk Hill.

Scott thought to himself. He looked ahead down the street toward the entrance to the inner town—then into the eyes of a female statue, identical to one he had seen behind the altar in the underground temple in Izmir. The statue was obviously a modern replica, placed strategically to welcome tourists to the town.

"Where are you staying?" Ahmet asked

"At the Tusan Efes Motel."

"Yes, yes, near the ruins," Ahmet confirmed, as he restarted the car.

"How far have we come?"

"Eighty kilometers."

At the small but cozy twelve-room motel just west of Selçuk and north of Ephesus, Scott exited the car and stretched his aching body.

"It's peaceful here," he commented.

"Yes, Mr. Scott, it is very peaceful," Ahmet agreed, as he opened the trunk. "It's why so many tourists come here. And to see the ruins, of course." A boy came out of the hotel and took the suitcase and bag from Scott, who followed in his wake.

Inside, he was greeted by a smile from the desk clerk.

"I would like a room, please," Scott said.

"Your passport, sir?"

Scott drew his passport from an oversized belt pouch and handed it over.

"Ah, yes, Mr. Frank," the clerk said after examining it. "We have been expecting you. Your room is ready, and I will inform Mr. Ruffescott that you have arrived."

"Is he here?"

"No. He was here, but he had to depart. He has called, however, and he has asked me to welcome you and see to your comfort."

"Thank you," Scott said with feeling. He turned to Ahmet. "I'm going to get some rest now. I don't know if I'll need your services any longer."

"Yes, yes I know. I have a friend in Selçuk I stay with. Tomorrow morning, at nine, I will return. We can tour if your friend does not return. Okay?"

"Okay. I'll see you tomorrow. Do you want me to pay for today's trip now?"

"No. No. You pay me when we have concluded our business. Not before. See you in the morning, Mr. Scott!"

He left, and Scott followed the clerk to room twelve. It was an end room, looked comfortable, and Scott noted with pleasure that it had its own bathroom. He started to undress and remembered Rebecca's words about their leaving a note whenever they changed locations. Returning to the front desk, he asked the clerk if Ruffescott had left a message for him.

The clerk turned and stared toward the wall boxes.

"Yes, he did," he said pulling an envelope from the box with Scott's room number on it. Scott returned to his room and locked the door. He sat on the bed and opened the letter:

> You made it! Good. I must depart unexpectedly, but we can talk when I return. Meanwhile, the area is rich in history and guides are available at the ruins. You should tour Ephesus. Gratefully, Ruff

Scott noted that the brief note was not dated as he folded it and placed it in his belt pouch. He shook his head. Here he was in Turkey, near some ruins he knew very little about, searching for the burial place of the Mother of Jesus and hieroglyphics her son of God may have left here on earth. And a rock. Not only that, he was searching for someone he'd never met, someone who had summoned him here through a secret code that involved a message under a stamp. He loved everything to do with travel, but on this excursion, he had stumbled through a series of incidents which left him banged up, fed up, bewildered, and exhausted. At that moment, Scott felt he would gladly trade the totality of his worldly possessions for a bottle of Old Crow and a ticket home.

# CHAPTER NINETEEN

## AUGUST 11, 1980

Professor Meister sat down to rest on the small bench in the remnant hall of the Ephesus Museum in Vienna. It wasn't much of a hall, as its name implied, but rather a series of untidy, dusty vaults in an unattractive warehouse structure. The locked vaults housed antiquities of dubious value. He was looking for the lost lidded jar, but had little expectation of finding it, or anything else of interest. As an archaeologist, Latin translator, and art historian, his life had been consumed in removing the sands of Turkey that had, over many centuries, buried the ancient city of Ephesus. Only ten percent of the city had been uncovered, and he had resigned himself to being little more than a footnote in the epic tale of how a once magnificent city was recreated.

The Turkish government had long realized the value of the Austrian Archaeological Institute to the history of their country. More than a million visitors ventured to Ephesus each year, and tourist dollars, lira, pounds, and yen were a significant source of income to the Turkish economy. This was why so many artifacts were allowed to be removed to Vienna for study, and reconstruction and display.

The professor realized that he had become too focused on the journals. Exactly why he had mailed the one by Herbert Weber to his wartime assistant puzzled him at times. But in the past few days, he had time to consider what it was he was actually seeking, and to blame his aging mind for perhaps misdirecting the hunt. He did not, however, share his latest thoughts about the mysterious jar and lid that had disappeared in the waning years of the 1800s.

Dr. Meister knew that when the English had first excavated at Ephesus, they had carted off the finest of the relics they had uncovered. The Austrians had done the same thing, until the Turkish government put a stop to that practice after the Turkish Republic was established and President Ataturk came to power. However, the Turkish prohibitions did not occur until years after the 1898 excavations. Meister had scoured the records and journals of the artifacts preserved in Vienna, but he could find no references to a jar with writing inscribed in its lid. The professor had persisted, however, until only these non-catalogued artifacts held out any hope of surrendering something of value in Vienna.

Professor Meister had entered the last vault to study broken pieces of terra cotta pottery, among the so-called "non-treasures" put there by volunteers from the Austrian Archaeological Institute. He expected no return for his efforts; this vault in the remnant hall was simply the last place to look.

Meister stood up from where he was sitting on the bench, walked to a wood storage box, and removed the fasteners that held the lid in place. Inside he found an eyesore. Someone, at some time, had pieced and glued together one side of a vase or jar. It was nondescript, and caught the professor's eye only because it had been so poorly reconstructed. Shaking his head in disgust, he picked it up primarily to curse whomever had done such a miserable job of restoration. As he studied its poorly aligned exterior, the light from behind him cast tiny shadows that revealed what appeared to be marks scratched onto the jar. Holding it up to his eye, he determined that it was not just a series of scratches, but a verse of an old Latin inscription. His heart skipped a beat. The inscription read, "Language of the God."

The professor laid aside the glued remnant and searched through the remaining pieces in the wooden trunk. None appeared to have come from the jar. And the jar had no lid.

He returned to the bench and sat there, examining his finding. The top portion of the jar appeared to be composed of terra cotta with a thin, black, glass overlay. There was one small sliver of the jar, located where the lid would have been fitted, that flared out slightly, then turned down toward the base. This suggested that the lid was also flared, and made of black material, perhaps the same terra cotta, also with a glass overlay. Such a lid would be somewhat unconventional both in shape and in embellishment.

Dr. Meister continued his search through the other wooden trunks in the vault, to no avail. He carefully placed the remnant of the jar in a burlap sack that he found hanging on a wall hook and carried it home with him, and placed it carefully upon his dresser. Then he went to bed.

The next morning Frau Weber looked at her face reflected in the bathroom mirror. She had arisen earlier than usual, awakened by the whistle of the kettle and the sounds of her distinguished tenant clattering around the kitchen. *He seems to be getting along better. It must be all the excitement concerning the journals, searching for some artifacts of significance, and his being enlisted in the cause championed by Jay Youngquest.*

"Then there is the involvement with the police from Salzburg, the dead man, and who knows what else?" she mumbled to herself. "I'll be right there!" she called out as she pulled on her summer bathrobe. In response, she heard the front door being opened and closed.

Professor Meister felt no discomfort in his lower back as he rode a bus to his office, with the remains of the jar now carefully packed inside a thick leather bag. When he arrived at his office building he found it locked.

"This," he chuckled to himself as he unlocked the door, "is my first early appearance in many years!" His secretary would be most surprised.

He entered his office, turned on the light, and heard his primary research assistant, Bassam Safar, singing in a low voice next door. Within a minute he was at the professor's door, giving him a surprised look.

"I thought there was someone in your office," Bassam said, "and I came to check."

"Why? Am I too old to enjoy time at work without the distractions of students and staff?"

"No," Bassam countered lightly. "I always expect you here two hours early."

"Well, I'm on a mission and I need your assistance."

"How can I help you, sir?"

"Close the door. I have something to show you."

Bassam closed the door as the professor placed his bag on the desk, opened it, and unwrapped the remains of the jar. He handed it to Bassam and pointed to the thin line of almost indiscernible text. Bassam read it several times, and then carefully inspected the entire jar. Finding nothing else of interest, he looked up with a questioning look.

"Now all we need to determine," said the professor to his doctoral candidate, "is where the rest of this jar and lid are located."

Bassam set the jar remnant on the desk.

"I found this yesterday," the professor explained, "in one of the many trunks of remnants from Ephesus. It was with the 1890s artifacts. The uncatalogued, broken pieces. Some fine work of reconstruction, eh?"

Bassam shook his head. "I don't think that we have the rest of this jar here, Professor. Otherwise, wouldn't it have been kept with this piece? The rest may not have been found, or else discarded. Workers looted many pieces as you well know, and the lid may have been illegally sold. The glass overlay is somewhat unusual, and the cover may have been all glass, or perhaps had a glass handle. I don't believe that the inscription was a part of the original design; it's too primitive, and appears to have been added in some haste. So if the cover, the lid, were made of glass, I doubt it would have had any such writings."

Meister nodded in agreement, but added, "At least not on the outside of the lid. But what if the inside was made of terra cotta?"

Bassam gave that some thought, and then stepped to the small chalkboard that hung on the office wall. Slowly he drew what the complete jar may have looked like. Several inches above it, beginning at the left side of the board, he drew sketches of how the flared lid may have appeared. His fourth drawing had a curved handle on the top of the lid, and the fifth had a handle that looked like a pumpkin stem. He paused with that sketch and stared at it. Professor Meister stood up, took the chalk from his assistant, and turned the stem into the neck of a cobra. He finished by sketching the body of the snake, coiled around the jar's lid.

Both men nodded thoughtfully at the sketch, and then at one another. Bassam went to the drawings and erased them. Then he took a cleaning cloth from a small cabinet in the professor's office and eliminated all traces of even the chalk dust.

"Good idea," the professor stated in a low voice. "Now, without attracting attention, let's walk past the display and see..."

"We should wait until the museum is open," Bassam said. "We don't want anyone wondering why we are there so early. We will have to get the key to open the case, so first we must turn off the alarm. Also, we have to consider the cameras and security personnel." Bassam paused, then continued.

"Perhaps we should contact the supervisor of the display section and request the piece for our private study. They could replace it with another artifact, and we would probably have it in our hands in a day or so. I can go over and see about it in a few hours."

"It may not be the right lid," Bassam cautioned.

"It's the lid. I am sure of it. It's a very unusual lid, and I seem to recall that it is made of terra cotta, maybe with a black glass overlay."

"This is unbelievable!" Bassam exclaimed. "One possible key to the sacred writings is displayed in plain sight within our own museum! I wonder what is inside of the lid."

"And why any inscriptions on it, or in it, were ignored?"

Two hours later, doctoral candidate Bassam Safar was led into the office of Dr. Evren, the museum official in charge of the display section of the Ephesus antiquities. Dr. Evren listened to the request for removal and study of a small second century AD terra cotta oil lamp.

"Of course," Evren said expansively. "How fares the good Dr. Meister these days? He was my doctoral mentor, you know?"

"Yes, I do know," Bassam replied. "Dr. Meister is doing exceptionally well. He asked me to convey his best regards to you, with the hope that he will see you again soon. He has renewed energy, Dr. Evren. He would like to have lunch with you sometime."

"Oh, oh. He must want to revisit my decision from last year to cut the spending for bringing in artifacts for temporary display from Istanbul. But, tell him that I will make myself available at his pleasure. He was the chair of the committee that reviewed my doctoral thesis. I found out well after my studies that he came to my defense against Dr. Hummel."

"The evil Dr. Hummel," Bassam remarked knowingly.

"I'll bet you're relieved that he retired two years ago?"

"Yes, indeed," Bassam Safar responded.

Dr. Evren thought back to the period in his life when he was an insecure student at the university. He smiled at Bassam.

"As soon as we close today, please meet with security at the display. I will see to the arrangements."

The two men shook hands. Bassam, relieved, returned to his office.

Shortly after the museum closed for the day, Bassam and Dr. Meister were at the glass display case. Two security men had the case already unlocked and the door open. Bassam removed a small clay lamp that had an unusual design, while Dr. Meister stepped forward to remove the small statue and the card with the typed description, "Coiled Cobra, 1st Century."

"Thank you," Dr. Meister said to the uniformed guards, after signing the receipt for the clay lamp. "We will be on our way now."

"Thank you," the guard responded, and the professor led the way back to his office, carrying the unsigned-for object firmly with both hands.

The guard with the clipboard signed his own name where the conveying official was to sign, and the two guards strode back to the archive office.

"That older man is the famous archaeologist, Dr. Meister," the guard with the clipboard remarked to the other one.

"Yes, I know," came the response. "A very influential man."

Once back in the professor's office, Bassam closed the door.

"Look at this," the professor said, as he turned over the object. "The bottom of the lid has been filled with wax! Probably to keep it stable. Some curator thought it was a figurine. We'll have to remove the wax."

"How?" Bassam questioned.

"With a hair dryer and soft tissue," Meister said. "I have a dryer in that old desk– second drawer, right side. Bring the tissues, too. And that empty fruit bowl. And get a spoon."

Bassam went to the break room, and found a spoon and a butter knife. He also checked the other offices and found that the rest of the staff had gone home for the day.

Professor Meister flicked on the hair dryer, and after a few minutes, the wax began to soften enough for them to begin extracting it with the spoon and knife. It was a wax of some constitution, but once the outer layer was deposited into the bowl, the task grew easier. After an hour of meticulous work, only a thin layer of wax remained. The hair dryer was used close in, and the wax dabbed out with the tissues, until the writings were as apparent as they were going to get. The two peered into the lid at the inscriptions.

"Where can we find black rubbing wax? The type that the tourists use to make impressions of brass icons?" Dr. Meister said this more to himself than his student.

Bassam departed and returned with rubbing wax, and the proper white paper. Somewhat later they heard the outer office door being opened, and the voices of men talking. Someone knocked on Professor Meister's door.

"Please, come in," he called out.

The two security guards looked nervous as they walked into the office.

"Sir," the taller of the two guards stammered, "I am sorry to bother you, but we failed to get your receipt for the snake sculpture that was removed from the case."

"Oh, dear me!" the professor exclaimed. "Thank God you two are doing your jobs with such attention to detail. I just wanted to look at it, and to correct an error on its typed description. Please take them both back to the display case, they are over there on that desk," he said, pointing to the two artifacts. "The inscription should have read: 'Coiled Cobra 1st Century BC,' which it now does. Please accept my apology, and I would appreciate your discretion with regard my oversight."

The two guards visibly relaxed.

"You may, of course, count on us, Professor."

With that, they left the office.

"I'm glad that we went to the professor before admitting to anyone that we failed to have this snake sculpture signed for!" the guard with the clip-board said. His partner nodded in agreement as they proceeded to the glass exhibit case, carrying the lamp and the Cobra-topped lid that had been repacked with wax.

# CHAPTER TWENTY

## AUGUST 11, 1980

Salzburg Chief of Police Honaker reached for the telephone in his office and signaled to his temporary secretary that he wanted privacy. She departed the room, closing the door behind her, noting that the chief had picked up line three to dial. She felt somehow miffed at being excused from the room. She would be the last person to divulge police secrets learned on the job.

"Professor Meister here."

"Good morning, Dr. Meister. This is Chief Honaker. How are you, sir?"

"I am doing well, thank you. Doing well. Are you calling to tell me that our books and journals are ready to be released?"

"No. I am calling to ask if you are planning a trip?"

The professor hesitated a moment. "Why, yes. I have decided to go to Turkey and visit the crew working this summer at Ephesus. I believe that the university's travel office has already purchased my ticket, and I leave this Thursday. Why do you ask?"

"Have you been contacted by Jay Youngquest?"

"I have not," Meister stated as a fact. "I have not spoken to him since the day before he left Vienna. Why do you ask?"

"I ask because the Turkish authorities have been less than enthusiastic about assisting us with this murder investigation," Honaker said with equal equanimity. "We have been monitoring certain events, but so far without results. I have therefore decided to go to Turkey myself, and have already sent two men there to assist me with my investigation. I thought I might travel there with you, Professor, if you don't mind."

"Not at all," the professor said, his voice masking the suspicion in his thoughts. "I will enjoy your company. It is a relatively easy trip, but I always appreciate company."

After hanging up the telephone the professor of archaeology walked to Bassam's office and tapped on the door before entering.

"I'm being watched by the police," he stated, as he slumped down on a chair. "They don't trust me and they have no word about the return of the journals. What do you make of it? The chief of police wants to accompany me to Turkey!"

"How did he find out you are going there?"

"The police have their ways. The point is, I don't like being watched. They may even have a wiretap on my telephone for all I know. He asked if Jay Youngquest had contacted me, which he hasn't. So maybe there is no wiretap. Nonetheless…" He left the sentence unfinished.

Bassam shrugged. "Look at it from Honaker's perspective. There has been a murder, and this is an unusual case. It's indeed a mystery! Besides, how often does a police official get to travel abroad as a part of an investigation?"

"True," Meister agreed. "But, I don't think we should divulge what we found here in the museum."

Bassam nodded. He wasn't sure why they weren't being open about finding the jar lid. However, there were competing interests involved, and a great deal of money, prestige, and notoriety if hieroglyphs from Jesus were found— or *any* artifact linked to Jesus Christ or the Virgin. The archaeological articles, presentations, and follow-up research would be worth a fortune to the university and the Austrian Archaeological Institute. He might be offered a full-time position with the institute following graduation. This thought had crossed his mind more than once since they had discovered the cobra right under their noses!

"Bassam? Are you still with me?"

"Sorry, Professor," Bassam said, flustered. "I was distracted there for a moment. My mind has been racing of late."

"I understand. My mind has been racing as well. But here's an important point: I have been contacted by Rutheford Ruffescott. He apparently knows more about this matter than anyone else, and he has acquired this information in an amazingly short span of time."

"He called you?"

"Yes."

Bassam appeared taken aback for a moment, before leaning back in his chair and asking, "Are you still leaving for Turkey this week, Professor?"

"Yes. On Thursday."

Dr. Meister paused and looked at his assistant. Bassam was young, bright, and would be an asset to any university or museum interested in Roman history or archaeology.

"You will have a fine time at your brother's wedding this weekend. Please give my best regards to your parents."

"I shall, Professor, thank you," Bassam said.

# CHAPTER TWENTY-ONE

## AUGUST 13, 1980

Scott Frank woke at seven and lay on his bed, staring up at the ceiling through the mosquito netting. Several lizards clung to the wall above the headboard.

"All right Mr. Rutheford Ruffescott, I'm here. Where the hell are you?" he whispered. He rose and turned on the light, then noticed the note that had been slid under the door. He picked it up, and unfolded it. The handwritten note was from his tour guide.

"I will be here at nine o'clock for your touring pleasure. Ahmet."

Scott smiled, crumpled up the message, and threw it in a high arc toward the wastebasket. It missed the basket, hit the wall, and dropped in. After dressing, he went to breakfast, and on the way checked for messages at the front desk. There were none. Promptly at nine, as if on cue, Ahmet arrived with that perpetual smile of his.

"Have you found your friend?" he asked.

"Haven't heard from him yet," Scott responded.

"Good! I will show you the ruins and the museum, the place of the Seven Sleepers, Mary's home. Everything of interest, and all in English."

"Maybe we should agree on the cost of this day tour?" Scott hedged.

"Only thirty dollars including petrol, plus admissions, and I will purchase my own meals."

"Thirty dollars seems expensive for a tour," Scott responded.

Ahmet shrugged. "Okay. Let's make it twenty-five dollars plus tip then."

"How much do you expect for a tip?" Scott inquired warily.

"Only twenty percent for you today, and you can pay me in American dollars."

"You win," Scott said, waving away negotiations that still pegged the price at thirty dollars. "Where to first?"

"To Meryemana, where the Virgin Mother lived."

Twenty minutes later, Scott was walking uphill through a corridor of trees to a small T-shaped residence that had been converted into a chapel. It was a hauntingly tranquil setting for a home, reflecting peace, comfort, and serenity. Scott looked around the grounds and saw that there was an active archaeological dig going on adjacent to the house. Surely it was occurring in the same general area as where archaeologists had dug up the earthen vase almost a hundred years before.

"Do you know about this place?" Ahmet asked, breaking Scott's concentration.

Scott shook his head. "Not really. My understanding is that St. John brought Mary here after the crucifixion."

"You are correct. In approximately 40 AD they came here, to live. Not in this house, though. It dates from the seventh century. Only the foundation is from the time of the Virgin Mary."

"How do they know that this is the place?"

Ahmet launched into what was by now a well-rehearsed answer. "In the nineteenth century a German mystic, a blind nun, had a vision that the Virgin lived in this place. She described it in great detail. Later, Lazarist fathers came here from Izmir and found this place, which perfectly matched her description. For many years before that, pilgrims had been coming here in mid-August, on the day of the Feast of the Assumption of Mary. Many of the Muslim faith came as well, and still do, to honor the mother of the great prophet. The Lazarists keep the site open to all pilgrims. Some have been cured of disease while visiting this site and it is holy ground."

"It *is* peaceful here. The trees are beautiful. Have they excavated this area, looking for artifacts?"

"I have never seen them digging here before today," Ahmet confessed. "There must be millions of artifacts hidden beneath the ground from here to Istanbul, and all over our country. It is a serious crime to search for them without official permission and supervision, though."

"I wonder if the Virgin Mary died and was resurrected here?" Scott mused, more to himself than to his guide.

"It is believed that she was taken to heaven upon her last breath," Ahmet answered him. "She is said to have arisen from that room inside to the right. It was her bedroom, or so it is claimed."

Scott noted the confidence with which Ahmet spoke. As he walked slowly around the site, he felt himself reacting to the same sense of holiness and sanctity that so many before him had experienced. A shiver ran up his backbone. He had left his home in America and had flown to Turkey on a furtive mission. Somehow, just being here for a short period of time made the entire unsettling excursion worthwhile. He sat under a large tree and stared at the home. Even the arrival of a busload of tourists did not disturb his inner thoughts and emotions. Ahmet stood apart from him, not wanting to bother his benefactor, who was deep in thought.

Some time later Scott rose to his feet. "I'm ready to go, Ahmet. Where to next?"

"To eat lunch. I'm hungry."

"Already?" Scott checked his watch and then checked it again. "My Lord, we've been here two hours!"

"Time melts away in this place," Ahmet said sincerely.

"Obviously it does," Scott responded.

Ahmet avoided the small restaurant at the site, and drove back to Selçuk where they ate in an open-air café near the turnoff to the motel.

"Now let's go through the ruins," Scott directed, when the meal was over and he had paid the tab. They drove west to the Tusan Efes Motel, where they turned south, and then parked the car a distance away from the tourist shops and restaurant. The vastness of the ruins surprised Scott as he gazed upon them.

"I don't know how much time we'll have before I must meet my associate," he said. "So take me to the ruins from the first century. I'm most interested in what sort of community was here when the Virgin Mary lived in Ephesus."

"Fine, but you should also see what has made these ruins famous: The Library of Celsus, Arcadian Way, and other places. We will have time to see many things before it gets dark."

He led Scott south, away from the Gymnasium of Vedius, constructed in AD 150 by Publius Vedius Antoninus Pius, to the stadium. There, Ahmet stopped and spread out his arms toward it. "This stadium," he said, "was built here during the time of Nero, around AD 60. It replaced a much older stadium. Ancient civilizations raced chariots here and gladiators engaged in mortal combat at the foot of Mount Pion."

"So if Mary did come to Ephesus with St. John, she might well have come to this very spot?"

"Yes, yes, of course!" Ahmet enthused.

They walked past the remains of a large sixth century building, and down a paved street. Scott was guided to the right, and led onto a path toward the ruins of the church of the Councils.

"This entire area was an ancient oak forest before Ephesus was built," Ahmet explained. "Before the coming of Androcles thousands of years ago."

"Who was Androcles?"

"A son of Codrus, the king of Athens. Legend has it that an oracle told him to settle in a place indicated by a fish and wild boar. He and his followers came here, and found people roasting fish near the shore. A fish fell out of the fire and knocked embers into a thicket that soon was consumed by flames. The fire forced a wild boar to run into the open, where it was slain by Androcles. The Greeks took these events as fulfilling the prophecy, and they settled here."

Ahmet paused and pointed toward extensive ruins.

"Church of the Councils. Early second century. Rebuilt in the fourth century, and again in the sixth century. I brought you here because this was the first church built to honor Mary, Mother of Jesus. The Councils of Ephesus convened right here. The first in 431, and the second in 449."

Scott was momentarily distracted by a large group of tourists walking quickly, to keep up with their tour guide. The guide periodically held up a white stick so that those in the rear of the gaggle knew they were proceeding in the right direction.

"Tourists. English and American. I know this guide. He is terrible. They will leave here learning nothing. The worst are the ship cruises. They dock in Kuşadasi, charge here in buses, see a few broken pieces of marble, and then race back to their floating hotel to eat before their next adventure."

Scott laughed and wondered what his guide thought about him. His gaze was then drawn toward a man sitting close by on an unusual one-legged stool. The man was obviously listening to their conversation. He waved and smiled at Scott when they made eye contact. Scott smiled back and then looked away.

"What were the councils about?" he asked.

"Bishops from the Catholic Church first met here to debate the nature of Christ. The second Council was the so-called 'Robber Council' which removed the patriarch of Constantinople."

Ahmet was about to continue when they both noticed the man on the makeshift stool get up, snap two sections of the folding seat back together to form a handle, extend the leg to form a walking stick, and proceed toward them. He addressed Scott.

"Excuse me, but I could not help but overhear your question. The Council in 431 was presided over by Cyril of Alexandria and included many bishops. It was convened by Theadosius II and held under the watchful eye of papal legates. During the bitter debate, the patriarch of Constantinople was condemned because he preached that Jesus was two separate persons, one human and one divine. He taught that Mary was only the mother of the human Jesus, and therefore should not be called the Mother of God. The second Council in 449 deposed the patriarch, and replaced him with a heretical priest whose name would only confuse you. Thus was the war of words fueled between Ephesus and Constantinople. It is also believed by some that the body of Mary, or at least some artifact from her, was buried here in Ephesus after the construction of this first church dedicated to the Virgin."

Scott stared at the finely-attired man for a moment before extending his right hand toward him. "Scott Frank," he said.

"Rutheford Ruffescott," the man replied. They shook hands firmly.

"I'm glad you found me," Scott opened. "I am having quite a time, at your expense, and don't really know why I'm being treated so royally."

Ruffescott chuckled. "It wasn't hard to find you because you were brought here by my new friend Ahmet, and you arrived only a few minutes late," he said, consulting his pocket watch as he spoke. Ahmet had walked a discreet distance away and stood there, smiling.

"I talked to Ahmet last night, after he dropped you off," Ruffescott went on to explain. "He left his number with the front desk. I have delayed formally meeting you because I wanted to be certain you are not being followed. Apparently you are not," he added in a low voice.

"No, I don't believe I am," Scott answered in the same hushed tone. "At least not anymore. But I was followed from my home to the airport, and again on the airplane to London, and yet again to Izmir."

"You were followed?"

"Yes, I disguised myself and lost them in Izmir."

"Damn. That explains it then. I underestimated you, Mr. Frank. I was sure they would follow you here and if they did, I would then know who had taken Jay. I miscalculated your resourcefulness. Did you take note of their description?"

"Yes. It was one person, a woman. I found out where she works in Izmir and I followed her there. She is involved with a strange group of women. A cult of some sort I believe."

"Her name?"

"I just know that her first name is Helen."

Rutheford Ruffescott placed a firm hand on Scott's shoulder and nodded knowingly.

"Congratulations," he said. "You may not realize it, but you have filled in a large piece of this puzzle. Your services have already been of great value to me. In addition, I now know why you no longer sport a mustache. Yes, very resourceful. A true soldier. I have many questions, but we must continue on with our little tour here. Ahmet and I will show you more ruins, then we must go to a place where I will ask more questions about your journey. Tonight, I have a joint mission in mind for us. Say nothing to Ahmet about any of this. We will discharge him at the end of the day. He can find someone else to guide tomorrow."

"He brought me here from Izmir."

"Izmir? You mean to say that you hired him in Izmir?"

"Yes. At the airport. He's taken me everywhere so far. Quite a nice guy."

"Does he know you were being followed?"

"No."

"Good. Do you think there is any possibility that he is being paid to watch you?"

Scott paused to consider that. "I don't think so. He was at the head of the taxi line, and I approached him. But I suppose there is the possibility that someone could have contacted him here, just as you did."

"Yes. Well, we'll see. Time should tell. The ruins provide no shade and it's hot. To see Ephesus at its best, we must not be exhausted from the sun and the walk up the hillside." Rutheford Ruffescott turned toward Ahmet and motioned to him to join them.

Ahmet walked toward the two and stood a few paces apart.

"Ahmet," Ruffescott said, "please drive us to the Magnesian Gate and then pick us up where the car is now, in three hours."

"Yes, yes," Ahmet agreed.

The three men walked back to the car. Scott noted that Ahmet was scanning the groups of sightseers. Suddenly he excused himself, apparently having spotted a friend. Ahmet hurried toward him and engaged in a muted conversation in Turkish. The friend rushed ahead as Ahmet rejoined Scott and Ruffescott. A few minutes later, a dark-green, 1950s vintage Chevrolet pulled up in front of them, and the driver jumped out to open the car doors. Scott recognized him as the man Ahmet had spoken to.

"This is my friend," Ahmet said, motioning to the man. "He is a good driver. He will drive us to Magnesian Gate so that I will not have to locate you later."

Ruff nodded slowly as he got into the backseat of the Chevy. "Good idea, Ahmet; we can always use a good guide." He winked at Scott. Then the three of them got into the car.

It was a short trip along the Aydin Road to the rubble and stones that marked the entrance to Ephesus that Ruff wished to begin at. It had once been the beginning of the ancient road to Magnesia.

"There isn't an actual gate here anymore," Ruff explained for Scott's benefit as they stepped out of the car. "The ancient road was constructed around the middle of the first century during the reign of Vespasian."

They thanked the driver, and along with Ahmet trailing a few steps behind, started walking down the marble roadway and past the East Gymnasium built in AD 200.

"This city must have been magnificent," Scott ventured, as he scanned the ruins on both sides of the roadway.

"It still is!" Ruff insisted. "And look around us at the hills covered with sand. Who knows what may lie beneath these sands!" He lowered his voice and said, "You spoke of a cult – say nothing about such things now. We must assume that we are being overheard wherever we are." Scott nodded his understanding, feeling a sense of excitement bubbling within him. *This is better than army officer training, any day!*

They walked past the ruins of the city's law courts, utilized in the first century AD, past the ruined foundations of a temple dedicated to Isis, and stopped at the Pryteneion dedicated to the goddess Hestia or Vesta. In its time it had contained the sacred flame of Ephesus, which was never allowed to go out. Hestia of the hearth, was the sister of Zeus and Hera. The hearth was the center of domestic worship not only in temples, but also in the ancient homes of Ephesus.

"Official guests and dignitaries were received here, in the Senate Hall, by governmental and religious leaders," Ruff put forth. "Lysimachus re-founded Ephesus in the third century before Christ, though the ruins visible to us probably date from the reign of Augustus between 27 BC and AD 14. In the museum in town, there are two statutes of Artemis that were discovered here; one from the first century, and a second one that had been hidden beneath the ground in a small room in the sanctuary, over there." He pointed toward the spot.

"There was also an altar here where, I believe, Amazons may have performed initiation rituals for young women entering their Order."

"Rituals!" Scott stated as a fact. "What sort of rituals?"

"The taking of vows, and a ceremony to prepare them for archery combat."

Scott's mind flashed him back to the ceremony under the museum in Izmir, but he decided to wait to make his revelation until they were no longer being listened to by Ahmet.

A short walk farther on, Ruff gestured toward the remnants of a small temple. "Temple of Hadrian, early second century," he expounded. "It was dedicated by Publius Quinctilius to Hadrian, and the goddess Artemis. Those reliefs show the fight between Hercules and Theseus, and the Amazon dances or battles with various gods."

Rutheford Ruffescott chatted as he walked.

"There on the left, are the remains of three tombs, one of which was discovered to hold the skeleton of a young woman about twenty years of age. The tomb is believed to be from the end of the first century."

They had walked on a short distance when Ruff abruptly halted and turned around.

"Ahmet," he said, "please tell us about these ruins."

Ahmet nodded. "Yes, yes, an interesting place. Here a marble arch remains, and across the street was a brothel, and a public latrine with running water. In the first century both were in use. The brothel's rooms were built around an atrium; some downstairs and some on the first floor. What you see there," he pointed at a small circular structure, "is the well which is still in use, and in which was found the Priapus figure, the small carving of a man with an enormous penis, which is copied and sold at the shops."

They continued their walk and spied a magnificent-looking building.

"Now *this* is beautiful!" Scott exclaimed.

"Indeed," Ruff agreed. "The Library of Celsus is the centerpiece of these excavations, and has been extensively restored by the Austrians. Consul Gaius Julius Azvila erected it in AD 110 as a memorial to his father who at the time governed the Roman province of Asia. It also served as a headstone for his father's body, which was discovered in 1904. The body lies in a coffin beneath the west apsidal wall of the library. At one time, the library contained more than twelve thousand scrolls. Those four statues you see there depict Sophia, Arete, Ennoia and Episteme. They are Homeric heroines who in turn represent wisdom, valor, thought, and knowledge. Excellent reproductions, don't you think? The originals are in the Ephesus Museum in Vienna."

"Are the library scrolls in Vienna too?" Scott asked.

"No. The Goths attacked and ransacked Ephesus in the third century. Then there was an earthquake in the tenth century. Not to mention Christians who were continuously looking to burn pagan works while fighting Muslims. No, the scrolls were all destroyed."

They proceeded from the library along the marble street to the theater of Ephesus.

"Here is where St. Paul preached against the goddess Artemis, or Diana as the Romans called her. This magnificent theater held twenty-four thousand people," Ruff said, as he sat down on a smooth slab.

"It's beautiful," Scott half-whispered, staring at the open theater. Ahmet stepped forward to offer his own commentary.

"This is where the Arcadian Way ends. It was a great marble street going from here to the middle harbor gate. It was built in the early fifth century AD and was once lined with shops."

They proceeded down the Arcadian Way toward the church of the Councils and Ahmet's taxi.

"It's overwhelming," Scott muttered.

"Yes, it is," Ruff concurred. "We could spend days here talking about the ruins, weeks speaking of the history, and years excavating the area. I have only included the history that is directly relevant to our quest."

Scott looked dumbfounded and Ruff patted him on the shoulder.

"It will all make sense later, I hope. Now let's drive by that wonder of the ancient world, the Temple of Artemis, before heading back to Selçuk for dinner."

"Good!" Ahmet snapped. "Tomorrow we can visit the museum--with your permission, of course, Professor."

"I am no professor," Ruff corrected him. "But perhaps we can employ you through tomorrow after all. You bring a certain perspective to these matters, and that perspective is appreciated."

Ahmet started the engine, and a short time later pulled the car over to where they could see the foundations of where the Temple of Artemis once held sway.

Ruff pointed across the tiny Selinus River and shook his head. "If you can believe it, Scott, what once stood there was one of the seven wonders of the ancient world."

Scott noted only one incomplete column standing, and the base where the altar building once stood just west of the temple.

"Imagine if you can, what it must have been like here twenty-six hundred years ago. The Temple of Artemis was the largest building ever built by the ancient Greeks."

"Artemis must have been quite a lady, to have that built in her honor."

"She was. In Greek mythology, she was the goddess of the hunt, the daughter of Zeus, and the sister of Apollo. She was also the protector of women; young girls in particular."

"So Rebecca informed me. I'm a little disappointed that there aren't any real remains left of the temple," Scott allowed.

"Did Rebecca happen to tell you about the residents of the temple?"

"No. She didn't."

"The high priest was the Megabysos; Persian for 'set free by God.' He was a eunuch, and was aided by a staff of virgins and minor priests known as the Essenes.

"A statue of Artemis, surely a magnificent sculpture, was the most-revered object inside. It has never been found. A series of them were erected, the first of which was fashioned out of wood, and the later ones of marble and onyx. Huge marble columns supported the roof. They contained beautiful sculptures carved into their bases, one of which is at the British Museum.

Artemis was also the goddess of childbirth. When Alexander the Great was born in 356 BC, Artemis is said to have attended his birth. At that same time, a lunatic named Herostratus decided to become famous by destroying this temple with fire. Years later, after Alexander had liberated this area from Persian rule, he came to Ephesus and asked local authorities if he could rebuild the temple and have his name carved into it. The Ephesians did not want Alexander meddling in their affairs, so they told him that they could not accept such a magnificent offer because it was not proper for one god to present gifts to another. Quite the flatterers, weren't they?"

"Many of the temple's treasures were subsequently moved to Rome. During the Byzantine and Ottoman periods, the fine marble of this temple was hauled away to build mosques and churches, including St. Sophia in Istanbul. Silt from the river covered this site, until archaeologist John Turtle Wood rediscovered it in the mid-nineteenth century."

"How was he able to find it out here, away from the city?"

"There was an inscription in the theater that said, at the time of performances, holy images were brought from the temple along the sacred way, past the Magnesian Gate, to the theater. Mr. Wood located the sacred way and followed it to this location. Wood, then D.G. Hogarth, and now the Austrians, have carefully searched and re-searched this site. Wood, however, paid a price for his discoveries. He was the victim of disease, broken bones, theft, and an attempted assassination. Others involved in the discovery were murdered."

The three men gazed quietly upon the ruins for several more moments before returning to the car and driving back toward Selçuk. As they slowly made their way through tourist traffic and past the Ephesus Museum on their left, Scott suddenly stiffened and grabbed Ruff's arm.

"That white Chevrolet over there, do you see it?" he said excitedly.

Ruff looked to where Scott was pointing. "Yes. What about it?"

"It looks like the same car that picked up the woman who followed me from Minneapolis!"

"Your friend is right, Mr. Ruffescott," Ahmet commented from the front seat.

"Take us into town, Ahmet," Ruffescott demanded gruffly. "And keep your eyes on the road."

Then, looking askance at Scott, he raised a finger to his lips.

After supper, Ahmet was paid in full for his services. It was apparent, however, that he would be available if needed.

Scott followed Ruffescott, on foot from the restaurant, along a series of narrow streets to a seedy-looking establishment. They entered the building and then proceeded to a back staircase, leading down to a basement storage area. Against the far wall, was a small door that appeared to be the entrance to a closet. Ruff stepped into the area and glanced up, listening intently for footsteps on the floor above. Hearing nothing, he removed a key from his pocket and unlocked the door. The closet was small indeed, but Scott was directed inside, with Ruff following behind holding a pocket-sized, but powerful, flashlight. He closed the door and then, reaching up, turned a hidden latch behind a coil of rope on a shelf above his head. He pushed against a shelf on the opposite wall, which pivoted ninety degrees, to reveal a narrow passageway. Standing stock still for several moments, his ears pricked for any telltale sound, Ruff motioned to Scott, and led the way down the passageway, after closing the entrance behind him. They went down three stairs to another sloping passageway. It led them beneath the roadway, and into the basement of another building. They exited through a similar storage closet, went up two flights of stairs, and entered a small windowless room furnished with two chairs, a small desk, a cot, and a single naked light bulb dangling from the ceiling on a frayed cord.

"Home sweet home," Ruff chuckled. He motioned to Scott to sit down on a chair. Ruff sat down opposite him.

"This room is safe and soundproof," Ruff said. "I want to hear everything relevant that you can remember from the time Rebecca left Minnesota. Tell me the events in order, and be as detailed as possible. But first, what about the cloth I sent you?"

"The cloth!" Scott exclaimed. "I had forgotten the very reason for my being here! Analysis shows that it's about two thousand years old."

Rutheford leaned back, smiling. "Of course," he whispered.

"Of course?" Scott stammered. "What's that supposed to mean?"

"Not yet. First, tell me about your journey here."

Scott recounted the details of his journey without interruption from Ruff, who leaned forward with his hands folded over the top of his walking stick. He rested his chin on his hands and closed his eyes, as if trying to visualize in his mind what Scott was telling him.

"Very interesting," Ruff said at the conclusion. "We have many, many pieces of a puzzle lying all around us. Many of these pieces are unseen, and our mind toys with us to divert us from the real quest."

"Which, I assume, is finding the writings and the grave of the Virgin Mary?"

"Correct. So after a thorough examination of the pieces at our disposal, what do you think we should do next?"

"Well," Scott said hesitantly. "I would like to know the reason I was being followed. And, of course, it's critical to locate Jay. And these ruins are fascinating. But I confess, I'm at a loss as to how all this ties together."

"Understandable. At first, my mind wandered from one plan to another. Now, with the pieces you have added to the puzzle, I believe we must refocus on the basic facts of the situation. Without more information, any search for a gravesite would be purely speculative. I suspect that Jay has essential information about the site, but we don't know where he is. This we do know: the cult of Artemis had you followed to Izmir. Then, they presumably followed you here to Ephesus. I have long studied cults, mythology, and religion, and you describe a ceremony that is only hinted at in ancient mythology. Today is August the thirteenth, the day of special significance to followers of Artemis, who is also known by the Romans as Diana of Ephesus, goddess of the crescent moon."

"Why is this day so special?"

"Because it is the day of the Nemoralia, or Grove Festival. It takes place at midnight under the crescent moon when neither Scorpio nor Orion appear in the sky. On this night alone there are no reminders of men and the perils of their pride anywhere in the heavens."

Scott paused a moment, summoning up a long ago lesson from the depths of his memory.

"Scorpio, Scorpius, the scorpion sign of late October and most of November. I read about the myth in Mrs. Nerum's Latin class. As I recall, Zeus and his brothers, Hermes and Poseidon, were walking on earth as mortals when they became hungry and asked for food from a poor farmer."

"Hyrieus," Ruff filled in. "The farmer's name was Hyrieus."

"So you say. He was a poor widower and had no food, but killed his pet ox to honor his guests. He didn't know they were gods until after the meal, when Zeus offered him any gift his heart desired. When he asked for a son, he was told to bury the ox's skin and after nine months, it would turn into a son. Zeus touched the skin with his staff and the three gods disappeared. The farmer buried the skin, and nine months later found a baby on that very spot."

"That would be Orion," Ruff informed him.

"Orion grew into an excellent hunter who wandered the world. He met Artemis... I can't remember where."

"On the island of Crete."

"Yes, Crete. They hunted together and became lovers. Then, to impress the goddess and to show off, Orion killed all the animals on Crete. Unknown to him, Artemis was also the protector of all wild things. She was furious with him for killing the animals and stamped her foot on the ground. A giant scorpion sprang from the earth, and before Orion could lift his bow, the scorpion stung and killed him. Artemis placed the scorpion and Orion among the stars to warn against killing wild animals, and the risk of pride."

"Very good! Very good!" Rutheford Ruffescott exclaimed, slapping the side of his left knee. "My God, I had no idea your range of knowledge was so vast. Odd for a lawyer and an army officer."

"Not so very," Scott said. "Where and when will this festival take place?"

"Good question. I listened with interest to your account of the ritual that took place under the museum in Izmir. Years ago, there was no museum here, and the artifacts were taken to Izmir. Today there *is* a museum here, and it may also have a lower level. However, I tend to believe that tonight's ceremony will occur at midnight somewhere out in the open."

"In the outdoor amphitheater, perhaps?"

"Perhaps. But more likely somewhere else. I must add, that while I remain impressed with your interest in mythology, your knowledge is... well... somewhat superficial. There are a number of accounts regarding the story of Orion and his relationship with Artemis. For example, one account says that Orion perished for touching the goddess while hunting with her on the island of Chios. Still another is perhaps the most interesting. According to this one, Apollo was jealous of his sister's attention to Orion, and challenged Artemis to hit a fish that was swimming far out at sea with an arrow. But it was no fish. It was Orion. And the silver arrow Artemis was tricked into firing, hit him in the head and killed him. So you see, there are many versions. Truth is often a matter of collective faith. The facts are hard to know. As lawyers, we are used to seeking only the truth that supports our position. Good for our clients, bad for justice."

Scott frowned at the admonishment of him as a scholar, and an aspiring attorney.

"I don't know why I'm here," Scott said matter-of-factly. "You are right. I am into an adventure that I am ill prepared to understand, let alone participate in. I should be at Fort Bragg."

"Don't be so hasty," Rutheford Ruffescott chastised. "And so negative. You bring other assets to our quest: a new perspective, the vigor of youth, and a mind that is open to what it perceives. Now, my friend, we must go hunting."

"Hunting?"

"Yes. Do you hunt ducks?"

"I'm afraid I don't."

"Well, neither do I anymore. But when I did, I went to where the ducks would most likely flock. I'd build a blind, and then shiver and freeze for many hours until the ducks either came or did not. Tonight, in less then five hours, the flock we are seeking will be somewhere nearby. In fact, if my instincts are correct, they will descend upon the ruins of the Temple of Artemis. I have prepared a duck blind there, and hopefully we will observe something interesting. Does this sound like a plan?"

"Of sorts," Scott said dubiously.

Scott followed him back through the maze and into the street where Ahmet had left them. From there, they walked out of town, across the countryside between the fortress upon Ayasuluk Hill and the Basilica of St. John, skirted the Isa Bey Mosque, and approached the narrow Selinus River from the north. There, among the ruins of the temple, Rutheford motioned for Scott to sit beside him on the ground. Cars passed by on a roadway that ran parallel to the river on the opposite side. Rutheford pulled a small pair of binoculars from his pocket, and scanned the area around them.

"Good," he chuckled. "No sign of ducks."

"Are we near our objective?" Scott asked.

"Over there," Ruff replied quietly, nodding toward a spot nearby, where what looked like a piece of heavy canvas, had been partially covered with sand. The stiff canvas was about the length of a man, and over a meter wide.

"Is that your blind?"

"Our blind, yes. Lift the edge and try rolling inside."

Scott did as bidden and soon found himself in a wide, damp hole.

"Does feel rather like a swamp, doesn't it?" Ruff chirped good-naturedly as he rolled in beside Scott. "Perfect for attracting ducks."

"Am I the decoy?" Scott asked.

Ruff chuckled at that, but said nothing.

"How long do we have to hide out in this place?" Scott groused. "Until midnight?"

"That should do it." Ruff went on, "Do you see the small visual ports in front of you?" Scott found the small openings, fashioned between the canvas and the ground. "I have with me a night observation device that will allow us to observe if anything unusual is happening at either the altar site or the temple."

"We're directly between them, aren't we?" Scott asked.

"Just so." Ruff stifled a yawn. "I suggest we rest and relax a bit. I am rather worn out from the day, and we may have a long night ahead. Wake me if you hear or see anything, but be quiet. We talk in whispers from now on. In any event, be sure to wake me when it's dark." He handed Scott a small waterproof bag. Scott watched as Ruff blew a second bag into a pillow, sealed it, placed his head upon it, closed his eyes, and was soon snoring softly.

*The sleep of the innocent*, Scott thought to himself. He was far too keyed up to sleep.

Every now and then, Scott listened for sounds, or peeked out from under the tarp at the remains of the Temple of Artemis. But mostly, he lay there in the mud, wondering what the hell he was doing there. He fell into a fitful sleep, only to awaken with a start. Immediately he sensed it was pitch black outside.

"Damn it," Scott whispered to himself.

He stared at the luminous dial on his wristwatch. It was nearly ten-thirty. He lay there shivering for another few minutes before reaching out and nudging Ruffescott.

The older man stirred. "What time is it?" he asked, suddenly alert.

"Going on eleven."

Ruff turned on his side. "Good thing you woke me. My left leg is asleep and I'm a bit waterlogged. Rather cold, too." He shifted his weight and raised his arm to lift the cover. Seeing nothing but blackness, he brought the night-vision device to his eyes and scanned the area.

"Nothing yet," he reported softly, as he lay his head back down upon the waterproof bag. "Here, you use this." He handed the night-vision device to Scott, who peered through it. He could see the terrain as if through a heavy greenish snowstorm, but the device worked amazingly well. He could make out considerable detail. From high above, a crescent moon suddenly appeared from behind a cloud. Looking through the device, it was as if the night suddenly glowed a yellowish-green, chasing the darkness away.

"Amazing," Scott whispered. "The army needs a few of these." He watched on and off for some time, as Ruff lay beside him, eyes closed, hardly breathing.

Scott drifted off for a moment, but woke as a result of Ruff's hand covering his mouth.

"Quiet now," Ruff admonished, and released his hand. He gave Scott the night-vision device and motioned to him to look through it. Scott did. At first he saw nothing. Then he noticed a group of people heading toward him carrying what appeared to be a small, wood statue. They were all wearing ankle-length garments with hoods that hid their faces--and they looked to be forming a circle where the altar to Artemis had once stood.

Scott watched intently as the statue was held aloft, and turned from side to side. Again, the moon escaped from behind a cloud, adding light to the darkness, and Scott saw that in fact, there were two rings of hooded figures. No one spoke. It was deathly quiet. Suddenly, the figure holding the statue moved from the inner ring toward the middle of the circle, and knelt down to place the statue there. Scott could make out little beyond the contours of the statue, and handed the night-vision device to Ruff.

"I don't need it," Ruff whispered excitedly. "I can see well enough with the binoculars."

Scott pushed his air bag as far forward as it would go, and peered through the device again, as the moon became partially hidden by a passing scruff of high cloud. In the center of the circle a light appeared. Someone had apparently turned on a lamp of some kind, Scott assumed. But then he noticed a mist that seemed to glow and seep out from between those forming the circle. Quickly, the mist morphed into a dark-green fog. Scott placed his elbows on top of his inflated bag and arched his back to raise the canvas top a little more for a better view.

Suddenly, there was a loud 'pop!' Scott's face dropped into a muddy puddle. The device's right eyepiece struck him hard, just above his right eyebrow, and he felt a dull pain throbbing near his temple.

"Crap," he cursed softly. "The damned bag popped." Hearing no reply, he reached out to make sure that Ruff was all right. He felt only ground and water. Scott pushed himself up and peered out of the blind. To his surprise, the canvas top was gone and everything was black around the altar. The green mist was gone. Scott found the night-vision device. It was damp. He wiped it off with his shirt and looked through it, but again saw nothing but blackness. Apparently he had ruined it.

Scott glanced up into the moon's soft light, and then it struck him a sickening blow. Suddenly he understood why he could see nothing. He was looking directly at the black robes of the hooded figures, who had by now formed a tight circle around the blind.

"Hello," he greeted them with forced good cheer. "Seen any ducks lately?"

Scott Frank felt pain as the point of a dart pierced his neck. Moments later, he lay unconscious on the ground.

# CHAPTER TWENTY-TWO

## AUGUST 14, 1980

Scott's dream was a long series of single-frame photographs that flashed through his mind. Everything he could remember since the time he was an infant was depicted, together with memories he did not recognize. They marched into his mind one after another, and he marveled not only at their clarity, but also how detached he felt from them. He was able to recall whom he was with at each event, as well as what the occasion was. Many events flashed by in an instant, while others seemed to stay with him for a while. Most had been pleasant experiences. Some were not.

There was a voice guiding him, and it was a soothing voice of comfort and solace. Sometimes the images became blurry, and his explanations became confused. At such times, the voice would guide him back to the last vivid frame of mind, and he would again be able to detail events with clarity.

Scott grew weary of going backward to his boyhood, then forward to his flight to Izmir. He longed to awaken. To relax and rest his mind.

Finally, the dream had run its course, and he woke in a dimly-lit room. The room was encased in stone and had no windows. He was lying on his back in a small rickety cot that was a foot too short for him; his feet hung over the end. His mouth and throat were parched, and his head ached something awful. He could not move at first—more accurately, he dared not move, for the simplest of motions caused the room to spin about. He felt exhausted. He was somehow reminded of his youth, when as a little boy, he would blink his eyes as fast as he could, while spinning around in a circle on his heels, until he fell down, laughing at his dizziness.

Scott sensed another presence in the room. He did not move or attempt to speak to whoever it was; surely it was not a friend.

After what seemed a very long time, the pain in his head subsided a little, and he swallowed and tightened his lips to force his mouth to salivate, to generate moisture. As Scott yawned out loud, he heard from behind him the sound of a chair being pushed back. A middle-aged man walked over to his bedside and gazed down upon him, concern written plainly upon his face.

"Are you all right?" he asked with a slight British accent. Scott did not respond. Closing his eyes, he willed his headache to vanish and leave him be. When he opened his eyes, he saw the man sitting beside him on a wood chair, the look of concern still evident on his face.

"I would offer you some tea, if I had any," the man stated, seemingly to himself.

"I'm afraid I left the box that my betrothed gave me in Vienna."

Scott closed his eyes again and slept peacefully for a span of time he could not determine. When he woke, the man was asleep in the chair, snoring softly. Scott studied him and then looked around the room, moving his eyes more than his head. He lifted up his head slightly, and noted the outline of a door in the faint light of two candles burning on a small table next to his companion. Scott wiggled his toes and flexed his fingers. He raised his legs one at a time, and bent them while lying down. The man, whoever he was, had awakened and was staring at him in a kindly sort of way.

"Well, young man," he said, "I had hoped you weren't going to die on me, and it appears my wish has been granted. You've been swooning in and out of consciousness for some time, but I must say, you now look a bit more chipper than when we first met. If you can sit up, I believe it might be good for your circulation."

"Where are we?" he asked, his head pounding from his meager efforts to sit up.

"I really don't know, though I suspect we are somewhere in Turkey, perhaps near Kuşadasi. I say, how are you feeling?"

"Terrible, thank you for asking."

"Who are you, and why have you been taken?" the man wanted to know.

Scott thought back to however long ago the waterproof bag had exploded. He looked at the gentleman sitting beside him. "If I may, sir, *who* are *you*?"

"I am Joseph A. Youngquest. Most people refer to me as Jay. I am an American citizen, although I was born and raised in England. Now it's your turn. Who are *you*?"

Something about this man did not sit well with Scott. Instinctively, he didn't trust him. "I am Scott Frank, from Minnesota," he said simply.

The two men stared, each sizing up the other. Scott was first to break the silence.

"Why are you in here? I assume we are in a prison of some kind."

"Very observant of you." The man smiled and then continued. "I was in Vienna doing research on the tomb of the Virgin Mary when I was brought here against my will. I have been of little use to them though, and find myself in this underground prison, without the benefit of even a window to tell if it's day or night. They've taken my watch and everything else I own except these clothes. I have friends who I believe will come looking for me, but I am losing hope that they will find me."

"Is this place bugged?" Scott asked. The question did not seem to ruffle the other man.

"No. I'm certain it is not," he said. "During my rather long stay here, I have searched the floor, walls, and ceiling. I can assure you there is no one listening in on us."

"Then I will tell you everything," Scott avowed.

"I would appreciate that," the man said, leaning in expectantly. "Please, launch in, by all means."

"I am an undercover detective on loan from the Minneapolis Police Department to the DEA. We have been searching for two years, trying to find out how illegal drugs are being smuggled into the US from other parts of the world. I came to Turkey searching for a connection, but was trailed by a drug courier. I began following her and was led to Selçuk. I followed her one night, maybe it was last night, I don't know. Anyway, she met some other men, and I believe that they were signaling an aircraft with a light when I was spotted spying on them. They captured me and here I am."

Scott settled his head back against the pillow and closed his eyes. He only meant to rest momentarily, but soon felt himself slipping into a deep abyss. He struggled against the flow, and opened his eyes just as the Englishman was about to jab a hypodermic needle into his leg.

Scott threw his weight to one side of the cot, and it collapsed as the startled Englishman lost his balance and plunged the needle into the cot's canvas. Scott swung his fist at the man's face, but he was too weak to have much effect. The man stood up, towering over Scott, and threw the syringe onto the floor. He reached down with both hands for Scott's arms as his victim rolled off the collapsed cot. Scott Frank lay there helpless and did the only thing his weakened state would allow. He smiled broadly up at the man who growled down at him.

Suddenly, Scott heard a sort of "snap!" The fellow looked perplexed, and his eyes rolled back up into his head as he lurched forward, falling diagonally across Scott who lay upon the collapsed bed. The man's body went limp, and Scott tried to push him off his own numb body.

Then suddenly, he was staring up at Rutherford Ruffescott, holding his folding one-legged stool like a sword.

"Mr. Scott Frank, I am pleased to introduce you to the *real* Mr. Jay Youngquest," he said, as a second man entered Scott's view and looked down at him.

"You carry him," Ruff said. Scott looked askance to his left, at the first Jay Youngquest who lay next to him, mouth agape. Scott then saw Jay bend over and unbutton the shirt of the unconscious imposter, and pull it to the right side of the chest, revealing a scar where a female breast had once been.

"Excellent male impersonator," Jay said. "She has been employed at the British Museum for some time. Gives tours on objects related to Greek and Roman antiquity from Tuesdays through Sundays, between ten and four-thirty. What she really has been doing is keeping watch over the Ephesus gallery in London for them."

"For whom?" Scott asked, as his pounding headache returned with a vengeance. "Who are you referring to? What in hell is this all about?"

"Not here!" Jay responded firmly, as he picked up Scott, turned and carried him through the doorway, and around several right angle turns before they burst into sunlight.

They were on a hillside above the Curettes road, and across from the Temple of Hadrian. As Scott was to find out, he had been imprisoned in a flank house built thousands of years ago for a rich merchant family. He had been held captive in the center of the ancient city.

Scott was lowered by the two men into a wheelchair, and a broad, drooping straw hat, several sizes too large, was placed upon his head. Rutheford pushed the wheelchair down the rough marble roadway, and out of the ruined city to a car. Scott was stuffed into the backseat, Ruff started the engine, and they sped off.

Scott lay in an uncomfortable heap on the Fiat's backseat as the small car pitched and lurched with each bump it encountered. He clenched his teeth, and with considerable effort sat up.

"Don't be hasty, Mr. Frank," Jay said, as he glanced back at Scott. "I know that drug takes time to wear off. I hope you don't experience the same wicked headaches I had to endure."

"I already have endured them," Scott groused, "I still am." He stretched out his arms to increase circulation and dissipate the drug.

"Where are we going, and where did you find Mr. Youngquest?" Scott asked Ruff.

"I found him thanks to you," Ruff told him. "I merely followed your captors from the Temple of Artemis, to the ancient wall home where you were taken. I watched and waited and listened, learning with great relief that Jay had recently been brought to a home in Selçuk. Amazing timing!"

"Wasn't I being guarded?" Scott questioned.

"Yes. But only by the male impersonator. They utilized drugs to keep you as a fly in a spider's web– sedated and quite under control. You were questioned extensively."

"Those dreams."

"Yes, precisely. Those dreams."

"Did I tell them much, do you think?"

"No. You were so detailed that after many hours, you were still relating your early childhood and couldn't be coaxed into the present for long before digressing back."

"How do you know all of this?" Scott challenged him. There was a pause. "How did you hear me?" he repeated heatedly.

"I placed a bug in the heel of your left shoe the night before we hid in the blind." More silence as Scott felt anger surge within him.

"The waterproof bag didn't burst accidentally, did it?" he asked evenly.

"No. I popped it with my Swiss army knife," Ruff responded.

"So you could follow them to where you hoped to find Mr. Youngquest."

"Precisely."

"I was just a piece of bait to you, wasn't I. Bait thrown out to the sharks."

"Not by any means. You have played a critical role in all of this."

Scott sighed. "I'm a pawn in an intricate game involving Jesus Christ, the Virgin Mary, fallen gods, Amazons, dead archaeologists, and others I can't presently imagine. I've been played for a naive fool."

"Don't be so quick to condemn yourself, Scott Frank. I listened to your clever explanations to Jay's imposter. You must tell us how you knew it wasn't Jay locked in that room with you."

"I'll keep that secret for later when we are enjoying a beer together back in the real world. By the way, you're treating."

Scott raised both hands above his head and arched his back in order to stretch his muscles.

The two elderly men in the front seat glanced at each other as the car sped toward the coast. A short time later, they turned from highway E24 down the hillside and into Kuşadası. Ten minutes later, Ruff parked the car on a side street and switched off the engine.

"We'll help you out, Scott. Then try walking. Jay and I will steady you."

After a few turns, Scott found he could walk adequately without support. So the three of them proceeded the short distance to the waterfront where they joined throngs of tourists flowing in and out of quaint shops. They arrived at the walkway on the top of the giant bulkhead that kept the Aegean Sea at bay, then they walked toward Pigeon Island. They crossed a street near the town's edge, and walked up a set of stairs into the Hotel Efe. In the small but cozy lobby, they took the elevator to the third floor and room 308.

"This is your room, Scott," Ruff said. "Rest to your heart's content. Jay and I will be right next door. But keep your shoe on, just in case," he added with a chuckle.

"Did you kill her?" Scott asked suddenly. "That impersonator?"

"No, I didn't kill her. I just gave her a small dose of a drug to assist her in falling asleep. My walking stick is not only convertible to a convenient seat, but its leg also contains a pressure-activated syringe. She'll be fine in due time, have no worries." Ruff smiled and departed.

Scott sat down on the bed, removed his left shoe, and inspected the heel. *Have no worries*, he mused. The tiny transmitter's location was easy to spot for someone looking for it. He considered singing into it, but decided to just lay back and relax. He wasn't sleepy, but it felt good to do nothing. A few minutes later, he got up to answer a rap on the door. Jay was holding a tray of food.

"Eat, shower, and then get some sleep. We will wake you. We still need your help."

"To find the writings?"

"Yes. And the grave."

Scott was ravenous and ate all the bread, the lamb kabob, and cake, and drank the bottled water. He took a hot shower, laid down on the bed, and soon fell asleep thinking mentally, saying over and over; *The writings and the grave, the writings and the grave, the writings and the grave.*

At five o'clock the next morning, Scott heard another rap on the door. Groggily he slid out of bed and shuffled over to the door, unlocking it.

"I know you could use some more sleep, old boy," Ruff said, as he entered the room, impeccably dressed as always. Jay followed behind, equally well attired. "But we need to talk before Jay and I embark on a mission involving some negotiations. A remarkable opportunity has presented itself and..."

"I know, I know," Scott interrupted. "And we must take advantage of this opportunity. Fine. I've heard of your modus operandi, and I have learned of your motives, of which there are the apparent ones and the not so apparent ones. Save me the introduction, I beg you. Save me the marketing and just tell me, number one, what you want, and number two, your hidden motives for doing what you're doing? I'll accept the mission or reject it, although I must say—and I must state it clearly—that I've been manhandled just about enough! I've just about had it. I admit, it's been quite an experience and I have no regrets. But I'm done in, and if your mission, as you call it, has any hidden motives, such as once again using me for a decoy, or a piece of bloody bait, tell me now and let me go home to Minnesota, where I can lead a relatively uneventful, but happy and safe existence."

Scott glared hard at Ruff and at Jay, who returned his hard stare with a broad smile.

"I completely understand how you feel, Scott," Ruff replied graciously. "Be assured that my colleagues and I view you as an equal, and not as a decoy or piece of bait. Jay, after all, has suffered much worse than you have. Do you think I view him as a decoy or a piece of bait?"

"No," Scott had to admit.

"You are now one of us. What we have involved you in, Mr. Frank, is one of the greatest religious quests imaginable."

"The written words of Jesus Christ, and the human remains of his mother," Scott said softly.

"Quite right," Ruff said. "Do you remember Rebecca telling you about a jar with writings on it, and inside, its lid?"

"I do, yes."

"The jar is made of terra cotta or fired clay. Its function is quite similar to the ones that housed the Dead Sea Scrolls. And it contained, originally I believe, a small scroll with hieroglyphic writings."

"Written by Jesus," Scott half-whispered.

"Some have come to believe that," Ruff responded.

"Do you?"

"The jury is still out, as we lawyers say."

"Is the jar in Ephesus?" Scott asked.

"It may be. My belief is that it was guarded by the cult of the Virgin Mary, following her death or assumption. They may have kept it in her home until the riot, instigated by Demetrius, erupted in the theater. When St. Paul departed Ephesus, the jar containing the writings, I believe, was buried. Then, it was unearthed in 1898."

"Why does the Artemis cult want the writings?" Scott asked.

"What religious body, cult, group, or person wouldn't want them?" Jay responded. "But, they are also on their own centuries-old quest. They are seeking the statue of the goddess Artemis that fell from the sky."

"The idol?"

"Yes."

Scott sat back in his chair and sighed. It was hard to get his arms around all this, but it was beginning to make a modicum of sense to him.

"One fell from the sky," he said, to which Jay nodded.

"Not surprisingly, there are theories about this, too," he added.

"A finished statue of the goddess Artemis fell to earth from some unknown planet?" Scott chuckled.

"Not from some unknown planet – from Mount Jupiter, or from heaven," Jay countered quite seriously. "Perhaps it was a meteor that was seen streaking to earth that was fashioned into a statue. Do you remember the small wood statue that you saw held high during the temple ceremonies?" Scott nodded. "Perhaps that was the prototype for the one sculpted from the meteor. Then again, what if a completed statue appeared suddenly one night – the wooden replica could have been made in its image. We don't know. It was a miracle, and all religions have miracles to confirm their validity. It was a sign and a gift from on high, whether it arrived in finished form, or was fashioned from a heavenly body. Without the opportunity to study the statue, we must rely on faith. And faith, after all, lies at the root of all religions."

Scott questioned what role faith might play in all this, but he let Jay's explanation stand without further comment. His mind raced back to the Artemis worshipers and their ceremonies under the museum in Izmir, and then to the idol held aloft at the Artemission. He thought about King Arthur and the Knights of the Round Table... searching for the Holy Grail. How was the cult of Artemis searching for their statue from Mount Jupiter any different? Scott Frank glanced at his small suitcase on the floor next to the bed. Home felt to be on another planet.

"So, let me see?" Scott Frank said, scratching his chin thoughtfully. "The oddly-shaped book Rebecca read to me told of a jar with a lid--both of which had inscriptions on them. Now we think it may have once held a scroll with hieroglyphs? There is also a statue of Artemis. Then there are the directions to where they are likely hidden together. Am I correct so far, more or less?"

"Frank, you are a true venturer," Ruff said in a most appreciative tone. He eyed Scott with apparent pride.

"An adventurer, you mean, Ruff."

"We prefer to use the noun 'venturer.' It means one who emits good fortune and who succeeds by taking chances that others might not have the courage to take. You are, after all, a Special Forces soldier."

"You call what has happened to me *lucky?*" Scott scoffed. Despite himself, he felt a tinge of pride at Ruff's words.

"Yes, most definitely," Ruff replied smoothly. "You have always acted as though you have nothing to lose, and at the same time, everything to lose. You do not attach well to others, but follow curious leads, without much regard for the consequences. Relatively few people in this world of ours would leave home and studies to take a stroll into the unknown."

Scott met Ruff's hard stare. "It's not possible that I was selected by you to become involved in this venture, is it?"

"Well, of course," Jay chuckled. "Ruff recruited you just as he did Rebecca and me in Paris."

"But, I found you through my response to an ad!" Scott shot back, before he paused to reflect on the circled words and telephone number on the card, that he had found on his desk. Scott Frank tried to remember if he ever knew who had left the magazine on his desk. Then he questioned whether he had ever actually opened the magazine to see the ad that the card referred to."

"How did you even know that I existed?" he asked. "Who referred me to you?"

"We can discuss that later, but not now, my friend. It is someone you met, a number of years ago, before law school. While you were serving in the army," Mr. Ruffescott offered.

Scott Frank shook his head slowly.

"Okay, but promise to tell me later, or I won't be able to stop thinking about who that person is."

"Agreed," Ruff said.

Scott shrugged. "I wish that I could at least pretend to be upset about all of this. But the honest truth is, I can't."

"No," Ruff responded. "You have always been able to see the humor in every situation, which, by the way, is not typical of venturers."

"But," Jay added, "it is a trait we four share. And because we do, we have decided to share with you the identity of those who are racing against each other to find the antiquities." He glanced at Ruff, who gave him a brief nod in reply.

"Scott," Jay said, "we believe that the relics that we have discussed do, in fact, exist. And they may be located near to where we are at the moment. However, we won't be shocked if a pathway leads us in another direction. Obviously, we are in competition with others who want the relics for themselves. And each party, so to speak, has a claim to ownership, or at least a claimed right to study the objects we are all seeking."

"Unfortunately, it is also in the best interests of those seeking the objects to withhold relics from the others, to keep them for themselves. This perspective is grounded in historical animosity. In mistrust going back thousands of years. It is also the result of a continuous battle for suppression that began with the founding of Christendom. The quest we share pits a number of societies and cults against one another."

"Like the cult of Artemis," Scott thought out loud.

"Exactly," Ruff offered. "And the Roman Church, and the underworld seekers of artifacts, who would sell the items to the highest private bidder, which could be a private collector, or a museum, or even a government."

"Why the competition? Why the intrigue? Why not cooperate to find these priceless treasurers for the sake of all mankind?"

"Spoken like an idealist," Ruff said. "And not as a lawyer. Lawyers understand the mistrust, and greed, and envy that unfortunately blacken the souls of too many people. History, alas, is full of such miscreants, from certain kings down to the lowliest cobbler. What you are witnessing here, is the latest battle between the two primary human groups populating our earth."

"The Catholic Church and the Amazons?" Scott asked, without conviction.

"Well, no. They are two of the organized entities on the front lines of the struggle, but we are talking about the battle between the sexes, the fundamental battle between men and women, and the inherent struggle that began for the Church when Eve purportedly offered the apple to Adam."

"I do not wish to offend you, sir, but that sounds like a bunch of sexist nonsense!" Scott said, his hands raised, palms up, in utter disbelief.

"What seems so preposterous is so apparent," Jay stated emphatically. "Let us assume that the Roman Catholic Church was created to serve at the forefront of the battle between the sexes, its mission to keep man dominate at every level of society. Think on it: the Church was founded by twelve disciples, all men. They do not allow women to assume any meaningful leadership positions within their organization. A woman cannot become the pope, or cardinal, or archbishop, or bishop, or even priest. Throughout early history, freethinking females in Christendom were sought out and killed."

"Church leaders, meanwhile, have established kingdoms on earth, and they have crusaded, plotted, and allied with governments. Their methods and philosophies have been copied by other religions, even to more of an extreme. Consider Islam, for example. Not always by doctrine, but in practice. How are women faring in the world's other major faiths? Name a few high profile women in Judaism, or Hinduism, or Buddhism. What about the other religions... those which have survived in the world?"

"Set against these male-dominated religions, we have scattered matriarchal communities, and little known organizations. At the point of the spear is the cult of Artemis; the Amazon fifth column, the suppressed remnant of the Amazon kingdom that was the last significant female-dominated nation with an army of archers and mounted cavalry. They are known to have fought in Athens hundreds of years ago. This nation of female soldiers was systematically attacked, and its inhabitants hunted down, at which point the nation went underground and survives today as a cult of bright, dangerous foes to many religions and to the societies they have created. This sect is so secretive that in order to gain admission, you must literally be born into it, educated in its beliefs, and may then join only through an initiation that marks you for life as a fighter for Artemis against the domination of men and their religious doctrines."

"Jesus," Scott whispered reverently. "I've never heard such a story. The way you lay it out, though... it does make me wonder."

"Their society began near the Black Sea," Jay explained. "They were, and remain, warrior women described by Homer in the *Iliad* as those who fight like men. They were also called "androtones," or killers of males, as recorded by Herodotus. Where they first resided is unclear. However, there is evidence that they developed a culture in Pontus, here in Turkey. We believe that Themyscira was their capital, and that they built ancient Ephesus when it was a coastal harbor; one of the very best harbors in Asia Minor."

"Why do they cut off their breast?"

"The name Amazon is derived from the Greek word *amazoi* which means 'breast-less.' They removed their daughter's right breast so that it would not hinder the drawing of their bows. The bow and arrow were their primary weapons, and they were particularly good archers, on foot or on horseback. They were masters of the horse and fielded the first cavalry on earth. During the Bronze Age they occupied Libya, and may have even had colonies in Egypt. Amazons worshiped Artemis, and continue to do so, and refuse to enter into traditional relationships, like marriage or even long-term relationships with men."

Rutheford took advantage of Jay's pause, and went on with the recitation, "Yes, this is a very real group of survivors who are taught their history well. They take great pride in the fact that with Penthesilea, they marched to Troy to aid King Priam. During the Trojan battle, their queen was mortally wounded by Achilles, the greatest of all warriors, who fell in love with her great beauty as she lay dying."

"Let's examine the greatest tales of antiquity. Hercules' ninth labor required that he travel to the land of the Amazons and capture the Girdle of Hippolyte, which had been given to the Amazons by Ares, the god of war. The girdle was a sword belt, the finest ever fashioned for any warrior. He captured the girdle, but Hercules had to kill Queen Hippolyta. Theseus, Hero of Athens, then abducted the dead queen's sister, Antiope, and took her back to Athens. The Amazons marched on Athens, and their greatness in battle and defeat, are reflected in Greek art and the marble carvings from the Parthenon. Even today, that particular form of marble sculpture is known as Amazonomachy."

Jay paused and Ruff picked up the story. "Historically, they held men in such contempt that after getting pregnant with the man of their choosing, it was said that they would either kill him or banish him from their society. If the child they bore was a boy, paternal societies preached that they would kill the child, cripple it, or even blind it, and it would become a slave. However, those tales regarding their treatment of male children were greatly exaggerated. Enemies such as Genghis Khan promulgated such tales to whip warriors into a frenzy before joining battle with the Amazons."

Rutheford Ruffescott paused, then continued.

"More probable, is the theory that the Amazons wished to continue their matriarchal society, but as a practical matter, they needed to fight alongside certain patriarchal societies such as Sparta. They did manage to hold out, but today are few in number. Such a society would, over time, become stagnated by limited population growth, and their numbers dwindled."

"And Ephesus is their holy ground, where the Temple of Artemis was built, and where they pilgrimage to worship," Scott added.

"Yes," Ruff agreed. "They come here to worship the ancient Artemis, the chaste protector of wild things, the hunter with bow. She was the Greek and Roman local rival to the Virgin Mary. Both women were chaste, immortal, but fundamentally different in every other respect."

"The statues here depicting Artemis are of a woman who seems more preoccupied with representing food abundance, and does not look like a warrior," Scott remarked.

"Good observation!" Jay exclaimed. "They are not one and the same. The Diane, or Artemis of the Ephesians, whose sculptures are here, is a separate deity, or a later transformation as male dominance grew. The wildness was taken out of representations of Artemis, and replaced by a more tranquil, harvest deity. This is not the Artemis of the Amazons... this is the fertile goddess, the mother goddess of abundance, known as Artemis Polymastros."

Scott looked into Ruff's eyes and nodded. "You know, I remember at the initiation there was a statue like the mother goddess, with multiple breasts or something, and also one of Artemis with a bow and quiver of arrows."

"Yes, the assimilation and worship of the separate deities was common in ancient times and is, apparently, still being practiced," Ruff answered. "Scott, I believe that you have witnessed what no other man has seen for centuries."

Jay leaned forward, addressing Scott in a quiet voice, "We are arguably at the modern world's flash point in the ageless struggle between the sexes, and what we are witnessing is the latest chapter in the great struggle. We believe that a container lies somewhere at Ephesus, and that it contains priceless relics: words we see in the Bible, and the bones of the Blessed Virgin Mary hidden by the cult of the Virgin Mary. Then there is the original statue of Artemis sought by the cult of Artemis. A statue that survived the seven destructions of the Temple of Artemis."

"A statue that fell from Mount Jupiter, or heaven, as set forth in the Bible at Acts 19:35, where it is says, 'Men of Ephesus, doesn't all the world know that the city of Ephesus is the guardian of the temple of the great Artemis and of her image, which fell from heaven?' These relics would be priceless to their faiths, and worth their dying for..."

"Or to any robber, or to any serious collector of antiquities," Rutheford added.

"Unfortunately, yes. They would be three of the most priceless treasures ever found, and they are being relentlessly sought by a number of people who set out on their quests because of Professor Meister's discovery," Jay Young-quest mused.

Scott Frank sighed, "And those people are the cult of Artemis, and the Church of Rome. Who else?"

"Yes, Artemis worshipers, the Church, organized international antiquity thieves, and by now, certainly the Turkish government, and maybe even legitimate artifact seekers like us," Ruff winked.

A thought popped into Scott's mind. "By the way, what was that piece that I had carbon-dated in Phoenix?"

"That was a portion of the cloth that was found by Ruff that was fastened to the inside of the back cover of the Weber journal," Jay replied.

"Thank you for having it carbon-dated," Ruff said. "I knew it was from the time of Christ, and that verification of the date lends credibility to our claims about what we are seeking."

"What was it originally from?" Scott asked.

"It was from a large cloth used to cover the jar or vase. Herr Weber cut a piece from the cloth that wrapped the vase and hid it in his journal. We cut off a small piece to have analyzed but ran out of time, due to circumstances. We left it to you to have it carbon-dated and its age confirmed."

"It is the lidded jar described in the octagonal journal which first sparked our imagination. The writer, Herbert Weber, assumed that it was from the time of Christ, or perhaps just before," Jay responded. "He was clever to realize that part of the cloth covering might be removed without arousing suspicion. It is a most sacred relic in its own right."

"Yes, and your dating, well it may prove essential to demonstrate to the Turkish authorities that an excavation is required, and soon," Ruff added. "Otherwise robbers might find the site and illegally remove the artifacts."

"Will my services continue to be needed?" Scott asked, half-smiling.

Rutheford Ruffescott ignored the question. Removing his pocket watch, he opened its cover and nodded toward Scott. "How do you feel?" he asked.

Scott stood up, and was pleased to find that his strength and coordination had apparently returned.

"I'm feeling fine."

"Well then, here is the situation," Ruff said. "Jay has been accused of murdering a man in Vienna. Actually, the alleged victim was attempting to kidnap Jay in order to coerce information about what we are seeking here in Ephesus. The chief of police in Salzburg, who is conducting the investigation, and two of his finest, are here with Professor Meister, who carries with him valuable clues concerning our quest. Others, most fortunately, do not know what he has brought to Ephesus, so we have the upper hand at least temporarily. In addition, the cult of Artemis is now searching for you two."

"Who is on our side?" Scott asked.

"The local police are being of some value through the efforts of the Austrian Archeological Societies' chief archaeologist who resides here. We also have an associate who is trying to arrange a meeting with the key actors so that our position is understood, and a possible agreement can be made. However, we need today to work on that possible agreement. It is critical in all of this that you are not found out. Can you remain here in this room until tomorrow?"

"Absolutely."

"Good. We will bring up some food for you. Do not leave the room under any circumstances, and don't answer the door. Don't even call the front desk."

"You have my word."

# CHAPTER TWENTY-THREE

## AUGUST 14, 1980

On Thursday, August fourteenth, Chief Honaker picked up Dr. Meister at the professor's home and drove to the airport. They flew to Munich, and then on to Izmir, where the Chief had a rental car waiting. They drove to Selçuk and arrived at their hotel an hour later than planned, but in plenty of time to relax before a late dinner in town. The town was bustling with vacationers.

When they arrived back at their hotel, two men stood up from their chairs in the lobby and approached Chief Honaker.

"These are my men, here to assist me in my investigation," the chief announced to Dr. Meister, who was introduced to Hans and Karl. Neither of them spoke nor offered to shake hands. They simply nodded in acknowledgment and looked at Honaker, who had moved a short distance away from the professor and motioned the two men over. He whispered something to them, and both men departed, without reply or good-bye, to either their boss or the professor.

Dr. Meister had not disclosed any information concerning the partial jar and its cobra lid to Chief Honaker, nor did he intend to. He resented that he had come under scrutiny. During the flights, and even at the airports, they had exchanged few words. The tone of their relationship had turned even more distant by the time they reached their hotel. The professor was concentrating on how he was going to use the information he carried in his pocket. And Chief Honaker was off on his private thoughts. He seemed far removed, as though preparing for something.

Dr. Meister went to his room and called Dr. David Freiberg's local residence near Ephesus. As the senior archaeologist in charge of the excavations for the summer, Freiberg was the man with whom Dr. Meister intended to discuss certain theories, while not divulging his mission until the time was right.

"Hello, my friend!" Freiberg said. "I have been awaiting your call. I know where you are staying, and I want you to pack your things and stay with me, in your old room here."

Dr. Meister had not intended to impose on his associate, and so had not requested a room at the institute's residence. Now however, he wanted to get away from Chief Honaker.

"I'm packing as we speak," he replied happily. "I'll await your driver."

"He will be there within the hour," Freiberg said. Then added in a more cautious voice, "But do not check out. When you hear a car's horn honk twice, go out the back door. It's a white Mercedes. Also, leave the phone off the hook."

Professor Meister smiled. "Understood," he replied.

An hour later his phone rang again, and the hotel's desk clerk asked if the room was acceptable. He said that he loved it, and then laid the phone down on the table.

Five minutes later, a horn honked twice. Quickly he exited the hotel through a rear door, and placed his bags into the open trunk of a white Mercedes. The rear door was opened, and he climbed in and closed the door as the car accelerated rapidly. He turned to look at the passenger beside him and stared into the face of Rutheford Ruffescott.

"Good evening, Dr. Meister," Ruff said. "I am delighted to see you, again!"

"Well, well," the professor said in reply. "I am most surprised to see you this evening, Rutheford. Are you staying at the residence?"

"No. But Dr. Freiberg and I are collaborating on a project that you carry the keys to, I believe."

The professor noted that Ruffescott was smiling in a most non-threatening manner. Nonetheless, he chose not to respond.

"In fact, Doctor," Ruff added, "you are now the most valuable archaeologist in the world, I do believe!"

The professor glanced into the car's rearview mirror to see if the driver was listening to their conversation. What he saw there made him pause. It was the reflection of Jay Youngquest, who briefly shifted his gaze from the road.

"Good evening, Dr. Meister. I hope you had a pleasant flight from Austria."

"Oh, my God!" the professor exclaimed with a laugh. "Who's next? My dog Artifact, who died twenty years ago?"

"Artifact? Yes, we hope so," Jay said. "But we can't resurrect that particular one, at least not now."

Meister sighed. "I'm afraid I have bad news for you, Jay. The chief of police of Salzburg, and two of his most solemn subordinates, are in town to have you arrested for murdering some thug in Vienna, and depositing the body into a sarcophagus in Salzburg--the very body that dripped blood onto my old journals!"

"I have heard those unfounded rumors," Jay responded. "I look forward to setting the record straight."

"I hope you do," Professor Meister replied.

Ruff gave the professor a sober look. "Dr. Meister," he said slowly, "we need your help to clear Jay, and you need our help to find what you are seeking. We know what you have on you and how you traced it. We are prepared to assist you, but what will occur may, in the end, not be to your liking. However, the outcome will be fair and justice will prevail--or so I hope."

Professor Meister suddenly felt very tired. He was in no position to argue. Strangely, he didn't feel threatened by either of these men.

"What do you need me to do?" he asked.

"You'll soon find out," Ruff assured him.

As soon as the Mercedes was parked next to the institute's residence, Professor Freiberg hurried out to greet them. Jay remained behind the steering wheel, and Rutheford Ruffescott carried the professor's bags onto the porch.

"Jay and I cannot linger here, even for a social drink," Ruff told the two professors. "I'm sure you understand. We can't trust a certain individual from Salzburg, and we must make arrangements for tomorrow night. Or maybe the next night if our negotiations move slowly. However, we thank you both for your participation, and we strongly advise you to say nothing about our activities."

"Good night then," Dr. Freiberg said calmly.

"Yes, good night," Professor Meister encored. "Watch out for the dogs. They are out tonight!" he warned, as he stepped into familiar settings.

Professor Meister smiled when he saw that his brandy had already been poured over ice, and was waiting on the coffee table near his favorite Turkish chair.

Back at the hotel, the light on the telephone in Chief Honaker's room was flashing red when he returned to his room after meeting with his two associates. The chief of police of Salzburg had been disappointed at the report delivered to him that evening. Not only were the local police completely ignoring his requests for assistance in locating the Americans, but the professor no longer seemed pleased to be around his former student.

The chief called the front desk. "Do you have a message for Chief Honaker?" he asked.

"Yes, sir. Mr. Jay Youngquest left a message for you. His message is that he would like to talk to you, and that he is sorry that you were not in earlier. He will call again tomorrow."

"What time tomorrow?" the chief snapped.

"He did not say, sir."

The chief hung up the phone in disgust. He'd be stuck in his room until the call came in. The operator probably forgot the time that Youngquest said he would call tomorrow. The American would have been specific on that point. "Damn it!" he whispered, pounding his fist on the desk next to the telephone. *Damn it!*

Honaker considered calling the professor, but thought it best to let the old man get his rest. He was surely asleep. In the morning, he would invite the professor to breakfast at the hotel. The chief realized that he had been consumed with his own plans and had been callous with the professor. He needed cooperation and he needed to make amends. The chief called his men, issued instructions, and then went to bed.

At eight the next morning, he called Professor Meister's room to invite him for breakfast. The phone was busy, so he waited for ten minutes and called again. It was still busy, so he called the operator and alerted her that he wanted any calls to him forwarded to the dining room. She agreed to his request and the chief went down to breakfast. *The professor may have taken the phone off of the hook so as not to be disturbed*, he thought. His men were to report back at nine, so he had an hour. He picked up a newspaper, sat down, and ordered his meal.

At nine o'clock the chief returned to his room where he found his two associates waiting for him in the hallway. Their meeting lasted nearly an hour. The two men reported no headway on finding the whereabouts of either Jay Youngquest or Rutheford Ruffescott. This despite their contacting in person, or by phone, every hotel, motel, and rental home in the Ephesus area. Chief Honaker instructed his men to call him every two hours. The expected call from Mr. Youngquest could well be their link to locating the American's whereabouts.

After his men departed, the chief proceeded to re-verify arrangements for their eventual departure from Turkey. Then he called Dr. Meister's room, but the line was still busy.

The chief decided to pay a visit to the professor. He went to his room one floor up and knocked softly on the door. There was no response, nor did he hear any activity inside. When he noted the "Do Not Disturb" sign on the doorknob, he returned to his room.

*Let the old man sleep,* he thought.

An hour later, the professor's telephone was still busy. The police instinct in Honaker clicked into gear and he called the front desk to ask if Dr. Meister's telephone was working. Yes, he was informed, but there was no one talking on the phone. The receiver was off its stand. Honaker hung up, went to the archaeologist's door, and knocked on it. He noted that the handle sign requesting privacy had been removed, but no one answered the door. Had he gone out? Seeing the floor maid at the end of the hall, he walked to her and asked if she had made up Meister's room.

"Yes," she replied. "I opened the door to ask about cleaning up the room and found that it was empty. I think he may have checked out."

"What makes you think that?" he asked.

"There was nothing in the room except the hotel's property," she responded.

The chief walked hurriedly to the front desk.

"Did Mr. Meister check out?" he demanded of the clerk.

"No, sir. Dr. Meister is still a registered guest."

An angry and frustrated chief of police returned to his room, slammed the door shut, and dialed the local police. He would report the professor missing and implicate the Americans in order to receive local police assistance. When the telephone in the Selçuk Police Department was answered, the chief thought better of his hasty decision and hung up the telephone. He had come with a good plan, his window of opportunity was still open, and he had no reason to panic. Perhaps the professor was now with the Americans. If so, that could work to his advantage. Patience was a virtue in police work, he reminded himself. Jay Youngquest would call, as promised.

The rapping on Chief Honaker's door was gentle, but firm. He admitted his man, Hans, who entered and then glanced around, verifying they were alone.

"We got a break," he said. "The museum here has an employee who I spoke to three days ago about Ruffescott and Youngquest. This morning, Ruffescott was looking at Egyptian artifacts and asked this employee if they had an advanced book on hieroglyphs. She told him no, they did not carry anything beyond some simple examples of Egyptian writings as they pertained to a specific exhibit."

"She remembered my telling her that I am working for the chief of police in Salzburg, Austria and so she asked him if he'd like to order one, hoping to get his name. Ruffescott told her that they'd have to rely upon his friend's memory about Egyptian hieroglyphs when they made findings, as they soon had to depart for home. She smartly introduced herself, and when they shook hands he said that his friends called him 'Ruff'."

"When are they planning to leave?"

"She didn't ask him that, but had the feeling that it would be within a day or two. She also said he acted very nervous and was constantly looking at people, as if to see if they were looking at him."

The chief looked out the window. "This Jay is searching for the artifacts with Rutheford, and I am beginning to suspect that Professor Meister knows far more about all this than he has told me. I wouldn't be surprised if they are together at this very moment, planning the excavation."

"Are the travel arrangements made for us?" Hans asked. "My partner wants out of here as soon as our business is finished."

"Yes. Everything that I promised you has been arranged. Now is as good a time as any to give you the vouchers and travel options. They were delivered to the hotel today."

He went to his briefcase, dialed in the combination, and pulled up the leather top. He retrieved two packets of documents, checked the names on the front of each, and then handed them to Hans.

"We are just a telephone call away from the beginning of the final stage of this task," he stated. "I have a strong feeling that everything will work out in our favor. Not having the local police involved may have been fortunate for us."

Hans looked through the documents in his packet, nodded in approval, and left the room to meet with Karl.

At five o'clock the telephone rang and Chief Honaker answered, "Yes?"

"Chief, I am glad to find you in. This is Jacob Youngquest and I understand that you need to speak with me."

"Yes, Mr. Youngquest, I do," the chief said. "Thank you for calling back. As you probably know, I am here to investigate a homicide that some people suspect you were involved in. You do have friends who insist that you could not possibly be involved in such a tragic event, so I decided to come here, with our friend Professor Meister, to locate you and hear your side of the story."

"I appreciate your openness," Jay responded, in as serious a voice as he could muster. "I have business to attend to here, after which I would be pleased to accompany you back to Austria."

"I am relieved to hear you say that," the chief responded. "I have extradition papers from the Turkish court, and if you agree to return voluntarily, perhaps I can give you some time to complete your business here," he added, wishing that in fact, he had such an extradition order.

"I am in your service!" Jay responded. "Just give me a day or two, and you have my word that I will come to your hotel and we can return together. Do you need to handcuff me for the flight back?"

"Not if you come voluntarily. Two police officers have accompanied me here and the last thing we want is to make a scene. If you cooperate with us, our trip back to Austria will be a comfortable one. We just want to obtain the information necessary to arrest whomever committed the crime."

"You are a reasonable man, Chief," Jay said. "I am sure we can wrap this matter up quickly. I will be back in touch shortly."

"Where are you staying?"

"I am in Kuşadasi, but I have checked out of the hotel. I will call or leave a message tomorrow." He then hung up.

Chief Honaker sighed. Things were going well all of a sudden. He called the rooms of his two associates, but they were both out. So he decided to stretch his legs and contemplate his next move. As he entered the hotel lobby, he saw one of his men, Karl, coming in the front doorway. He had an excited look about him and the chief motioned him into the hotel's bar.

"I found Professor Meister, Chief," Karl said. "He is staying at a home leased by the University of Vienna for the use of archaeologists. Hans is there now, watching the house. The professor is a fool. He must know that you are searching for him, and yet sits outside on the porch. He looks rather frail, and there is a truck on the premises that's got shovels in it."

"Hans is watching the house?"

"Yes. He'll follow him if he leaves and call your room with any new information."

"Shovels. Tonight may be the big event. This is all coming together. You have done well, Karl. The bonus may be larger than promised."

"I have the key to Hans' room. He wants his things brought to where he is at the moment. I am inclined to get my belongings, also."

"Don't check out," the chief warned. "I will pack my bags. We will both join him. I think something is planned for either tonight or tomorrow morning."

Both men returned to their rooms and packed. They were traveling light.

Within fifteen minutes, both had departed the hotel with the bags from their three rooms. Chief Honaker got into the passenger seat of a rental car, and Karl drove them to a location well behind their second rental car that the chief noted was occupied by Hans. The truck that Karl had described was parked in the driveway of a home, which was hopefully occupied by the professor.

Hans acknowledged the arrival of the second car by a quick wave of his hand through the driver's window. Honaker took a small pair of binoculars from his bag and peered toward the house. There was no movement that he could detect. When Hans next looked back, the chief motioned for him to come back to his car. Hans exited his vehicle, slowly walked back to the chief's car, and slipped into the backseat.

"I last saw Meister about half an hour ago," Hans reported. "He was standing by the window, with his back to it, and I think he was on the phone."

"Something is up," the chief said. "Hans, is there a back entrance to the house? I don't want him slipping off again."

"Yes, sir. But the backyard is fenced, and we can see the only gate from here. Hans paused and pointed toward a wooden gate. "And in his apparent condition, he's not able to walk far, so I doubt he would leave the house on foot."

"Shovels," the chief reflected out loud. "A telephone call. A truck ready to go. I'm hopeful we will score our goal very soon. I want to review our plan for when Meister leaves. We will have alternative courses of action, depending on whether or not he travels alone, and whether or not Jay Youngquest is with him. Also, if something unfolds tonight, I suspect that the two Americans, and our esteemed professor, are hoping to make a significant discovery, in secret. Otherwise, why wouldn't they go to the site during the day and have the Austrian excavation team bring shovels? They are up to something. It will all work to our advantage!"

An hour later, Chief Honaker watched a car slowing as it approached the house. It was driven into the driveway and parked alongside the pickup truck. Two men got out of the vehicle and went into the house. The three observers recognized Jay Youngquest from photographs the chief had obtained. Now, if the three known occupants of the house left in the truck together, Plan B would be implemented.

The chief was not to be disappointed. Professor Meister soon emerged from the home, followed by Jay, and a man that matched the description of Rutheford Ruffescott. He even carried the combination walking stick/stool for which he was known. The professor locked the front door, suggesting that no one remained inside. The three men walked to the truck and Youngquest slid into the driver's seat. The truck exited the driveway, turned away from them, and proceeded down the hill. Both rental cars followed the truck at a discreet distance.

Jay drove the truck to an empty parking lot adjacent to the Ephesus site, which was now closed. Signs indicated that the site had closed early due to maintenance. The last workers were departing in a van.

The first car, with Hans driving, pulled up directly behind the truck. The second car parked adjacent to the truck driver's door. Chief Honaker and his two officers got out of their cars and approached the truck, with their right hands close to their concealed weapons.

Rutheford Ruffescott opened the truck's front passenger door slowly and got out, looking quite surprised. Dr. Meister then got out of the truck, followed a moment later by Jay Youngquest, who frowned at the three men as Professor Meister walked over to the chief.

"Let's not have any trouble here, Chief Honaker," he said boldly. "Jay has told you he will return to Austria with you. So leave us to our business here this evening. I need his expertise for at least a few hours."

Youngquest and Ruffescott were approached by the chief's two men. Karl patted each down for weapons, while Hans looked on from a short distance, with his right hand on the handle of his automatic pistol.

"My man will need to check you for weapons, Professor," Honaker stated.

The professor raised his arms away from his body and was patted down, to his obvious displeasure.

"I understand that you are here to look for something, and we will accompany you in your search. If what you seek is not found this evening, you may have to go forward without the assistance of Mr. Youngquest. However, Professor Meister, I want to give you an opportunity to find whatever it is you came all this way to find. Do you need your shovels?"

Just then, a young man approached them by foot from the roadway. One of the chief's men raised a hand and Scott Frank stopped.

"Do you want me to raise my hands?" Scott Frank asked hesitantly.

"This is my associate, from the United States," Ruff said matter-of-factly.

"Mr. Scott Frank is a recent law school graduate."

"What is he doing here?" the chief demanded.

"He wasn't feeling well in the car, so we brought him here first, to rest," Ruff offered.

Honaker looked at Scott, who appeared to be tired and somewhat out of sorts. The chief motioned Karl over to frisk him. Karl found no weapon. The three Americans and Professor Meister were of no apparent threat. The ancient city appeared to be deserted, and the chief decided to question their purpose in being there. Honaker's gaze took in the three Americans and the Austrian.

"I understand that you are here to search for some ancient objects of great value, and that Mr. Youngquest has some special knowledge of Egyptian writings that may assist you, Dr. Meister."

"Yes," came the flat response from the archaeologist.

"As I said, I am here to take Mr. Youngquest back to Salzburg, and I have extradition papers and airline reservations for tomorrow's departure," he lied. "Having said that, I don't want to sabotage your plans for this evening. My men and I will accompany the four of you to find what you are looking for, and then we must take Mr. Youngquest with us. Are you ready to proceed?"

Rutheford frowned. Jay and Scott stared blankly at the policemen.

Finally Dr. Meister said, "That plan is more than considerate, Chief Honaker. I do not want to lose the opportunity to consult with Jay during the search as I have reason to believe that hieroglyphs may be involved. He is an expert in that ancient form of writing. But, I am a bit taken aback by the time restraints that you are imposing on us, and I therefore suggest that we proceed to the site and see where the clues lead us before you make a decision concerning Mr. Youngquest."

When the chief of police did not respond, Professor Meister proceeded into the ancient city of Ephesus. He reached into his pocket and retrieved a hard-shelled pocket case, which contained the impressions from the cobra lid. Opening the case, he removed the paper.

"I think we will need the shovels from the truck," he called back over his shoulder.

At a signal from the chief, Hans procured two shovels from the back of the truck, and the group of seven proceeded along the marble pathway.

# CHAPTER TWENTY-FOUR

## AUGUST 15, 1980

Father Antonio Gianti, Jesuit Priest recently assigned to the Missions and Marian Authority section of the Vatican, under the supervision of Father Jerino Martelli, came out from under the influence of the drug very slowly. He couldn't remember where he was, or how he got there, but was aware of the fact that he was in a bed, under a sheet, with all of his clothing on, except for his shoes. He was also aware that he was not alone in the room. Shadows were cast on the wall next to his bed, a twin bed. Shadows of people moving slowly. And there was snoring. Loud snoring coming from his left as he lay face up. He assumed that it was the snoring of Father Joseph Baronio, who had a reputation for snoring loudly whenever he was unusually tired. *He must be very, very tired*, Anthony thought. Then he opened his eyes and looked into the concerned face of a woman nurse, or maybe physician, who shined a small flashlight into each eye, and suddenly looked relieved. She stood up straight, and nodded toward the other side of the room, before turning her back and bending over the bed that he could now hazily see next to his.

"Father? Father?" she said. "Can you open your eyes for me?"

Something that could have been interpreted as a "No" seemed to be the response. *It really doesn't sound like Joseph at all*, Anthony thought, as he drifted off into sleep again.

Father Joseph Baronio emerged from his drug-induced state feeling extremely itchy. His entire body itched. He tried scratching to no avail. His arms and hands would not obey his orders. He opened his eyes and a woman was looking down at him, a stethoscope dangling from around her neck.

"Feeling better?" she asked.

"Yes."

"Good. I am going to help you sit up. If you can't hold your position you can lay back down again and get more rest."

With assistance, Joseph was able to sit up, and although he wouldn't want to try standing, he indicated by holding up a hand that he wanted to remain up. He looked at the bed next to his, and saw that Anthony was sitting up and smiling at him with a blank stare, as though he was pleased but did not know why. An hour later, they were both able to turn sideways and place their feet on the floor of a very pleasant bedroom. Another hour passed, with the milestone that each could stand up, walk around the room, and then sit back down again. They were instructed what to do by the woman, as two muscular and very serious looking females stood by the door, watching them intently. Neither man focused on anything other than driving out the drug through movement and circulation.

Both however, were planning to somehow break out of the room, to be free of their captors. Their unspoken plan was reaffirmed every time the two Jesuits glanced into each other's eyes. Finally, just as Anthony Gianti was about to grab their attendant and begin their escape, an additional woman came into the room carrying black priestly attire, and clerical collars.

"Please, get dressed," she seemed to almost plead. "And wear the collars. I will explain what you must do after you are dressed. Also, the drug is not fully dissipated and won't be for some time. If you try to escape, or physically confront us, it will go poorly for you I'm afraid. Don't force us to place you under the drug again, or force us to bind and gag you. Simply comply with our commands, which you will find to be reasonable. Do you understand?"

Before either man could respond, she said, "Good." Then she handed them the clothing and indicated they should change clothes immediately, and in the presence of their captors.

They complied, finding that the clothing was the appropriate size, and that the collars felt good around their necks. Each felt somehow protected by the garb that they now wore, symbolic of the Society of Jesus to which they had pledged their lives. They each hoped that their service would be allowed to continue on Earth.

# CHAPTER TWENTY-FIVE

## AUGUST 15, 1980

As Professor Meister walked slowly into the ancient city, he studied the impressions he had taken from the inside of the jar's lid. Once again, he was surprised at the directness and simplicity of the Latin directions.

He looked up, shaking his head.

"The key, my translation indicates, is buried at the sunrise corner of a mausoleum, originally built as the replica of a lighthouse. It is an octagonal structure, and surely an Egyptian burial place. Further, I know where the most prominent of such structures is, or at least was. It was built before the coming of Jesus Christ, and is located directly across from the Scholastikia Baths."

"A key?" Chief Honaker inquired. "A key to what?"

Without responding, the professor began to walk down the ancient Curetes Street, passing beneath Hercules Gate. Professor Meister strode to where the Octagon, now in Vienna, had once stood. They gathered at where he indicated was the eastern corner, and stared at the ground, seemingly expecting that a key would mysteriously appear.

"This is why we brought shovels," Professor Meister said matter-of-factly.

Chief Honaker nodded at Hans, and he and Scott stepped forward and began shoveling dirt away from the location indicated by the professor. They were down about two feet, just off of the original Octagon's corner, when the blade of Scott's shovel struck something hard. As they dug around it, the top of a marble column, approximately six inches square, was revealed. After another round of slow, careful digging, the dirt was cleared away, down to a depth of nearly two additional feet. Scott signaled to Hans to stop digging, and laying aside his shovel, grasped the top of the column and gently moved it forward and back, right and left. It moved slightly, and they resumed digging until so much soil had been removed that the column began to sway.

"Let me try again," Scott said, and he dropped to his knees and rocked the column until it appeared ready to be pulled out like a loosened stake.

"Professor, should I just pull it out?" he asked.

"Yes," Dr. Meister replied, "I believe that will be fine."

Grasping it firmly, and with some additional rocking and considerable lifting, now with the help of Chief Honaker, Scott withdrew the marble column slowly. He stood it on the ground, next to the hole. It was approximately one yard in length, made of black polished marble, and it appeared to Scott to be slightly tapered toward the bottom, which came to three separate points, placed irregularly, and of different lengths.

"Where is the key?" the chief of police asked. "Inside, somehow?"

"Oh, no, no. This entire column *is* the key," the professor responded, with excitement in his voice. "This is what we need to open the chamber, and to raise up its treasure. First, however, we must look for an inscription as to where we insert this ancient key."

After brushing away most of the dirt on the marble key with his hand, the professor withdrew a handkerchief from his pocket and carefully wiped the sides of the key. Near the center on one side he found what he was seeking.

"Look here!" he exclaimed. "Egyptian hieroglyphs and Latin script. If I am reading them correctly, they indicate that we are to proceed first down Curetes Street, and then left to the end of Marble Road. Jay, do you concur?"

Jay Youngquest studied the markings. "Yes," he said slowly. "Apparently, the treasure is hidden in the theater!"

With surprising speed the professor set off, with Scott Frank beside him, carrying the heavy marble piece. Hans came up to help Scott. In short order, they had the obelisk positioned so that they could walk swiftly, but they had to work in order to keep up with Dr. Meister.

As he walked along, Scott Frank noted to himself that Rutheford Ruffescott and Jay Youngquest had been very quiet during the excursion in the ruins.

The seven men entered the ancient theater, located on the slopes of Mount Koresson, and followed Dr. Meister into the semi-circular orchestral area. For centuries masked actors had performed here before audiences numbering twenty-five thousand. Spectators had sat, and stood, in the wide bowl-shaped cavea, looking down onto the orchestra from the hillside.

Scott and Hans gently stood the marble piece on one of the many large, square marble slabs that covered the floor of the orchestra pit.

"And now, Herr Professor, what do we do with this big marble key?" the chief asked.

"We find the keyhole," Meister replied. "It is a marble-lined vertical shaft into which we drop the key. The keyhole lies beneath a marble slab, like the ones we are standing on!"

They all contemplated the many large tiles that covered the thirty-four-meter orchestra area. Their eyes then returned to Dr. Meister, who stepped to the center and scrutinized the tiles.

"Obviously," he said, more to himself that anyone else, "the resurrection of the vessel, or marble box, or whatever is down there, would require some space, or distance around, to allow the workings of the mechanism. Such devices helped build the pyramids, raise giant monuments, and close massive doors to safeguard the pharaohs as they embarked on their journey to the afterlife. I believe we are looking for an original marble slab, which would have been green in color and positioned near the center of this amphitheater."

Meister beckoned Ruffescott over. "Ruff," he said, "I see that you carry that unusual walking stick of yours that folds into a seat. Perhaps you could tap these center slabs and see if any of them sound particularly solid."

Rutheford Ruffescott nodded his understanding and stepped to the center of the orchestra pit. He soundly struck first one slab, then another, as he moved toward where his calculation suggested the center was located. At what seemed to be the center-most slab, which was green in color, his walking stick struck a tone that sounded different from the others. It just sounded denser. He walked around that slab, striking those adjacent to it. Each emitted a higher pitched sound when struck. He returned to the center piece, and struck it three times. No doubt about it: it was comprised of thicker marble.

Scott placed the blade of a shovel under the corner of the slab and pried at it, without success. Hans took the second shovel and they pried at the same corner until the slab began to rise, ever so slightly. They worked the opposite side, and within a few minutes, the heavy slab was loosened, but obviously too heavy to be pried out with just two shovels. Jay looked around the area and spotted a worker's chest near a stairway. He opened it and removed a long tool.

"Let me try this," Jay said, as he stepped forward with the long pry bar he had found. He slammed the pry bar into the ground close to one side of the slab and pulled back. The slab raised up and the shovels were thrust into the gap. After a series of lifts, and the use of rubble and other wedge material, the slab's base was finally above the surface of the ground. Within a few minutes, with assistance from everyone present, the slab was raised further, and pipes from a scaffold were positioned under it. The slab was then rolled to the side of the pit.

The men grouped together and peered down into the hole over which the slab had rested for centuries. Jay took a shovel and carefully scraped away a layer of crumbled clay that may once have been a solid piece. His efforts exposed a square marble plug, that was about ten inches across, and had a bronze handle recessed into its center. He used his hand to brush off the dirt from around the plug, and then blew away the remaining dust. He glanced up at the professor, who was examining the obelisk and frowning.

"Pull out that stopper," Chief Honaker commanded, as he picked up the marble key and moved toward the keyhole.

"Stop!" the professor countered. "If you are hasty, all will be lost. The key is square at the top, but as you can see, it has a number of characteristics toward the bottom where the three prongs are located. The key is dropped into the opening and falls to a chamber, many meters below, where each prong must strike its intended target. If they strike correctly they will break special containers. The containers then release sand and start a chain reaction that will expose the treasure we seek. However, if the key is dropped incorrectly, it will jam before it reaches the bottom. That may lead to the sealing of the lower chambers, and perhaps even the destruction of the artifacts. The treasure could be lost forever."

"How do we know which side faces which direction?" Ruff pondered out loud.

Professor Meister walked over to a stone bench and sat down. He placed his elbows on his knees and his chin in the cups of his hands, and stared at the marble drop key.

"What do you think, Jay?" he asked after a couple minutes.

Jay Youngquest got down on his knees, and carefully inspected the top and sides of the marble key.

"Look at this," he said slowly. "On the side next to the inscription. It's a hieroglyph of a falcon. An Egyptian hieroglyph representing the sun god, Ra. My guess is, that this side must face the direction of a rising sun, or east."

There were several more moments of silence before the professor stood, stretched, and sighed in exaggerated fashion.

"We are done here, for today," he stated. "Let's put the slab back in the ground, and make the area appear as if we had never been here. I need to do further research. I want to consult experts on the workings of such keys. Perhaps the area should be the subject of a careful excavation. We don't want any artifacts damaged or destroyed."

"Professor, we cannot wait," Chief Honaker retorted. "I am willing to take a chance that you are correct. We must act now!"

Scott Frank noted that only he and Professor Meister appeared to be surprised at the chief's outburst. The chief walked toward the key as Dr. Meister moved to block his way.

"You can't be serious? I forbid it!" he shouted. "We cannot risk loss or damage to this obelisk. That would be irresponsible to the extreme, even if we did manage to somehow succeed!"

The chief thrust out his right arm to push the professor aside, just as Scott and Jay sprang toward the two men. Honaker quickly backed off a few paces and drew a 9mm semi-automatic pistol from its holster. Simultaneously, his two men drew pistols and pointed them at Scott, Jay, and Ruff.

"I am sorry, gentlemen," Honaker said in a hostile voice, "but I am exercising my authority to recover these antiquities, to safeguard them, and to ensure that they are not trifled with by you or anyone else."

The professor's jaw dropped. "I can't believe this, Chief. Surely you are joking? You can't possibly have any jurisdiction here! You would jeopardize everything that we have worked to preserve if you act as rashly as you sound!"

Ruffescott had a different interpretation. "Perhaps, Chief, you have received an advance payment on some promise to deliver the artifacts to an unscrupulous collector? Otherwise you would not be so irrational."

The chief snorted in response.

"Don't pretend that you have no secret desire for these objects, or that you have not made inquiries as to who might be willing to pay for them. I know your reputation. During the war you served in the Arts, Monuments, and Archives section of the American Military Government in Berlin. I know that you almost got the golden Trojan treasure out of Berlin before the Russians shipped it to Moscow in 1945, the one that Heinrich Schliemann excavated from Turkey in the late 1800s. I understand that they emptied the underground bunkers that were filled with King Priam's Trojan gold just one day before you and the American army got to the bunkers where Hitler had the priceless objects hidden in 1941."

Jay nodded. "You see, Professor Meister," he said matter-of-factly, "your former student here did take up an active profession in archaeology and antiquities. Years ago, when he was a detective investigating a possible insurance fraud case, Officer Honaker found out that the owner of a museum was making a false claim for stolen artworks that she had hidden away. She sought to collect millions of deutche Marks from insurance coverage, but died unexpectedly of a heart attack. Prior to her death, she allegedly confessed to your former student, Chief Honaker, where the stolen art was located."

"Well, the temptation proved to be too great. The chief never reported that he had found the art works, the estate received the insurance money, and the paintings surfaced years later, when an unsuspecting owner tried to sell them at auction. Your former student learned from the dying woman who she was going to sell the paintings to. Two or so years later, he sold them to those underworld figures. Thereupon, an alliance was formed between an international black market organization, and a young police official who would later become a police chief, and someone in a perfect position to assist them, in many devious ways."

The professor's eyes bore into those of Honaker. "This cannot be true?" he said softly.

"It is the way things worked out for me!" Chief Honaker barked. "This is my final act before retiring to a new life that I have been planning for many years. So do not attempt to stop me, as I have no reason now to care if others are killed."

"Others?" the professor could not help blurting out.

"The man who died trying to kidnap me in Vienna was one of his men," Jay stated as a matter-of-fact. "I am afraid that it is the chief who was responsible for getting blood on your journals, Professor."

A dark cloud crossed Meister's face. "You put that man in the sarcophagus in Salzburg, to make Jay a murder suspect?"

"It gave me official reason to pursue these antiquities. And it would have gone according to plan, if not for your meddling American friends. If you cooperate with us now, we will have no reason to harm you. If you refuse, you will regret it."

He waved his gun toward a row of benches. "Now, if you four will please sit together on those benches, we can get down to business."

"Shoot them if they move," he commanded his lieutenants. "And make sure the silencers are secured to your weapons."

"Be careful, Dr. Meister," Jay told the professor. "These two men are not police officers. They are robbers employed by the chief to do his bidding."

Chief Honaker stepped to the keyhole, grasped the plug's handle firmly with both hands, and pulled hard. Surprisingly, the plug withdrew easily, nearly causing the chief to fall over backward, and causing him to bite his lower lip. Blood appeared at his mouth and he wiped it away with the back of his hand. The police chief of Salzburg looked crazed as he stared at the blood, and then looked at his stone-faced accomplices who were covering the others with their pistols. He went to the marble key and carried it to the square hole.

Having already determined which direction was east, he rested the marble key next to the opening, before locating the side with the sign of the falcon. That side, he turned toward the eastern horizon. It was very late in the evening, and light was fleeing fast. A drop of blood from his lip splattered onto the top of the obelisk as he placed it over the keyhole.

"Wait, stop! It is facing the wrong direction!" Jay cried out, as Honaker allowed the key to begin slipping through his hands. "You'll destroy everything!"

"I don't believe you," he hissed.

"The falcon does not represent Ra," Jay protested. "It is a depiction of Horus, and shows the left eye of Horus. Look at the eye! It is shaped as a circle depicting the white eye. It is the eye of the moon, the lunar eye, and is a device to thwart robbers!"

"Horace the protector!" the professor shouted in support.

Jay quickly added, "The eye on the other side of its head, unseen to us, is the eye representing the sun; the solar eye. That eye must face east!"

"My God, he is right!" the professor shouted out. "Look at the eye. The key must be turned! Pull back the key," he begged. "Please, it must be turned!"

Chief Honaker studied the hieroglyph for a moment, and then spun the key around and dropped it into the shaft. Professor Meister and Scott Frank gasped. They heard the sound of marble sliding against marble, and then silence. They held their breath, listening for... what?

"You lied to me!" the chief angrily accused Professor Meister, when silence was met with more silence. "What happens now?"

The professor did not appear to be listening. He was looking beyond Honaker, his eyes sweeping the orchestra area.

"Sand apparatuses take time to work," Ruff responded for him. "In some cases they can take hours before anything happens. You must be patient. Your actions were not well thought out. I am afraid you may have confessed being a criminal for nothing, Chief Honaker."

The chief gave Ruff a fierce glare.

Suddenly, the ground began to tremble. Stones and bricks began to move. The earth seemed to buckle as four holes gaped open in the orchestra pit's floor. As if of one mind, the men scrambled up into the lower seats of the theater, the hired gunmen keeping their pistols aimed at the three Americans and Austrian. A fifth hole then suddenly appeared around the keyhole. In a matter of seconds, the keyhole and its marble slab tumbled into the earth, and the theater became silent.

The chief moved toward the hole into which the marble key had been dropped, but stopped at Professor Meister's command.

"Wait, you fool!" the professor yelled at him. "You'll gum up the mechanism of retrieval if you fall in. It's not safe there."

Honaker stopped, and then backed up a few steps, as additional slabs of stone collapsed into the earth.

Then, a portion of the flooring near the stage entrance slowly caved in as a harsh grating noise was heard coming from the expanded key shaft. After what seemed to Scott like an eternity, a form began to rise in the center shaft. Very slowly, the top of a white marble ossuary came into view and gradually came to a stop above ground level, fully exposed.

Only one path led to the chest. From the other side, a path led to the stage entrance.

Scott Frank stared at the white marble chest that surely served as the final resting place of human skeletal remains. Its sides contained relief carvings, and on one corner stood a small statue of a man, staring across at a figure of Artemis, that was at the opposite corner.

"Watch them!" the chief commanded, as he walked through the lower aisles of the seating area and onto the actor's entrance.

He strode to the marble ossuary, and was about to attempt to remove its cover when Jay shouted, "Get down!"

Scott saw Professor Meister stand up, contrary to the warning, just as Hans turned toward the archaeologist and fired. The weapon recoiled slightly and silently. The bullet cracked against a bench support behind the professor, as Scott threw himself at Meister, knocking him over while Ruff and Jay hit the ground of their own accord.

"Kill them!" the chief shrieked, as Hans and Karl fanned out beside him to get a better line of fire. Hans fired and his weapon kicked back, just as Scott noticed a figure above him and to his left. A dark figure with a bow unleashed an arrow that struck Hans in his upper right arm. Hans, cursing, turned on his assailant and fired two shots just as arrows unleashed from the other side of the theater pierced his neck, legs, and chest. He fell to his knees as if in prayer, and collapsed in a heap beside Karl.

Karl and Chief Honaker crouched low and fired deliberately at the silhouettes that seemed to disappear into darkness, just as each pistol was fired. Karl sensed a figure behind him, spun around and two arrows pierced his torso. He lost consciousness and died as his head struck the orchestra pit floor.

Scott carefully peered around the theater as he crouched over the professor, who had not attempted to move since being pushed to the ground.

Chief Honaker, realizing his plight, turned and ran, weaving from side to side, while firing over his shoulder. He glanced back, and in his distracted haste, failed to see that he was running directly toward one of the open shafts. When he finally looked forward, he was unable to check his momentum, and toppled into the hole. Scott heard a thud as Honaker's body apparently hit bottom.

Scott then became aware of the muffled voices of Jay and Ruff. They were apparently talking to the archers. He looked in their direction, and saw a young woman with a drawn bow close by. The arrow, with a point fashioned into the head of a cobra, was pointed directly at his face. Scott shrugged, smiled at her, and raised both hands in surrender. She looked toward

Professor Meister, who sat up and nonchalantly began brushing dirt from his face and clothing. Scott perceived a slight smile cross her lips as she relaxed the bow, turned, and assumed a position facing the edge of the cavea. Other archers assumed similar positions around the theater, creating a perimeter of eyes and ears alert for intruders.

Jay walked briskly to Meister. "Professor, are you all right?" he asked with concern.

"Yes, yes. I am a bit shaken, but serviceable," Meister replied, as he studied the strange gathering and the disrupted orchestra area of the ancient theater.

Scott noticed that a female archer was staring down into the pit into which Chief Honaker had fallen. She looked up at an older, unarmed woman standing next to Ruff and shrugged her shoulders.

*Apparently, the city of Salzburg is now in need of a new chief of police,* Scott thought.

A small band of women armed with bows entered the theater, with two men about Scott's age between them. Jesuit Fathers Joseph Baronio and Antonio Gianti walked unsteadily as they were led to the path leading to the marble ossuary. They stopped behind the raised bow of a woman warrior, who smiled at Father Baronio, who looked into her face and then appeared to turn crimson.

It was getting very dark and Scott noted that the number of women in the gathering had greatly increased. Some sat in the cavea. Others stood upon the ruins of the stage building. Some were archers guarding the perimeter of the amphitheater.

"What a play," Scott whispered to himself. He noted several women talking to Ruff. And there stood Jay, with his arm around Rebecca Solmquest, who looked over at Scott and smiled, as though in complete understanding of everything spinning through his brain. He felt a presence to his right. An attractive woman, somehow familiar.

"You are a hard tag, Lieutenant Frank," she said quietly. It was Helen, the woman who had trailed him from Minnesota.

"I was caught up in a fast game," he replied.

"How is Rose?" Helen asked.

Scott felt a chill radiate down his back. "She died, but many offspring still live in a school in Germany. Where are your mirrored sunglasses?'

"Vietnam." She replied, as their eyes locked together.

"I owe you a drink, don't I?" Scott offered with a smile.

"I haven't forgotten," came a most inviting response. "Perhaps one evening, beneath the painting."

Scott's attention returned to the group assembling at the foot of the path to the ossuary. Ruff and Jay approached it carefully. They tried to lift off the lid, to no avail. Jay placed the pry bar under one corner of the chest's lid and pulled up on it. The top opened just enough to insert a wood wedge, placed by Ruff. He repeated the process at the next corner until the cover broke free, and the two men were able to lift off the top and carefully lean it against the side of the ossuary. They both peered into the ossuary before glancing into each other's eyes with apparent satisfaction.

An Amazon, watching over the priests, said something to Father Gianti, who then walked slowly down the path to stand before Ruffescott. Ruff bent down, took a wrapped bundle from the ossuary, and handed it to the priest, who was visibly shaking. The Jesuit turned and rejoined Father Baronio, who recited a prayer over the bundle as tears streamed down his cheeks. Their female escorts stepped back and away from the priests in respect for the treasure they held.

A large man appeared, wearing a red fez hat reminiscent of the Ottoman Empire. He shook hands energetically with both Jay and Ruff, who then removed from the ossuary what appeared to be a leather tube about two feet long. Scott assumed it was a sheath protecting a papyrus scroll. Ruff handed the casing to the Turk, who bowed low in appreciation, and then walked toward the priests and their escorts.

Ruff then nodded toward the elder woman wearing a white peplum. Scott recognized the high priestess that had presided over the ceremonies under the museum in Izmir. With grace and dignity she came forward to the marble box, kneeled, and removed something heavy that was wrapped in layers of silver cloth. She cradled the image in her left arm, as a mother would her baby, and rose. She looked from Ruff to Jay, and then across the short distance to Rebecca, with whom she seemed able to communicate without speaking. Turning, she walked a short distance down the walk, and then stopped. She unwrapped the top half of the image, and holding it aloft, she slowly turned in a circle for all the followers of Artemis to see that she held their sacred idol: the meteorite image that had fallen from the sky, thousands of years earlier.

As he watched her, Scott realized that a brilliant crescent moon now pierced the deep darkness that had settled over them. He turned back toward Helen. She was gone.

"Interesting," he heard Professor Meister say, apparently to him. "It is the fifth night past the new moon, and here we are, most coincidentally, returning the sacred idol to its worshipers under that proper moon, following a two thousand year quest."

Scott stared at the professor. "I'm surprised it has been preserved for so many years."

"Thousands and thousands, my boy. This is the meteorite that fell to earth in the shape of Artemis. It was taken from the temple in Pessinus and brought here. It was later taken to Rome at the bidding of Attalus, king of Pergamum, in the hopes that its presence would help end the war between Rome and Carthage. With a Roman victory, of course. That statue was highly prized in Rome and records reflect that Emperor Elagabalus cut off his male organ, as required by the highest worshipers of Cybele and presented it himself to the world's supreme mother goddess."

*Ouch,* Scott thought, as he watched a contingent of the followers of Artemis depart the theater along the marble road leading to the single remaining pillar of the Temple of Artemis. Scott Frank realized that the guards on the edge of the amphitheater had vanished, restoring the area once again to a state of peace and disheveled harmony. Recalling the recent battle, he reluctantly looked to where the bodies of the two police officers from Salzburg had fallen, but they had been removed without his noticing. He walked carefully to the hole containing Chief Honaker's body, but could see nothing much below the Earth's surface due to the shadowy darkness.

"This site should be left exactly as it appears this night," Professor Meister said out loud, as he seemed to almost dance with arms waiving.

"What an opportunity for visitors to experience the latest drama to take place at Ephesus. What an opportunity! Imagine the sound-recorded description, the illustrations that could be drawn and the painting of the last performance... the earth crashing down, the ossuary arising..." He stopped, smiled, and looked to the four Americans who were watching him and listening to his enthusiastic vision for Ephesus.

# EPILOGUE

Scott walked over to where the three other Americans stood together. They were just standing there, staring at either the torn-up orchestra area or the crescent moon, as if simply enjoying an ordinary summer evening out in the country.

Rutheford Ruffescott smiled at Scott Frank. "You have questions, no doubt, and we are here to answer them. Fire away."

Scott nodded in appreciation. "Right. My first question is, were those the remains of Mary, Mother of Jesus that you gave to the priests?"

"They will have to determine that for themselves," Jay replied. "These were the remains originally buried at the home that you visited recently, where it is reputed that the mother of the historical Jesus lived after her arrival here with John, shortly after the crucifixion. They were later dug up, and then most likely placed into the ossuary, and laid to rest at the Church of Mary, now also known as the Council church, which as you now know was the world's first church dedicated to her."

"Her mortal body was said to have been taken there and re-buried under the altar. Then, when the Constantinople authorities sent for the body to consecrate a church in their city, the remains were secreted away, hidden together with the other precious relics relied upon by the Ephesians to protect them."

"Do you believe those were the bones of Mary?" Scott Frank asked.

Rebecca answered, "The Vatican will take years to analyze the contents of those wrappings. Look how long they have been examining other artifacts, without allowing outside experts to know of their progress, let alone assist them! However, they have pursued the remains in such a way that has not threatened the other artifacts and in the end they cooperated with us."

"Cooperated?" Professor Meister scoffed. "Surely you jest. The Vatican sent Jesuit priests to spy on us, and who knows what they would have done had they had the opportunity to snatch the whole marble container."

"Well, now. Who did the Marian Authority send?" asked Jay. "Thugs? Secret sergeants? Swiss guards? No, it sent two very bright but inexperienced young Jesuits who could be relied upon not to physically harm us or the Cult of Artemis. They were dispatched to observe, report, pursue, and await orders. Moreover, they are agents of impeccable credentials to whom the remains could be entrusted. Their historical adversaries, the Amazonian cult of Artemis, are guarding them now. We expect that an aircraft, with a flight plan approved at the highest levels of the Turkish government, will soon be transporting them to a Vatican meeting with perhaps the pope himself in attendance. They played their roles well, even if they did not know what their roles were."

"The superior general of the Jesuit Order, however, has most likely retired from his position," Ruff added. "His secretive actions resulted in two deaths. And Jay is lucky to be alive. Trying to emulate the bold actions of other Black Popes will cost him dearly."

"Okay," Scott said. "So why didn't the Vatican demand the original writings of Jesus– those Egyptian symbols or hieroglyphics?"

The three others smiled at Scott Frank and gestured with their hands to indicate he should answer his own question. The answer suddenly seemed obvious.

"Okay, I see! Jesus was of a Jewish culture with a strong oral tradition. However, he was most certainly illiterate. He left no writings, in Egyptian, or in any other language!"

"Yes, that is our conclusion," Jay stated matter-of-factly. "It took many years to train an Egyptian scribe, as there are over seven hundred hieroglyphs."

"Something else was in that tubular case that was turned over to the Turkish authority," Scott surmised.

"Very good," Ruff chuckled. "You are beginning to understand. There is, at least we trust that there is, a scroll of hieroglyphic writings in that casing. Read without a thorough knowledge of the history of Ephesus, and the Egyptian pharaohs, it can be misleading, as it contains declarations similar to those made by Christ. References to everlasting life after death and resurrection, and about the living god, and about rendering unto Caesar what is Caesar's, and rendering unto God what is God's. However, these were pronouncements by someone long before the birth of Jesus of Nazareth. Writings about, and for, an exiled Egyptian princess banished to the Temple of

Artemis. Hydrographs written by Cleopatra VII, the last of the great Greek pharaohs of Egypt."

"*The* Cleopatra?" Scott exclaimed.

"Yes, as a matter-of-fact," Rebecca interjected, and then continued, "Scott, you know of my weakness for details, so bear with me, for all listening will marvel at this tale chronicled in many histories of Egypt. You see, Cleopatra was the last of a long line of pharaohs that began with one of Alexander the Great's generals, named Ptolemy. His dynasty reigned for more than two hundred seventy years and Cleopatra was the seventh pharaoh of that name; a woman jealous of her position and power. And she was justifiably paranoid. Family members before her had conspired and murdered each other to determine who would become the ruler of the Nile. She was only seventeen when she assumed power and soon had to deal with the Romans, the other great world power, as well as conspirators in her own family who sought to displace her."

"Cleopatra had a younger sister, Princess Arsinoe, born about 60 BC. They had the same father, but were only half-sisters, having different mothers. Cleopatra and the Roman ruler, Julius Caesar, met in Alexandria, became lovers and had a child. That solidified her support from Rome, but she soon discovered that an Egyptian rebellion had arisen against her and the revolt was nominally led by her sister, Arsinoe. Caesar's army marched to support Cleopatra and captured the rebellious sister, paraded her through Rome and she was sure to be publicly strangled, as was the Roman custom in dealing with those who committed treason."

"But, the parading about of the chained, young, and very beautiful Princess Arsinoe touched the heart of the Romans, who cried out against her execution. Caesar was mindful of the masses and the pleas of the senators, so he exiled the princess to... where do you think?"

"She was brought here? To Ephesus?" Scott questioned without conviction.

"Correct. In 46 BC she was brought here in a Roman galley, and was led from the nearby port, past this theater, to the Temple of Artemis. There, she entered the temple of sanctuary and was assured safety as long as she resided within it. The temple priest, a man named Megabyzuz, welcomed and treated the princess like a queen, much to Cleopatra's displeasure." Rebecca paused, and looked toward Ruff, who continued the story.

"Unfortunately for the princess, two years later Julius Caesar was assassinated in Rome. His heir, Octavian soon began fighting with Marc Anthony for control of the empire. Whoever won would control Egypt and Cleopatra made the fateful decision to support Marc Anthony. Her military support, however, was contingent upon Marc Anthony removing the threat that Princess Arsinoe posed to Cleopatra's reign."

Rebecca continued, "Cleopatra believed that a carefully worded condemnation of her sister, addressed to her and to the Romans and Egyptians, would deflect any criticism of her actions. She signed the death warrant of Princess Arsinoe, but also promised that a temple would be built in Alexandria to honor her. Her crime, so it is reported, was that she had not worshiped and honored the Egyptian gods, as was required of all Egyptians, particularly members of the royal family. Also, that she had betrayed her own religion in favor of the goddess of another kingdom– the goddess Artemis. So she was condemned to death not by Cleopatra the civil ruler, but by Cleopatra as high priestess, in order to placate the Egyptian gods, and the true believers of the Nile Valley."

"Thus, to the untrained and rather undereducated members of the expedition who found references to the papyrus scroll on the jar and inside of its lid, they came to the incorrect conclusion that Jesus was the author."

"To return to the story: Under orders issued by Marc Anthony, Romans entered the sanctuary, and presented to the unsuspecting princess the pronouncement of her death and promise of life after death. All this is written on that scroll, in hieroglyphs. They dragged the princess out onto the temple steps. There, legionaries used their swords to brutally stab the beautiful eighteen-year-old to death."

"Cleopatra and Marc Anthony had lived in Ephesus for a number of years, but underestimated the reverence that the world had for the sanctuary rights afforded to the Temple of Artemis. Even criminals who entered were afforded protection from arrest. The world roared in condemnation of Marc Anthony and Cleopatra. They were declared enemies of Rome and outcasts."

Rebecca looked at Jay. "You tell of the sea battle."

Jay smiled.

"In late summer of 31 BC the Roman fleet gathered here at Ephesus. They remembered the princess of the Nile, her bloody demise, and paid homage to the goddess of the Ephesians. The Romans then set out with two hundred fifty ships. They passed the island of Samos and sailed against the combined fleets of Egypt and Marc Anthony, which outnumbered them two to one. They saw over five hundred warships arrayed before their fleet."

"Some said that Artemis, long enraged by the desecration of her temple, and mindful that the Romans had worshiped her in the temple before the battle, intervened. The greatly outnumbered Roman fleet won the battle at Actium, south of Corfu. Their commander, Octavian, was honored with the title Augustus Caesar, returned to nearby Samos and planned for the final defeat of the rebellious lovers, Anthony and Cleopatra. Recognizing that their defeat and executions were inevitable, they committed suicide. Cleopatra was killed by a cobra."

"And," Scott Frank said, "that octagon-shaped tomb where we uncovered the key was the final resting place of Princess Arsinoe of Egypt. Her tomb was originally a replica of the great lighthouse of Alexandria, also one of the seven wonders of the ancient world."

Rutheford Ruffescott looked appreciatively at Rebecca Solmquest.

"How sad it is," Ruff said, "that only we few, gathered here tonight, were able to witness this spectacular unveiling of those precious objects, sacred to two religions. This was to have been witnessed by over twenty-four thousand onlookers, invited from throughout the Roman Empire! The religious leaders of the world, as well as the secular leaders of all nations, were to be invited. Unfortunately, the original invitations to this spectacular event, the resurrection of the ossuary, were never sent out."

"You see, Scott," Rebecca continued, "this theater was never intended to be a secret hiding place for these objects. There wasn't supposed to be a conspiracy to protect the remains of perhaps the mother of Jesus, and the Artemis meteorite, and the words of Cleopatra. No, no. We believe that this was to be the most spectacular public event ever held. Hosted by a prestigious society that flourished in the Roman Empire thousands of years ago. Unfortunately, peace ended between the religions. Unscrupulous rulers sought to acquire all religious artifacts for themselves and to destroy the treasures of competing religions. Those hostile actions created religious chaos in the empire. And so the event was indefinitely postponed. Until tonight..." her voice trailed off. "It's too bad that the greed of the chief of police of an Austrian city prevented this unveiling with the whole world looking on. It is truly a shame."

Professor Meister looked with admiration at Rutheford Ruffescott, Jay Youngquest, and Rebecca Solmquest. "How have you acquired such knowledge? How did you piece together this puzzle with so many missing pieces?"

Rutheford looked down at the marble slab that he was standing upon and then looked up and smiled at the professor.

"I based my theory on a number of factors. I could not think of how such preparations could have been undertaken in this theater without anyone knowing about them. They surely dug out the entire orchestra section in order to place the ossuary underground. Well, the reason, I surmise, is simply that there was no secret. This was to be a very open and public event. One sponsored by the so-called emperor's cult."

"Another religious cult?" Scott asked, disbelievingly.

"No," Professor Meister broke in. "The emperor's cult was never a religion. It was a society formed within the Roman Empire, centered around emperor temples, to give honor to the emperor, but not to truly worship him."

"These temples were only constructed by direct authority from Rome and a city's right to be an emperor's city was limited to a specific time period. This city was allowed emperor status by only three separate caesars."

"Yes," Rutheford continued. "It was a society to unite the people of different religions and cultures and to help guarantee the unity of the Roman Empire. Unfortunately, the spectacular ceremony planned for here was never to occur. The invitations never went out and the emperor's cult resorted to hiding this resting place until after the reckless destruction and looting by certain religions passed. Also, to be honest, there was a clue to this on the drop key. Below the falcon was the crest of the emperor's cult."

"It is amazing that they were so successful," Jay said.

Rutheford Ruffescott nodded. "Yes, an entire city kept silent, fearful that without holy relics their protection would diminish. Other artifacts, such as the large statues of Artemis, now in the museum, were taken from the Artemision and actually buried in the Senate Hall near here so that the Christians would not destroy them. They survived largely intact for many hundreds of years, buried underground, with the prayer that one day they also would be uncovered and cherished."

"How did the bones, meteorite, and scroll find their way into the hands of the emperor's cult?" Scott asked.

"Now, I can only offer a theory on that question," Professor Meister said. "If you will permit me?"

"Well, of course," Rebecca Solmquest responded.

"My educated guess, based partially on what Ruff here has so ably conjectured, is also based upon my previous thoughts. Each artifact that was in the ossuary found its own path to the theater. Let us start with those human remains, the bones of, let's assume for now, the mother of Jesus. She died in about 40 AD, at the age of sixty in her home not far from here. She is buried on the grounds near that home. Then, the church of the Virgin Mary, the Council church, is constructed. To consecrate the ground she is disinterred and reburied within that church, at its dedication. The Roman Church is aware of the remains and has consented to the reinterment."

"Meanwhile the Artemis Cult continues to worship at the Artemisian, where the great Temple of Artemis once stood. The statue that streaked to earth from Mt. Jupiter was worshipped there. And, among the many artifacts guarded by the priests and attendants was the death pronouncement scroll of Cleopatra, written by her in hieroglyphs, reading very much like the words spoken by Jesus of Nazareth, but written to justify the assassination of her half-sister."

"Hundreds of years passed, and there was jealousy and turmoil in the Roman Empire. Constantinople and Rome competed to acquire all true religious artifacts. They made plans to acquire the remains of Mary and to destroy all pagan idols. The emperor's cult was viewed with suspicion as it attempted to quell the growing discord. Its plea to respect all religions and all religious artifacts was openly criticized and it lost its power."

"Meanwhile, assimilation occurred. The cult of the Virgin Mary largely absorbed the descendants of the cult of Artemis, while respecting their admiration for certain relics such as the statues of Artemis, the Mother Goddess, the fallen star, and the Cleopatra scroll."

"Word spread in Ephesus that their artifacts were threatened with destruction or removal. The emperor's cult, priests of the Church of Mary, the cult of the Virgin Mary, and the worshipers of Artemis all joined in a plan to hide and protect their precious artifacts."

"The marble ossuary, constructed for the jubilant celebration of emergence, was placed in the now secret chamber under the orchestra in this theater. Mary's bones were quietly removed from the first church dedicated to her and placed in the marble, along with the meteorite likeness of Artemis and the pharaoh's scroll, which was interred without the jar and its cobra lid."

"They knew that some hidden clue must remain as to the whereabouts of the ossuary. The drop key was buried in a place where it could be found in the future, at a place directly associated with one of the artifacts, at the eastern corner of the lighthouse tomb of Princess Arsinoe. The riddle as to the proper direction that the falcon side must face may have been to thwart those who might threaten the remains. No one will probably ever know. Perhaps it wasn't a riddle at all, perhaps any person knowledgeable about such drop keys would have understood the proper orientation without giving it much thought. We don't know."

"However, some directions needed to be left where they could be found. The jar would survive underground for centuries. Its cobra head would signify that it was a most important object and they may have assumed that any discoverer would instantly know that a pharaoh of Egypt was involved and therefore protect it. Then, the terra cotta portion of the jar's exterior was etched with a message and the inside of the lid was etched with directions to the drop key and theater."

"The lidded jar was then buried in, or near, the home of the Virgin Mary and it was forgotten."

"It was, however, discovered by two young Austrians in 1898. They sought to keep their discovery a secret, but it became known to Herbert Weber who wrote about it in his eight-sided journal. By the way, Jay, I would appreciate your returning it to the university."

Jay smiled, "That is our reward!"

"Well," Dr. Meister replied, "Keep it. Without your meddling about the jar and cobra lid may never have led to the artifacts. The next earthquake could have broken the mechanism. I'm amazed it still worked."

"By the way, Mr. Ruffescott," Scott said, "how did you manage to get the cooperation of the Amazons, and the Catholic Church, and Turkish officials to do what was accomplished tonight?"

"They were each presented priceless treasures which they may never have found on their own and they understood that with one mistake, all might be